Red in Tooth and Claw

Paul West

Onager Editions
Ithaca, New York

Onager Editions
PO Box 849
Ithaca, New York 14851-0849

Red in Tooth and Claw
Paul West

Copyright © 2015 by Paul West
ALL RIGHTS RESERVED

First Printing – May 2015
ISBN: 978-1-60047-745-4
Library of Congress Control Number: 2014956966

This book is a work of fiction. Any references to historical events, real people or real locales, names, characters, descriptions, places, and incidents are either the product of the author's imagination or are used fictitiously. Any resemblance to actual events or locales or persons, living or dead, is unintended and entirely coincidental.

No part of this book may be reproduced in any form, by photocopying or any electronic or mechanical means, including information storage or retrieval systems, without permission in writing from the copyright owner, except in the case of brief quotations embodied in critical articles and reviews.

Cover artwork Copyright © 2015 by Paul West

Printed and bound in the United States of America

First Edition

0   1   2   3   4   5   6   7   8   9   10

About Paul West

He now lives in Ithaca, New York. ("I'm a country boy, born and bred," he says, "I like trees and lawns, animals and huge silence.") West has been the recipient of numerous prizes and awards, including the Aga Khan Prize in 1974, a National Endowment for the Arts Fellowship in 1979 and 1985, the Hazlett Award for Excellence in the Arts in 1981, the Literature Award from the American Academy and Institute of Arts and Letters in 1985, a 1993 Lannan Prize for Fiction, and the Grand-Prix Halpèrine-Kaminsky for the Best Foreign Book in 1993. In 1994, the Graduate Schools of the Northeast gave West their Distinguished Teaching Award. He has also been named a Literary Lion by the New York Public Library and a Chevalier of the Order of Arts and Letters by the French Government. *The Tent of Orange Mist* was runner-up for the 1996 National Book Critics Circle Fiction Prize and the Nobel Prize for Literature. He's working on his fifty-third book.

BOOKS BY PAUL WEST

FICTION

The Ice Lens
The Invisible Riviera
The Shadow Factory
The Immensity of the Here and Now
Cheops
A Fifth of November
O.K.
The Dry Danube
Life with Swan
Terrestrials
Sporting with Amaryllis
The Tent of Orange Mist
Love's Mansion
The Women of Whitechapel and Jack the Ripper
Lord Byron's Doctor
The Place in Flowers Where Pollen Rests
The Universe, and Other Fictions
Rat Man of Paris
The Very Rich Hours of Count von Stauffenberg
Gala
Colonel Mint
Caliban's Filibuster
Bela Lugosi's White Christmas
I'm Expecting to Live Quite Soon
Alley Jaggers
Tenement of Clay

NONFICTION

The Left Hand is the Dreamer
My Father's War
Tea with Osiris
Oxford Days
Master Class
New Portable People
The Secret Lives of Words
My Mother's Music
A Stroke of Genius
Sheer Fiction-Volumes I, II, III, IV
Portable People
Out of My Depths: A Swimmer in the Universe
Words for a Deaf Daughter
I, Said the Sparrow
The Wine of Absurdity
The Snow Leopard
The Modern Novel
Byron and the Spoiler's Art
James Ensor

Red in Tooth and Claw

1

Weeks later, as he bled through clumsy necktie tourniquets into the makeshift bed of a big wooden drawer hauled outside by the few surviving Red Cross nurses, Ludwik Czimanski remembered the golden Poland of before, and the bicycle festooned with his suits. The land had been alive with doomed people full of flamboyant bad humor, dryly joking about motor torpedo boats, the famous statue in Warsaw of Kilinski brandishing his saber at the sky with a face of invitational outrage, and the invincible yellow-capped national cavalry whose red and white guidons flapped above their heads like swallows' wings. How uncanny the sky had been, stunning him like a blue gas his mind's eye inhaled again and again: the drug from nowhere that wiped out the ills of the land. Everyone had looked upward, inhaling hard (at least as he remembered them), looking not for the first wave of bombers but for scrubbed and rosy refugee camps arranged in vistas tapering infinitely up to that comfy otherwhere in which, as legend said, everything went right.

Now, fading away in the big drawer that once held toys or starched and ironed bed sheets, he wondered hopelessly about his wife and son, lost somewhere in the broken landscape, and the suits with which he had tried to bargain before the Huns moved in. In spite of the smoke and brick dust obscuring the yard of the first-aid station that used to be a school, he could see yellow, green, and pink auroras, arcs and streamers and rays of bouncing pearl, and he told himself it was indeed cold enough for northern lights, the summer was a summer only of the mind. The dusty smell of blood would never go away, but like some maroon revenant had ousted for ever and ever the sweet scent of water the burial service invoked. His eyes brimmed as he heard, at a colossal distance, the lazy swish of intact trees bloated with chlorophyll, then teared when he gazed, with head propped up against the end of the drawer, at the sun lolling fat on its course beyond the smoke and the auroras. *I am who I am*, he coerced himself, *I am who I have been. That much remains, and wherever I go the land will fall away steeply to the pond at the bottom of the garden and the hill shall rise from there until it meets the sky.* And now it was as if the colored lights in his head had begun to squeak; he felt with one hand for the other and, in a spin of silly mental momentum, winced at the thought. Which was worse, the gone hand feeling for the still present other or vice versa? To grope for something with nothing, or for nothing with something? It was not a vital distinction now, even though something comparable had gone wrong with his feet as well, where the cold began that bulged upward along the length of him inside the shreds of his major's tunic. Having gone to war in full regalia, like a throwback to the nineteenth century, he judged he had no right to decide what explosive engine of war had hit him as he galloped southeast from Warsaw, bidding his mother and war adieu to refind his wife and son somewhere in the bloody mark of the small town where they had last embraced, a slewed tripod of love in the garden at Kazimierz, leaning their bodies blindly together while some passing bird, as they discovered a moment later, released a pellet of white wet lime that landed on his shoulder: a portent of good luck at which they miserably grinned before embracing again, and he'd left it there to dry in the sun, like a tiny additional epaulette.

Assistant Military Attaché in Berlin, which he had been, before removing himself fast, with wife and son, as the Nazi design upon Poland became grossly clear, he had thought as logically as he could, getting them all three out of Germany, then from Warsaw to the countryside on the fringe of an old city on the Vistula. All pacts wither in the making, he'd decided. Let's make one of our own, even if it postpones an evil day for a week only. *Evil day? Devilish eternity, more like it.* So he had, as it were, put away both wife and child, like a cache of gold and cream in a land awaiting heathen predators, and had gone to do his duty with pistol, sword, fire iron or gardening fork, he whose métier for years had been the desk, although he had kept in riding practice at the Krampnitz cavalry school, so at least he would not be unseated while attacking a tank or machine gun nest. Something huge-feeling in his eye, like a reified whirl of light, made him wince, reminding him of an engine cinder which, in boyhood, hit his other eye as he leaned over a bridge to watch a train, and the wince shook loose a few forgotten words, which he lip-formed with almost holy slowness: Poland, Switzerland, Admiral, the suits, the boy, Wanda, the bird-lime, the pigsty, the bank, the money, the farm, the telephone lines all cut.

It was no use: the part of his mind which identified gibberish and denounced it, pitching it out from his sleek diplomatic-military chessboard of ideas, no longer functioned, and the dead came back to haunt him, to be worried about, even as his conscience let slip the living, on whose behalf he had invented so many paper stratagems, including a small cave dug in one of the ravines near Kazimierz and use of the twin-engined courier plane to get them all away, northwest to Denmark, southwest to Switzerland. There had been no time to make the cave, and the plane, on one of its shuttles between Warsaw and Berlin, had vanished, shot down for target practice by a Luftwaffe pilot on the prowl. Not that Ludwik Czimanski knew this, or any longer cared; his father, who had died in his chair, drumming his fingers incessantly on the arm in a tattoo bespeaking helplessness and diffident rage—*thrim-thrum, thrim-thrum* until his wife facing him held both of his hands still—came back to life as a hostage to fortune, to be smuggled out by airplane or squirreled away in a cave. Indeed, a line of people formed in his head, his father first, then his mother still creaming her arms with an imported aloe lotion (she who crooned in her sleep, in a half-dream repeating that voluptuous motion along each arm, although untidily), then these two followed by his grandparents, fidgety cardboard caricatures with wolf-head canes and spilling samovars, behind whom came the living such as the Sakals, both teachers, and she part-Jewish, with a single child, a girl sensuously named Myrrh with whom his own dead son had played and walked and (he'd supposed) mildly necked. But, in the sea-changes of his delirium, while the sun of his last day bloomed and waned behind the smoke, the dead and gone did not come to life only when the living gave up the ghost. It was more complicated than that. Instead of life-for-death exchanges, these beloved phantoms rang the changes in a parody of resurrection, and a host of proverbs turned morbidly inside-out: after God's finger touched them, and they were no more, God's finger touched them again, and they asked to be saved from Adolf Hitler; in the midst of life, they were in death, and then they were not, and they asked for visas to America. Even worse, while this chop-and-change ensued, blighting with fickle guilt what he no longer even recognized as the drift into coma, he somehow found the head of his dead wife, Wanda, on his live grandfather's trunk, and one dead grandmother's arms on his dead son, Izz, at all of which in his enfeebled dither he rebelled, and in so doing rid himself of all categories, at the almost very last abolishing the category into which he slid. And so, dying, he could not die, he had never been alive; indeed, so far, on the planet, there had been no life at all, but only a flicker of a promise decked out with plausible ghostly faces, brought into being by a Creator whose main purpose, initially, was to try out the capacity of humans-to-come to love one another. Then, the test over, these figments could vanish. And they did. One day during some effusive eon there'd be humans. *Oh yes*, he told himself, *there are going to be people, the rocks will no longer be lonely, the water will be drunk, the birds will finally have heads and shoulders to squirt their whitewash on, the first onion will be fried, the hops be brewed into beer, the mice be trapped, the moss in the woods blot the first wound.* On it went, a vast anachronistic alibi that piled up the more his blood became a drizzle, the last of it arriving in the open air mist-slow because there was no longer anything behind it to push it along. Major Czimanski died in a bloodless plethora crammed with the evidence of things not seen.

2

Yet what he had hoped, finally, to register with tender completeness, and then to set it up before his mind's eye as a Polish Palladium—an improvised sacred object having the power to preserve a city or a country like the famous statue of Pallas Athene that protected Troy—was still there in his head, frozen among the engrams along with the classical learning he had brought into play at embassy cocktail parties, with a Latin tag for this, a Greek one for that. Major Epigram, as they nicknamed him, had wished to see, and, having seen, had convinced himself that the seen was never lost. Let someone witness a thing, he'd taught himself, and it endures: there is no time, no loss, no waste. So, just the same as two weeks earlier, people still trudged from farm to farm, bartering honey for apples, balls of whitewash for birchbark strips from which to make sandals. Stranded at the tilt like outsize palm leaf crosses from an ancient Easter, the windmills had no motion. Sagging at their long middles, the milk wagons had nowhere to go, and they sagged from long use, from being overloaded in days gone by, not in any way from the weight of empty churns. Like propped-up coffins with little roofs, the beehives seemed to invite new tenants in. *Go anywhere, get out of the way,* were the messages everyone was whispering, but no one knew what to do first, and so clusters of farmers and farmhands dawdled about in the landscape, guessing and arguing, and only in Kazimierz-like places were the prudent busily pasting brown paper over their windows to save the glass from blast, the occupants from splinters. The banks and schools were closed, but the stores were open, though with little to sell: no sugar or liquor, no canned goods, just the pots, pans, files, vises, pincers, choppers, and shovels pictured outside on a placard for the benefit of the illiterate, whose visual abstractions had more flesh and blood, or at least more shovelly shovels, than the verbal ones of their betters did. WODA SODOWA read the sign on the soda water stand on the edge of the closed market, but there was none to sell. The pharmacies were out of bandages and iodine. Repaired clocks went uncollected while time dilated or shrank. And those impulsive ones who had fled, moving so as to be on the go at any rate rather than knowing exactly where to go, trundled with them barrels of salt herrings, heirloom pictures of Christ gazing blankly at some conifers (a standard icon), and chickens in improvised wire coops. The departing trains, all headed east or southeast, toward ghoulish Mother Russia, would never return, and folks who stayed behind slur-chanted the shallow hairsplit last-ditch litany "With the Germans we *may* lose our freedom, but with the Russians we *shall* lose our souls." The

Germans were everywhere, the rumor said, but they had not yet reached that disk of magical ocher and russet landscape, or were hovering at its perimeter, joking harshly and goose-stepping in circles, as if loath to interfere. It looked so German anyway.

Nourished by a mind's eye full of this drawn-out idyll, Major Czimanski, after irritably hunting through the drawers and walk-in closets of the rented townhouse on Pulawy Street, hung his suits in heavy parcels, done up with cord, on the crossbar of the bicycle he had found out back, unoiled and dusty and upside-down as if ready for conversion to another purpose such as spinning or water-pumping. "Perhaps," he said, "they're not all mine, but no one will ever come back, not for their suits. I'm sure the owners wouldn't mind."

"They won't even know," his wife told him distantly, as if accomplishing hard mental arithmetic. "Ever. If it doesn't work, bring them back. We'll find a use. Oh for a car. Will you just look at all this stuff they left behind." She motioned at an untidy array on the couch of books, silverware, cut glass, gramophone records, trumpets and clarinets. As if a high-living musical quintet had left in a hurry. "Remember, Ludwik, he has the gold already." She twanged the bell for him as, rather like someone leaving a funeral or a hospital waiting room, he wheeled the bicycle away, a display frame with wheels, the strung-up parcels like dun-plumaged headless birds. Minus his tunic and cap, he looked to her rather ordinary, a well-groomed repairman removing his equipment from the premises after fixing the elephantine trumpeting noise the bathroom pipes made when the faucets were turned full on. "What?" he called behind him, thinking she had spoken, and almost collided at the gate with two Jews walking backward in front of a spinning wheel on a small cart and tugging hemp from their waist bags, twisting it deftly into strands and feeding it to the wheel run by a third man in a cloth cap too big for any skull. At these three he stared, amazed by the somnambulism of their toil, three of the doomed anxious to earn their keep even while backing into the inferno. Spinning the thread of destiny, he noted with a classical smile: Now which of these three Fates is the one who snips? The bicycle fell into line behind the spinning wheel on the cart as if not he but some more appropriate force were moving it along, shoddy bargain with an even shoddier destiny, and his mother's disdainful shade hectoring him with "Is this you?" and his father's cannonade: "Servants do *our* wheeling for us, and that is not an exhortation to *ride* the foolish thing."

Ludwik Czimanski advanced with his mind shut off, reaching the edge of town after ten minutes, glad that the trio of hemp spinners had provided him with a rhythm to walk by, but gladder still they had gone the other way. Now he stared, pausing, at rye-thatched haystack covers, like the roofs of an African kraal. *This year of years they will stay empty.* Farther along, hemp was soaking in the ditch along the roadside, and bundles of it lay unattended on the bank. Overtaking him with smothered gurgles, half a dozen sprightly men in cloth caps that might have come from the same box on the same day (uniform buff twill) forged on ahead with bundles of coat hangers slung over their backs and half a dozen in each hand as if in search of an army eager to strip naked and air their battle clothes. It's all half-dozens, he told himself sardonically, and looked at their hands, half-expecting each to have a sixth finger. Or did they take six steps and then halt, as if walking to bars in music?

What sharpened his deep-buried, deliberately minified distress, after he turned into a lane flanked with crude houses for sale, perched on diagonal brackets built into the walls halfway between the ground and the roof. Bigger coffins, arranged on carefully folded sacking spread over pairs of trestles, he just blinked at heartlessly, but the little ones dismayed him, tugging at his mind with a pertinence too keen to bear. He no sooner passed one set of them than he saw another, planed and sanded but still the post-mortem minimum, just enough in the shade from the eaves not to reflect sunlight. *Prophetic greed,* his mind told the lane. *They might need them for firewood before the week is out. Cold always by the end of this month.*

Fifteen minutes later, in a black sheepskin hat and a holed plaid shirt encrusted with a complete range of droppings from egg and mustard to whitewash and manure, Gnonka the pig-farmer untied the cords and began to finger the five suits, one with satin lapels, one of a tweed perfumed with Baltic heather, a third with two vests of which one was velvet with maroon pearl buttons, while the other two were ordinary and a bit worn at the cuffs and elbows: these two culled from the house, not his own at all, and certainly not his taste, which did not run to tree-bark brown.

"Worn," muttered Gnonka thickly into his splattered shirt, then added that the gold didn't amount to much either.

"All there is." At this they began to argue, the one voice raw with clumsy sullenness, the other clipped-brisk and only letting the words out a little more than it drew them back in again, as if communicating only through tone. *What you expect—The bargain—Which was?—Two children—Two!—Two—,* as he had said the last time, ashamed and half-willing to kill, to walk away at least, as if he had caught himself making overtures to a pig.

"Two's a lot. Which's the Jew?"

"Part-Jewish."

"You don't need to worry, squire. They've nothing against Poles, why should they? But Poles that have Jews in tow... They sell better things than you in Kazimierz market. Why don't you go and peddle your suits where they belong?" Gnonka, who had a pea-sized polyp growing either side of his nose where it joined his face, scratched them both with slow, studious vexation, savoring the gulf between his customer and himself. Then, as he saw the suits go back into their brown-paper, "Well, maybe for a few more. I've a busy winter ahead of me, see, I'll be a man in demand, what with *visitors.* I can't be signing milk contracts in my working clothes, can I, my lord?"

"Yes or no? For two?"

"I've sacking aplenty."

Promising to return in one hour, Czimanski rode away on the disencumbered bicycle, eager to breathe a different air, and Gnonka's German shepherd chased after him until Gnonka slurred a one-syllable command, at which it loped back and followed him into a low rickety barn between a root house, already covered with sod and straw, and a rye-thatch granary stacked high with firewood.

"All you have, there's no time left," Czimanski told Wilson Sakal, his old classmate, professor of economics who spoke lispingly from around the stem of an unremovable briar pipe actually replaced each December with stealth and much misgiving as he put the old one in the flames and turned it to charcoal and bubbling Bakelite. "No, keep two for emergencies."

"One to be buried in. Why two?"

"Don't be romantic. Suits, please."

"My dear fellow, you're streaming with sweat. Have some barley-water."

You go and deal with him, Czimanski's dry-mouthed rage began to form, and Wilson Sakal would wheel the bicycle and ride it back, superciliously prevailing over the earthenware ogre in the encrusted shirt, burying their joint ten-twelve-fourteen years of education, the grades the prizes the fellowships the rabbit fur hood the silks, in a transaction that might have earned a headline in Sodom: I do not have a disgrace-meter, Wilson, but it couldn't measure what I feel, if I had one, if one existed, I am beneath the bemired hooves of beasts of the field, I *am* a beast of burden, a deliveryman, an errand boy, with the ghosts of my ancestors rearing up around me in paramount, mahogany-headed, bloodcurdling rage, asseverating—isn't that what the dead do once their gums have rotted off?—asseverating *Best die, shoot the children, there are poisons.* I, Wilson, am sucking the snot from Gnonka's nose when only recently in Berlin, I was closeted with the *Admiral* for two whole hours, and the future was within our grasp; he kicked the dog turds off the little rug in front of his desk and said, *We won't let anything happen to you, Ludwik, no matter what the thugs let loose, I know they have some dastardly things in mind: if only they'd had forts and toy soldiers to play with when they were boys. I have an eye on every millimeter of their doings. Now, leave Berlin and stow your loved ones safely away, but remember: When the caravan comes through, there will be a camel for you, not a leopard and not a giraffe. Camelopardalis,* he'd blathered on, near Ursa Major and Cassiopeia. *A giraffe with horns. Do you ever look at the northern sky? Without the stars, and Greek, and saddle of wild boar in a croûte of black breadcrumbs and red wine, and a little croquet with the Heydrichs in Augusta-Strasse (their henhouse adjoins our garden)—well, the list is longer, but without such things, my dear, the atrocities would be unbearable. I use the word advisedly, in its metaphorical sense of course. They have even saddled me, aha!, with field gendarmes of my own with whom to sniff out spies and saboteurs. Dogs, horses, they're the cream; the rest is degradation, black tar between the teeth, compost 'neath each eyelid. Beware, my dear. Now go.* Well-connected as he was, Czimanski sometimes felt he had lost contact with his own memory; the things that had happened to him had surely happened to someone else who had given him a garbled, pushily vivid account of them which he'd made his own; or they were things he'd invented because his work in Berlin was so dull, an orbit of German-style cocktail parties (raucous, in a formulaic way jolly, and weighed down with fair skin excitably flushed). As for the Admiral, that pill-popping introvert with the lisp who hated people who had small ears or who were tall and lived mainly in a boyhood world of invisible inks and uncatchable spies, he came from the dimension of wizardry, a freak, a hyperbole, a hybrid right out of Hans Christian Andersen, yet he controlled the fates of millions, deviously interfering and undermining by means of a staff deployed throughout the civilized world. A tip here, an overture there, and someone either died at the frontier or came sailing through it in disguise, and most of his relatives worked for him as well. The master of fair-weather machination, he was a man not only worth cultivating, but worth priming and sweetening as well; the Admiral was the ghost of intrigue past and of subterfuge to come, when the entire world ran according to bits of cardboard (fake of course) stamped with hieroglyphs entitling you to grass, a roof, the right to breathe last outside a jail.

But now Major Ludwik Czimanski plied his skill, and his incredulous memory, in a different world, wheeling the next batch of suits to Gnonka's farm, there on the crossbar like excerpts from a careless taxidermy, for Gnonka's enormous, stone-rough hands to palp and stretch, maiming whatever ghost-human might be left within.

"You've come, and to prove it," he murmured with harsh peasant levity, "you're here." It was one of the countryside's honored formulas, a ham-fisted redundancy that gave both speaker and listener time to think up something else to say.

"Well, it'll rain or go dark before morning," a far cry from the svelte ripostes of Polish intellectuals feinting amid the brass eagles of ambassadorial Berlin, where the Poles and the Germans pavanned through the marble hallways like teams with separate destinies, the latter eyeing the former like meat, the Poles responding with aphorisms borrowed ("To goodness we make our promises; pain we obey," from Proust) or conjured up in a desperate mental squirm, as when Major Czimanski scandalized an entire dinner party, including the Admiral and Heydrick, by announcing "Self-abuse is the ultimate compliment." Time and again he had said such things just for the sake of something to say, not to have the silence balk him or the reiteration of Nazi pieties numb him into an oral acquiescence that was the prelude to the military rape with tanks and dive bombers, an event he had been able to nose in the very air of Berlin for months before September 1st, 1939.

"A bit better," Gnonka was growling. "Not much. But...."

"Two. And food. Agreed?" Yet his mind was on an already dead dilemma that had made him choose between his own son Izz, Myrrh, the Sakal's child, and his own wife, the theory behind his and Wanda's final decision having been the adult ability to fend for oneself, together with the superior chances of hiding a child rather than an adult whose name would appear on lists (lists, the Admiral had told him, already being compiled by his agents in Poland) of businessmen, doctors, priests, landowners, teachers, and civil servants. Who, after all, listed children by profession? Besides, there was the ulterior plan, something nimbly and almost mutely rigged with the Admiral: a so-called deposit, left in his safekeeping, not as a trophy or as spoils to the victor before the victor had vanquished, but something akin to that, in the form of a cashbox containing 25,000 American dollars and fifty gold ducats. *We'll stay in Germany, then*, he'd told the Admiral in a desperate flurry of resolve only to hear, as the bushy white eyebrows came together and then flung themselves upward sideways, *Messing one's own doorstep*.... To which he could find no valid answer save some babble about a plane, or a train, as the other's demeanor seemed to preclude whatever he meant to say next: a look of astute tolerance backing him off, tacitly pleading *Do not put words to it, let it be, we shall provide*, and in spite of himself he began to smile, to begin a grave giggle, because he knew then that an outsize German eagle, complete with armored satchel holding beer and liverwurst both of which he loathed, would come whizzing out of the night, smoothsailing through the fires of his homeland, and snatch them up painlessly. Several thousand leathery wingbeats later they would all be lunching with Madame Kollontay, the Soviet envoy in Stockholm, a dab hand at bridge who thought the Soviet system was doomed, anyway, and was thinking of buying a house in Germany, well within her means, which amounted to over three million dollars. That easy it would be, easy as Madame Kollantay's changing her mind.

"Safe as houses," Gnonka kept saying with intricate conviction, as if yearning to be only half as safe himself as whatever he was recommending. A lighthouse? A treehouse? (Surely not?) An attic with no window, disguised as a piece of the chimney?

"There is nothing safe about houses," he heard himself retort. "There is a certain finality about houses. They do not take off, like the planes that pulverize them."

"No faith, my lord, in the brains of a poor farmer. *As* houses, I said. I didn't say *houses* as safe as houses. It was what you'd call a comparison. Something else, safe as houses, see, but also safer than houses, because it doesn't fall down. It might fall in, of course, but not down, not down like a house falling down, and you couldn't fall off it neither."

Oh, Major Czimanski yearned, for rescue by wizard, right now, whatever the price: never eating *Kutia* again, and, right there in the noxious presence of Gnonka, the earthenware deathshead, his palate longed for *Kutia*, a whole plateful, honey and poppy seeds and boiled wheat. Not much to ask for, perhaps not much to give up, then. What had the Admiral said, with that Delphic obliquity peculiar to his trade, which kept him sane even while he was not safe? *In the circumstances, Major, although that phrase implies a complete knowledge of them I neither possess nor aspire to (some of our most decisive gambits float above an unknown sea, happy over seventy thousand fathoms as the Danish philosopher Kierkegaard puts it, it may have been sixty or eighty), anything concrete or precise* (at this point his two dachshunds, Seppel and Sabine, yapped in unison and he bent from his chair to comfort them) *might generate too exact a longing, even a requirement, which as well as capable of being elicited by torture, or alcohol, might end up disappointing the client himself. Although free, he might wish to have been freed in a different way, the way he contracted for with certain deposits, as snails do, although a snail catapulted, say, or slingshotted, ten thousand meters might object. Take my word for it. So, in the circ—as I mentioned, there is no way of being specific beyond reiterating the, how best to say this without offending the Chopin in you (My wife is an accomplished musician, and one of my daughters plays her violin all day, which is why I'm at the office so much!), I can cite*—and he leaned on the verb as if coming to rest on a smooth rock after a long swim—*only the Platonic form of the undertaking: you will be saved, you and yours, of course you shall, and that contract between us is pure as crystal, which nonetheless I would not want flawed by pedantic recitals, of the exact measures that might suit best at a given time, and only the stars give us time, they cannot be bribed (not that I imply you have bribed me). Have you ever bribed the stars? I know the best astrologers. In short, my dear man, leave it to me. Even if I hated you, self-respect would guarantee my part in this. If you die, I die; if you live, then so may I.*

"Earth like a fox's." Gnonka had begun to push him in a certain direction.

"I don't follow."

"You'd better. See yonder pigsty? A nice dry hole, been empty since an old helpmate of mine used it years ago when he wanted a bit of privacy from his wife, and the police. It's a gift from heaven." All Major Czimanski could see was a low, ample hut behind a hip-high stone wall. Nearer, he discerned a planking floor beneath fouled sawdust, a lid coated with slop, and he cried out with revulsion as the nature of this bargain, compared with the Admiral's labyrinthine reassurances, began to sink in. Prying up a plank, Gnonka motioned grandly at a dank earthen cellar beneath: a manhole, a catchment trough, a grave.

"It's wet," he cried. "It's waterlogged even now, and this is summer."

"You know the seasons, Major, I'll say that for you. A bit of sawdust and some sacking, it'll be as clean and comfy as a nun's armpit."

"And air to breathe, with the top on? In place?"

"That pipe, it comes out round back. There's air galore. You could run a windmill in there."

Stifling the dry heaves in his throat, Czimanski tested the pipe by shouting the phrase "fresh air" into it, then having Gnonka do the same while he, Czimanski the customer, applied his ear to the other end, "round back." What he heard was an irrefutable proof that the pipe conducted both air and sound. "You, you," bawled the farmer, "got no choice, have you now? Will you be moving a lot of furniture in, my lord?" All this time, fat white pigs were shuffling and waddling about, butting one another or colliding, and their noises, which he heard through the pipe when he went to its other end and shoved the farmer away, merged into a stifled gargle as of a rumbling belly heard close up. Try as he did, he could not banish from his mind the children's coffins for sale along the roadside: something the Admiral had never seen, although, Major Czimanski fantasized, he was capable of using any one of them as a mail drop for a local spy. With Gnonka beside him, whose ruddy face announced the fatuity of the whole plan, he walked back to the hole in the ground and stared at it in disgust, his eyes wet with rage. Next he decided against installing his son and his friend's daughter in any such place, only to have to wonder what else he could do. Would things be that bad? Would there, as the Admiral had warned him, be not only a prompt, steamrolling invasion with orthodox military maneuvers in the course of which soldiers aimed at and killed one another, but also indiscriminate shooting, the casual pitching of hand grenades into houses for fun, the dive bombing of suburbs whose only offence was to have a couple of statues and an ornamental fountain? There would be even worse: the deliberate abasement of the Polish people in free translation of atrocities which, the Admiral had confided to him, Germany itself had already seen; the malevolence at home would pour across the frontier, and any Pole, boy or girl, Polish horse or dog, would be fair game for the horde of psychopaths assembled, of course, just to do them in. There was nothing rational in such a prospect, but, for a moment, as he peered wordlessly down, Major Czimanski foresaw the fool he would make of himself, the only parent who secreted his child whereas, only a week after the occupation of Poland was complete, happy families would be strolling about on Sunday afternoons with tricycles and kites, tots in creaky little strollers, and small brothers and sisters toddling along hand in hand. *There was no need for that, Ludwik! Fancy a military man like you panicking! The Germans have nothing against our children.* The voices he heard were those of common sense and worldly well-adjustedness. What would happen if all the parents in Poland buried their children alive? The Nazis would notice and dig them out, then win them over with a big party-picnic, all fizzy lemonade and chocolate-covered buns! Only a few could get away with it, only a few parents; and, if they were right, there would be virtually no one left to tell them so, and, if they were wrong, they would never live it down. Either way, a father had to guess, which Czimanski was now doing, both at speed and with stupefied slowness on the caked mud of Gnonka's farm while the farmer stared at him, meanwhile thump-fondling whichever pig came to hand as he leaned his paunch over the low wall, certain this fool would never take the suits away now, whatever else he decided. He wouldn't want to be seen wheeling them home again.

Major Czimanski's brain was burning. What had seemed a reasonable plan, ensuring the children would survive, was really a brain-sick aberration on the part of someone who took his metaphors too seriously, and whose child, instead of surviving with some inconvenience above ground, was doomed to freeze or choke to death underneath it, or to starve, be drowned, nibbled on by rats, infested with lice, maybe even rooted out by the pigs and bitten to death. All for what? His premise, he suddenly realized, was his assumption that he, the father, and Wanda the mother, and the Sakals, had virtually no chance of surviving themselves. The Admiral had schooled him well in prophetic fatality. No, that wasn't quite right: the Admiral was going to get them out, of course, he had promised to do so; but when? Strictly speaking, then, until rescue they should *all* disappear, which was out of the question. Major Czimanski had a sudden ridiculous vision of underground families communicating with one another through carefully reinforced tunnels and dining in well-appointed burrows. *Not on this earth*, he thought, at last realizing that his highly trained mind kept refusing to tell itself what was obvious and could be formulated as follows: as an officer, called to the colors (in that mellow phrase), he himself could not go into hiding without committing treason, or showing unforgiveable cowardice in the face of the enemy (a phrase less mellow), not that he knew exactly what to do, but he would find something, even if only work as a courier. So he would be absent anyway. In the ravine caves, Wanda would have a chance; but, if she were caught, the children would still have a chance.

The same was true of Wilson and Suzanna Sakal. The buried logic of his motives, impressed upon the hard-headed Sakal who nonetheless was no man of action, found the pigsty less obvious, less known, than the ravine; and so, in spite of all the objections his mind wincingly rehearsed right there in front of Gnonka's contemptuous stone-age gaze, he began to see that he had been right all along, so long as the Admiral's people knew where to find Izz and Myrrh, so long as the two children stayed put. *Children?* No, they were very grownup, he told himself. Twelve and thirteen aren't as young as they used to be, and their brains added up to twenty-five. Unlike an ancient Spartan, he was not going to expose his offspring, but inter him genially, with supplies enough for a month at least. He could hardly phone the Admiral about something they hadn't even dared to mention bluntly in private, but the Admiral's resources were legendary, with thousands working for him all over the globe. Almost convinced, he sighed, only to begin tormenting himself all over again, this time with the question—*What if Izz and Myrrh refused?* He could hardly drag them screaming and kicking all the way to Gnonka's farm. The farmer wouldn't stand for it, and he might hand them over to the Nazis anyway once he, Wanda and the Sakals were out of the way, in one sense or another. There were better schemes than this, but he could not think of them; having weighed the chances of the children being found against those of the parents' not being snapped up in a Nazi purge, he had come to this undignified point, of bargaining over a pigsty with a lout, with his own death in action uppermost in mind like the only card he had left to play, and so his thinking, he told himself, was desperate, lumpish, flawed; a man contemplating the scenario of his own end as vaguely as this could hardly accuse himself of being self-centered, but he felt he was, against his will soothing himself with that finality instead of bracing himself with what the Admiral had said: *We'll pick you up in Kazimierz, remember; in Warsaw it won't work at all, there won't be any Warsaw left. Just think of it: a million fewer violins!*

Right where he was, Major Czimanski wanted to cry, because highly evolved human companionship, sustained across frontiers through several languages over many years in complete accordance with elaborate protocol, should not (he said "must not" aloud and made Gnonka flinch) be subject to something essentially barbaric. It was as if crocodiles were running the world, who could not be swayed, argued with, or bought off; and men of brains and sensitivity found themselves driven to inventing gruesome and unseemly plans, primitives all over again in a world gone mad.

3

"Take it or leave it," Gnonka said, as if taking his cue from the major's thoughts. "Now."

"I'll bring them," Czimanski answered, having nothing else to say, and meaning, *You barbarians have won.*

"And then you'll stay away, elsewise—"

"I'll be gone," he said, still as a kernel in its nut.

"They'll fend for themselves too. I won't go near." Gnonka dramatized his made-up mind by holding up two flat hands, thumbs linked as if to suggest lacework done in stone, but meaning only a flat manual, *No, they'll rot before I'll budge.*

Glad the deal was clinched, or at least that the verbal fingering of it was over (no more suits to wheel across the landscape, no more gold to surrender in small felt pouches, either as coins, bracelets or rings), Major Czimanski took a deep breath, at once felt light-headed, and walked back to his bicycle, worry still about something clouded in his logic, maybe even something too lucid in his hunch. *You are obeying an ancient impulse* he chided himself, *to hide what is yours, like a peasant hiding his money in a sock and stuffing it into the mattress. You may have exaggerated the danger, but you still want to get your son out of harm's way. Lions, kangaroos, wild boars, do just as* you. You are using a burial ritual on behalf of life, and the overtones keep on nagging at you. What you have to be clear about is something else, and that is being certain you don't see the boy as some kind of sacrifice: fruit of the earth rammed back into it, son of man obliterated to keep the man alive. An exchange, another filthy bargain. No, that kind of mumbo-jumbo was as foreign to him, he decided, as wandering about without his jacket and tie, as now, with an ungainly bicycle between his legs, clicking and whirring as he looked up to watch a white eagle which swam in on a thermal from the ravines. That was his chosen mode of travel, six times higher than the highest steeple. Working at it hard, he suppressed his civilized man's worry that he had undertaken, and was going through with, an act generated deep within the shadows of the race, founded on some unverifiable churlishness of the heart which only human contemporaries of the saber-toothed tiger would recognize. Whatever the horrors of being shut away in the ground, even with a Myrrh for company (and she chilled out of her wits after the second night), the just-imaginable nightmare of his son wandering aimlessly through the wreckage of bombed-out houses, with only the bereaved and the insane and the SS for company, outweighed them, oh yes: as an iceberg an icicle, as a tweak of angina an ache in a tooth. One thing Ludwik Czimanski knew about himself was paramount; since he was doomed, since in the popular idiom, his number was up, he would go to any lengths not to have his son dragged after him, and if accomplishing that entailed uncouth and drastic measures, then uncouth and drastic he would be, a colonel in his last few acts as a major. And if that were self-promotion, after a long stint of playing second fiddle to the military attaché, himself a colonel whom the government had already transferred to Sweden, he would accept the honor with poise: just so long as the Admiral's men came and did their part, sleek to save, night-stalking with whispered directions to the nearest airfield, this to be followed by cashing the first check in the bank in the free world. For that glowing alternative he would be glad to ride sidesaddle against a dozen Tiger tanks, with the second-beat stress of a mazurka floating on his lips, his eyes on the pregnant space where a bone-white eagle was bound to appear. That he would see auroras instead, he had no idea.

All the way home, past the children's coffins (from which he again averted his gaze), he heard something going flip-flap in the rear wheel and then, the closer he got to home and the more the sheet of badly printed newspaper worked itself toward the axle, flip-flip-flip, which just had to be removed, so he stopped, dismounted, and removed the paper by dismembering it. The big letters of the hastily printed broadside informed him that the mayor of Z----- W-----, a town halfway between Warsaw and the border with Germany, had been sat bare-buttocked in a red-hot skillet, God alone knew to affect what change in his mind. Itself grotesque, this culinary sadism told him more than he needed to know, and any misgivings he had about being uncouth or drastic, the heavy father prophesying Armageddon or the fussing semi-diplomat trying to forestall every rotten chance, fell away. The brutality he expected, the Admiral had tutored him about Hitlerism; but that element of the ludicrous got him on the raw. If mayors could be fried, then assistant military attachés could be poached, and professors of economics roasted on the spit, and, just possibly, Admirals keel-hauled for being tight-mouthed. Leaning the bicycle against the open gate, left thus as always by the uncaring Izz, he strode into the house, full of news and love, already murmuring a dinner-table speech that went gravely from a pretty thought into the baleful never-never: *Once in a blue moon, my darlings, the blue moon being a storyteller's daub for almost never, a lively boy like you, Izz, taking your bicycle lamp to pieces in order to rub the copper flanges bright with a strip of emery paper, and a blooming girl like Myrrh Sakal, playing at being older by holding plasticine nipples against the slight swell of her chest, having to be told that the future might not be theirs after all. The future might not happen, my loves. It may never come, wrapped or unwrapped, in a blueprint, or fleshed down to the most minor detail.*

Yet, at table, he said nothing of the kind but told them the mayor of Z----- W----- had been fried butt-naked, and so they heard all over again about history and war, none of which Izz and Wanda found half as interesting as they would have found the blue moon itself, an azure figment rolling between never and now; yet the tutorial in disillusion went on, in words which in themselves made sense, about a future which did not, and in which they showed less than little interest, heedless of the basic maxim that you are obliged to show some interest in whatever is going to wipe you out. The Admiral had found Ludwik himself a less than avid student of these textbook horrors, yet had persisted until his Polish major had mentally woken up before his eyes, murmuring *A staged event at the border, with corpses dressed in Polish uniforms? I can't believe it.*

And in German uniforms too, the Admiral had told him. *They will be the victims of this dastardly attack.*

Izz himself was saying grandly, out of a naturally exotic intelligence fidgety with boredom, "Then we'll just clear out, to Greece or the West Indies. I don't mind which. Somewhere warm, like now, please. Poland's not so bad, but the horses are still scared of the cars.

That's not my idea of a modern country. Maybe the cars are scared of the planes as well."

"Don't dream at table," Wanda scolded him, for lack of something with which to expunge the image of the mayor in the skillet. "It's no laughing matter."

"I wasn't laughing, I was—yearning, see."

"Don't tell him," Ludwik says tenderly, "not to yearn. You're as good as dead if you don't yearn, even if what you're yearning for is in another universe altogether."

I'm no fool, Izz decided. I know what's crazy. Cheese mold doesn't grow on brass. Axiomatic. The Pacific Ocean is blue, and it does not wash the coast of Florida. A piano has twenty-four keys, doesn't it? No one comes after you, to kill or burn you, without a reason to, I don't care what history says. I'm thirteen and I don't have to. Or is that where my upbringing has let me down? A better training for life as it is would have been a daily smack across the mouth for no reason at all. Then I would have been better prepared for my bare bottom in a red-hot skillet. He must have howled his head off, yet it wasn't loud enough for us to hear in Kazimierz. Pain has such a short range. Away into one of his lunging, never confided reveries, in which precocity skywrote its compensations against the blank of an uninquisitive adult tolerance, Izz reminded himself of the year, 1939, added up its digits to twenty-two, and then made four, wondering where to go with that. What was four the number of? Perhaps it was the quartet of locally based PZ fighters, gull-winged and radial-engined, whose image haunted him all the more because he never saw them in the skies, but heard them as noises off, a blurred gobbling buzz, beyond the horizon. They reminded him of gulls, except these were gulls with their noses chopped off and replaced with the fat round cowling of the engine, so they were gulls that had flown headfirst into small saucers, which had stuck. Not content with imagining how they looked, although not tumbling in flames, he flew them in his mind, especially one with a Vee engine, so-called because the engine seen from the front resembled the letter V, whose angle matched exactly the angle of the full-wing root, giving the pilot a perfect forward view, whereas the big cubby radial engine blotted out so much that in some versions it had to be lowered, while in others the pilot's seat was raised, even as Izz was growing from a small plane-infatuated boy into a big plane-infatuated boy. Preposterous, he had long thought, to be shuffling the engine up and down, and then the pilot, just because some fathead had decided Poland would use the Bristol engine dreamed up by the British and not the elegant, self-effacing Hispano-Suiza Vee. Even worse, he had told himself repeatedly as he planned his career as an airplane designer, the Bristol Jupiter pulled with the strength of only 485 horses whereas the Vee pulled with six hundred, a neat round figure, making the model he personally flew twenty-eight kilometers an hour faster. One breezy day back in August, he had taken off from the aerodrome in his mind and, banking sharply left to get the sun behind him, had seen two teams of horses tramping in a race across a fallow stretch of land dried saffron by the heat, six hundred versus four hundred and eighty five. When he swooped low, the smaller team scattered and ran all over the plain in twos and threes, at which, having been influenced by his father, the military classical scholar with fluent German and Latin (still, as it were, awaiting his first posting as military attaché to the Roman Empire), he murmured *et dissipati sunt*: and they were scattered, an expression his father had in fact gleaned from an account of Sir Francis Drake putting the Spanish Armada to flight in 1588.

4

"Pulawski," Iz blurted into the middle of serious words between his parents about his immediate future underground, "he designed the PZL series, didn't he?" He knew the facts by heart, of course, but it was his way of beginning, Zygmunt Pulawski, born in Lublin in 1901, being his main hero, already dead, killed in a two-seat light amphibian he had designed for his own use. Yet, now that Pulawski got no older, he, Izz, kept on catching up with him, and in a profound infatuation Izz had no plans for living beyond twenty-nine, the age at which his hero died. Only sixteen more years to go, he told himself: *I'd better get moving if I want to amount to something half as good.*

Now he said "Dad, why did Poland have to manufacture the Bristol Jupiter Seven-F nine-cylinder radial engine, when the Hispano-Suiza Vee sat beautifully in the contours of the nose?"

His mind on subterranean flooding, the amount of food needed by two children for at least a month, and his own shaky notion of why he wanted to hide the children at all (as if a ghoulish fairytale and an ancient Biblical practice had fused), Ludwik Czimanski answered absentmindedly, "Oh, politics. It's always politics, my son. And business. I don't exactly know, but I think it was one of those government decisions based on a private deal struck up over the dinner table." He coughed, somewhat awed by his son's grasp of technological history and his passion for facts which, as Nazi Messerschmitts and Heinkels poured up into the sky over Poland, five hundred at a time, had no future and would survive, if at all, as abstract emblems whispered about in the hospitals and morgues of recent history: The Polish Air Force never exceeded three hundred and fifty kilometers per hour.

"Whatever happened," Izz persisted, "to the Rolls-Royce Kestrel engine? Liquid-cooled and shapely! Or the Lorraine supercharged Petrel? Eight hundred horses? Why are we horsing around with the Bristols? Why have a man invent a good thing, then make him a bollocks of the whole thing?" His mother smiled the smile of patient assimilation: one thing Izz could be, besides being factual, was obscene, but he was invariably more factual than obscene; she thanked her maker that he had never graced the embassy receptions in Berlin.

"The model I fly," Izz began rapturously.

"Have you built a model airplane?" his mother said.

"The particular PZL P.8/II I take up," he began again, "has a liquid-cooled engine, and I can see all round me. Do you think it's symbolic that our best fighter plane happens to be one the pilot can't see out of? Up they go and they see less, the pilots I mean, than if they'd sat behind a garbage can at home. Does it mean Poland's willing to fight but not to see what's in front of it? Here we are, with one of the best (and first) all-metal monoplanes in history, and we squash its nose, which is like sending up a hundred and fifty potato-mashers!"

"Poland," his father instructed him with bemused sternness, "isn't quite so stupid. There are dummy planes positioned all over fake airfields."

"Yes," Izz insisted, "but I'm talking about what happens in the air. The poor bastards can't even see what they're shooting at, and they bloody well can't see what's shooting them down. You tell me Poland isn't stupid. If Zygmunt Pulawski were alive today, he'd ground the lot of them and sell his services to Willi Messerschmitt, and who could bloody blame him? Whoever runs Poland, Daddy, is full of pizz."

"*Izydor!*" Wanda had grazed her lip with her fork.

He said it again, word for word exactly, adding, in the lofted tone of a priest reciting pious formulas, something he had even tried on his teachers at school, translating it into bogus Latin in a two-hour essay: "In the Pulawski wing, the inboard panels taper sharply in chord and thickness towards the root, their thinnest sections sloping down to join the fuselage immediately behind the cylinder—"

"You win," his father told him distractedly. "You always win. You win before you open your mouth. You were winning long before you had a mouth. You were a winner long before there were mouths for humans to have. Even in the time of the blue-green algae, when mouths were only little suckers, you were winning hands down. *Semper ex—*"

"Don't say that again, Dad. Listen." And he resumed in Latin, carefully rehearsed, while his mother yearned with all her heart for the Sakals to arrive for their council of war and peace, while his father, in the one moment of levity he had allowed himself in the past five weeks, wondered if his son were not some kind of secret weapon, exerting many times the horse power of the renowned PZL P.8/II and with visibility exceeding three hundred and sixty degrees in any given—but the family secret weapon was now going off, at the mouth anyway, and both his parents looked away.

"*Cylindri ripae machinae erectae, sic amoventes visus*—er—*obstructum, ala impositum, sicut omnibus adumbrationibus!*...the cylinder banks of the upright-Vee engine, thus eliminating—"

"We know," his father sighed. "We weren't exactly picking turnips when we were your age, and younger. But I am going to have to change the subject. Just so long as you know that I know, and your mother knows, this little voluntary finishes as follows: 'the obstruction to vision imposed, by God, by the wing, as was common in all other layouts.' Or something such. Satisfied?"

For a thirteen-year-old boy's, Izz's face revealed little; cheerful but aloof, it seemed always in the midst of beginning to stir, and this worried Ludwik and Wanda when he was seven or eight, because it made them listen too hard to what he said. Then, because he said so much, although rarely about his inmost feelings, they became used to him: the sounds he made replaced the motions of his face. And, as strangers found to their discomfort, the big dark blue eyes, while seeming to look right into their own with voracious appeal, actually looked beyond them, and people who thought hard about his phenomenon felt they had merely intercepted twin, parallel rays or beams; his field of vision was a tunnel not leading to him at all, and the most enterprising of those who talked to him found themselves in the odd predicament of wanting to ask him not to look them in the eye, as an honest boy should, but to please look away. When he did so, they felt the kingfisher's wingtip of his glance just graze by them, puzzling, eerie, yet seductive as milk. He was not shy, but he was working up to it. His hand, however, perhaps because there was not eye in it, was always there to be held, and alarmingly warm, as if it had just come out of a nest or the inside of a newly baked loaf. As for his hair, so curly when he was a tot that it earned him the nickname Goldilocks, it became a darker brown each year, and, cut severely short, revealed its true nature only in the crop of coils on top of his head, which he diligently plastered down with brilliantine: solid, heather-scented, and for some reason water-soluble, which made his curls feel like something carved, beading or fretwork; Izz didn't care so long as the wind blew nothing loose. When it did, a rare event because he water-greased the mat of it down hard with the back of his comb, he became unduly disturbed, thinking the loose forelock might tangle in his eyelashes (which were long and paler than his hair) and tear them out, then his eyelids, and the skin of his forehead. What pleased him most was, in his room or the quiet of a library, to tap a pencil against his hair and hear the faint, precise clicking sound as painted wood met the carapace created by a product called *Fixfirm* and another called rain, tapwater, or spit.

Small feet, small hands; a nose always cold; medium-sized ears with always a bit of a flush; a wide, sensual mouth with an upper lip thinner than it should have been, and suggesting a ripple of disdain along the cutting edge where lip met skin: such was the rest of him. Slightly below average height, he sprinted superbly and, for the past two years, had sprouted a blondish fuzz as yet unshaved, which in face looked darker than it was against the often-queried sallowness of his face. Izz was tired of being asked if he felt all right, if he was sickening, about to throw up or (by boys at school) if he hadn't been overdoing it, playing with himself: it hollowed your spine in the end, he heard, and even the big boys stored it in stone jars under their beds in case it had to be replaced. A strong wind could snap a boy in two, they told him; but he was too precocious and well-read to care, though he did smile at his private vision of the biggest boys in the act of thrusting fistfuls of a lard-like substance back into the tubes of their backbones, out of the wind of course. Having discovered a year ago that he could produce a new liquid from himself, a nacreous ammonia-like gruel, he inspected a half-dozen samples of the yield, and then got bored with it. Only five years ago, when Izz was eight, Willi Messerschmitt had invented the jet plane, and that was of more interest to Izz than his own puberty; or, rather, Izz took his puberty so much in his stride, with in every sense a helping hand from Myrrh, who was as casual in these things as he, that he came to regard sex as merely laxative (while remaining a virgin) whereas aeronautics made him thrill indefatigably; the air was skin, the plump cross-section of a wing was the tumescence of desire, and a silvery mote droning high over a map on which *it* could not see *him* gave him his first metaphor for the mind of God.

His non-aeronautical treasures included a plywood fort complete with American Indians, cowboys, tigers and lions and zebras, all of whom he blasted to bits with a small green anti-aircraft gun aimed low. The bogie wheels which allowed his long red locomotive to negotiate the circular track without coming off, or losing speed, dangled loosely and rattled when he lifted it up to peer at the men in the cab, and he hated that, afraid the entire locomotive was coming apart; but that was better than having a four-square engine with no bogies at all, always toppling off the curves with the dry, spluttering noise of a bee on its back in the raw sun. When his father moved to Berlin, Izz began to appreciate the quality of the German toys, which were built as if intended to last the owner until he was fifty at least: German locomotives were heavier, German sulfur (in the chemistry sets at least) smelled stronger, and German books, reinforced with headbands that reminded him of the furry part of a bell-rope, and glued so tight he couldn't split their spines, could resist monsoons and fire. Always, when Ludwik brought them back to Poland on leave, Izz spent the time with Myrrh; so, at first, they had been together day in, day out, while growing up, and then they saw each other only for short, intense spells, during which each noticed abruptly how much the other had changed: Myrrh more voluble, less untidy; Izz less of a tease and more upright (for years he'd seemed to crouch, as if to ward off a blow or curl up round a tummy pain); Myrrh darker than ever, from deep walnut brown to sooty mahogany hair, her fair-skinned face a little more broken out than before, her gaze even more direct and, unlike Izz's, halting at the other person's eyes, making them almost lean toward her to make the contact.

"More or less," Izz answered the question his father had put to him a thousand years ago, "I'm satisfied. I think my Latin's full of potholes; I do it as some people play the piano, by touch, by ear. But that isn't what bothers me. What does is what I said about our own air force, and something else—why aren't the Germans using jets? If they're going to come flying all over us anyway, I'd rather they did it with their very best, with something worth looking at."

The Sakals arrived in a flurry of kissing, he overheated in a suede jacket he at once removed and laid across his knees like an emaciated animal run over by a truck, she trim and jocose yet rickety, not so much a woman in a floral dress as a floral dress by chance having landed a woman and wormed its way over her. Myrrh winked at Izz as if to hint: the syrup of your loins has wet my hand, so what the hell do they know different? "I don't like weather," she told him in a haughty voice. "In winter I long for what it's like now, but I'd give anything for a snowball to rub across my face. Yes, Father?"

"I was only agreeing," Wilson Sakal said. "I grunted."

"The future." Ludwik whispered when everyone had tea or ginger beer. It sounded like a toast in reverse.

"Small topic." Wilson was not wasting words today.

"What we agreed upon has come about. There's no time to go through it all again. We must tell the children now and then install them, before it's too late."

"I thought we were all going to Switzerland. Your mother too."

"No, Suzanna," Wanda said acidly. "We are going nowhere at all. We may get our moneys worth later. Grandmother refuses."

Wilson just added, "They mostly do, grandmothers."

"What about your precious Admiral?" Suzanna didn't like this business of the suits, on top of gold paid out in this way, then that. "Is he going to deliver or not?"

5

"That's the Admiral," Izz butted in, "who gave me toys. He has two daughters, one of whom is an invalid, and he always wanted a son. He showed me how to use invisible ink and how to feed sugar lumps to his Arabian mare. I think he's been in every country of the world, and actually in some countries no one's ever heard of, where the rivers flow uphill and the natives live on liquids only. If you take him with a pinch of salt, he's quite all right. Anyway, *I* don't call him Admiral, I call him Uncle Wilhelm. Or I did."

Sighing at the practical uselessness of their all three having been on almost intimate terms with the head of German Intelligence, Wanda put an old velvet cushion behind her head and settled back, the very picture of offended resignation. It was too late for anything good to happen, and all they could do now was shuffle second bests. Her jewelry had gone, her hair was short, already trimmed to help her pass muster as a man, unless it got her into trouble she might otherwise have avoided. There in that uncomfortable, essentially *rented* chair with the high carved wings and the hard narrow arms, she let her left arm rest across her waist as her eyes glazed and her nose lolled into a shaft of light which made a brief stripe from bridge to tip, then vanished as she moved.

"We'd be better off in Warsaw," she said to no one.

"No, we wouldn't. Why do you think I pleaded with Mother?"

"The apartment," she began again, but Ludwik cut her off.

"Will have to take its chances." Now she had a distinct image of time, a viscous fluid rolling forward like lava with its leading edge, several hundred kilometers long, hot and steaming, and her mind filled with favorite drawers, towels, brands of soap, truly comfortable chairs, and the piano on which she played Chopin and Liszt. She even caught herself longing for Berlin, its receptions and dinner parties, where all the trouble came from, a panther from among suavities.

"I don't want to live in a ravine like a savage," she told them all. "I wouldn't know how. Your mother's better off."

"You'll be lucky if you get a chance to," Ludwik said. "But he'll find us, I'm sure he will. He's a man of his word."

"He sounds might distant to me," Wilson said loudly. "Maybe we'll have to join the Nazi party before he'll do anything at all. They might not be so eager to have Jews with fully paid subscriptions. We'll take a ravine any day. Just lead us in. Now what about the farmer?"

"If you don't want them to get you," Izz announced with cantankerous brightness, "hide in a museum, among the statues, still as stone, and someone will bring you a bagel at night to keep your tummy from rumbling during the day." Shushed, he subsides, but mouths his impatience to Myrrh, who giggles, then says her piece: "I know, we're going to be invaded. We already have been. Do all Germans have blue eyes and flaxen hair?"

"Perhaps," Wanda said with a slow, stretching wrench of her full lips lined with millimeter marks, "by the time they reach here, well, everything might have calmed down."

"You know better," Ludwik told her. "Count on the worst, just in case. Any other way is reckless. Now, let's get down to business. I beg your pardon. I withdraw the metaphor."

"I could always," Izz began, "go and stand naked in the public fountain, like the boy in the Tivoli Gardens in Copenhagen. You know, the one on the way to the tennis courts. I'd just spurt away and they'd never know."

"Find the words, for God's sake," Wanda said, "before he gets really funny."

He tried. "Any day now, any hour, it will be true, as much a fact as the honey in that jar or the mole on your mother's lower cheek, Izz, or the pollen that fell from the overhang of the roof, where the bees got in last summer, back in Warsaw. Carpenter bees, who push the sawdust out."

"Husband, you haven't told anybody anything yet."

"I think he means," said Izz with an elaborate, cunning look at his mother, "the domestic form of emigration! That's what the Germans call it, isn't it? You vanish without going away."

"The domestic form of evacuation is more like it." Ludwik looked at his son with unfocused eyes. "How ironic that you have come to know German so well. How elementary some mysteries are."

"Are we going to take poison," Izz asked. "Like Socrates?" Heroic nausea made him rub his mouth and then, even as he looked up to watch his parents watch him, halted with his wrist in front of his lips, as if stifling a burn.

"You and Myrrh are going to hide." Ludwik thought he was going to faint, and abruptly fixed his gaze on Myrrh, who had stood in order to fidget about, and now faced away in profile with one hand on the smudged veneer of the dining table, fingers together in a trowel shape, as if imperceptibly nibbling across the surface to a bowl of grapes. God save us, he thought. How scraggly and golden she has become. She reads Verlaine in French and draws penises freehand with her eyes closed. They think they have secrets, but they have none from me. Imagine a regime, to which I myself have been some kind of *cavaliere servente,* or go-between, wanting to wipe out the likes of her, just because her mother descends from Shem. It's unbelievable. The light doesn't refuse to shine on her. The air allows her to breathe it. Water doesn't rebel when it enters her mouth. The table reflects her without demur. Why, she looks more Slavic than anything, yet she's one of the doomed. Look how her lower face falls away, from its natural sit, but because she sucks in her mouth and tugs back her chin when she's lost in thought, as if she's just swallowed the idea of death and is waiting for it to go down. She could stand there for ever against that folded screen, a long black-haired pixie lost in cogitation. She knows. And so does he. They pick things out of the air. They receive our transmissions before we even formulate them. That's what adolescence is for: the intuition of essentials while the grownups shuffle their vocabularies. "Hide," she said in belated echo. "What are we doing now? Advertising where we are?"

"Underground," he told her, told the room, with lips like slabs of cement. "Briefly, until help arrives. And then another country where," he let the limp joke out, "for once I have no diplomatic privileges."

"Then," Myrrh said, again sitting, "tell us where, and we can all begin learning the language. Is it where the rivers go uphill and the natives live on liquids only?"

"Cuckoo clocks," he answered, desperate for something precise, unwilling to admit he didn't know.

"Or sleds drawn by reindeer?" Izz had come back from a reverie so intense his top lip shone and his incipient mustache looked plastered down. "Give us a clue, Dad. Cancer or Capricorn? North of the Arctic Circle or south? Is there an Antarctic Circle too? If so, why don't people mention it?"

6

Passive in exasperation and with a plucking sensation in his chest which he knew was heartsick taciturnity, Ludwik looked through the violet-plastered wall of the dining room, all the way to the farm, with his abstract gaze averted from the coffins for sale, and found Gnonka's walnut of a face, the face of one who did not need the gold or the suits, but who could not resist yet another transaction, a joke to him whereas to everyone else involved it was a matter of death and life. Do it with dignity, Ludwik told himself; do it with so much dignity it transforms the raw material into a tender legend which, one day, someone will remember, incredulously touched by it. *Once upon a time*, it will begin, *two children, a boy and a girl,* and then he gave up.

"It's a living space the farmer has used before," he said, as if construing difficult Latin with a hangover. "It needs sprucing up a bit, but it won't be too bad in summer. Think of it, my loves, as a dugout, the sort of place you might otherwise have in a tree, for example, or along a river bank. Where you can picnic or spy on people. In the right mood, I could even envy you, but I have other things to do above ground. Don't worry, we'll look after you. It's been arranged."

Over steamed cabbage, boiled potatoes, and a stewed chicken brought by the Sakals, the six of them ate supper in numb silence as the evening sun poured undwindling through the stained-glass fanlight above the westward windows. It was too hot a meal for such an evening, but a hot meal somehow reassured them, getting them in the right frame of mind for the enemy outside, far less gentle than winter, yet comparable in that it had to come, it had to be heeded. Next year, perhaps, things would be back to normal, Poland would not be cratered like the Moon, swamped with lethal visitors barking in a foreign tongue (yet not foreign to the Czimanski's), and disfigured by such minor things as an old Renault tank parked at an angle across the entrance gate to the citadel of Brest or the bicycles dumped in a heap by the Polish company captured by Guderian's tanks across the River Brahe from Hammermühle. Next year the blown Vistula bridges would be up again, Polish forces would not need to go to ground in the famous forest of Bielovieza; the Primate of Poland, Cardinal Hlond, would have returned from Rumania. Better, Ludwik was thinking as he re-chewed what he had already chewed but couldn't swallow, to make sure: we can always bring them out, with a cheery proverb or two. We *can't* revive the dead. There is almost no water, no food. The end of the world arrives on cue tomorrow. No newspapers, no radio you can trust, no air cover, and no Admiral arriving at the front door in some inconspicuous German car with passports in his hand, money up his sleeve, a flask of cognac to keep us brave.

With feverish giddiness Izz was airing his knowledge, although this time not of planes. "In the Boer War, between Great Britain and South Africa, the Boers rang a bell every evening, and after that there was no more fighting until the next day. Why not do it here?"

"Horsemeat," Myrrh half-giggled, "all next year. Sometimes I feel all scrunched up and want to let the light into myself. As if I were a scarecrow in a field and the weather had plastered all my rags together and I itched like mad just to have daylight running through me again."

"How did all that come from horsemeat?" Wilson noticed that her left eyebrow was thicker than the right and, near the nose, did an unpruned upward run as if it came from a different face. His wife saw a tear land on his chicken and lose its shape, rolling down a bit of sinew. Their stares interlocked as Wilson, pronouncing each word with willful slowness, said "Tomorrow, the new world."

"Eat up, you two," Wanda told Izz and Myrrh.

"It's only four o'clock, and the meal's nearly over." Izz mock-cringed before his mother's congested, tender face.

"We want you," Ludwik said, "we want you safe before nightfall."

"Underground?" Izz asked. "In our dugout," he said.

"Just to try it out. Mainly that. Think of it as an adventure."

"While we wait for the Admiral—for Uncle Wilhelm?"

"In a sense, yes." Ludwik palmed the flames in his face.

"Both of us, Father? Just like two seeds?"

"Why, oh why," Wilson Sakal suddenly roared, dropping his pipe, as if all his education, pride and sense of congruity had come to bear on this fleck of history, like sunlight focused through a lens, "should our bright and wonderful lives all of a sudden be so full of *merde*, just because we are here and not somewhere else? It's obscene how geography makes clowns of us. Who knows, if we ignore it, the war might just pass us by, or come infiltrating among us like a new style in dress, with a few changes here and there but nothing much to tear your hair about." Then his face seemed to dry from within; a withering in the bone made him add "Sorry, I know I'm talking rot." He set his hand, as if it were no longer his, on the bread plate and froze in that posture. "Would we like to sing?"

No one answered, but Izz, in a little flurry of valiant irrelevance, chanted "the fox's coppery tail, against the sunset black," and then seized up.

After deep, protracted looks, they all stood, shook hands, forbearingly hugged one another, and then Izz and Myrrh stood aside in vague embarrassment, caught between a pout and a smile of radiant apology.

"It's not," Izz scoffed, "as if we were going to separate boarding schools. Is it now? Or as if *we* were going back to duty in Berlin? We'll be down the road, at the jolly farmer's. Whole families can't go underground after all. Just promise us: if you have to get away, then go. We'll keep. That's the whole idea, isn't it?" His half-broken voice fluted, then went dark again.

"Why not leave now?" Myrrh was trying to see the whole stratagem from the parents' point of view. "You'd have more time."

"We're hedging, my darling," Ludwik sighed. "We're still hoping there's no need for any of it. But I, I'm afraid, will have to report to some Polish unit or other, not that I'll be of any use." Now they moved outside, as if to breathe more easily.

"No, not now," Wilson kept saying, "not yet."

Now the laying-on of hands began again, an enfeebled rigmarole for last-things unrehearsed, and the six of them felt like pulp to one another, groping, hugging, mumbling; but the tears had gone, and they all looked up as a honey-colored bird squawked over and something splashed on Ludwik's shoulder, quite detonating the solemnity of the moment.

Back inside Ludwik produced a bulky waterproof kitbag: "Army issue," he said. "Two bottles of water, a knife, crackers in cellophane, a dozen chicken sandwiches, to be eaten first, a Polish ham complete with key, some aspirin, cough linctus (you wouldn't want to be heard, my dears), two toothbrushes, some sanitary towels (*I* know, *you* know), soap, and the last of a plum cake, to be eaten with the sandwiches. Well, if not with, soon after. A mouse trap. Of course. The rest is blankets, pullovers, heavy socks, gloves, and two groundsheets. Two flashlights with extra batteries. Candles. Matches in an old tobacco tin. Toilet rolls. The theory is this: by the time it's all gone, and you need to forage for whatever food the farmer doesn't bring, you'll be gone too. You won't be in Poland for the winter, or even the chillier first nights of autumn."

"A clock," Suzanna said, turned to salt. "I brought one just in case." Then she handed over a radio with an earpiece. "One of the first things they'll do, when they come, is confiscate this kind of thing. I'm being realistic."

"Toffees, a rarity." Wilson brought a handful from his pants pocket. "Eke them out, you two."

"You know what," Izz murmured at his most subdued, "I feel like one of those old German heroes they floated out to sea in a skiff full of gifts—gold and corn and fancy swords. After they had died, I mean." A full, sapless minute of silence followed that, until Ludwik coughed, then said, "Pencil and paper for any messages." Somewhere the Polish army awaited him with his death.

"We have it," Izz snapped. "And books. We've probably overlapped on a good many things. Are we coming out tomorrow, after the test, then?"

"Will there be mice?" Myrrh sensed the presence of a joke, a romp, but cannot locate either. *"Mice?"*

"Watch the light, though," Ludwik cautioned them.

"I'll kill that bloody farmer," said Wilson, his eyes beginning to steam.

"You'll do nothing of the kind." Myrrh was anxious to go and see, mice or no.

"We're all going," Suzanna said. *"Aren't we?"*

"No," Ludwik whispered in orotund apology. "I'll do it. The fewer the better." After that, it did not matter who said what. A valedictory babble filled the room, not so much a six-way exchange as desperate speech flung or skimmed at the unknown like flat stones against the sea to skip-skip-skip, then sink.

"The damp most of all."

"And wipe yourself clean, remember."

"Batteries don't last forever."

"Codeword *Pulawski*, to be whispered."

"We're not exactly babies, Dad."
"And not to cough if you hear voices."
"The middle plank."
"We're not exactly babies, Mamma."
"Pigs, she said pigs."
"Misery, joy, death, it's a motto."
"Some sort of adventure."
"I'd rather be at the Berlin Zoo."
"OK, we'll listen."
"And no reciting of poetry."
"And no airplane noises either."
"*Pulawski, Pulawski*, yes."
"It may get colder, so—well, you know about body heat."
"We've been studying it for years."
"Love you as long as God endures."
"Never out of our minds, remember."
"Go now. Already? Well, a kiss for Grandmama."
"We need the light. Not too much, but enough."

Three from three they went, walking through a sunset bright enough to read by, at a slow, impeded gait, using the bicycle as trolley for the crammed kitbag which sagged on either side of the crossbar, and both children touched the bicycle, Izz the handlebars, Myrrh the back of the saddle, as if to maintain contact with the only concrete thing in the morbid, nebulous legend they felt fast-growing about them, like a half-sadistic joke which had suddenly enveloped its teller, depriving them of everything save incredulity as, watched and watchful, they trudged off into the night, going horizontally but, in their minds, beginning to sink into a fog of soot and shame.

7

When they arrived, Gnonka came out to chain his yapping wolfhound and eyed Izz and Myrrh as if intending to buy them as livestock. Leached-out sunlight made the barnyard and paddock seem almost two-dimensional, burying figure and ground in a brightness impossible to behold, and staining a few high points salmony violet. Ludwik longed suddenly for flowers with which to clinch and grace this awkward ceremony, and, unable to find the right words, or indeed any, he sensed babytalk beginning to form just inside his teeth. "Dere, den" or "Diddums," only to suppress it with a firm bite that dragged on his nostrils a little. West of here, he thought, geography is changing hour by hour, and some of those people who, in panic or spurious zeal, lay flowers on the chugging, backfiring tanks of the invaders will be machine gunned or mutilated by breakfast-time tomorrow. In his mind's ear the text of an insufferable interrogation starts up, erasing the moos of milking time, the plump flutter of hens. According to our population roster, prepared by agents of the *Abwehr*, there is a male child at this address. Missing. Unreported. Where is he? Have you done away with him, Pole? They twisted Wanda's arms behind her back to egg him on, but he refused to tell them anything except his rank and number.

Izz and Myrrh stared again and again at their place out of the sun. "It's awful," Izz whispered. "We'll grow tails in there." Wrinkling her nose at the stench of hogs, Myrrh nodded and said, "Do we smell half as bad to them?"

"See," said Gnonka in a hurry, "the water's out. I've even put a board across the bottom, just like new. I make a bargain, I keep it. They'll be dry in there." But all Izz and Myrrh can focus on are the pigs, shoving and wobbling at the hole's ragged edge, their spliced hooves driving the slop to and fro and teasing Ludwik's mind with a memory of overweight women's legs in overhigh heels, trotting thick-ankled and ungainly through the Warsaw rain. Or was it Berlin, on the Ku'damm? Where those women sat and spooned up cream, nibbling a flake or two of pastry to keep their palates clean.

Clambering over the low wall, Izz tested the planks with both feet, then lowered his legs into the gap, bracing himself on his elbows, both sides. Then his drowning face vanished as he ducked down to investigate further.

"Quite light down here," he called. A big horse lumbered past unled. Down went the kitbag.

"You ready?" Seeming to convulse, Myrrh knelt, then eased her way down, down, and under.

"Are you comfortable full-length?" Peering with wet eyes into the horizontal dumbwaiter in the earth, Ludwik decided he would never do this kind of thing again, then corrected himself wryly: You'll never have chance, major, it will be beyond your control.

"On our backs," Izz called. "We can smell the pigs."

"All right. Come on up and we'll lay the blankets." Down went the two groundsheets, the blankets, and Myrrh could hear the scuffling, hollow sound as Izz arranged them over the board in the bottom.

"I forgot," his father shouted with unnecessary volume. "Newspapers make good insulation." Turning to Gnonka, who was watching all these preparations with a fecund sneer, he asked him to fetch some only to hear "What passes for a newspaper these days wouldn't keep a rabbit warm."

"Old ones then."

"*Now*, my lord?"

"It will be harder later. Now is right."

Gnonka shuffled away, red-faced and grumbling in dialect, on his way managing to collect the stationary carthorse and lead it away.

"In this order: groundsheet, newspaper, blankets." To Izz, still out of sight, the strained voice of his father had almost no human quality, but seemed made of straw and clay, a turkey croaking in the distance, a waste pipe right on top of him, refusing to flow. A piece of that dazzling, static landscape had moved, slowly as if peeling and swaying low, but it was a familiar human pair, Wilson and Suzanna, coming into view round the corner of the whitewashed cowshed, he wheeling a wheelbarrow, she burdened with a leather satchel. *I wish you hadn't*, Ludwik began to say, but the afterglow calmed him and the sigh of Myrrh fleeing from the hold in the ground toward them sliced through his heart. I have no gift, he decided, for severing people from people, people from anything. And he gave them an agonized nod, but, having embraced Myrrh with elaborate curling motions of their arms and little supplementary hugs at the knee, they had already begun to leave, with Myrrh following until she realized what she was doing and scurried back only a few paces ahead of the returning Gnonka with four or five newspapers under his arm: "What if the Germans catch us now?" He dumped the newspapers into the hole right on top of Izz, whose complaint rose and faded like a bouquet of dipthongs. There on the ground in front of Ludwig sat an eiderdown of mingled Egyptian-Burmese motifs (a pyramid grew behind an elephant) and four hot-water bottles of ruby rubber wrapped in felt or flannel, which Myrrh at once began to open, only to have Ludwik caution, "No, don't they—"

"You don't understand." Each one she twisted open and sniffed, exclaiming softly with a limber smile that made her look half a dozen years younger: a child who had fallen asleep at a picnic and awoke with a voluptuous grin of self-rebuke, already hungry again. "An old family trick," she said. "They're full of hot bouillon."

And where would they get more water? But he didn't say it, just made sure the caps were screwed in tight again, tamping the wingnuts deep into the rubber vulva-like ovals. Then he gave Izz the eiderdown, draping it downward into the hole and Izz's hands after untying the cord that held it in a double fold.

"Smooth it out," he called. "Is it really dry in there?"

"Really dry," his son answered from the bower in the bowels of the earth. "Come and see. Come and enjoy the fun, Dad!"

8

Instead, Ludwik lowered to him the hot-water bottles, calling "These to drink, as well as keep you warm. Hot broth," he inaccurately added, "to keep your strength up, even when it's cold." *It* is the broth, he told himself, not the weather: you are becoming woolly, Major, you soon won't know a German from an eiderdown, a live burial from a deathwalk to the paradise garden. Surely, he pondered, feeling tense and faint, they would never wet their beds at twelve and thirteen; the bed, so-called, would never dry, and then the aroma of putrefying dandelions would be with them both until winter began.

"I've even tucked the bottoms in," Izz called up to him even as Ludwik motioned Myrrh to go down now, and the face she pulled had equal parts of loathing, levity, and grief. One long voracious gape at the sunset was all she took. The pigs had moved inside the sty, from which a mild, quarrelling multiple snore rose and fell, almost human yet falling short by something too dense, too close to jowly flatus. Already Izz was using his flashlight in the gloom, now leaving it in one place to shine evenly, then aiming it here and there in swift ephemeral ribbons through which blanket fuzz and tiny feathers strayed in a languid zigzag. When he tested the candleholder, an eerie slab of yellow slid into place at ground level, a human touch beneath the planks, although all Ludwik could see of the children was a heaving, lion-like shadow as Izz continued arranging things while Myrrh lay on her back with goosebumps, trying to persuade herself she was on a school camping holiday in the course of which she would again see boys peepee into bottles, insert the stems of eye-sized daisies into the peephole in the glans, shove cherries into hysterically giggling spreadeagled girls, herself included, and offer tiny acorn-cups smeared half full of fresh-milked sperm.

"How about some cigarettes?" Izz called bravely, and Ludwik felt an inexpressible pang for something lost in childhood: cozy, lamplit, secret. Was it a snowhouse? A tent in the rain? A crawlspace with his birds' egg collection in it? Gnonka, however, was conducting a lugubrious debate with himself which become the more violent the further it went: These middle-class kids are pampered to death, yes milord three bags full, but who'll get shot if they're found, one of them Jewish, the girl, that's for sure? Whose land are they on when all's said and done? Not for a few cast-off suits and only gold enough to buy a pre-war birdcage. I'm a soft touch through and through, I ought to nail them in when he's gone and drown them with a hose, then we'd all have peace and quiet, a nice invasion. But the parents would blab. Right. Wait till the SS have whistled them off,

Gnonka my lad, as they surely will, and then I'll water the children. Or I'll gas them. No, just nail them up tight and leave them to practice their praying. The shouts would soon stop. Why don't I dump a load of manure right on top of them and shift the pigs out for a day or two? What the hell have I been and gone and done? I didn't have to do anything at all.

His rudimentary mind aglow with vicious plans, matched only by the mawkishness of his self-congratulation, Gnonka patted Ludwik on the back in the twilight. "Comfy now," he growled with caustic chumminess. "I'm half-tempted to climb in there myself. Who knows what we mightn't get up to after lights out."

"Goodnight," Ludwik said. "We will come and go as discreetly as we can, if we can come at all. They have food for three days at least. They will come out only at night. When you're close by, say hello. Just say *Hello, it's Pulawsky*. They'll understand. Ask if everything's all right."

"This," Gnonka told him in a sly, punitive whine, "is a cheap lease. It'll upset my pigs for sure, and there's no crop going to come up. It's not as if we'd planted a root crop, is it now? The price might even increase if the going gets tricky" (he winked in the gloom) "during the national emergency. You've heard the radio no doubt. One of our famous artillery regiments ran into some German tanks, and only two of its guns managed to fire. The German generals are putting themselves up, by invitation, in grand old castles all over the place, like the one they say Napoleon used, way back when. You can still see the scratches his spurs made on the wooden floor. Now the spurs are different."

On went the middle plank over the hole, leaving only a thin streak of yellow along either side. The airhole worked. Then the candle went out, snuffed so clumsily Izz burned his finger and thumb. It was nine-fifteen on his father's watch. The farewells came in muffled pitch, from below to up above, from there to three hardly visible planks. Ludwig rode away weeping quite openly in the dark and did not hear Gnonka roar angrily, for reasons unknown, at his dozing pigs. Then Ludwik stopped, wiped his face on his shirt sleeve, switched on the bicycle lamp, stopped again, switched off the lamp to comply with wartime regulations, found he could not see his way, and flipped it on again: he was not a military target, the war was virtually over anyway, and he was damned if he ride blindly, after interring his son and one other, into a display of coffins for sale. Flares twinkled along the horizon, indices (he recklessly thought for a moment) to all the other fathers riding home on bicycles after seeing their children into places of safety, in good hands, with four square meals, clean ventilation, vermin-free beds, and good thick walls against the bullets and the winter.

9

"They've gone," Izz said, "they have actually gone," testing his voice for loudness, with Myrrh on his right. The ground seemed to suck all the edge, the timbre, from his voice.

"Are you scared? It's sort of fun, I suppose, but all I can think of is mice and spiders. I'm tucked in all right, it isn't anything like chilly, but I don't want a spider coming up my nose while I'm asleep. Izz? Are you awake? You must be."

"You flick them away," he told her with a firm pat on her blanketed stomach, "or you squelch them between your fingers and tell yourself they're bits of bacon or bread. Think how small *they* are, and how big you."

"Not when I'm asleep I can't. Never mind. It's not like being buried, is it. I can hear the pigs. They're company in a way. And any time we want we can sit up and climb out. Shall we do it now?"

"You've only just settled in. We ought not to show a light as late as this. I suppose it's early, though. Silly, isn't it: the only time you're not supposed to show a light is exactly when you need one. When you can, you don't need one. Let's stay put this first night."

Her voice thick and forced, as if straining into some antiquated long-distance telephone system, Kazimierz to Berlin, she said, "I don't want the pigs to root us out in broad daylight."

"Like a sandwich? Some hot-water-bottle soup?"

"Izz, I can't see. Switch the flashlight on, please."

He dazzled them briefly although pointing the glare at their feet, then aimed the stubby fan of light sideways and upward, but all they could see was spade smoothed earth with tiny crumbles here and there, landslides made by earthworms. The soil looked unusually pale, as if tinged with lime. Myrrh's face, as he peered at her, lost proportion in the gloom, her chin and nose lengthening as he looked at her. Then, for a joke, he popped the head of the flashlight into his mouth, making a pink gargoyle of his cheeks, and she laughed smoothly, trying to make her breath frost in the rosy light. "Crickets," she whispered. "Listen."

"It's the pigs," he said. "They must have colds."

"Just think," she began, letting her mind roam, and then forgetting to say the rest aloud.

"I'm *for* that," he said. "It's one of the things you can do in here without getting into trouble. Well, maybe not. Depends what you think about."

"The end of the world." She sounded husky and self-hurt.

"Is that all?" I sound too snide, he thought.

"Isn't that enough?"

"There's always something left, I can't *see* any such thing, Myrrh. It's an exaggeration."

Pretending to take the huff, she went one better, as always becoming more complex and allusive when he quibbled at one of her phrases. "I didn't mean that. It's more like something in music, after music is over, a vibration in the air of a concert hall. Well, in this case, the vibration seems to be there before the music begins. Know what I mean?"

"Of course, but if we're lucky we'll never find out."

"We can't stay here forever, Izz. We'll be found. We'll soon be back in school, it's that time of year already. Or we'll die." How easy it was to say that word, just say it.

"We won't die, we'll never die. Our luck is good."

He yawned, not so much from fatigue as from lack of decent air, then said it again, to convince her. "Our luck is really very good. And I know German, after all."

"So do I."

"Yes, Myrrh, my precious, but mine is the German of Berlin, see, where the whole thing begins. Mine is diplomatic German."

"Then you'll never offend anyone. Do you think, Izz, if the whole of Poland had spoken diplomatic German we'd ever have been invaded at all?" Was she joking as her mind began to drift before the siege of sleep?

"Once," he told her, going in a quite different direction, "I slept in a little loft when I stayed with an aunt in Warsaw, and you couldn't walk more than a step in any direction. There was all sorts of stuff on the floor: empty coal-scuttles, tiny stools, trash baskets, an old sewing machine, a broken samovar. Even the standard lamp had a big ribbed base, like a pyramid of weights. The walls were covered with the sorts of reproductions you never look at. The window was small and so high in the wall I couldn't see out. But I didn't mind, I pretended I was in a lighthouse, and then in a submarine at the bottom of the Baltic Sea, and I began to enjoy everything because it was so close to me. After a while I couldn't tell where it began and I left off. I'd never felt so safe. I suppose I could even feel like that in here, though I'd rather be at my aunt's. I never knew, there, if going out made the room seem smaller when I got back into it, or if staying in all day, when it rained, blinded me to how small it was."

"And did you talk diplomatic German?"

"I talked lighthouse-keeper-ese."

"Izz, you don't listen. Screw your aunt and her room."

Izz was thinking of the mayor in the skillet, unwilling to concede the ridiculousness of the thing that happened.

"I don't want to talk about it. Go to sleep, Izz."

"I can't, I thought I heard guns going *wump-wump*."

"Guns don't go *wump*-whatever, they go *boom-blam*."

"Honest?" Now he listened with his nose pinched and said, "If you do that it's like the sound of the sea in a shell."

"How far away, Izz?" She was whispering and sounded cold.

"Fifteen kilometers maybe."

"Then they're not coming peacefully. There will be killing and things will get blown up."

"Those Huns are crazy. They have an army and they want to use it, they want to show it off."

"You should have stayed in Berlin."

"No, I was scared to death, in a quiet sort of way. All day they banged through the streets with brass bands, and they kept lifting up their shiny boots like storks do with their legs."

They tried to come up with restful thoughts, thoughts they kept to themselves, neither speaking, but each listening to the sound of the other's breath: pulmonary smoke blown against an unseen moon. Brislings, Izz thought: we're just like brislings in a can, waiting to be opened up, have the oil drained off us, and then squashed with a fork onto toast. One of these days, soon, I'll have to go up for water unless that farmer brings it, and in my experience you can't rely on farmers. We'll both have to go up, too, for calls of nature. Unless we live like pigs.

"Myrrh, do you need to *go*?"

"Where shall we go when we go?"

"Not with the pigs. Promise to tell me when you have to, and I'll come with you, only a certain distance, of course."

"It's supposed to be at night, but who can wait all day?"

"We might have to."

"Well," she said with aggressive hauteur, "I'm going to get out and do it when I have to. If they want to, they can shoot me for doing it. I won't be filthy, I won't."

Again there came the bloated thump of gunfire, but the ground did not vibrate, and Myrrh grunted amiable disapproval as she vaguely flapped a hand against his side. "Come closer," he said with a blocked-up nose. "You needn't do anything."

"On a night like this! It would be better in here, Izz, if it had a name. Dugout. Burrow. An earth like foxes have."

"Then we'll be foxes if you like." He hugged her head, restrewed the invisible long black hair, trying to weave a dream in which the impractical and its opposite had equal force, in which they could lapse into a simultaneous sleep that no pig and no bomb could spoil. "Your chin is hurting my collar bone," he told her gently. "Better. If only we had a gun." The thought had spun into his mind unbidden.

"Our parents don't have guns. Who has?"

"There's always the knife, I suppose," he said floatingly.

"You want to be heroic."

"I want to sit and read books in a tropical garden full of red flowers shaped like ears. Is that heroic?"

"Am I invited? Or are you going to be a hermit?"

"Only if you'll cook. No, we'll dine out all the time."

Into their developing, fitful dream-sleep, a faint land-tremor intruded about one in the morning as the Polish remnant used their mortars against the tanks which just kept on coming over and through them. Izz and Myrrh slept on, stirring only to nudge back into contact with each other, breathing each other's mildly sour breath with incurious abstractedness. The space they lay in was not even whitewashed, but at least below the level of the flying shrapnel. At dawn the pigs woke, though, and trotted about above them with dismal squeals, making the planks rattle and sending through the cracks a faint drift of sawdust flakes. The whole landscape was astir in the rosy half dark, churned up and smoking, with ragged shouts, white and yellow and vermillion flashes, bangs and cluttered-sounding thuds, with sirens blowing both the alarm and the all-clear at the same time. In the midst of all this, doors were being slammed, horses were running amok, riderless, through the streets, and Major Ludwik Czimanski, waiting for his one cup of lukewarm coffee to activate his system, was trying to hitch a ride in full dress uniform from the corner of Pulawy Street back to Warsaw and his invalid mother. His ride eventually came in a motorcycle sidecar whose driver offered the handlebars to the dapper, cool-eyed officer who had appeared out of nowhere and must know where to go. Refusing ("Drive northward, man"), Ludwik held his sword erect between his knees, point upward, already considering, half giddily, a mode of attack in which a motorcycle charged while the sidecar passenger pointed his sword forward, ready to impale. The stink of sulfur and burned manganese had ousted the damp aromas of late summer and, along with them, for the major at least, of his son cached like a termite, of Wanda ordered to the ravine but refusing, and of the Admiral who was bound to come, or send emissaries, sooner or later, skilled in half a dozen languages and strong to save.

When Izz woke, his head full of webs and his right leg numb, it was with an extraordinary sense of desolation, not so much from being where he was as from having done what he was told to do. He felt very much in his place, into which for reasons good or bad he had been put; a world gone awry had somehow deprived him of his individuality, and here he was in a category: waif, refugee, fugitive, with so many questions never even asked, so many other possibilities shunned. Trying to wake, or at least to muster some version of alertness, he summed up what had happened in a series of thoughts which appalled him with their severity: *Our parents have planted us like two flowers, two seeds, two bulbs; we are probably more conspicuous down here, because obviously we are going to have to come and go so as not to live in filth, than we might have been either at home or hidden in a barn somewhere else on the farm; we have no information about the war, our parents, our home.* He felt suddenly relegated to the back of his father's mind, a man who, though Izz knew nothing of this, was in the act of commandeering a horse in order to lead a few stragglers against a crossroads held by the invaders, a phantom doodle executed by automatic-minded dreamers intent on doing something, anything, as distinct from just giving in. Major Czimanski's best thought, new that morning, was one he wished he'd had time to savor, but then he convinced himself that what was more human than anything, on the level of mind at least, was one sharp aperçu registered in the midst of turmoil, in this instance a flower of war that ran: *As if life itself were not frightening enough, along comes history to frighten you even more*, which he then had time to refine into *Both life and history can frighten you to death; either is lethal; but being scared by the one distracts you from being scared by the other, so we actually thrive by having the horrors divided.* He knew that, if he subdivided the horrors enough times, he would come out the other end in a state of giddy euphoria, ecstatic to be alive enough even to theorize; and then, as severe with himself as with a schoolboy, he ordered himself to compress the notion into something small enough to chew on, like a pellet of gum, in the act of riding against a barricade, with perhaps even a riding rhythm to it, such as "Trauma has two heads," which he found satisfactory and said aloud several times, knowing that he knew more about it than it said. Then he thought of Izz and Myrrh, smiled at the outsize tumbleweed of barbed wire up the road from him, and knew he had done the right thing. Back in the house on Pulawy Street, according to instructions, Wanda had already scrawled in lipstick letters a meter high, in each room, PULAWSKI and the farmer's name, GNONKA, but not that only: each room bore the name transliterated into Greek, —NONKA, redundant surely, in its pedantry, but Greek was a language the Admiral knew, having diligently acquired it since spending a summer vacation in Greece with his parents in 1902 and becoming entranced with the story of a certain admiral's heroic feats in the Greek War of Independence, especially his night attack on the Turkish fleet in the Channel of Chios, June 18-19, 1822. Major Czimanski knew his Admiral well; anyone visiting the house on Pulawy Street, an address the Admiral had, would at once flash the weird word to the eccentric mastermind back in Berlin who always knew what to do. The daubs done, Wanda could go to the ravines, but it was too late, there was fighting in the streets, which was why Wilson and Suzanna Sakal sat in the basement playing dominoes, having spent the night reading to each other from their holiday books.

"To neither ravine nor farm," Wilson told her. "There is nowhere to go. *Yet.* Once the first wave has passed through, we'll be able to move about again."

"We could have kept her with us all this time, husband."

"I speak confidently, which comes from being who I am; but there is no telling what just might happen to us, and therefore not to them, in the next twenty-four hours. Don't worry, we did the right thing. Or, rather, confronted with various things, some worse than others, we did one that's half-decent. Wait and see." They played the radio, nearly all of it scattered atmospherics with here and there a phrase or two, announcing, as curtly as possible, the transfer of a Polish HQ from Center City to Lublin Union Square, say, all of it news from Warsaw, and all bad. Then came a few bars of the national anthem followed by a plea to stay tuned, indefinitely, for the Mayor of Warsaw, who would speak, but then a burst of static blotted out the rest of the transmission, while from Kazimierz itself there was nothing, only the frayed thunder of motorcycles from above as advanced Nazi units moved through en route to Brest Litovsk.

"Well," said Myrrh without even looking sideways at Izz, "we didn't die in our sleep. How long have you been up?"

"Half an hour. I think the Germans came and maybe went around dawn. It's quiet now. The bouillon's still warm. Here." And she drank messily from the mouth of the hot-water bottle while Izz, with one leg prodded the underside of the middle plank and managed to raise it a hand's width, letting in dribs and drabs of early morning light, fits of birdsong, and some bracingly cool air touched with smoke. Then he sat up, stood, and peered out with the plank raised no higher than necessary, but all he could see was smoke from Gnonka's chimney, twirled away by a faint northeast breeze. The pigs were silent, even when he clambered out and, crouching by the low wall, added his water to the crumbly slop already on the ground. Coming back, he skidded and nearly fell, which drove the pigs back into their shed. "Your turn now," he called to Myrrh, "the coast is clear." Up she came to squat, her face contorted in aversion, by the wall while Izz, half back in the hole, kept an eye on the landscape. Over toward Kazimierz there was another kind of smoke, like broken charcoal bubbles that would not disperse on the breeze but just expanded without seeming to thin out.

No horse, no German shepherd, no Gnonka. "Do you like anticlimaxes," he asked Myrrh, "in the middle of Armageddon? I mean, how about some breakfast? Chicken sandwich? Then some plum cake?" He drew the plank over them again, fixed the radio's earpiece in his ear, and switched on, slowly rolling the tuner to and fro.

Not having slept enough, Myrrh began to doze, hugging herself with both arms and trying to use the blurred rumpus from above (or was it the sound of homesickness, magnified, doing an incessant flux and reflux in her ears?) to calm her twitching mind. Sounds heard horizontally, she told herself, seem bedraggled. Far from sleep, Izz badgered his mind's eye with frightful images, as if to guarantee a mellow outcome by harping on the worst: the town on fire, his parents' rented home gutted, the menfolk lined up against a wall daubed with patriotic slogans.

"I can't sleep," Myrrh complained. "Kiss my nose," which is what she frequently had asked him to do when strolling together or cuddling at the movies: a refinement, a variation, a tender ritualizing of their bond, and always supplemented when in private with an equally ritual bit of talk.

"Kiss my nose," said with imperious nervousness.

He did, then always had to ask "Where do you come from?"

"I come—" always the voluptuous pause, "from Nosekiss, in Bessarabia." Why she had chosen Bessarabia, instead of some place in Poland, they never wondered; and the exchange went on, relaxing because nothing random could invade it.

"What's your name?"

"Kiss Nose," she said, "I'm Kiss Nose from Nose Kiss" (this latter being the only acceptable alternative to Bessarabia).

"And where are you going, Kiss Nose?" Always that query.

This could always be factual: she would say where or invent a destination. Today she whispered "Underground."

"Who with?" He kept his lips on the bridge of her nose until she responded, and afterwards as well.

"With my sweetheart, Izzie." Unsure if that last word explained who, or was a vocative to renew his attention, Izz removed his lips and gently pinched the bridge of her nose between finger and thumb, varying the contact and prolonging it in the manner of someone seeing a person for perhaps the last time ever.

"What's up?" she asked.

"I am. The Germans have gone through—sorry, I told you that. Maybe we have to be told things again after each sleep. People who insist on the truth also come to terms with death, and if they know they have they try to forget each time they go to sleep. And then they remind themselves all over again. It's only human."

"You're more awake than I am," Myrrh answered. "I'm silly. I want people to be happy. How innocent I suppose I am, to want that when the whole world's coming apart. I first realized it—that I wanted it—when I was watching skaters compete in Warsaw for the national championships, years ago. I couldn't have been very old. At certain times they seemed to flat over the ice, with every motion beautifully weighed, no sag, no slip, nothing abrupt, and I thought something like—They are in perfect harmony with the world of things, never mind how much strain and effort's underneath. It's hard to explain. Then I had this weird thought next: I wanted the whole world to be in that kind of harmony all at the same time, even if everybody was cursing under their breath about what hard work it was. I mean, people as much at home, and as graceful in place, as a rabbit scampering. In Biology not long ago, we had photographs of the South African springbok's courtship ways. The male stands behind the female and with his front leg taps the outside of her left rear one, then does the same on the right. Then the left again, and the right again, for quite a long time until she gets the idea, as if she didn't get it from the beginning. Well, what I like about it is the—serenity of it all, the poise, the way it's completely itself and nothing else. So much of what people do is mixed up with other stuff. Discords all the way."

"One day," Izz murmured, "I'll stand behind you, then, tap your legs. Tap, tip, tap, tip!"

"Don't make fun."

"Not making fun."

"Not making fun, I'm responding. I wish you ran the world. If you did, we wouldn't be down here, like a couple of silverfish in the ashpan under a roaring fire."

"With earthworms, which admittedly don't hurt you, curled up into the walls only inches from our faces. Ugh." Myrrh faked a sob, but not the revulsion behind the impulse.

"Try a sandwich, they're still fresh."

"No, I can see the little bird the chicken was, clucking about and flapping."

"They're not *that* small." He reached sideways and found one of the two water bottles. "I'm itching again," he said. "One of my blasted allergies, I suppose." Izz regularly came out in hives in response to humidity, fruit, cheese, preservative chemicals, wool, and mere agitation, against all of which he swabbed his skin with calamine lotion, none of which he had with him in the hole. It had always seemed to him "manlier" to blame his hives on anything but agitation; now he said "I'll have to will them away or scratch them to death."

"Smear them with spit," she said unsentimentally as if emerging from a trance. "Here," and she applied spit of her own, and kept on applying it while resuming her initial idea about the skaters. "That is also how people die, buoyed up by all the love they've had in life. See what I mean? Unloved, they have nothing to hold on to when they...go over."

Still raking his fingernails over his wrist, Izz came up with an image of his own, which he stated even while fidgeting against the histamine that coursed through his body and gave him brief, stud-like shivers. "When you see squirrels foraging about, up and down the trees, or woodpeckers hacking away for grubs under bark, that's your harmony, I guess. But does what you were saying apply as well to a lion jumping a gazelle and ripping its bowels out? I think you only like harmony when it's inoffensive."

Quite through with argument, or at least with pursuing this particular one into the far reaches of hair-splitting (as she saw it), Myrrh told him to kiss the bridge of her nose again. "Twelve nose-kisses now!" There in the opaque gray glow under the planks, he complied, ignoring the sudden scream of the pigs in panic, and shutting his eyelids tight until carmine or vermillion shreds seemed to float across his sealed-up vision; when he looked at her again, after number twelve, he saw segments of her face in split-second glimpses, as if, in parody of his antic with the flashlight in his mouth, she had managed to make bits of her skin luminous. She twinkled, she spoke, "I have to go. Again."

"Too much water," he said in mellow blame.

"No, I'm just scared to death." Up they went, crouching, and he looked away as she explained to him, "Girls can't do it into bottles, Izz. We tried. Remember the Kimskie picnic? Put in a complaint to God Almighty, if you have one."

"What if you get us killed?"

"Then the complaint will get there sooner."

10

When, after an inconceivably distant series of explosions, something jagged, light, and warm landed on his chest, like a small conical finger done in bronze, Izz stowed the thing in his back pocket without saying a word. "A spent round," he told her "flattened where it must have hit something."

"Where is it? You put it away really fast." With her tongue lolling on her bottom lip, she sniffed at it. "It smells like linseed oil. An oven burner just switched off."

"It's been fired from a fairly new barrel."

"We're still alive, still here." She kissed him on the cheek as if in specific gratitude to him, and then wailed upward at the planks, blaming and interrogating them with "How much longer? How many days more?" Then she turned to Izz again. "Did you pray?"

"Who prays? It seems to me that, for prayer to be effective, you should be able to pray before you're born, and after your death. The rest's all imagination, and in the end it's almost a relief to know you've just been talking to yourself all along." Lying on his back, he shrugged, only to realize that the gesture meant nothing unless you were standing or sitting.

"When we're asleep, Izz," she said tentatively, with a pulsing frown that kept the bridge of her nose in motion, "we sort of plunge through the darkness. Praying isn't much different."

"Just being alive's the same as well."

Myrrh groaned as if everything had suddenly come clear. "I think God ought to pray to us, all of us. I think, to answer my own question, I *would* pray if I didn't have you to talk to. Is that you scratching, Izz?"

"It's a specially trained mouse who rubs hives on his days off."

On it went, this diffident whistling in the dark, not only refusing what was obvious (a war raging across their world), but also taking refuge from each other's worst guesses beneath an eclectic numbness in which what was trivial was up front, what was intimate was all of a sudden oblique and courtly, and what was preposterous became the bridge of life, while time itself, only dimly apprehended on either side of a fitful sleep, was a silk stocking that stretched and stretched, but never broke. Every human born had died, Izz thought; no one escapes. It's just the waiting period that's different.

It was not a situation of which children could make the best, nor was it, however, one for which they were wholly unfit, both of them having in appreciable measure the gift for improvising dreams in the slack no-time between the ironclad hashmarks sketched on the faces of clocks. The waiting was all, and in the mother-of-pearl marrow of their bones they knew it, Izz schooling himself in how best to use the amplified calm of a drawn-out second, seizing his idea of what that instant had been like and folding it back into the instant itself, Myrrh in her own way trying to listen to her cells as they grew, silent as oysters, making her frame and flesh swell just fractionally overnight, between ten to nine and nine minutes to nine, to make room for them. "Oh my knee," when Izz groaned, it was one of those iceberg statements, of which they both knew the full depth, because his aching knee was his father's knee, his mother's, the knee of the young man he was going to be, clad in pilot's leathers and ferrying airmail over the Carpathian mountains, and if she only misheard the groan, she filled in the words, wishing away the big bubble that had lodged in the top of her chest, just inside the bone cage, a couple of millimeters in from the heartspoon at the root of her neck. Her own best wizard, she removed herself back to the cradle, faintly tap-tilting her nose against one of its sides with a little comfortable snuffle that brought no one running from the neighbor room, but was through and through her own sensation, incommunicably mild. And, if the pilot of any overflying dive bomber had been able to see through the shield of earth into their burrow, he would have observed them side by side, obedient to the grand scheme which put them there, white and listless and holding hands, flat on their backs as the planet spun them and, as he banked the plane to get a better look, twirling at the bottom of the cone whose upper perimeter his flight traced out. Two small islands in some grubby Micronesia of the heart, they lay and thought their thoughts elastically: *Oh my knee*, said as if the knee belonged as much to the crumbly clay around him as to the thigh and the calf, and *That bubble hurts*, left unformulated because the bulge of the discomfort, prodding and threatening to choke her, was engram enough; to feel it was to register it enough, enough her sore body arranged about it, from her toes to her scalp, and her entire nervous system was telling itself that something was wrong. There was a hiccup that wouldn't come.

"Here today," Izz said, hoping she would complete the proverb, but having to wait until she answered, instead:

"I know."

"Do you believe it?"

"I won't say it. That proves I believe it." But did the proverb mean rescued tomorrow? Saved tomorrow? Or something much worse, unspeakable and raw? That double echo haunted them both, almost dumbfounding them with its half-and-half notion of mortality or absence. If *gone tomorrow* meant *freed* instead of *off the planet*, they need not blanch; but language itself seemed likely to undo them when even a proverb smacked them back and a simple hello, spoken at such close quarters, brought back to mind how they might never use it again to greet each other at a distance of several meters.

"Gone tomorrow," she said, finally daring to say it, "gone among the gone, gone into a tomorrow that isn't the next day after this, but feels like what comes after everything. If you say a thing enough, it doesn't feel so bad. I'd rather say something else, though. Here today, that's enough for me, not that I like it here, or that I like today, Izz, but being able to say it is something." Her blood moved, her lungs breathed, her nerves helped her to ache, and her nose, her eyes, her ears, got on with their jobs, even as she lay there telling herself to pay proper attention: *This is me, this is how it feels to be me this is how no one else in the history of mankind has felt, I am unique, I am beautiful, I am irreplaceable.* When, in fact, at Myrrh's age, all that should have been beside the point and her life from day to day a thrilled insouciance, a romp, a cavort, an adding of this to that without the faintest grip of pattern, but just her smell, her quivers, her moist athleticism, running into his, twelve into thirteen, thoroughly wound up and never running down. She seized his hand, almost mortally aware of the act as a hand-seizing: an act whose category she knew before she even moved her wrist, and squeezed it until she heard it crack, when he snatched it away murmuring, "I'm real, I'm real, don't test me." And she put the hand over her mouth as if she, and not Izz, had spoken.

"I can't get comfortable," she said, squirming on her elbows. "I never thought I'd long to be standing up."

"It's best," he told her in his sagest voice, "to pretend you're standing up close against a wall; but, if you want to lie on your side, you really have to dig out a hollow for your hipbone." That much he had learned, in resentment, camping.

Only half a kilometer away, after an interminable night which she should have spent in a ravine, Wanda had decided that another hour in an empty house whose walls were decorated with Gnonka's name would send her clean over the brink, so she gathered up her things into an old shopping basket with high hoop handles, slung it over the handlebars of the bicycle, and pedaled off on an empty stomach to the Sakal's, through the smoke-swathed debris and with obvious casualness past a group of German soldiers in green-gray tunics, who only whistled after her. On the unsteady saddle she felt as buoyant as a mushroom in water, but the basket kept bumping against her knee, reminding her that she was a woman whose child was underground, whose diplomat husband had gone off to war, and who, if she wasn't careful, would tumble straight into a shell hole in the road. We have all been blown away, she told herself in an imperious hum that matched the rhythm of her legs, and things have ended which will never come again. It does not take a shell or a bomb to do it, only some general who draws an arrow on a map that doesn't show the people living on the land, in the streets; their names never show on the maps until they're dead and gone. Being alive is no qualification for anything. Next thing, she was presenting a face that felt thick and unwieldy at the Sakal's door, as if she had come to borrow, or was reluctantly returning the bicycle and viewed the walk home as an insufferable chore which a woman of her standing should have been spared. "Oh," they said to her, not smiling at her, not inviting her in but motioning her at the same time out of the street, which surely meant into the house, or into the hedge, so Wanda just walked past their aghast gazes, past their tucked-in stomachs, into the house, her mind suddenly flooded with the risk she was taking. Not only that: she had now severed the line of contact between Izz and the house on Pulawy Street; but she also knew that a woman can wait only so long alone, listening to the blood hum in her ears, her breath like some malfunctioning cistern, the small-arms commotion in the streets, the occasional shriek, the abrupt uncoordinated creaks of the house settling.

"I've come," she told them needlessly, but it did not sound enough to say it, it was not over, it had not (in some ways) even begun, so impetuous her leaving had been; and it sounded as if they had asked for her and would be glad, or as if she had arrived with a scheme for reaching the ravines, or with word from the Admiral himself, wuff-wuffing from Berlin: *Madame, the dogs may bark, but the caravan passes on, your new name is Björnsen, or Cholmondeley (pronounced Chumley) if you prefer.* "I have come," she told them, "but that is all. I am as helpless as you; and you, being two, are twice as helpless as I am. Simple arithmetic has brought me here. I'm sorry. We are all insane."

Now started, Wanda could not stop. "And may the Lord God in His provident upstream majesty lay His curse, from Alpha to Omega, on all rented houses, on all accommodation that seems as ephemeral as human life itself. I have allowed my child to be put into a manhole, along with the rich ripe beloved of your own heart, like gold into filth, and unto snorting pigs. I have nothing left except to let my head spin and give off sparks. I have slept the sleep that makes wakefulness itself seem an act of sloth. I have heaved into the unflushable toilet what I am convinced are portions of my most intimate anatomy. I have waved my husband off, not to his next diplomatic reception, but to some boyish expedition which will net him the dowdy-looking Cross of Valor, the white and maroon ribbon of which is not given for the reading of books, the shaking of hands, the turning of phrases, not even at its oxyacetylene finest. Major Epigram they had the insolence to name him. If they had only been respectful, he would be with us now, and not whoring away after that other bauble, the Order of Military Virtue, given in five classes like so much taffeta. The chances are, he will not have a chest to pin it on. His only son will wear it on state occasions round his neck, and the taller he grows the more we shall adjust it to hang not too high, not too low. I have simply, in goodness of heart, and having nothing else to do, nor anyone to do it with, arrived to inform you that we have all taken leave of our senses when we might have *negotiated* this matter on the local level, and Major Ludwik Czimanski could have plied his trade if he wished in a rented uniform from the old French army, in which as you know, at least until 1912 or -13, Polish men actually served, with a tall blue hat like an inverted fez, an azure tunic with scarlet lapels, and a cloak to be worn over one shoulder, casually, so as to expose the sword where it kisses the boots. All this he showed me. There was no need to ride off into the smoke before the coffee was even hot, as if God had called him from on high with massed hunting trumpets and baying angels. All I had to say to him was 'We need you' and saying it should have sufficed, but it did not, and I said it, I said it on the stairs and in the kitchen, in the garret where he was unpacking military things he brought with him from Berlin. I said, 'Ludwik, these militarists have made you military, which is not your forte,' but he only said 'I have been mocked, my love, and I am simply taking my turn, it is my turn to go, there are no quotations left.' There are no Admirals. I have no child. This is not any year at all. Something swollen and disastrous, like a bleeding goldfish, has come swimming through our lives. I have come, but there is nothing of me left. I need no bed, therefore, no meals, no chair, no breathing space. I am a little Polish ghost who suddenly has learned to cry in every language in the world. I am here, but I do not have to be spoken with, any more than Mucius Scaevola, about whom Ludwik spoke, who thrust his hand into the fire after failing to assassinate Porsenna. I have had so much pain. Look how dusty I am. First I died, and now I have come."

"You have come," Wilson Sakal said, "in style."

Throughout all this she made as if to sit, backing to a chair and dipping her elbows like someone testing bathwater, but then drawing away in a ponderous twisted flutter while her head kept up a fast nodding which reminded Wilson Sakal of some mating bird, he could not remember if it were a dove or a pigeon. Still not accustomed to seeing her with short hair, they felt in the presence of some prolix stranger who, while stopping short of verbal abuse, talked with such tearaway vehemence that they felt rebuked, got at, put upon, even though what she said was vividly impersonal—indeed spoken thus, toward some point on the wall behind them, because she did not think them worth addressing, or because she was even more impersonal than that and was a tide returning that had years ago gone out. Hardly aware of their eyes fixed on her with incredulous commiseration, she sensed an erratic heat moving through her as she talked; she wanted to squeal or shriek, but she kept on saying things in that same percussive monotone of perpetual afterthought, with no idea of where she would end, but quietly yowling because there would never again be sprightly little sallies between Ludwik and Izz, at table or over fizzy drinks in the garden, whether madcap exchanges about Pulawski the airplane designer or about how the wildebeest gives birth, shaking its rear end about until the newborn falls away. All that was done with. The three of them had gone separate ways as if at some barely audible starter's signal, and all she had remaining was a traumatic sense of inappropriateness, a fiendish version of what had happened in their first apartment in Berlin, where, trying to set out her toiletries in the bathroom, and Ludwik's, and Izz's, she had found every surface—the washbasin, the top of the toilet cistern, even the sides of the lilac-covered bath—convex, so that everything toppled off, could not even be balanced with a steady hand. The same feeling of not being wanted, of having been born to be humiliated by trivia, came to her more strongly now: the world itself was not designed for living in, and the only accommodation she could make to it was to mouth her rage in long, curling, poignant commentaries meant to empty her out, of love and fury and ideas and desire, until she had become the consummate husk, chaff of history whose wind could blow her right across the Polish border into the wastelands of Russia, where a niche in the snows awaited her and she would pass away with a self-inflicted snowball in her mouth.

"Imagine," she hurled at Wilson and Suzanna, in quarrelsome postscript with her eyes trance-thickened, "over in London at this very minute they are having picnics in blue blazers and gingham frocks as if the rape of Poland were part of the Oxford-Cambridge boat race! Thunder," she said, "I heard it, thunder or gunfire it's all the same to me, it's ogreish and dumb, it knows nothing about us."

"But," Wilson said in a voice gravelly and weak, "the British have declared war on Germany, they really have, not that you'd know the difference. They have carved their name on a tree somewhere, it's about as consoling as that. Wanda, won't you sit down?" She did, but with mouth still working although her voice had ceased. Then she began again, in a truculent whisper, bewildering the Sakals into the same disheveled mental state as herself.

"The thunder is the sound of the British declaring war."

"Pens are quieter," Wilson suggested, thinking *Anything can be said now; here we are with all this grammar, to put words together with, and none of it matters. Meaning is over.* "We were going to celebrate at the Savoy Hotel," he said with a sleepwalking mouth. "I was going to speak on the BBC. By invitation."

"And the only peace is between thunderclaps."

"Perhaps not even then."

"And all the children are buried, the fathers all have swords. Are you going to answer me or not?"

Wilson knew from his silence that he was not, and Suzanna had closed her eyes, shutting in the horrors she dared not mention.

"In that case," Wanda said, "you had best offer me a cup of tea. I am close to being an hysteric. Before that, however, I would like to propose that we stroll over and visit the children with just a few things they might need, some hot soup, some toothpicks, a few handkerchiefs, some envelopes and stamps." In just this tone of diffident efficiency she had spoken all her life, and Wilson could not stand it, not today; it was as if a polar bear had quoted Homer. "Yes, Wanda," he said, "yes, Wanda.

My God, Wanda, you are really being Wanda today. Isn't she, Suzanna?"

11

But Suzanna could not find the syllable with which to start an answer, and just let the pent-up tears roll from behind closed lids, with no attempt to mop them as they came.

"The children," Wilson tried to tell her, "are like letters *poste restante*, waiting collection," but wishing with the back of his mind the farmer Gnonka didn't stink of vinegar and dung, wishing with all of his mind that, when there was nothing to do, he didn't feel willing to do anything, no matter how reckless, useless, vain. "There's time yet," he said. "We just have to hold on."

"Hold out," Suzanna said in a stifled, urgent whisper, at which point Wanda prodded and shoved them under the kitchen table, made them crouch and hug one another, and then embraced them with a fierce vague almost painful hug which reminded Wilson how Wanda used to throw the discus and set his wife audibly weeping while repeating "I know, I know," as if the two words kept the tears going, and the tears the two words, in miserable unison.

"If only," Myrrh was saying, "the sheep was here, the one on my bed at home, with a fluffy lamb inside a hatch under its tail. In the store they called it Lamb with Baby, which is stupid.

It's Sheep with Lamb, of course, for when I'm lonely, when you were in Berlin or some place equally revolting. I lift its ears and seat it on my shoulder, and I sometimes make the lamb milk it. I make it nurse." Soothed by a memory more potent than absence, she slumped against him, breathing hard and warm into his neck while he, trying not to hear the pigs thump-trotting on the planks above them in what sounded like a squish of liquid which so far hadn't dripped through onto them, told himself The rain, the rain, it's the rain that puts everyone to sleep.

The 'rain' worked. Just before ten o'clock Izz and Myrrh were sleeping the kind of sleep that resembled floating forward over a shallow seafloor whose patches of alabaster sand distracted the sleeper with reminders that such sleeping, whatever anyone else said, was nearly a deliberate act. With vacant, aching eyes Wilson was looking through the boarded-up window at dead horses in the street, over one of which a tank had ground, leaving the carcass as only a swollen looking bearskin. Upstairs, Wanda was lying face down on the bedroom floor with a mound of bed sheets tugged over her while Suzanna kept watch, trying to knit, but making mistakes galore. In his fatigued mind's eye he inched out of the door, decided against the bicycle Wanda had brought, and stumbled through the pitted streets, past several gutted still-burning houses, inadequate chains of men with buckets who hailed him and asked him to lend a hand, past the gasoline station, the bicycle-hardware store, over the failing wooden bridge, the disused water mill, past the street of the coffins, and so arrived at Gnonka's farm, raucous with horses, cows, pigs, and the wolfhound all going mad. Thank God the dog is tethered, he thought, as he swung himself stiffly over the pigsty wall, only to be felled by bustling pigs, and he started calling "Pulawski, Pulawski" right away. Then he knocked on the middle plank.

Stirring, Izz waited for a bayonet or gun muzzle to prod down at them, but then heard the airplane designer's name, shoved the plank upward and said "Hello, Uncle Wilson. How's Poland? Where's the farmer?" They hadn't seen him at all, all day.

"He's asleep," he said.

"Look, it's your father. Shall we invite him in?" Izz asked Myrhh. And Wilson lay down between them like a bolster.

Only then, lying there rigid as a stave in a pigsty of his own imagining, did Wilson know finally that he should not go, and that they should all three close their minds. He felt as if he had ground the peas in a pod to pulp with the heel of his brown and white paneled Oxford shoe, and he punished himself again and again with the off chance that something grievous as distinct from uncomfortable would happen to Izz and Myrrh: a bomb or a shell, discovery and capture prefacing some Teutonic atrocity, but he reasoned himself out of such dread anticipations and in the end talked himself round: left alone, the children were much less at risk than if visited, and the visitors would be safer at home too. It sounded what Ludwik, the bizarre scheme's architect, would have said: *Leave well alone, Wilson, you can no more help it along than you can help a solstice, a dawn.* Then Wilson, half ready to congratulate himself on having nosed his way to the sagest position, realized that what all of them, perhaps even Ludwik included (wherever he was), were waiting for was the quantity of the Germans' behavior. All depended on that, on outbreaks of amused, lazy bullying, but no more than that, or systematic and inventive atrocity that went on for months and as time went on became more codified, more systematic. But, somewhere in Berlin, an introverted, lisping admiral who headed German intelligence, no less, was not finding time to open the mental file that would save them from either eventuality. It seemed to Wilson as if the disaster had to be full-blown before the Admiral's absolutist German mind saw any point in getting them out of it; unless he had just pocketed the money and decided to keep quiet, buying a truckload of dog food with it, a new Arabian.

(Wilson sometimes felt he knew the Admiral better than he knew Ludwik himself, having heard so much about him as Ludwik became expansive during leaves, citing the man's hatred of paperwork, his passion for visiting Southern Europe on a fake Chilean passport, calling himself Kika and visiting apartments he rented under the name Reed Rosas, and on one occasion, while driving through the Black Forest after a foray into Spain, encountering a snowstorm so severe that he took refuge in an isolated farmhouse where a peasant widow insisted on nursing him back to a health he was in no danger of losing: "Sir, you are soaked to the skin"; "Do you think," he'd responded, "pneumonia...?"; "A hot bath, sir, at once"; and she had undressed him, bathed him, and later on, as the Admiral intimated, accorded him extraordinary privileges and such use of her body, such ministrations to his, as he had never dreamed of, even in the fleshpots of Paris and Estoril.)

Such was the man, the figment of Arabian myth mounted on an Arabian mare pampered with sugar, on whom their lives depended; would he perhaps arrive incognito, disguised as a peasant woman from the Black Forest, offering unprecedented sexual adventures printed crudely on a piece of cardboard? Wilson felt betrayed. The bargain in Berlin had been too sketchy. Ludwik was exactly not the man to negotiate such things. If only he, Wilson Sakal, professor of economics, had been dealing with the Admiral, both children would be safe in bed in the Savoy Hotel in London, dreaming of Oliver Cromwell, Stratford upon Avon, the Changing of the Guard, and Dick Whittington, three times Lord Mayor of London. He even knew the telephone number of the hotel, but how glacially remote it seemed, how luculent and useless and blank.

"Now I know how the weak feel," he told Suzanna, who reported that Wanda had begun to sleep. "The flightless birds of New Zealand. Like the kiwi, the ostrich, the emu. We run in circles on the ground, but we cannot flap and go, and anyone, just anyone, can take a running kick at us, or a potshot, or tether us with a cord, dig traps for us to run into. I tell you: we should have gone when there were trains, when there was fuel for the car, when—when there was a direction to things. The Germans from the west, in a week's time the Russians from the east (you see if I'm not right), and what's left? A nonexistent Polish Corridor, leading from nowhere to nowhere."

"Don't grumble, Wilson," she told him with motherly aplomb.

"Grumbling's the rhetoric of being ridiculous," he told her. "There's nothing else left. I'm grumbling about having to grumble."

She stuffed his pipe for him, produced matches, and with a neat smile lit it up, taking a few puffs with an eager look of overpowered solicitude. "Come out of the rain, Wilson. Smoke your pipe. Be a good professor."

"That slimeball of an admiral," he said with only token vehemence. "He lets us dangle."

"Penises dangle," Suzanna told him. "Not people."

"Are you," he said affectionately, "speaking from experience, Madame? Or is that a rebuke to me? I admit I've not been especially active since we let Myrrh go. What did you expect?"

"Nothing," she answered so fast there seemed no gap between the end of his question and the first syllable of her retort. "Then I'm grateful for anything that comes along."

"You wait," he said, "there are things coming you won't be grateful for. Here we sit, just waiting. At this very moment, they are probably mopping up the ravines at bayonet point. They will be listing the local Jews. They will have commandeered the water, the gasoline, the bread, the radio, the telephones, the trains, the buses, the undelivered mail from the past four days. The newspapers will be theirs, not to mention all the fretwork saws, the typewriters, the public fountains, the sharp wheels that slice ham, the pickled fetuses in the University pathology laboratory, the skeletons in the graveyards, the dogs in the kennels, the babies in their cots, the cigars in the wooden boxes, the cancers just beginning to eat their way through the bowels of some of our dearest friends, the wax in the ears of the man who conducts the autumn symphony concerts, the termites in the logs, the trout in the rivers, the wrinkled faces august and impenitent and elegiacally over-attentive of all grandparents in their photographs in heavy metal frames more lasting than bronze—as if to turn back time itself, fold it over, sew it down, make a hem against mortality—"

"Wilson, you miss lecturing. It shows."

"No, I thank God your parents are in Canada. My, what prescience I used to have." Montreal seemed out in Andromeda.

"Your own would have joined them, had they lived."

12

Wilson's face halted all its motions, dwindled, flushed, trembled, stilled itself again, then with taut forlornness put out a few more words: "I do not like to thank a car accident for sparing me embarrassment or grief. If I had my choice, I would still prefer the problem of having to try to save them now to the awful miserable blank of living through all the years they thought they would live to see." His pipe had gone out, but he made no effort to relight it, just puffing and sucking at it, making a spittle-whistle into a tuneless composition rehearsed ad infinitum.

"Parents," said Wanda huskily, who had come downstairs, "mine do not speak to each other, nor have they spoken to me in years, one in Poznan, imagine that, and my father in Munich, married to some whore or painter. He might have joined the Nazi party for all I know. Our German connections have not exactly paid off, have they? Not that, over the past ten years, I have been easy to speak to, considering how uppity life on the diplomatic circuit is supposed to have made me. 'There are some cakes which she positively disdains, those with cherries or dates, for instance. Nor will she touch a drop of Indian tea. It has to be China.' When you are reviled simply for having been a good, competent, gracious wife to the assistant military attaché, who after all is a diplomat of sorts, you have to redo your register of friends. You must be among the lucky ones, my dears. Some Poles I no longer even know, and some I address in German. These are the drunkards and the *sportifs*. I have come to prefer the serious people and the wits, such as yourselves, most of all the serious who take themselves with a little levity and the wits who do not think of themselves as essentially funny. How many enemies I have made this way I have no idea. I have been busy cultivating my garden, helping my son plan his career as a great aviator, and most of all supporting my husband in his aspiration to rise from assistant military attaché to attaché full blown, at the same time trying to persuade him not to devise for the entire Czimanski family a coat of arms half Polish, half German. King Edward the Third of England claimed the crown of France, and so he divided *his* coat of arms into four, quartering the lilies of France with the lions of England, and so the English coat of arms remained for nearly four hundred years until it became clear, even to them, that France was a mere pipe dream after all. With Ludwik, though, things were quite different. He wanted to dramatize his ambivalence as neither fish nor fowl, the fence he had to straddle, and there they were, planning and plotting all the time. Next thing you see German soldiers hoisting a Polish border turnpike out of the way, one of those with the fluffy Polish eagle that looks rather like a cockatoo, doesn't it, and you know that a man such as Ludwik, with inverted nipples and prone to migraine, might have found something else to do, like dealing with a country you could trust. Just think: all those cocktails, for a cockatoo!"

"Just think," Wilson sighed. "Who the hell can think?"

"Yet it must have had," Suzanna said with envious affability, "its exciting moments. It must have been a zoo, a proper circus."

"I don't know about that," Wanda said in a sudden shift to a more responsible-sounding tone, "it was more like a ballet. You never saw so many epaulettes lining up to kiss ass, if you get my meaning. All the time, Ludwik worried about his mother, frailer and frailer with heart palpitations and some awful virus infection that left a cavity above her eye. We could hardly take her to and fro to Germany, and she wouldn't have gone there anyway. 'I'd sooner die in a Polish sewer,' she'd say, 'than float in German beer.' Tough old stick, but he adores her, and she fanned him upward to a career when nobody else gave a damn. Actually, she has lots of friends in Warsaw. She must have a dozen callers each day, and she doesn't so much occupy the apartment as tinker with it, teasing the ghosts out from between the cushions and the arms. Her friends are much more capable of looking after her than Ludwik is, or was, but he worries. He argued with her for hours, but she wouldn't budge. She's a born survivor, anyway. A great polisher of ashtrays. And when she draws the drapes, she pulls the cord in a slow even sweep because, she says, she doesn't 'like the light to jerk.' Well, my darlings, I don't give a pigeon's claw if the light jerks or not. I miss the life in Berlin, and there are no doubt thousands of Poles willing to shoot me for saying any such thing. I find the war an enormous *nuisance,* but I am being brave, I may get my own Cross of Valor yet."

"You are being braver than brave," Wilson said evenly. "I don't see how you could be better. Did you sleep?"

Instead of answering, Wanda pushed her bloodshot eyes close to his and blinked repeatedly, in evident acute pain.

"I see." He brushed away invisible pipe smoke for lack of anything to do. "We'll soon all be gone, I'm convinced. Ludwik isn't the sort of man to let us down. nor, from what Ludwik said, is his Admiral. Sounds like a doer to me."

Wanda jeered, seeming to halt traffic with one hand placed flat against the tide. "If we were dogs we'd be in Iceland. Don't you put too much trust in old Uncle Wilhelm, he's got an iron in every fire in hell. He's a meddler of the highest caliber, and there is absolutely no way of telling what will interest him next. If it happens to be you, that's lovely. Each hour he has about a dozen that strike his fancy. One of his habits is to go home, exactly when everybody's looking for him, and sit in the garden in front of a tree, leaning back in his chair and contemplating—I don't mean just looking at either—a bowl of flowers. *That* was what mattered to him. Motte, his Arab mare was called, or Moth. Imagine. All white, like her master's hair. I've seen her come through the French windows into the dining room to get a lump of sugar from his own hand. Take it from me, if he's not frolicking with his dogs, or feeding his mare sugar, or staring into a bowl of flowers, or not preoccupied with something going on in a country you'd take fifteen minutes to find on a map, he might just have time to do something about us. Otherwise, my loves, we're out of pocket and, like the mayor of wherever it was, into the fry pan. Is there any more tea?"

Nodding, Wilson confessed that, in his mind, he had visited the children, whose current life was dull rather than dangerous, and in the course of that magic-carpet fantasy had learned it would be better if they all kept away. "The whole ploy," he said, "depends on our having enough courage to wait it out here, or at least away from them, in other words matching them in courage. After all, in terms of resourcefulness based on experience, we are far better equipped than they are. Relatively speaking, they are newcomers to the planet."

Inhaling the vapor from her teacup, Wanda stared at him neutrally while her face tightened and suffused with amber. "On the basis of a dream, you know all this? In your mind's eye, that scruffy little waiting room for the train that goes to nowhere, you read all this in leaflets nailed to the wall? In your imagination you have gone and come, like the mailman of chaos, and the entire business is open and shut, just like that? My God, man, if Christopher Columbus had just dreamed about America instead of being so rash as actually to go there, that entire continent would be a useless wasteland even now, dark and dead."

"Intelligent hypotheses are—"

"No substitute for lived experience. *Professor!*"

Wilson subsided into a downward glare, murmuring "Well, I dreamed a dream, you dream dreams, you don't experience them in any other way, do you now? A dream is a dream, there's no harm in that. And I'm sure I dreamed the right approach, and that is: to keep away, for the first few days at any rate."

"Butterscotch," Wanda told him, using one of her euphemistic words of blame, much more telling than *poppycock* or *fiddlesticks*.

13

"Well," he said lamely, as Suzanna frowned at him to desist, "at least I'm talking about the right subject. *Somebody* has to fiddle while Rome burns."

"You are fiddling before the fire has begun." Wanda seemed lit with a new fury now, not the headlong oral semi-dementia of before, but something more like common sense gone punitive. "The real truth of the matter, Wilson, is that you go looking for fires in order to have an excuse to talk. In fact, you go looking for fireplaces to make speeches into."

"He misses lecturing," Suzanna said, hopelessly cowed. "He has not been himself for weeks."

"He was never himself," snapped Wanda. "Were you, Wilson? You have always been a rumor to yourself, and a mere working hypothesis with your friends. I am sorry, but, as I see it, there *is* no fire, there *is* no Rome, there *is* a good case to be made for keeping an eye on our darling children. And don't you go thinking I'm just another mother half out of her mind. The whole business is exaggerated."

"Mayors in fry pans?" Suzanna had gained a second wind. "Wanda, my dear, haven't you noticed the bombs and the shelling? The streets are full of dead horses. And dead people. A war has blown through town and you think nothing's happened?"

"A mother has her reasons," Wanda said, appealing to the half-authority of misquotation.

"As I said," Wilson complained. "You're every bit as locked up in your own head as you tell me I am. Just look outside."

"I refuse."

"Then, sooner or later, *it* will come to *you*," he said, "and it will come with a little swastika armband, not with an olive branch or a winning little posy. I may shrink from the horror of it all into rhetoric, but I don't forget the horror is there, and my advice to you is this: When dealing with the abominable, play safe by using as many models as you can. If you want to get some idea of what it's like to be disemboweled, stick a carving knife into a lump of dough." He mimed the plunge, the slash.

14

Suzanna wailed, then began to laugh hysterically, in little twisted yelps, patting her hands together in some terrible fusion of ecstasy and applause, at least until Wilson seized them, took them to his lips, and ritually kissed each of her knuckles in turn, at once calming her although her eyes still churned and her nostrils seemed to pulse. "There, there. Just an example. You see," he said turning to Wanda, "how much pain is underneath. Being Jewish, she is in a special position, and she doesn't forget it. Neither should we."

"If I choose to go and see them," Wanda said rigidly, "I choose to go. At my own risk. *Some*body must."

She made as if to leave, intending only a token gesture indicating that she was able to move across the room in mild enactment of a bigger and more dangerous departure, but Wilson stood up and fell upon her, pushing her back into the chair, knocking the cup and saucer into her lap and ramming her back against the chair with rhythmic force even while, half-babbling to herself, she sank her teeth into his wrist at the abraded place where no hair grew, and he let her bite on while he shoved away at her, muttering as if to a pet, "Down, down, not today, Wanda, bite me if you must." She did, as if at last discovering a physical focus for her sea-changing misery, in which pride, tact, gentleness, helplessness, indignation and high-spiritedness had come together and gone sour, driving her into madcap blather which blew like foam off the periphery of her being while she remained cold, inert and unvented at the core, awaiting an explosion, a heart attack, a stroke, even an implausible rescue by an Admiral to whom her pain gave a dramatic armada, and all its galleons flew the same pennant, the name Pulawski lettered on a square quartered red and white like raw beef against snow.

"Bite me," Wilson told her, amazed how little it hurt him.

"Please," Suzanna cried, "No more!"

"She must," he said, "She's burning up!"

"With fever?"

No, he told her distantly as if anesthetized, Wanda was aflame with unformulated rage; tempted to envision the most abominable thing in the world (and she fresh from Berlin, though he doubted the freshness of anything, anyone, coming from that chamber of horrors), she had been unable to, but had then found the nightmare walking about inside the chambers of her head, a bland invited guest at a diplomatic reception, and with seeming diplomatic immunity: the devil on summer furlough; and she had recoiled—"Unlike you, she still had hope," he said—in too much pain now to utter what he registered mentally: *she thought armbands were colorful, she thought armies were nice.*

Then Wanda, opening her eyes, saw the blood seeping from his wrist and let out a compassionate, unsteady scream, only to hear him say through tightly aligned teeth, "Rather you make me bleed than anyone out there. Now rest."

15

As if she had no bones in her, Wanda flopped into the armchair, shocking from it a faint mirage of dust; and, while Suzanna wound a bandage round his wrist, all he could think of was an image of Adolf Hitler he had seen in some illustrated magazine of the year before: permitting himself a sly enervate simper, the dictator cuddled himself with both arms crossed, his fingers thrust out in an extreme of saintly orgasm culled from a medieval painting; a small psychopath had received for his birthday, or whatever the occasion was, exactly what he had demanded, and Europe (Wilson thought) was the unhappy donor.

"Coffee," Izz was groaning. "I'm sick of bouillon that tastes of rubber and stale beds. I'd love some black and sweet, like the Turks drink it." With a clandestine bit of his brain, he was reciting to himself what he thought was true, what had become true overnight and during the morning: the hare-brained scheme had not produced a tragedy after all, against which thought he staged in postage-stamp size images another fate, which told him the worst was yet to come, after the ordinary troops moved off and the SS arrived, in no hurry, to "pacify" the area. "I suppose I'll drink it anyway," he said. "Want some?"

"You first," Myrrh was not even thirsty, but some inchoate, superstitious impulse made her do the same as Izz.

"*You*," he said, half giggling, and she took a sip or two.

Now, as Izz yearned for antihistamine ointment, the sun began to liquefy, dazzling and harsh, heating up the trench in which they lay, Myrrh intently visualizing her parents' faces, both weirdly streaked with flour as if the lens of her memory were defective, while Izz wondered how many parents all over Poland had cached their offspring in pigsties, cellars, garrets, roofs, aviaries, monk's holes, airshafts, derelict gazebos, and heaven only knew what else. His fidgeting mind lifted clear of his skull, turning into tattered windblown streamers which melted as he stared at them. *That was sanity taking leave*, he told himself. I still can't roll an *r*, I'd still like to live long enough to own a car, even a plane. Then he realized Myrrh was talking to him, with some impatience, jabbing him with her fingers grouped in a trowel shape.

"Dead things," she said loudly, "I can hear them"

"You're dreaming. Come on, let's do our walk. Now."

"Our walk?" The sound of Myrrh's bafflement was more telling than its expression on her face in daylight.

"Face me. Put your feet across mine. Yes." It was an old game, first played when they were ten or so, in which he pumped his feet slowly up and down, lifting hers fractionally until she chuckled and tried to anticipate his next upward motion, so that when he lifted his foot hers was already a toe's width ahead of it. The she paused and asked him about the hollow for her hip, without which she could not possibly be comfortable. "My hips are bigger than yours, Izz!"

"Don't let it begin," he said. "We have no way of digging." Telling her not to let it begin was his formula for dissuading her from the first words of a crescendo complaint; and, made self-conscious in this way, she usually cheered up, not letting "it" begin. Once Myrrh felt that someone cared how she felt, she was willing to care less about what she felt; as long as it was known that she felt, *that* was enough, almost as if someone might have supposed feeling was unusual and that her birthright was flawed, making feeling only a privilege.

"All right, I won't let it begin. Once it's begun it gets out of control. So what else shall we talk about? Do you want to play word games? Am I good-looking? Will I become a doctor or an economist? Is my father a conservative? Does my mother defer to him too much? Why does *your* father do so many things? Why does he always seem to take the initiative for both families? Does your mother defer to *him*?"

"Those," Izz told her genially, tapping his foot against her ankle, "are instances of conversation. I think I'd rather just lie here and dream, or snooze. It's getting hot." He rubbed the outside of his calf against the comforter like a restricted pedal-pusher, and her feet obeyed, carried up and down, up and down, their rhythm constant even when, with a grin just visible, he thought how he and Myrrh were symbolic creatures on a coat of arms, freezing in the act: two treadmillers *couchant* or two watertreaders vainly trying to stay put although actually treading air.

Now he applied a series of nose-kisses with his eyes closed, trying to enter her developing trance, but the daylight tugged at him, making him look past her forehead at the earthen wall itself. There was no harm in the wall, no threat; and he suddenly felt cheerful, convinced he would soon be back in school, construing, oh, Tacitus aloud, and using six words to one of the old Roman word-miser's Latin ones.

"Myrrh, you asleep?"

"No, just sideways-drowsy."

"At least we're not wet. It didn't rain in, *if* it rained." It was something to say, a mental loop his mind made while dozing.

"If it rained on my chest, my bosom would grow. That's my theory, anyway, I've heard of people rubbing a salve on their bald heads. Do you think there's a salve for bosoms too?"

"If there is, its internal."

"Then," she murmured with dreamy imprecision, "it must be something like reading that book on silence I found in my father's shelves. There was one lovely sentence, or phrase, that went something like this: The *something* absence of the audible is like remaining alive with a heart that no longer beats, whereas hearing everything is a *something... something* commotion in—the mind's ear. Sorry, I can't remember exactly what the words were. But it told me something that was only a bit more full of meaning than it wasn't. It was close enough to gibberish to make me nervous, Izz, but it almost actually said something so profound it made me wet-eyed."

Izz recognized the plateau she had reached. This soothed, semi-articulate rambling was familiar to him from many picnics together, sessions of homework done at the same table in his home or hers, or when, out of straying voluptuousness rather than urgent need, they had fondled each other under the table like two of the newborn—wrens or rabbits—fumbling around. "Necking," she had told him more than once, "it's repetitious. Like always having soup, whereas petting—"

"Yes?"

"It seems to have no identity, no shape, no music to it."

Izz inhaled, and he knew her aroma from that of earth and clay; Myrrh smelled of fizzy raspberry drink. "One day soon," he told her gravely, "we'll even things out. I'll find out how. From books. And if not from books, from boys."

Hugging her tight, with a benighted smile, he heard her once again attempt to quote from the book about silence, filling in her *somethings* with likely words: "The *heard* absence of the audible is like remaining alive with a non-beating heart, whereas hearing everything is a *golden*—no, a *heaven-sent*, or an *indelible*, and *indelibly hopeless* commotion in the mind's ear. It's gone, Izz, and it was so beautiful."

"When words fail," he said roguishly, "try something less abstract," and he peeled the summer shirt upward from her dewy waist, nuzzling.

16

Two thousand meters above their lair, the port wingtip of a Polish monoplane began to fall to earth, severed by machine gun fire, its camber flashing as it tumbled in the sun. The other plane curved away to watch the Polish one reel flamelessly smoking into a low hill lush with trees. Faltering like a small leaf, the wingtip sailed into the flank of an oblivious cow in Gnonka's main pasture, causing a minor stampede, after which it sat there on the grass, among the cowflops, arbitrary but final, the size of a breakfast tray, all of a sudden perched upon by haggling sparrows in whose landbound airscape it had become a permanent ramp, already subject to weathering, birdlime, and decay.

The Nazi fighter, its pilot unaware that Kazimierz had already fallen, cruised back low over the town and machine gunned the steeple of a local church, making its bells pong-pang and *en passant* shredding the skull of an old man in the belfry to repair sections of rope, which he did (and was doing that morning, Nazis or no) by rolling retied sections under the sole of his boot. Next the fighter redundantly shot up a stationary motor coach used for outings to Warsaw, only to pass through a fan of vertically fired rounds from an old-fashioned Lewis gun worked by a wounded Polish soldier cut off from his unit and just waiting for something to do, unable to carry the gun away, reluctant to leave it for the intruders, and uncertain how to immobilize it. Shot through the groin, all the way up into his trunk, the pilot clasped his belly, sagged against the control column, and dived the Messerschmitt right into the post office and the lending library. The gas mains exploded with a gigantic bang, scattering envelopes and stationary far and wide. Books flew through the air as well, more of them leaving the shelves in that second than Kazimierz took out each year. A copy of *Gulliver's Travels* done into Polish landed in the Sakal's back yard with a fluttering plop, just beyond the verandah.

"What on earth was that," Suzanna said, "I'll go and get it."

"Incendiary bomb, no doubt," Wilson told her. "Stay put."

"I can see it. It's a book. Or it was."

"Even so." He wanted the world to be still, to keep its distance from him, and his mind, recoiling from bangs and shots and bells and distraught women, had fixed on a big bowl of petunias, kept in the house for a month until they began to wilt and fade, then unleashed into full sunlight like a small wild animal incapable of being housebroken, and thereafter blooming a profound purple as never before.

"If it *was* an incendiary," Suzanna pursued her point, "then our children are not safe where they are. But it's a book, it's just a bit of a book. You won't have to throw sand on it to put it out."

With a pout, a toss of her shoulders, and then a gathering snarl she did not quite know how to complete, Suzanna went outside, picked up the half-burned book, brought it in and tossed it into his lap. "It's still on fire, Wilson."

"I've read it," he said proudly. "Long ago."

Deciding it was her turn to speak, Wanda said something mild and faint about the gift of life, the gift of a book, the way in which a book is the lifeblood of a stranger made available for a pittance. "Ludwik's mother," she said eventually, "once took a honeybee into her cupped hands and let it sting her, saying 'It's life, it's life. Why not?' "

"I'm not that disabused," Wilson scoffed. "Neither was the author of this burnt offering of a book."

"Disasters," Suzanna said, "ought to be in winter, not in weather like this. It's hot, it's glorious. It's obscene."

"A good sky for dive bombers," he whispered. "I don't want to see anybody heading for the door. Stay put. In light as good as this, a pilot can see for miles, and they'll shoot at any target that offers. I still can't fathom why they're shooting up the town after they've already taken it."

"It's because," Wanda told him curtly, "*because* the only people left in town are Poles. They're having target practice."

"If what you say is true," Wilson told her, "and it really is target practice, then what are they practicing for? What in God's name is the *real* thing?"

"In the name of the *Führer*, not of God. Don't make that mistake, husband."

Wilson stood his full height, aiming his pipe stem at her. "*Husband!* We are getting formal as the end of the world approaches, aren't we? Would you like me to call you *wife*?"

"Call me Jew if you like. It's likely to be my last formal title." She mimed throat-cutting with the edge of her hand.

"Darling," Wanda cried. "Don't be so melodramatic. That's just how they want you to feel. I know *I* would too, but *you* must not. I don't mean to seem imperious, but we mustn't let go now. The more I think about it, the more convinced I am that we shall all be saved. Somehow we'll get out and away, not in style, but in one piece. Just think of *my* poor husband, wherever his is, whatever he's having to do at this very minute. I wonder, did he go off after his mother or to fight the invaders? Perhaps a bit of both."

"Heavens, Wanda," Wilson exploded, "it isn't as if one is marzipan and the other pastry! You sound so glib."

"I only sound glib, as you call it," Wanda instructed him with raised eyebrows which made her look as if surprised by a flashbulb, "when I'm almost demented. Would you rather I chewed your arm again?" The eyebrows sank back to normal as she began murmuring inaudibly, and Wilson with a grunt drew back his arm, wrapped as it was in its ridiculous flag of truce.

"The day is young," he said self-consciously. "Praise God we'll see the next one."

"You and God," Suzanna said. "That old duo died many years ago. Your subscription has expired. You took no noticed of Him and he sure as death will take no notice of you. But you never know: a burnt offering might work wonders yet. How about me?"

Hugging her in mingled shock, self-disgust, and tingling bewilderment, he could find nothing to say beyond the fervent, choked repetition of her name.

"Gallows humor," Wanda said airily, "we had enough of that in Berlin. It's what those bastards are reared on. If it isn't the good old bittersweet, *Schadenfreude,* just listen to the word—it begins with spit and ends by chilling you to the bone—then it's bloodlust with a suntan, the killing of lovers in the interests of elegiac poems. Let's all calm down and have some tea. Cold or not. Cold tea is good for bruises, isn't it? It might be good for what ails us on the inside too."

A short, dangerous walk away, with Nazi fighter planes in squadron strength rasping above the town at steeple height, but no longer shooting, Myrrh squirmed closer to Izz.

"What are you thinking about? *What are you doing?*" It was an old, affable question, hers to him, his to her, usually put when one of them was bored and uttered with operative intensity, as if the other had suddenly been caught up in a ravishing pastime denied the other.

"I'm thinking, about some idiot from school who bashed my head with a rolled-up newspaper, a heavy one. One of their insane masculinity rituals, see. *Wanna fight?*—he said. I told him I didn't have the energy, as I had a perfect right to do, so he thwacked my skull and came after me when I tried to walk past him with both eyes running from the bump on the head. I tried to grab the rolled-up paper, but he smacked me across the mouth with it. I guess the slimeball was really hitting me with his penis, without knowing it. At school he actually jerks off in the cloakroom, and they stand and watch him, and then he and some others throw the smallest boys into the holly bushes with their flies yanked open and their penises pulled out. We would have more privacy in Papua. Are girls as bad?"

Myrrh laughed mock-sagaciously. "Poor Izz. I'm only a year behind you. You *know* what goes on. Underwear pulled down for group inspection, even in the schoolyard on warm days. Not half as many girls pull the pants off boys as boys do off the girls."

"One day, as if you didn't know the sort of thing that goes on, Miss Rypin who teaches modern history—you'll get her next year if we survive—called a big guy to the blackboard with a big one wobbling from his open fly. 'Come forward,' she told him, and he did, which is when she slung a piece of chalk, real accurate, and hit him right on the bulb. 'That,' she told the class, boys and girls together, 'was a bit of an ass's jawbone. Sit down, Turka,' she told him, using his nickname, 'and make your pet mouse behave. Or we'll have to keep him in a cage.' What a day that was."

Myrrh whistled a tune, complex and skittish as she peeked out from beneath the middle plank. "What?" she said. "Oh, Durand's *First Waltz*. Izz, I've heard planes. And shots. And maybe soldiers tramping about. We'd better stay put."

"In the old days, when I was a real kid, we used to run around in circles to kill the urge to pee. It works, but not for long. How am I going to run in here?"

"Like marking time," she told him. "Run in place."

He tried it, anxiously gyrating his knees, but this only made him feel wetter and colder, and more desperate to go. Then he had a brainwave. "Myrrh, I've solved it."

"You've solved it. The eighth wonder of the world."

"I'm solving it right now," hunched away from her with a precise angle to his back as if examining a specimen: a stamp, a minnow, a pine cone.

"I hear you," she said disgustedly. "You're using one of the hot-water bottles. So long as we mark them for which is which. I wouldn't care to be surprised by an unfamiliar taste." She began ferreting about in the kitbag and produced first a sawn-off umbrella, then the chamberpot, which she waved at Izz's back. "This is what we need." Next he heard a long, part-histrionic sigh of amusement as she produced a half-full bottle of what looked like water, which she opened and sniffed. "Izz, it's not water at all. Here." She put the umbrella down.

"Vodka," he pronounced. "Now maybe *that's* what we really need. Get ourselves plastered and then we won't mind anything." He took a swig, coughed, choked, then took another to ease his throat. When he was able to talk again, he wondered aloud: "I can't imagine who put it in. Perhaps it was there to begin with, a relic from another war, part of a soldier's battle equipment!"

"Izz, you shouldn't drink it. It'll make you sick."

"I've had it before, just a drop now and then." Several times, either in Berlin, Warsaw, or here in Kazimierz in one rented vacation home or another, he had untapped the household supply and shot the burning fluid against his vocal cords, not for stimulus or relief, but somehow to sharpen any day when he was bored. "I'd rather," Ludwik had told him after catching him in the act, "you took a sip openly if you want one. Not that it's any good for you. Growing boys do not need volcanic fire. That is Polish vodka, my son, a fact which may mean nothing to you, but even grownups take it with slices of black bread and cheese."

"I don't like it," Izz had said. "So the only pleasure in it is that it's forbidden, something done in secret. If I do it openly, Dad, the whole thing's a bore."

At that point in their conversation, although he certainly did not recall it while lying in his blood in the big drawer in the courtyard, Ludwik had gone to a parallel memory, not of alcohol at all, although during the event in question he had quaffed several steins of Berlin beer. Having, as his duties required, sat through a Nazi firework display with increasing boredom at the monotony of red-and-green, Christmas-type fireworks, he had come alive toward the end as the finale began with several gigantic creamy-gold spiders or anemones spread against the low cumulus, seeming to vibrate and quiver even as, between them and him, white and pink globular thunderbolts appeared and just as soon exploded, spewing rainbow streamers most of which died out fast, but a few of which developed a second life and went threading and looping away, ever thinner and finer, until they seemed to form an enormous web or nebula right above him, amber and rose and azure, still mildly spitting and crackling with the promise of infinite sputtering extension independent of the polished jackboots, the armbands, the Sam Browne belts, the black or field gray tunics with pastel-striped badges on either side of him. It was as if, he thought with exuberant surprise, a universe had come into being right before his eyes: stars where nothing had been before, bright red tracery that lingered in his retinas even after it had gone, and scores of outsize catkins glowing white-hot. All of a sudden, almost deafened and blinded, he felt a surge of joy as he realized the explosive universe included these petty explosions; the microcosm was made of the same bangs and black pothering smoke as the big one, and so any version of the big one included the little ones which people imagined in the big one, because there was nowhere else for the little ones to be. The universe, he decided, includes even our imaginings of it, and that means nothing ever gets left out. The remainder of that epiphany died a natural death as the neat ranks of dignitaries rose to their feet, with a Nazi anthem beginning to grind and rattle against the thunder and lightning of the last fireworks. How empty the pipes and tin whistles sounded in that arena of billowing smoke, how inconsequential the bass drums and the kettledrums calling the faithful to order. Yearning suddenly to be in a night club just as smoky, listening to a raunchy song from a blonde in leathers with a raucous, almost baritone voice, he nudged Wanda and said, to her amusement, "The volatile yell of the risen sun. These people are just tub-thumpers. Did you see the last few minutes, though?"

"How could I not? What are they celebrating?"

"I've forgotten." He guessed. "Hitler's birthday perhaps."

"Weren't they," she asked, trying in vain to make herself heard as the massed military bands achieved crescendo, "giving themselves a glimpse of Armageddon? Wasn't that it?"

All Ludwik could hear was the word 'Armageddon,' and his mind was suffused with something like a quotation from the Creation itself, also an affair of bangs and flashes, but with no politics announced. He nodded at her, confident that he could guess at most of Wanda's meanings, and then took his heel-clicking leave—a habit he had self-consciously acquired, perhaps to lull the Nazis into trusting him, perhaps to hitch his skiff to the galleon of local style, perhaps even to impress himself with himself. In some ways he was more German than many Nazis and (more important, he told himself) less Nazi than some Poles.

"You've enjoyed it," Wanda teased, "and you said how boring it would be. There's a small boy in you yet that loves a bang and a flash."

"No small girl in you?" He bowed at a general all in black.

"Whatever small girl there is in me has died a natural death: in this case, of headaches. The bands rather than the bangs. I keep forgetting to bring aspirin. Perhaps you should learn that technique of massaging the temples—how odd, it sounds like something you'd do in ancient Egypt or modern—er, where? Modern Yucatan!" Already Wanda sounded cured, ready to spar verbally again.

"I'm glad your sense of humor's coming back. Without it, you wouldn't last a week among these imbeciles. There's more sophistication in the trunks of trees."

Three years and a short train journey away, Izz was trying to define the exact noise of pigs: a tearing of thick paper, a wide-diameter pipe suddenly emptying, a rude sound made by that ancient water-lifting contraption on the Nile, the *shaduf,* going suck-suck-snogorrah-gorrah, schnunt; but none of these was right, so he finally gave up analogy and onomatopoeia for a couple of phrases: a gobbling snore, a gargling with coke. There were just too many elements in pig-noises for easy summation, and he told himself, as the heat in the hole made him doze, resting his head against the already sleeping Myrrh, Pigs sound more complicated than humans do. At least they don't invade. Well, they haven't yet. Nose-kisses now were of no avail, nor marching on each other's feet while staying horizontal, nor perfunctory orgasms on his part, nor dreamy acquiescence on hers, nor vodka, nor freewheeling reminiscences, nor even self-solace through imaginary feats such as recalling Columbus and rediscovering America, obliterating Leonardo da Vinci and reinventing the airplane, or, as Izz claimed to have done, lying for once, remaining constipated for three weeks on arrowroot just to see what being pregnant might be like.

"Goodnight," Izz told himself half and hour before noon. "The vodka did it, Dad was right about the black bread and the cheese." Remembering some vague behest to give his nose a good blow, but to blow one nostril at a time, he wiped his nose on his arm, wondering where the tears came from, his head was full of so many other things as well.

17

When the SS finally arrived, in order to 'pacify' those who had already adjusted to being invaded, overrun or whatever the gruesome verb was, they behaved with semi-intoxicated abandon, smashing in windows and doors, looting, and, in grotesque understatement of the real thing, bayoneting upholstered sofas and chairs, plumped-up pillows on neatly made beds. They moved through Pulawy Street in fifteen minutes, rounding up so-called undesirables. The mayor and his deputy they suspended upside down from one rope flung over the crossbar of a lamppost, a noose round their ankles, and their mouths swaying just above the rubble on the sidewalk, while their wives, bound back to back and screaming only a couple of meters away, watched them lose consciousness. A solitary SS private stood guard with a machine pistol and a cheroot pillaged from the nearest tobacco store, at his feet a box of fifty, suggesting that he intended to chain-smoke his way through the vigil.

Twelve others, local dignitaries but with a couple of intellectual-looking summer vacationers for good measure, grabbed right off the street, were made to stand against the wall of the municipal offices, presumably to be searched. Or so they might have concluded until shots hit them, the whole thing as casual and impromptu as a child kicking an empty can. Prodded with bayonets, twelve more, seized at random, shuffled up to where the bodies lay.

"Point out the Jews and intellectuals," the SS officer brayed at the assembled crowd. "Or these will get the same." At first, no one moved or spoke, but then a babble began of terrified accusation, of pointing and name-giving and helpful obsequious hand-motions. The squad of SS fanned out like crows, laughing and cursing among themselves as their day achieved momentum. Regular summer visitors took no longer to find than permanent residents did, while newcomers took an extra five minutes or so, which was also the time taken to establish that the half-dozen who had gone to the ravines were not in town. Pocketing the short list of those absent, which included Myrrh but not Izz, the SS officer, whose face had a dolorous tic that made him seem to be smiling, had everybody lined up and searched.

"We're doing better than those poor bastards by the wall," Wilson said indistinctly, having refused to surrender his pipe. He had lived this scene in his mind a hundred times, but the actuality sapped him, and his body did a dream-float which he could not control. Among all the ways he had improvised, this was not the one; it was too calm, too understated, too much like an air raid drill, as if they would all soon be returned to their homes, their unfinished cold lunches. Despite the bodies by the wall, at which he dared not look too closely, this could be only a head-check, a run-through; the atrocity had *been* committed, the warning given, and now everyone would comply, except for those in the ravines, who would be hunted down with dogs and shot in the mouths of their caves. Or would they torture him to make him reveal Myrrh's whereabouts? Would they defile Suzanna in front of him to make him talk? 'Your daughter is not with you.' 'No, she is out playing somewhere, but she comes home for lunch.' Was that really what he had said in response to their interrogative statement? The soldiers did not seem to care much; the NCO had shrugged, had even given Suzanna a rumpled, world-weary grin as if to intimate an affectionate exasperation with children and their wayward ways. "We'll see," he told Wilson. "You have an American name," he said in broken Polish.

"It's—"

"We know. You're in enough trouble as it is."

Suzanna looked frozen, searching Wilson's face for a cue that did not come; fifteen years of marriage did not lead to this summery anticlimax at the hands of bored soldiers, half of them reeking of drink, the rest behaving with concise disdain as if distracted from something far more interesting: a horse race or a parade.

She had expected knives and flames, not this sullen bureaucratic shuffle based on lists compiled in Warsaw by, in fact, the Admiral's agents, working on his behalf although without direct orders from the Admiral himself. Wanda had told her so, but Suzanna didn't believe that foreigners could care so much about who was who, and who was where. Having the more analytical and capricious mind of the two, Wanda was not surprised, having seen street arrests in Berlin, as often as not a couple of overweight men in raincoats, with umber Homburg hats and marmoreal drained faces, like fugitives (she often thought) from a bad propaganda movie or an unsuccessful furniture business, nonetheless propelling with trained shoves the day's victim, who spun his head this way and that in search of those coming to his aid with a brown waterproof pass, a bribe, a message from the *Führer* himself. Usually, if the arrest took place outdoors, the arrested finished their coffee first; they were allowed to; the favor gave the whole operation a polite, civilized air, as if the Gestapo men had brought news of a death and took their time about helping the recipient to walk steadily home. Oh, she told herself, then and now, *They are always so benign, they have nothing to lose, nothing to give, they are merely instrumental.* Only an hour ago the loudspeakers rigged on top of cars had told the town it had been freed by the armies of the Third

Reich; a band had played and gone; the Nazi flag had been raised; there were no local troops to be mopped up, only civilians in the ravines, and to be found out there was to be condemned before being even accused. Yet, looking at several mothers who glared at her in envious resentment without daring to say anything, she in turn envied them for having their children by them: company, distraction, something to soften the soldier's hearts. Her numb yet abstractly convulsive mind tried to formulate what felt wrong. *He is a soldier who has gone to war*, she had told the SS officer, who had clicked his heels, nodded, saluted, then slapped her across the mouth: "There is *no* war, you Polish bitch. Poland has been freed by the armies of the Third Reich. Now, where is he?

"Warsaw," she said quietly. "Somewhere there." They had asked Suzanna about Myrrh, but why no mention of Izz? Were their lists wrong after all? Thank God he's where he is, she told herself, or they'd have put him on their list. The secret was good with her even to her last breath. As long as he remained invisible.

"*Warsaw?*" the officer said. "Then he is ours already. Go and stand over there." Then she addressed him in German, she had no idea why, but perhaps to impress him, to curry some indefinable favor, even an apology for the slap. "I know Berlin well. We were intimates of the Admiral."

The boy-thug face tautened at her burst of near-flawless asides, then moved close to hers like a free-floating balloon. "Are you Czimanski?" He was looking in a small black book of the sort, she facetiously thought, bachelors are supposed to carry but never do. "Then your absent husband is not a soldier but a diplomat. Why is he not here, to surrender?"

"Because," she told him, feeling several things leap up her spine and through her open mouth before she could check them: pain, arrogance, pride, and the urge to be different. "Because, you face-slapping upstart, he is *heroic*." Wanda had always been a touch reckless, but today she was sublime, subject to no law on sea or land; she knew, she just knew, he would not shoot her on the spot, in spite of Wilson's hush-hush and Suzanna's immobilized gape. *It is happening*, she instructed herself, *it is happening exactly like this, and it will never happen any other way*. Do it carefully, Wanda, don't throw away a reprieve just by opening your big mouth; don't upset the balance of this ebonite Hun; your name means something to this man, he knows you're different. Don't make him slap you again, either, because he'd rather not.

All the officer said was "So he has gone to Warsaw...to be helpful." This in awkward, not quite grammatical Polish.

"He took his sword with him." She was still talking German, but others in the immediate group understood it too.

"To go on top of his coffin, after his hero's death." This he said in German, sardonic yet unoffended.

"Pulawski," she said, out of the blue, not daring to say the name *Gnonka*.

"I see," he said evenly. "It all fits. But, Frau Czimanska, you caused a German officer to slap you. The provocation was acute. And that is a crime. You are therefore in two positions at once: you are known to us, for good reasons, but you are also an ill-behaved sow of a Slav. Now, I could have my soldiers rape you for several hours, and then set you free to find your husband. Or I could have you shot on this very spot, but you would learn nothing from *that* lesson. You see, although I am not in the diplomatic service, I have power, of life and death, and I find it stimulating. You are a handsome woman with clipped hair. And you are a mother, about which there is nothing more to be said. How about a bargain, then? One for two? Or, if your husband has already found his military destiny, one for one?"

"Your arithmetic," Wanda told him in German, trembling, "is off. There are two—"

"Not a word more. One for two, as before?"

"What if I say no?"

"One for none." A year or two ago, Izz had confided to her a nightmare in which, while taking a bath, some imposing power had told him that, if after he lost the soap in the water he did not find it again in ten seconds, his mother would die, and for bath after bath, even while singing cheerily, he had tormented himself with this morbid game, and she his mother had died many times over. Now she sensed Izz frantically fishing for the cake of soap, ever slipperier, as the seconds trotted by, and failing even to locate it, never mind bring it from water into air.

"Come with me," the officer said. "Over there will do," indicating the open door to the local dentist's, actually a front parlor with a discreet small window-sign with italic lettering gold on black. The dentist had already been shot at the wall, and Wanda could not resist the ghoulishly flippant thought that the Nazis would have no one to take their teeth to; the same dentist had checked Izz's teeth for four summers running. Inside, apart from the Bakelite and steel chair, everything was gleaming mahogany, with rectangles of tile inset. Now the officer, instead of interrogating her confidentially in German or even his bad Polish, or explaining some message he brought from Berlin, flicked his pistol at her and told her to strip naked exactly where she was standing.

"Why? In the name of heaven why?"

"In the name of nothing why. If you refuse I will have to shoot. Now, if you please, above the waist first. You see, I am a connoisseur."

On he droned, telling her how different he was from the rowdies, the sadists, the butchers he had to mingle with. "Think of me as a non-practicing sculptor."

This is for Izz, she thought, and tossed her bra into the dental chair, noting how the inside satin was wet with perspiration. If this bully has to peek, he has to peek; I am not ashamed of what he sees. I have been a mother to men.

"My goodness," he sighed suavely, "Frau Czimanska, I have seen the varieties—the lemon, the bloated lemon, the pear, the oblate pear, the low melon, the melon high under the chin, the razor-strop and the saddlebag and the pimple, but you have something extraordinary: *the mango*. And what is even more amazing is the nipple: not the stud, the wild strawberry, or the radish, but the golf-tee. The exquisite." Seating himself in the dental chair, he set his pistol on the round mahogany tray beside him at chin height, and began to draw in his little black book, exhaling intently and letting his tongue-tip stray from the corner of his mouth.

"Now," he said brightly. "Let's get on with it." Once again he waved the pistol at her, then tapped her on the nipples, left and right, to speed her up. "Frau Czimanska, show me the Ganges delta, please." Her mind closed, yet standing in a sudden non-climatic chill that came up from the soft pseudo-Persian rug on which she stood, Wanda unbuttoned the side of her summer skirt, then halted. "Why? Cannot a connoisseur such as yourself guess? Imagine it, man."

His face gleamed with deviant joy. "Delighted, *gnädige Frau*." He knew that, if he wished, he could shoot her now, in the head, the stomach, through any bodily aperture, and nothing would happen to him; he had done it before, with or without sexual obbligato, and being free to do as he pleased bored him. So he warmed to the resistance she put up, almost fawning on her and launching into a peeping-tom symphony of anatomies he had known. "The thick head hair usually signifies the matto grosso below, like a black bison's back, with sometimes curly mustaches going up to the waist. But your hair is thinner, less coarse. I was insincere about the Ganges; you are more probably the tall narrow brush ascending directly from the cleft, or the crescent of patchy scrub. You do not use depilatories? No? Good. Some of these damned Orientals, they shave the entire mons pubis bare, making their frontal pulp into a kind of upper lip. A man of taste enjoys his undergrowth, though. I think, Frau Czimanska, you have the tall narrow brush, pale auburn perhaps, which when wet becomes an exclamation mark."

Yes, she told him, he was right.

"Then I must see. The proof of the pudding...."

With a shrug and a grunt of revulsion, Wanda peeled away what was left, only to hear him bellow with sly rage "You lied, you cheated, Frau Czimanska, you do have the matto grosso, and thick enough to comb. My, what an exquisite pelt!"

"I am modest," Wanda said, telling herself *Yes, he is one of them, I saw them in Berlin. Boy bully is a voyeur, but nothing worse. I am safe, I am going to live, I am not going to have to do anything more for him. I am going to see tomorrow dawn.*

"Wouldn't you," she taunted him, "like a handful, mein Herr? It would take an hour to get it all out of your teeth." All this, she harangued herself, I am doing for Izz, for Ludwik, in order not to have to die, in order to walk with them both into the paradise garden, holding crocuses in our hands, our mouths full of wild raspberries, our heads an interacting dream of the male, the female, and the little. Unless he shoots me on the spot.

What he did, however, was to advance with a folding nail scissors taken from a monogrammed leather case no bigger than his thumb. "A sample, for my collection." She sat, he pawed briefly about in her thatch, then snipped an outreaching curl, stood up, stowed it in the little black book, which had a small envelope between the last page and the inside cover, and gave her what she concluded was the connoisseur's smile. "In a short while," he murmured, with almost postcoital coziness, "we shall be in a different climate, where one's parts will all but freeze. What little life they have will demand a big supplement from the mind, a special stimulus. So my ambition has been, over the past week, to collect up enough—impedimenta erotica (I know you are an educated woman) to keep me going during the hard days. I will fondle the little clippings, dreaming I am roaming through a dozen pairs of thighs, and the brown flaps, mucous and fat, will be there to fondle between finger and thumb. Something for the cold nights, the boring days. Some of my colleagues find a sufficient stimulus in bloodshed, but I have a subtler nature. I have not evolved that far. My taste is not for Wagner or Beethoven, it is for Mahler, for Debussy. For which *I* could no doubt be shot by the orthodox lovers of porridge and drums."

A friend, Wanda thought madly, as he told her to stand up, stand still, and inhale while he took one final summary, blurred, lascivious look. I could shoot him now. He has left his pistol where I could reach it before he could. He would no doubt enjoy it until he realized he had to die of it. Instructed to dress, she let one hand drift toward the pistol, but he snapped it back in one motion and wagged it just below her chin. "Your problem, dear lady, is that you figure on two lists, one of which is that of Polish undesirables, which of course includes educated women such as you. We mean that you have no aptitude for becoming a beast of burden. Strangely enough, that list was compiled in part by the agents of the very Reich office which seems to hold you in favor. You have friends in high places. My own problem does not exist. If I shoot you, I shall be both carrying out orders and offending their source. But have you ever heard of an SS officer being hauled over the coals for an act of violence? You see the double standard, then. Either way, if I have you killed or let you go your own disreputable way, no one will much care. But I would hate to think of such a beautiful matto grosso rotting in a mass grave somewhere dug by idiots and unlocated on the map."

18

My little buried son, she mouthed, and his friend, the little Jewish girl; but she could not get the words out, she had better *not* get the words out.

"You looked so—sisterly. You see, one accustomed to Germans does not find them repulsive. But, please, do not confide in me further. There is a limit to how much I can ignore of what I know and am not supposed to know. All I know of you is gossip from headquarters. I have no authority to save you from the wall, but, dear lady, I have the taste to do so. Stay there in that chair. You will be fetched. See," he patted his loins, "I am not even hard. That is what beauty does, it cools the glans."

Caught between sickened hilarity and a terror so complete she could not focus it on any one event, Wanda flailed around mentally, trying to respond. Never mind her experience of diplomatic Berlin, amidst protocol elusive as marsh gas; she was living in a new age now, with new combinations of feelings, new paradoxes, for which there were as yet no names. The old terms, such as bittersweet or pleasure-pain, no longer served in this tricky hell conjured into being by sleek psychopaths with a license to do whatever they wanted, as if experimenting on the minds and bodies of whichever human crossed their path. Valiantly *wrong,* she found herself living on the edges of her mind, always spinning away from the responsible core into some skittish, gross enjoyment of things that would hitherto have made her scream or rave. This fatuous degenerate, for instance, prating about his glans with narcissistic grandeur, belonged in a night club farce, but here he was, making her strip, measuring and evaluating her nudity as if she belonged to some newly found tribe and his destination was not wherever the Nazi advance went next but the annual meeting of some royal zoological society. "Captain," she said, beginning to say something that might reassure her simply because she had been able to utter it, only to hear him correct her from the doorway: *"Hauptsturmführer."*

"SS, of course," she said in a dream, never having been able even in Berlin to figure out their titles and ranks, or interpret the various bits of tin with which they bedecked themselves.

"Well? I have duties, Frau Czimanska." It was hardly the same man, the one who had just ogled her body hair.

"You mean, just wait here. For what?"

"For someone to take you to where you are going."

"My son—"

"Is he also away, fighting the so-called invader? I told you, there is no war, there was merely an abortive Polish attempt to cross the

German border. Sit still and examine your teeth." She saw the tiny mirror, the probe, a roll of unused dental floss on the tray beside her, on which he had just briefly set his pistol, and she knew she could not go through with it, she could not ask about Izz. Instead she called after him. "Do you know of any word from Caesar?", using the Admiral's nickname.

Once more he stopped and turned. "Caesar? Any word from 'Caesar' would not come from me. Caesar's own people do Caesar's own work. They are in the field alongside us. Intelligence is being more cooperative these days. You will have to wait. The main thing is that, if Caesar wants to find you, find you he will; he has thousands to help him, and wherever you are—in a camp, or a mass grave in some Polish sewer, or even in the chair of some Jewish former dentist, never fear. You will be found. You must have mingled in high society in Berlin, so you are already aware that 'Caesar' both gives and takes away, and so do his minions, half of them relatives and Jews, the other half genuine party members."

"There were some cocktail parties," she said in a trance, more in the old Berlin than in the Kazimierz of now. "We got to know all kinds of people, and of course my husband made a lot of contacts I knew nothing about. Does the word 'Pulawski' mean anything to you?" As soon as she said it, she knew it was the codeword for Izz, and Izz alone; it had nothing to do with the Admiral. No, the SS officer did not know the name, and he was late. "Stay put," he said. "I may return."

In the meantime a small truck had moved through the town, collecting up all rings, pocketbooks, cutlery, pewter. Those who had been allowed back into their homes stood respectfully in the center of their living rooms or kitchens while the plunderers thundered in and out, up and down, very much the rough-and-ready SS of 1939, improvising techniques rather than putting into practice something formed back at home with deadly, logistical finesse.

Now those remaining in the square by the wall were made to undress.

"Here we go," Wilson said as cries of indignation gave way to those of pain amid the slack thuds of rifle butts. Everyone was shivering in the fitful summer breeze. Just off the square, where the mayor and his deputy were no longer writhing but dangled in mid-dive, and their wives had sunk into bloodless faints, a radio began to blare, quelled at once by a soldier who beat it with a rifle butt as if it were a human head. There was not a sound of bird, or dog, or cat, but only a whimper of children hushed but not subdued, as if to be alive on that day, and small, were grounds for involuntary complaint.

With a flash of his hand, the young *Hauptsturmführer* signaled that the march could begin, and the group shuffled off to the local cemetery, Wilson holding Suzanna's hand, each marveling at the goose-bumps of the other, each refusing to believe anything worse than this could happen, yet glad that Myrrh was missing. "It's just to humiliate us," Wilson whispered. "It's their idea of a joke." "They could have had their joke without undressing us, Wilson," she murmured as if intoning an endearment, "everyone here is a professional." "Including the professional children," he winced. At this moment an SS private was tying Wanda to the dentist's chair, as ordered, and gagging her with a fistful of gauze, as if in preliminary to something unspeakable; but then he left in a clatter of buckles and clips, slamming the door behind him.

Those at the cemetery, having been shoved close together as if for warmth, were also bound, with clotheslines round their necks, the children bound by their necks to their parents' waists or thighs, which gave the children an oddly supplicant, upward-begging look in the midst of a lowing, dense herd of snow-white Adams and Eves, massed round a tall sculpted angel with enormous unfurled wings, gray to the people's white. The sun died as a lump of cumulus floated over, but the cemetery birdsong went on and bees and wasps cruised among the upright bodies, making them flinch and try to waft them away, and flies touched down while dragonflies came and went in swift, angular patrols. Someone with a bass voice began to sing Ave Maria, wavering and hoarse, until a soldier slapped him in the face with not the butt of a rifle but its barrel, and he stopped singing, although the children picked up the tune and persisted with it, in spite of cuffings, as an uncoordinated wail from within a wound that had opened up in the great big world itself.

"We're going to get away with something after all," Wilson said. "Remember that. Come what may, my dearest. We're going to manage that at least."

"Why don't they do something?" Suzanna said, not especially to him; it was as if he had not spoken to her, she was waiting to be untied and sent home. "Why don't those mothers shut their children up? The soldiers might say something important and we might not hear it."

"Oh, I think we'll hear, one way or another." As Wilson looked at her, she became two-dimensional, limpid, and slight, as if no longer there, not even when the dousing with gasoline began, and the children forgot to wail, distracted by what was going on, this something new, but the adults let forth a mammoth, ragged exclamation in which prayers blurred syllables of outright stammered rage, squeals, barks, brays, calls of hello and farewell, incongruous sneezes and gasps of cardiac pain. A lighted newspaper, which had been blowing about the cemetery for over a week, its front-page photograph of Neville Chamberlain and Hitler, ignited the fluid on the group nearest the angel, these people tethered to its feet. The soldiers stood back as the roar of flame began, and the officer with equivalent rank to captain donned a pair of gold-rimmed sunglasses before he turned away half-wishing he were aghast, but knowing he was not; he had other work to do than waste their gasoline like this. But orders were orders: for every exception he made, he had to do his duty by the rest, and not every interesting instance—and unusual personality, someone with pull, a big enough bribe, or a magnificent body—could be an exception either. Already he thought he was on the verge of becoming indifferent to superlative human specimens; the entire human race was consumable in the end, and that was not his fault. So to postpone such rawhide and crystalline indifference, he had let himself be seduced by Wanda's low-floating smoky voice talking German, whereas, in fact, he told himself, he had not been unduly attracted to her. She was his gesture to himself, his penance for being so close to automatic, like his pistol. Pondering the eventual fate of Wanda Czimanska, who might have done better to stay on in Berlin and pass herself off as a German, he turned to study the effects of fire.

As the crescendo of human sound began to fade, the soldiers tossed in the remaining fuel, and the smoke thickened, going black; an exploding can next to Wilson seemed not there at all, but relegated to some shrunken continuum of inaudible death-in-life, but he thought he saw an empty chair enclosed within the framework of another chair, a chair with a seat inside a chair that had no seat at all. The angel was invisible. The flames wheezed and soared. The people seemed lower, the clotheslines no longer held them, and the stench drove the SS farther back, only to be prodded forward again by their *Hauptsturmführer*, telling them to breathe deep, this was their destiny, they had best get used to it. Then the angel reappeared, sooty and split from groin to armpit, with below its plinth an enormous black wreath of vaguely recognizable carcasses over whom a low, vestigial flame still played, nibbling and hovering. One young soldier, who had seen too much that day, muttered indignantly to the man beside him, who shoved the youth violently and began reviling him. "This one's training," he called to the sergeant, "didn't take. He doesn't like it." Their voices came to the officer in sunglasses like those of distant, quarrelling pheasants, and he continued to order several box loads of books dumped into the flames, *Gulliver's Travels* included, then froze with arm outstretched, index finger canted high, slowly aiming the finger at the culprit, whose fair-skinned face flushed from chin to temple.

Red in Tooth and Claw

"What have you to say, Kreideweiss? What did you object to?" *My own voice sounds too young*, he thought: *it's too affable.*

"To bonfires, sir. It isn't soldierly." After a quiet order, two soldiers held him while a third slammed a rifle butt into his kneecaps, then into his groin. Already the books had caught fire, and the SS dumped their comrade-in-arms on top of the blaze. The sergeant cocked his pistol, but the officer told him "No, no, he will have to learn the hard way." Then the soldiers piled into trucks while the officer rode back to the dental office, where Wanda sat bound and gagged, already numb and willing herself not to faint by fixing her mind on Izz and Myrrh, the mayor of Z----- W----- in a red-hot skillet, the mayor of Kazimierz upside down on the end of a rope, and Ludwik, surely by now in Warsaw to find and rescue his mother. *Sit as still as his mother does*, Wanda told herself: *your chances are increasing*, but there was the SS officer in the doorway again, mopping his brow, and starting to talk with the forlorn diffidence of the expert liar.

"Now," he told her, "you know the pleasures of being gagged. Women gag themselves at regular intervals in their other mouth, so why not the hole in the face too? Admittedly, the hole below does not do much talking, but how eloquent it can be. If I had more time to spend with you, Frau Czimanska, you would not feel quite so lucky. As you know, I am essentially a souvenir-hunter. I collect sexual quotations. I rarely read the full volume. All that is behind me or, in some much more voluptuous, ingenious form, still to come, in one of those Russian palaces with a big furnace going in the basement, and dogs leading Bolsheviks around on long chains with spiked collars. Have you read the memoirs of Catherine the Great? Or Kantorowicz's life of Frederick the Great? I thrive on the Greats, you see. One day I shall found a museum of war trophies." She rippled her face at him and let out a stifled rebuke that sounded to her like a distant wind blowing over the Polish plain, to him like what it was: an accusation. He had insisted there was no war at all, and she was reminding him. His hand smelled of disinfectant, an odd mixture of tar and quicklime, then the gag was out.

"You were telling me there was a war. Not yet there isn't. But there will be. How do you feel? You may consider yourself, and the matto grosso, saved, for the time being. Your friends have left. You wish to know my name. Ask others. I answer to several names, among them *Haarkünstler*, the Hairdresser. I was a student of philosophy once, but now I have a new career. Do you know why?" He slipped the bonds from her arms and knees. "If you become truly wise, you may end up powerful. If you become an SS officer, you get power right away and you can become wise or not as you please. Take you, in the dental chair, utterly at my mercy, and I am going to let you go. That is power. I would rather have that kind of life than sweat over books in a garret, living on crusts and beer, hoping one day to become a man of authority. We shall hand you over to the field gendarmes, who will take you to a camp. I am being generous because you please me: you speak German, you are not unacquainted with our country, just climbing up out of the slime as it is, and you have amazing physique. You should bear more children, and pass on to other generations the mangoes with the golf tees and the Persian rug below." Motioning her to stand up, and exercise her arms to get the circulation back, he bowed slightly, did the heel-click she despised, it was so puerile and so mechanical, and smiled broadly. "This is farewell."

"You mentioned a camp."

"Ah, not to intimidate you. A refugee camp. We have scores of them set up all over Poland, with hot soup, good books, and not a Jew in sight. I could still shoot you out of hand, as the saying goes, but don't you think a *subtler* exercise of power is to let you live, to go on and say how well you have been treated. I gather you have influence, so you are entitled to survive in order to use it. To give and receive, Frau Czimanska." He went to the door and called an order, in response to which she heard pounding boots and then the neat slam of a soldier standing to attention. "Your courier," he said, "En route to Warsaw. The way is now clear. If dead horses upset you, close your eyes during the journey."

"I am going now? May I go and collect some things from Pulawy Street?"

"Pulawy Street! We have been there already. There is no time for that. Did you not bring a bag with you in the first place? Hm, it will have been collected up now with all the others. Never mind, you will be provided for." She made as if to leave, already determined to talk the soldier-courier, certainly if not SS, into making a sweep through Gnonka's farm; but she had nothing to bribe him with, only her body, which seemed to appeal to a certain German type, at least to this green-eyed, light-brown-haired, long-legged psychopath with the thick, bulbous mouth, a mouth so burly it seemed to move in two directions at once and exhibit conflicting emotions: always an appraising lustfulness, but sometimes with it boyish insouciance, or sardonic mock-zeal; but he was showing her something, a custom-made ammunition belt with spaces for perhaps thirty rounds, and little flaps like ear lobes that snapped shut.

"My insurance against loneliness," he said.

"In case you are isolated," she said in baffled reciprocity. "Cut off, I mean. And there is no regular ammunition. I know a bit about soldiering."

Shaking his head with an almost fey grin, he motioned her to oblige him by removing her underwear again, and she thought, mother of God, here it comes, I thought he was going to leave me be; surely he doesn't just want to look this time. Then he handed her the cotton swab, told her to leave it in place for a minute or two, which she did, with shivering bemusement, and then took it from her, stuffed it carefully into his cartridge belt after a haughty, critical sniff, and put the belt back round his athlete's waist. "In Siberia,' he said courteously, "you will be the breath of life. Just think of how you will be being useful to a lonely man. I have done you no harm, and I hope you will inform the appropriate authorities when the time comes."

If he were not twisted, she thought, I would not be alive. I would not still have a chance. "Then," she said, loathing herself, "what about a memento of you?"

At once he fished a molten slab of chocolate from his side pocket and handed it over. "You could eat such muck with a spoon," he said. "Here, use this," handing her the dentist's tiny mirror on its strut. I could blind you with the probe, she thought, if I did it now, I would get one eye at least, if I got him to lean over me, but what use would that be? I could blind the field gendarme, though, I could kill him with it if I stuck it in the right place, but you have to be a surgeon to know such things. Here I am, eating soft chocolate with a dental mirror in the presence of an SS captain, to hell with their pretentious SS ranks, who has taken a curl of my pubic hair and a vaginal swab to keep him company in some future campaign, and my only son is underground with a Jewish girl half a mile away, and I have no idea where my husband is, or even if he is still alive, and all I can do is to premeditate murder with a spike. Woman, you are dreaming: the dentist is dead, murdered, and all those others by the wall, and this man, your vicarious rapist, is responsible, so who knows what else he hasn't done out there, or elsewhere? What is life worth if, to keep it, you have to suckle the devil, so that he can go marauding across the continent of Europe, pistol in one hand while they brand the mayors and execute the Jews, and an erotic toy of a nosegay in the other to keep his thinking sweet? Life is worth all that, and even more.

Preposterously bright in manner, she appealed to him on a level he might like. "Is there anything left in here I could barter with? If I have the probe and the mirror, which I'll clean, I might be able to trade them for food. Might there be a syringe?" At once he understood, thinking she had injections in mind, and flung open a drawer, grabbed the hypodermic, the needles, even a few syrettes of novocaine, and scooped them all toward her in one big hand, then handed her a waterproof bib that was lying on the table. No, she decided, I won't need the laughing gas now, I'm equipped to bargain, and I can even deal with local pain, the metaphorical nature of which mental remark made her smile feebly as he bustled her, with package in hand, to the door and her courier.

"That awful sweet smell," she said outside. "It could be rotting leaves, but it's early for that. The smoke still hasn't gone."

"We have burned some Polish poetry," he said in German. "And one Polish poet." She clambered into the sidecar of the motorcycle and sat down while the goggled driver stared ahead, one hand on the pistol slung across his front, the other on the thick rubber stub of the handlebar. The Hairdresser saluted, the driver kicked the starter, and Wanda tried to do something appropriate where neither thanks nor greeting nor facial expression would do, in the end just nodding at him as if she had finally remembered the name that went with a familiar face. Her heart was trying to flutter free. Her hands were trying to execute a gesture that did not commit her, which she accomplished by imagining them boneless and leaflike in the stalled fug of early afternoon, doodling, sapped, exempt from time's imperceptible weight and the sharp arbitrariness of all human signals. Then it seemed to her that, until she made the correct gesture at all, he could not go on to his next wall of victims, his next fire, his next curl of nether hair, his next swab of woman's holy mucus, his dreaded immolation in Siberia; so, in effect she had voodoo power over him, who claimed to have substituted power for wisdom, using his green eyes like primitive crystal radio sets tuned in to the unimaginable, speechless future, in which he might figure only as a criminal, a bogey to frighten children with; and she decided she would not let him go, she would keep him there, even as the motorcycle churned and raved like an animal biting itself to death. So she and the Hairdresser glared at each other, breathing wordlessly into the spoiled cube of air between them, he with his sunglasses in hand suspended from the linked earpieces like a rejected chemist's balance, while his eyes searched her face with indignant voracious dependency, she with both hands clutching the dental tools rolled up in the splash bib, neither willing to accommodate the other with insult or rebuke. Convinced that he saw her genitalia in her face, he wondered why this woman, out of so many, should have the power to hold him in functionless vacancy in this mildewed, smoking, lousy Polish town, tantamount to keeping him from ever making Major, while she, having just gone through the worst, although the sketchiest humiliation she had known, commanded herself to look her fury full into his undeveloped face (he could not be more than twenty-five), a look of blades, vinegar, and death-watch intensity that said *I could have killed you in there or blinded you at least,* and she saw herself gouging out his eye or, more appropriately, passing the probe through his genitals, except that might have gratified him in some unspeakable masochistic bloodlust he had wanted from her all the time.

"Go." She knew as soon as she said it that the Hairdresser was a virgin, and that was her power over him, but she had no idea that while he stood there stranded in the sun beside the throbbing motorcycle, with his own driver watching him intently from the door of the thrown-together-looking scout car, his truant military mind was trying to combine her with a memory that nagged at him from his last leave, in Munich, where some whore in a green wig had called him into the toilet to watch and hear her void her bowels, after which she made him pull the flush and then, in a voice befitting a disturbed lioness, bass-purred at him *There you are big-boy, now I'm made room for you,* as she wiped, at which point he had babbled to her about Hermann Goering's morphine-and-honey enemas, demanded of all his mistresses, and *Hauptsturmführer* Haarkünstler had fled into the night, using a bit of gossip as his ticket of leave. Then he had told the story, embellished for the slanted tastes of his fellow officers, but without giving the address. *You try them all,* he'd said, *until you strike pure gold.* At least, then, from that scene of coercive grossness, he had been able to go, but not when Wanda told him to, nor when she repeated it and began to revile him in German and Polish, in the course of which harangue he began to smile and sigh, almost ruefully, nodding as her vituperation increased the more she thought about her son underground, a prey to beetles and spiders and sow bugs, rheumatism and centipedes and wireworms, death by drowning, by shellburst, by a homicidal farmer more attuned to beasts of the field than to human beings. She saw and denounced the comedo in his nose, the cast in his eye, the lyrically cruel outfanning lines on either side of his mouth, as if compasses had described two intersecting arcs and let the lines trail on past the intersections. *The quim cut in your face,* she thought as he stood there, a marionette in leathers and buckles waiting for the strings to move him over the real-life model of the map he knew by heart.

What broke the spell, if so active a standstill on her part had any magic in it, was the driver's firing his machine gun vertically, as he had done before when his master became transfixed by a woman, a tree, an effect of the light; on each occasion, as the Hairdresser stayed out of himself too long, the fluid scurry of shots had brought him back, sometimes to acts of unprovoked frenzy, face-slapping and *schnell!*-shouting; but not this time. Peering at Wanda as if she were already in Warsaw, or at least in a fast-contracting dream, he gave her his overburdened boyish sneer, said "We both go to Warsaw, Frau Matto Grosso. From now on, you must learn to eat time, like a horse in blinkers at the treadmill." In two uncoordinated thunders the vehicles leapt away, and Wanda felt she had won, won something, she had no idea what.

That something stayed with her for the first ten minutes of her ride to Warsaw along ridiculously serene roads with craters in them where shells or bombs had landed, but the two vehicles, weaving and tilting, made fair progress and seemed at times almost to be playing tag under the big blue lid of a sky that promised a cooling-off by sunset. Whatever it was that had contracted in her chest, forcing her lungs into her heart, now let up, and the occasional pile of dead horses, sometimes alongside human bodies, arrayed in gorgeous colors and antique helmets, passed through her eyes into the ether again, all of them as she now realized part of the pattern-smashing she was obliged to live through, determined to be strong even in the dental chair, humiliated and awaiting the pistol-shot, and even more so in the creaky celluloid cabin of the sidecar, where she crouched with her legs drawn up underneath her as if preparing to vault clean out of it, her hands clenched knuckle-pale on the bundle of instruments as if they were her birthright, with which to pick, stab, inject her way into the next phase of what she already considered her new life. That she had survived, was in the process of surviving, she had no doubt, but she could not dismiss her last sight of Wilson and Suzanna, neutrally acquiescent, visibly sorry for *her* as the Hairdresser had her led away to some only too imaginable private horror; yet she put aside all guesses at their fate, telling herself that the main thing was to prevail through the next minute, and then the next, in dogged lumpish assimilation, hunched up on what felt like an antique sewing machine fitted with the merest pad of a seat, while the wind plunged past her with a flavor (stronger than a smell) of burning blossom and warm rubber.

If she had a plan, she let it float like water as it found a way here, an obstacle there, her main vow to herself being to go back, to claim her own with a towering shout of gratified mother-rage, but also to do something about Ludwik, who had galloped off the pages of an illustrated children's book on knights into what already seemed the aftermath of war: a few peasants, stranded by the roadside waving a welcome to the conquerors (among whom she rode like an incubus), some of them with panes of glass on which swastikas had been hurriedly daubed in whitewash; a few pockets of German troops, who saluted as the scout car and the motorcycle swept by; an ox at one crossroads, waiting for whatever oxen waited for, like an emblem of mindless durability that implied a whole landscape of polled Angus cattle, rye fields with drainage ditches, whitewashed property markers gleaming like malformed teeth in the afternoon sun, hemp tied in bunches next to rows of cabbages, straw stacks shaped like loaves, pumpkins piled on roofs like clumps of outsize frogspawn, windmills driven by a long wooden pole that sat unattended on the ground like some outsize abandoned seesaw, stacks of straw on stilts, unused by completed thatches resting against the wall of houses, other long poles to be used for beating out roof fires, coarse beans drying on a south wall, double gates for wagons, single gates for people, storks' nests on roofs, vertically woven wicker fences, windmills with balconies, one-story shops with wooden shutters, untidy hand-painted signs saying FRYZJER or hairdresser (she noticed them all), hydrants covered with straw figurines, a horse on a shaft turning a primitive mill beside which stood tall wicker baskets like open-air vases, and the water wagons, the well sweeps, the iron verandahs, the cobblestones with deep ruts, the tar paper on the roofs, the little Greek orthodox churches painted blue, the overhanging roofs that shaded the sidewalks, the beets, the maize, the mangled flax, the tin cans built into the roofs, the nailless ladders, the firehooks, the hand-made harrows, the clover, the wheat, the moss, the sawdust and the shavings that drifted about on the village streets after summer repairs. It was a landscape worth crossing borders for, she could see that, and it was where the abandoned tanks did not belong, although down the tunnel of history she saw how the steel panels would one day be used to fix a hole in a roof or shore up a slumping outhouse. She saw the land as a beloved skin, and the features implanted in it as akin to the little moles, like incipient grapes, that grew in her son's armpits, whereas Haarkünstler saw all this as only the texture of a map which he repeatedly checked as the sputtering scout car moved northward with the sun behind it, forcing its way repeatedly into a vertical postcard that receded with the sun full on it, remaining the same—pasture, field, village, pasture, field, village, town—and so on until he could stand it no more, called a halt, and went to relieve himself into a low hedge, whose lower scrub accepted his urine as if he did not exist, it was gone so soon; and then the two drivers did the same into the same hedge, rather less pensively, even as their officer waved at Wanda to do likewise if she needed to. I would wet the sidecar, she thought, if I didn't need to stay in it, I would pee on everything they have; but she failed to complete such thoughts of vengeful irrigation as he, her defiler, walked up and tossed preposterous bounty into her lap: a chunk of canned ham and a small wedge of fruitcake in which the dim red of a cut cherry caught her eye and held it. They had been cutting cake! Appalled, she gestured at him and went away to squat at the hedge, the two drivers having finished, but she still expected a bullet in the back as she turned away from them, even after Haarkünstler, as she now thought of him, transposing nickname into name, got back into the scout car and barked an order at her over the intervening grass.

She did not budge, however, clutching her food against her on top of the dental bundle, hearing only the whistle of her pent-up water into the thistles and the dandelions, seeing only a high bird cruising on a thermal. The scout car had already vanished, as she finally saw, and her own driver stood at an embarrassed distance, beating his boot on the ground, and still she did not move, except to stuff the ham and the cake into her bundle, from which she took the probe. Then, shivering in her perspiration, she half-stood, drew up her underwear, smoothed her dress, and then sagged sideways in a slow faint, which the driver saw, cursed at as he began to walk toward her with the aggrieved, blighted look of a farmer obliged to examine a crop that had almost failed. When he reached her side, she held her breath, and held it still as he slung his pistol over his shoulder in order to crouch, still not speaking but beginning to form an interrogative grunt as she continued to sham. First he shoved her shoulder, asked her what was wrong, then peered in exasperation at the horizon as if expecting the scout car to come back; but in looking away from her he had gone off-balance, not enough to topple, but quite enough to sway sideways, complementing with his weight the crossbow lunge with which she drove the probe into his windpipe, thrusting with all her heart for Izz and Myrrh, for Ludwik, Wilson, and Suzanna, and continuing to thrust until, she saw it, the point emerged at the other side during an instant of gruesome silence even as blood ran over her hands and the driver, a close cropped blond with dark brown eyes, held his stance, neither falling nor straightening, but remaining there as if the probe had speared his entire body to the ground, and all she heard was a series of swift violent hiccoughs, a gurgling, an attempt at speech, after which he fell. Allowing herself one brief glance in the direction of the scout car, but seeing nothing, she held the writhing head by the ears, stabbed each eye with the hypodermic, and ran for the motorcycle, which she now had to try to start, knowing only what she had seen him do during one start and one stop. At the third attempt, with bundle tucked inside her blouse, she got it to go and, thinking much more slowly than she drove, steered it off the shoulder onto the road and began to hurtle back the way she came, heedless of the blinded, choking driver on the ground, little knowing where to go, and in a panic recognizing she was heading south only because the SS car was heading north, whereas perhaps Ludwik was up towards Warsaw. Between husband and child, she accelerated south, cursing herself for having to choose a direction at all, as well as for not knowing how to stop. To calm herself enough to drive, she regaled her mind with one of her favorite dishes, crayfish in cold cream, both succulent and costive, and the very thought of it prompted her to go faster than ever as if the dish itself awaited her at journey's end, complete with a brand-new silver spoon cradled in white tissue paper of the gentlest weave, a gift from Ludwik on the occasion of nothing at all really, just the joy of being together in candid reciprocity, whether in Berlin, Warsaw, Kazimierz, or on the seacoast of Bohemia. Yet the driver speared through the throat with the slightly curving motion she knew she had to achieve, having thought about it all the way northward, came back to her, his windpipe like the shaft and crossbar of some stringed instrument. Past groups of Germans in new positions, but oddly lethargic (some of them actually dunking their feet in a stream), past a few peasants who waved and again brandished their swastika-ed panes of glass, and past the same dead swollen horses she sped, undulating as if drunk, but fortunately meeting no traffic going the other way. She steered by the sun since all the signposts had been either torn down or twisted the wrong way round, in some sly symbolic ploy to undo the invader, who of course had maps in great detail showing wooden or metal bridges, railroad signal boxes, even hunter's cabins and the location of all fresh springs. The wounded, and the dead, were all away from the main roads, having sought cover or been gently removed to a penultimate resting place amid the decency of shade trees; but of course the invaders had been more cavalier with their dead, the main purpose being to thrust on northward and eastward, whereas the losers had had time to lift the remains, rearrange the limbs and hair, the tunics and the boots, and the wounded, both German and Polish, being under a greater necessity than that of opposite sides, found themselves together, being treated by the same orderlies or (if they were lucky) doctors, again either Polish or German, and in some instances even being subject to the scribes of war who filled out Registers of Prisoners of War, Unwounded or Wounded (Separate forms are to be used for officers and for men.), which demanded more information than anyone wished to give or could be bothered to extort, the one significant column on the form (B 103A), apart from the serial number, being that headed *Discharged, Exchanged, Died, or Escaped*. The weird thing about these little chapels of broken people, scattered about parallel to the main highway, was that the Poles with prisoners felt incongruous, like bankrupts holding bullion, whereas the Germans (except for the SS, who had a short way with both prisoners and wounded, as with the populace at large) felt ill at ease just ministering to the wounded in the wounded's own country, which they had to concede had on that day an undeniable shimmer and wore its craters, its sundered trees, its plundered villages, its tiaras of broken glass, with indelible aplomb, as if, in the mildest way imaginable, to rebuke those who disturbed its peace exactly when the massive groundswell of summer paused to let a sterner season through the gate, and as the Germans were not autumn, they had no right to come bundling in thus personified.

A woman with more time to examine things, even though her knowledge of soldiering was scant, would have realized that what had clanked through Kazimierz was the rearguard of the forward wave, which in turn went forward, leaving behind a garrison with which she had not reckoned at all, equipped with loudspeakers, flags, curfew dogs, copies of the lists the SS had used, and a truckload of leaflets and posters which cajoled and threatened at the same time. But Wanda's head was full of the glue brewed by motherhood, which drove her homeward like a carrier pigeon in a frenzy to be doing something instead of being carried passively to Warsaw and its environs, with at the end of her journey a one in a thousand chance of finding Ludwik's mother sitting in her rocker, with a pile of family albums beside her and across her lap the fire irons she weekly washed, coated with furniture polish, and then rubbed into a fine gleam that never went near a fire, since fireplace she had not. If Wanda had calculated her chances, isolated at speed and unsure how to brake, not only in the middle of an occupied zone but also in the direct path of reinforcements, she might have chosen to turn round; already she had been prodigiously lucky: she might have been shot at the wall along with the local dignitaries, or burned alive in the cemetery along with Suzanna and Wilson Sakal, and the Orthodox Jews in skullcaps and black nightshirts, or raped and then quite privately done away with by the Hairdresser; her driver might have had better luck himself and machine gunned her as she swung at him with the dental probe, ignoring its presence in his windpipe so as to remove its amateurish wielder, or he might have, blinded as he was, nonetheless raked the area with bullets and picked her off at random even as she was escaping; and she might not have had the probe, or the hypodermic at all; she might have been machine gunned by a swooping Messerschmitt, felled by a sniper; blasted off the road by an anti-tank gun; she might even have gone headlong into a tree and broken her neck. Indeed, the Hairdresser might have turned the scout car around and come after her, which he was too busy to do, of course, but he just might have, a man so whimsical might even have staged an *auto-da-fé* on her by the hedge where they all relieved themselves, an orgy of mute rape with canned ham and fruit cake, plus a finale calling for dental tools used without electricity, and lethal in the extreme.

19

This last possibility floated through her mind like a leaf through a woodland glade shafted with sunlight, amounting only to a marginal horror while her misbehaving mind, matching her body as her hands tried to change gears, admitted a snatch of talk from an old Western movie, in which, after the stagecoach halted, the driver called out 'Watering place, folks: ladies to the left, gents to the right,' and she again heard the whistle of her water against the nettles and dandelions, the speargrass and the fumitory spread like a low cloud of smoke over the ground.

If only I had taken his goggles, she thought, I would see better instead of having my eyes blown shut. What was ahead of her, like an untidily built tower of dominoes wobbling in the heat shimmer that came off the road, itself a dazzling cream-buff, was what she had no means of construing, never having seen such a thing in her life. Now it seemed to come toward her, now to veer away and almost pause, but her own unbridled speed took her towards it anyway, along a straight five-hundred meter stretch of road which, in itself, might have been a relief, enabling her to wipe her streaming eyes and sit back a bit from her zealous crouch over the handlebars. It was an open dray, she told herself, stacked high with the things Izz and Myrrh had taken with them underground: bedding, cans of ham, hot-water bottles, candles, the radio, the clock, the bottle of aspirins, but the scale was wrong for that; nor was it a peasant cart loaded with furniture in a desperate bid to escape from advancing armies into the rear of any army that had already gone by. In the lead, as she now saw, was a low vehicle, in fact a troop carrier, crammed with heads, and right behind an armored car with a machine gun mounted behind a bulletproof visor, and behind that a tall tank whose gun turret seemed to her big as a granary. Superimposed behind one another as they advanced, these three apparitions had an unstable homemade air, and of course no one was firing at her; the only vehicles on the road were German, and what she rode on towards them was an official motorcycle with a big fat headlamp behind the front fender and, on the right side, a little like the nose of a truncated sailplane, the only non-aerodynamic feature being the steel bracket, an outsize staple, for the passenger to hold on with. But what the advancing column saw was a short-haired driver, plausible enough in summer and especially as far behind the front as this, but dressed in a blouse containing the mangoes admired by the Hairdresser in the dental office, and the bib-wrapped bundle too. Next they saw her wide-splayed legs, not those of a Polish witch riding a technological broomstick but simply those of a civilian doing something altogether contrary to the book, going much too fast, weaving all over the road, never changing gear on the downslope toward the front of the column, and, oddly enough (at least to Germans equipped with a limited number of invader-victim combinations) not being pursued by anything at all.

One accurate, scrunched-up glimpse was enough for Wanda, who, because of her slipstream tears, saw the apparition refracted and multiplied, as well as in hues and tints which came from the nature of light itself trapped in the water globules that coated the roots of her lashes. At the same speed she turned sharp left, over the grass verge, down into a gulley whose floor half a meter down was the sediment of a stream now dry, up the other side with a fearsome lurch that seemed to rupture her pelvis (a twisting jounce of the muscles), and into a small copse of widely spaced trees, through which she roared with not enough time to evade one trunk or another, simply trusting that, if she could skirt one or two, she might miss the next one as well, which she did, having hit the copse at its narrowest part. The low-hanging branches whipped her across the face repeatedly, bringing more tears, which became worse as she careened into a small pasture, uneven and rocky and littered with feeding troughs, into one of which she cannoned even before she hit the low whitewashed wall scrawled on with hearts and tic-tac-toe crosses done in charcoal, and went headfirst from the handlebars, over the wall, into a small playground which, in the fractional second of her being airborne and almost stationary at the top of her curve, seemed a ludicrous throwback to pre-invasion days: a garden fair, a many-family picnic, an outdoor wedding festivity, a scene so busy and so crammed it somehow needed a roof over it, or a tent at least, a red and white striped awning, at least something to keep the rain off and to give a minimal coziness to what was beneath.

Behind her, not that she knew or would have cared, at an altogether more prudent speed, fut-futtered another motorcycle, sent in pursuit by the colonel in charge of the column, which had already gone by with a stench and a commotion masked by the trees, through which the fumes now managed to drift and the noise bounced about like a series of backfires. Wanda's own machine remained on the other side of the wall, its wheels visible from where she had landed on her front, on asphalt, badly grazing her face, snapping an arm (whose click she heard without pain and registering it with heedless, almost procrastinating calm), slithering a couple of meters to the dainty summer shoes of a medium-height child who screamed and at once ran away into what Wanda, barely seeing at this point, found only a low-level assortment, a sideways slice, of blood, white, and blue, with big brown boxes obscuring the rest, although there were also bigger feet, in boots, and these included those of the German who had ridden after her and easily swiveled his butt over the wall.

Being now unconscious, Wanda did not hear the disheveled conversation that ensued. "Orders to follow her," said the rider who had come behind her. "A regulation motorcycle."

"A spy or saboteur," an Army sergeant announced. "These people have absolutely no right to be on the roads. She has destroyed valuable equipment, and there'll be hell to pay when it's established where she got it from."

"So long as you don't pay it," said the major in command, "you needn't worry. This woman is hurt, she may be crazy or even dangerous, but the paramount fear about her is that she is in no condition to help herself." Two orderlies in bloodstained white smocks lifted her aside gently, but almost without looking at her face, not because it resembled raw meat but because they had seen too many faces that day, too many men, women and children cut by shrapnel, glass, bullets, and blast, and had been able to do too little for them; what the ingenuity of hands had created, to explode or to pierce, the ingenuity of hands could not mend, and this depressed the major, an older man who did not in the least mind being put in charge of two kinds of wounded, as well as refugees, hysterics, vagrant orphans, and Jews in pathetically poor disguise. It was just that there seemed a lack of even-handedness in a world system that ruined more easily than it repaired, and he could only conclude that the saving grace of so much mayhem was the ease with which children are made.

When she came to, Wanda knew she must answer no questions at all, having disemboweled the face of a German soldier, SS at that, and stabbed him in the throat; she would not even be tried, and the facts were sure to come out when her driver failed to bring her in. Or so she supposed, imagining a blind man reeling about the landscape, trying to find someone to whom he could tell all, if only he could speak, instead of that stertorous gobbling noise he made each time he took a breath. The advancing column would no doubt find him, take him in, and ascertain the ghoulish facts perhaps in improvised sign language, or with a blackboard on which the poor wretch asked for his captain, to whom no explanation would be necessary. Then she would be lucky to hang from a lamppost upside down, with her pubic hair on fire, her eyes annulled, her throat and tongue impaled on wooden skewers, and, strange as it seemed, worst of all the dental drill entering her arm, then becoming a horn of plenty that widened until it split radius from ulna, transforming her arm into an atoll of bone enclosing only air.

"She's coming round," the major said. "Take over. I am not going to interrogate her if someone else wishes to. The trouble with interrogation," and he spoke this with sour commiseration to her burning, iodine-purple face, "is that you get answers, you always get what you are looking for. This poor, mad, insensate Polish woman with the well-kept hands was no more destined to be riding a motorcycle than these poor devils on the stretchers were destined to be blown to bits. The more wounded people are, the more they seem alike. I've seen enough exposed livers for one day, enough bone to last any ordinary mortal a lifetime." As if answering him, Wanda said "Pulawsky," and then "Pulaws-ky?"

"Take over," the major said again. "She's asking for somebody. It's no use asking for somebody here. Put her in the shade, let her collect her wits." He eased his palms together.

Wanda was plumbing a deep lake, as dense as anthracite, for other names, although unclear where she was, to whom she was speaking if the whole thing were not some evocation of another life not her own, just using her as its mouthpiece while she remained a mute witness of the milky cascade before her eyes, full of geometrical figures that melted and came again somewhat altered. Topaz wheels sparkled on what seemed to be the ground and a delicate buzzing was all she could hear as she murmured the signals that might get her through, to safety, or to do some good for others while she faded away for ever. Then she realized she must be feeling better: to be able to think of fading away for ever meant, surely, she was coming to, yet she felt much less lucid than what felt like only seconds ago. No one had taken any notice of the major; Wanda had received what medical aid there was available, and neither the young army surgeon, whose hands and wrists were limp from overwork, nor the orderlies, who were dog-tired, saw much point in lingering at her side. In the crude differentiation of things, she was alive, not dying nor badly hurt, whereas those stationed around her lay like waxworks in a fierce undertow they knew little of, each afloat in a morphine haze, and lucky in that; but the supply of medicine would run out, and no one, no motorcyclist, no dispatch rider, would come hurtling from the rear with fresh bandages, and if not for the half-dozen Germans lying there, maimed by a game of their own devising, then certainly not for the two dozen Poles who, mostly, had been trying only to get out of harm's way and had been engulfed. Evacuation by ambulance was the only way of preventing the major from becoming the head steward of a mortuary, a sorry fate for a fifty-one year old ex-lawyer from Bavaria, who at this moment longed to get back to his books, his almost bloatedly perfect collection of several dozen albums of German and French colonial stamps, gaudy and blithe and picturesque. A mental zone for which he felt much better equipped; but, at least, he half-reassured himself, he was not involved in the haphazard killing, the impromptu decision by so many army units to use Poland as a bloody doodling-ground where men could play with life-size toys denied them long ago.

"There will have to be a report," said the motorcyclist from the column, who had chased after her to this surgical playground with its hopscotch chalkmarks still visible in the small patches where no one lay. "She should be shot forthwith," he added with monolithic certainty.

"There has been shooting enough already," the major told him. "Get off back to your unit and report one fugitive now in custody, to be dealt with later. There is nothing here for you. Go and subjugate Poland. Please."

Puzzled by the elaborate verb, *Unterjochen*, which felt right while somehow seeming ironic, which it was, the SS motorcyclist, quite omitting any courtesies due to superior rank, waved at the array of wounded, and condemned the whole enterprise as a waste of time. "You are living in a dead world, Major." He donned his goggles as if to shut it out.

"When," the major said evenly, "I want advice on how to do my duty, certainly from a leprous dungspreader such as you, I'll let headquarters know. Goodbye." Soon the SS would be running everything, the morticians of the new era, he thought, and the lucky wouldn't live to see it or serve it. Even the survivors among his wounded would probably starve to death, he told himself; this was a holding operation, understaffed and ill-equipped, with no future and little point, and it had come into being more in order to find him something to do than as a consequence of military foresight. Without Hitler and his foreign adventurism, he would already have been enjoying his pension. Still, as a symbol, his receiving station wasn't bad; the breeze was willing to blow over it, the sun baked it, the night came down on it unresistingly, and a few assorted birds clucked about, looking to snap up whatever fell and actually sipped blood from the ground. He vaguely recalled the reason for his being in Poland, drafted by some old sentimentalist of a planner to liaise with the civil administration and get things working again; but the invasion had become so barbaric he had no role at all and certainly no say. Like a doomed elephant, he was apart from the herd, and he preferred it that way: I and the wounded, the dead, the dying, he told himself, are obsolete; we may well malinger together. There's no place better than a school, roofless and windowless as it is. If I have to end my days pottering about here, with a few young derelicts from my own people, a handful of war-torn civilians and soldiers from the losing side, then at least I go to my grave with an uncontaminated heart, like that poor swine of a major bleeding to death over there in full regalia, intercepted by gunfire on his way to a fancy-dress party (yet is their dress any fancier than our own brownshirts, the penguin get-up of the SS?). There are men, thousands of them, whose hands will never wash, whereas the blood on mine will stay put, not much of a badge of honor but a minor part of the panoply of good intentions. He yawned, sat on the edge of a big wooden drawer like an overturned sentry box, and then he saw the eyes perceiving him with distraught neutrality, behind them a fog of gradually failing narcosis and he got up, strolled to where the four children sat marooned in a close posy someone might have flung from a passing funeral, happy enough in the sunshine, unrelated to anyone else on the premises, and already, he theorized, oblivious of how from three different directions (the two girls together) they had wandered unharmed into an enclave of the hurt, perhaps even playing hide and go seek in the still recognizable countryside left behind by the advance army. Life was crisscross: there were little Neroes everywhere, counting up or chanting in the rigmaroles of play, to whom indeed a line was something you must not step upon if you didn't want to be 'out'. He knew no Polish, they knew no German (which was unusual, prompting him to think they were peasant children), and all he could do was to stand, try not to seem intimidating, and tousle the hair of their heads in a dumbshow of reassurance that only made them, in turn, lazily dislodge his hand without rancor or fear, but dislodge it all the same even as he pretended not to be doing it, looking away at the horizon, the just visible steeple of a church, the wounded in the wooden drawers, thinking himself every centimeter their shepherd, oh yes, just for having let them remain and be.

At this point, heavy with partly spurned affection, he walked with a brisker stride to where Major Ludwik Czimanski, as his papers said, lay in a near-coma, breathing a low breath of spliced murmurs and bathed in the aroma of blood sausage, and no longer with his remaining hand feeling for the hand that used to be there, or (even in his detonated mind) with the absent hand for the other. Major Czimanski did not so much lie at death's door; he blocked the doorway with his body, somehow convinced with the fringe logic of someone delirious beyond pain, that he could not go through the door so long as his body, *any* body, lay in the way. As major touched major, not in a laying-on of hands but the German announcing his presence in an involuntary way, in fact touching a brass button as if to touch the fabric that sheathed the body were too intimate and false. Wanda happened to look up, all of a sudden clear-sighted although fuzzy-headed, saw the German crouching over the rim of the wood, and felt something acute: a big air bubble choking her, but it was really a word. "Here," she croaked, "I have this stuff inside my blouse. It might come in handy. See here."

The German major was just thinking, *Here is another major who will never be elevated to lieutenant-colonel. The deep, true caliber of his heart will go to waste, the scope of his interests and zeal go unrecognized, his constructive sympathy for others be discarded as mere busyness.* Then he realized that the woman had spoken, called to him in fact across the playground, surely not with sexual innuendo in this place of the barely subdued agony. Her blouse? She was fishing a bundle out of it, something in faded pale blue, not very big, but handled tenderly as a grail, an heirloom, a dead baby's first shawl. As she staggered to her feet, almost tripping over a German soldier next to her, who raised one arm ruefully and tried to fend her off and up with the flat of his hand, she called out again, working her purple face hard as if not only the caked blood but some inward muscular spasm sapped her power of speech: "Something for what ails you," an expression so antique it seemed facetious, more appropriate to a glass of schnapps proffered in a small bottle. So she came over, her gait a knock-kneed wobble, and he thought, *She is hurt more than I thought she was, there could be internal injuries, which once again we are not equipped to handle.*

"Holy sunset," he exclaimed. "Look at that!" Already he was waving the surgeon to him with an arm both curt and urgent; he was still in command here, and, better, he was almost in command of himself again, no longer dribbling off into reverie about his hobbies and all the books he intended to read once discharged, and in which order, beginning with Adams, Henry Brooks, the American.

"She has novocaine and a hypodermic, which needs to be washed and sterilized." Her face blood, obviously, had leaked down to her chest, but surely that full bosom was not injured.

"No, no," she was saying in what he suddenly realized was good, idiomatic German. "It was really quite different."

"Are you a dentist?" No, she thought, but I know more than most about what can happen in a dentist's office: I have seen the living dead walk and talk, and clip my pubic hair with scissors, take quite unmedical swabs for unthinkable stimulation away in Siberia; I do not need to read Baudelaire to find out about degenerate proclivities or the exquisite's longing for mud. I have seen great stars turn into black coals, I have seen a big red eye peering up into my bowels, like a critical octopus, and several times recently, if I can trust my bruised and battered memory, I have gone clean off my head. That I have killed I have no doubt. Even if I have not killed, I have killed in my mind, and here I am surrendering my weapons. No: keep the probe, and use the mirror as a spoon.

Already the fluid in the syrettes was in the veins of those who needed local anesthesia. The playground was quieter, but she could hardly believe the sudden surcease in bitten-back moans was the result of hypodermic injections, it was because the sun had disappeared behind a cloud almost pale peppermint green.

"An angel of mercy on a motorcycle," the major was saying. "Where did you learn your German? You have a Berliner accent. I myself am from Munich. But I know. Who *are* you?"

Wanda blinked her glued-up eyes until they teared, and then she blinked hard to clear her sight, uneasy because just on the edge of her vision she could discern the bulge of her swollen cheeks, hemming her in like the face of someone who had come too close and was inside her focus blurring and looming. How odd that there should be both Germans here and Polish civilians, mingling, not with ready affability although they might be able to exchange a few words in German, but conducting themselves (at least those who could move about) like members of the same race, without tails or saber teeth, neither clad in bearskins nor carrying cudgels. Taking a breath of deep, near-rhetorical relief, she looked about and was amazed to see not only German nurses and orderlies but also nurses with Red Cross insignia, the clutch of children reciting something among themselves, which she wished Izz and Myrrh could hear, and (she moved on to another image, another thought, fast) two kinds of wounded, the erect and the bedridden, but the bedridden on blankets on the hot, almost fluid asphalt of the ground, or in huge drawers as if ready for burial, and she imagined a vast chest of drawers, a structure of slots like a skyscraper, kept in readiness for the day when all the drawers with their inert cargo would be rammed shut, after which the knobs would be removed in the interests of decency, aroma, and neatness. I am tired of clever minds, she heard herself reciting, of twists and maneuvers. It all comes to this, it all comes down to this, bandages and weeping, pain and silence. When was it that I last had a good night's sleep? Each day for months I seem to have woken with an immediate sense of not having slept enough, that grittiness, that hollowness between the nose and the brain, that sickening sideways feeling as if I'm not walking straight, always bumping into things, dropping them, putting them back in place upside down or at a slant. The body becomes its shadow's shadow. That is what it's like. To other people you look much the same, but you feel subtracted, and something inside, not the heart certainly, keeps on quivering and the quiver shows in the wrists, but nobody can see your wrists trembling. It's all on the inside, where your nerves no longer move to any kind of music.

How she responded to what she thought she saw next, or how she thought she was responding to it, not even the complete compound eye of the omnipotent Creator, that imaginary realist among dreamers, could quite set down; the deity would not have time, too busy keeping the world in trim. Her entire response, forming and dispersing, from million upon million of tiny heartfelt particles, some of which belonged together while others did not— a gray, a twang, a whiff of crayfish, an arm rubbed smooth with aloe, the taste of copper as if she had licked the flange of a flashlight— almost made her sick, it was too thorough, demanding that her blood no longer flow, her lungs go flat and snowbound, full of fluff. If she saw a face, she imagined it from the merest evidence, and if she held a hand it was her own. *Who am I?* Is that what someone asked me? I have just heard music, not just that of instruments, oh no, but that of the mind and the body joined, like a depressed dance tune heard from afar while I lean against a lattice of crystal against which someone bleeding has also leaned, witness the smears, the spittle, the still-enduring warmth from the hand that hungered at this lattice, as at a straw. Looking down at the face in the drawer, she fought off the tender condescension that went with peering into cradles, and instead, with the full volume of her will added a neck to that face, the shoulders to the arms, assembling the man of her dreams like someone materializing hair and teeth from a sample of St. Elmo's fire, she told herself, she told the major, she told the smashed face: "I am this man's wife, I am this Polish major's wife, he is my husband Ludwik Czimanski, father of my only son." There was nothing else to say about her life.

"I know his name," the major said. "Who else would claim him? There is nothing to be done. He is already far away. We have transfused all we have. You, who speak such gentle German, had better sit. Talk to him if you wish, but I am afraid I would be deceiving you if I let you think he heard." On he droned, as if captivated by this dizzying coincidence, half wishing something as arithmetically rare had not come his way; it tempted him to believe in something, not God, or fate, but a charity of swirling atoms. She would be better off not having seen him thus torn apart, whatever it was, a tank shell or something from an aircraft cannon, and yet how quietly he sank, how quietly she stands and looks her all into his face, unable to recognize that something is over, for ever, and ever, so that not even the full loving suction of her heart and mind, her faith and will, can pull him back from wherever it is he's gone. And now she blames me, she who leapt into the arena with novocaine and syringe. I wouldn't mind going home to my stamps, right now, I have no skill with carnage, and the subtler carnage wrought by the dead upon the living.

"What happened?" She saw her man setting out that morning, before sun-up, in his fancy costume, to reclaim his mother (no doubt) and then, after putting her somewhere safe, on whatever distant planet orbiting some unnamed star, to brandish his honor anew like a cap-badge coming to life, the eagle writhing from its metal frame, fluffing its feathers, and breaking free like a ghost made of iron filings. She saw him charge a barricade and execute a parabolical jump, leaving the saddle slightly. She saw him catch a falling bomb on the point of his sword, then flip it expertly upward into the underbelly of the dive bomber still above him, frozen in time before climbing, so fast his sword had been. She saw him blind the driver of an oncoming tank by catching the sunlight on the blade of that same sword with careful canny tilts until the beam went through the slit even as he, the relayer of light, kept his balance on the whirling Earth. She saw him dead, but not killed; she saw nothing happen, but saw her man in action, as he had never been in years, and then his one-armed body as a relict from a previous time, making her a relict too, in the sense of widow; and that one word, trailed like a crepe blindfold across the ends of her pent-up nerves, forced from her the most terrible shout the major had ever heard, a sound that began with the bottled-up shy bleat of an affronted child and ascended into the half joyful roar of a woman giving birth, each burst of pain a star, each intake of wind a gulp of hope. There was no answering this, not in any language the demure major knew, so he simply held her close, from behind, as if to keep her from leaping into the drawer, which indeed she tried to do, cocking one leg over the wooden rim, only to have the major tell her, *Don't do that, he isn't dead*, while he leaned backward with all his weight to keep her off the body, letting her scream her way toward the unthinkable, *schnell, laut, und brutal*, he told himself, but all she did was pull hard away from him and shout at her husband's face up close as if to shock him back to life, to wake him from whatever blood-sucked coma held him and have him jerk upright, asking for breakfast, complaining about a broken sleep, and then with only half-strength coffee to sustain him, boiled up from used grounds, go again about his heroic business against the invader, but this time with ammunition and a gun. Where, she suddenly thought, and the screaming stopped, was his pistol? The holster was empty. "I have it, of course," the major said. "After all, I am the enemy."

"You are," she said. "I wish to God you had stayed at home."

"With my stamp collection," he said, feeling ridiculous at the narrowness of his reference, but he had been eager to say anything so as not to appear to her a Hun, and then she would start to scream again. Oddly, no one else had responded to the noise; Poles were Slavs, and Slavs did a lot of screaming, and so did the wounded of all nationalities. "I just happen to collect stamps," he said lamely. "Just as I do not happen to be much of a career major. We have done what we could do for him. A miracle? If you believe in such things. Plasma would help." Out from her blouse, now stippled with her own blood and Ludwik's, she fetched the ham and cake, handed them to him with a face of obstinate, grave apology, and said, "It's real. But where it came from's not. Can you turn it into plasma?"

That done, she turned again to Ludwik's face, willing it in its mask of purple and red to be again the face of the frail, papery skin, almost transparent, which she delighted to observe during sunset, when the low light which had scarlet or vermillion in it caught him on the cheek, the lower jaw, and gave him color, made him solid. Then his big startled eyes closed down a bit and he seemed to begin sinking into a sleep from which he wanted no return as, with astute casualness, she patted his face this way or that just a degree so as not to waste the sunset. On a dozen balconies in Germany alone she had gone through this tender placement of the face in the rays, slow-fondling him as he lit up like some treasured icon, except of course that he was so much more: an icon with blood running through it, in conduits that had small internal fins to keep the flow one-way, and able to murmur slight, almost incoherent endearment as the sun went down, clasping his big hands together rather than holding hers, and nodding approval at the hemorrhaging crude sun as if it had done something unusual that day, which no one else had noticed, easing a millimeter nearer Earth or achieving an even more unviewably golden gold, at a given hour, than ever before. His big, thick, long-lobed ears matched his hands, but his chopped-off mustache, thicker and much wider than Hitler's, belonged to his job alone; it was the assistant military attaché's, and now as she caressed it, with her thumb purging it of dust and scabs, it felt artificial, a prop to get him extra attention in that grisly funeral yard where children had once formed a secret society and current enemies merely kept away from one another. Bending over him fully, she began to kiss him in one long surge, as if to push him through the bottom of his trance and bring him coughing to the surface. Five minutes of this brought no result at all, but even as she rose, dizzy, just to catch her breath, the German major pointed at an eye that moved, no more than a visual hum, and she at once thought of all she wanted to say, then bit it back to listen to him hard, whatever the tremor in the eye might be prelude to. *When this is over,* she heard herself forcing back the words, *we'll go on a reading holiday to the Black Sea, or go to Canada to see the stampede; our bodies will address each other in pure symmetry, time will melt, dimension likewise, there will be no sea level, no airlessness at the peak, we will be dazed by each other's radiance, and I shall turn you to the sun ever so gently as though you were my telescope. And I your—*

His mouth split open, though a thin membrane on the right failed to unpeel, and she dared not touch it to free it, though she hungered to part lip from lip. What one thing could she say that evinced, without blotting out his chance of answering or of having his answer heard, all he was to her? Mouth clamped tight, she heard the miscellany of late summer, bees and birds and clattering nuts, but no gunfire and no sound of engines from the not so distant highway. Then like some intoning priest he said her name, just once, seeming to dream the first syllable, then uttering the second as punctuation in the void: a shorter, sharper, but still dazed-sounding affirmative: *da.* Still she hushed, actually turning aside to mouth the milling words from her systems, while keeping both eyes fixed on him. Now was the time, she knew, so she said, fast as a lark's wing, "Your mother." She had meant to make it a question, but it came out as a clue, a signal, and he stiffened, began a series of tiny almost imperceptible shakes of the head, even as she resolved to tell him, as if he were going to get well, that the hand didn't matter, there were thousands of men with worse. "Would not go," she heard that carbon-pure disembodied husk of whisper tell her. "For anything."

Then she dared: "She is in Warsaw?"

He made an agreeing sound, then his mouth crumpled shut, his eyes closed as if she were not there, and she looked up to see the major, the surgeon, and a nurse stationed behind her, celebrants of what rite she hardly knew: the miracle of the word or the hell of pushing Ludwik to the edge to have him speak. She had kissed him into speech in a fit of conjuring sacrilege and they were waiting to see her turn into a pillar of salt or catch fire right before their eyes, the finesse-bound major, the unshaven blank-eyed German surgeon always appearing to stitch a wound in midair, the jowly young nurse with the brown hair drawn back punitively hard into a bob. "Izz," she said, determined to drop a few more words into the abyss between them, even if that meant lying and building up for herself a store of guilt which would make her stomach churn bleak and viscous in the nights, "he'll be all right." There was no sign of a response. The flash of life he'd show had made him seem wanner than ever. Yes, she said numbly, I'll pay for this: there are promises you just can't make, not even to sweeten the going of your dearest one. I'll die of it for sure.

It had all taken too long, not this exchange (if that were the word for something so tacit and skeletal), for there were some prolongations that should never end, but getting the children into the earth, followed by the ordeal with the pervert Haarkünstler, the ride north, the ride back south, the collision with the wall, the time lost while presumably she was unconscious in this way-station for the damaged and the doomed. For Suzanna and Wilson, whose end she had guessed at and at once suppressed, she had not a single thought, having already equated them with Myrrh in some backroom algebra that sealed one end of her conscience while opening the other. She was facing forward, yes: somebody had turned her head in that direction, but mentally she was down in the wooden drawer with Ludwik, willing to give the rest of her years to kissing him back to life, holding the tourniqueted stump and calling into his ear the names of a lifetime, enemy or friend or darling, it did not matter so long as she could bring to him the noises and the labels of life, saying it is still here, it is all going on without you, the world of the living is not as self-sufficient as you might think, its quality is much feebler without you. On went that spread-out silent cry, the dumbshow of the will, no longer prodding him or harassing him, but tuned in to all that had been secret between them, matters big and trivial, like the quarrel about whether her mouth was a fit place for his sperm (teething trouble she later called it with an ample laugh), like the tiff about whether freshly washed lettuce squeaked. What haunted her already was the slow-maturing suspicion that, in the overlap of souls known as society, and perhaps also in the universe at large (or nature at least), there was something like justice, which meant a life taken entailed a life given; and all she had to work out, like someone walking the plank while trying to solve a crossword puzzle in the mind's eye, was which came first. Had what ruined Ludwik preceded her assault on the SS driver, whom she still saw running amok over the ploughed fields blind and making the shuffle-choke of emphysema? Did it matter if Ludwik was dead or not? How could one solitary woman work out the blame for two men, both perhaps only dying after all? Taking her stand on primal fact, she opted for common sense at its most nostalgic: without the invasion, she and Ludwik and Izz might have been swimming in the Vistula this very day. That was clear. But some dangling long arm of fate, evident in the coincidence of her having driven the motorcycle right to where Ludwik lay, almost convinced her that nothing was random: she had been steered here to pay, to repent, to see what she got for having done what she had done, and Ludwik would die even if the SS driver survived in a sanatorium, knitting shawls into his dotage.

It wasn't fair. It wasn't wholly without justice either, and now she began to wonder how she could change justice, rough as it was, how tamper with how things panned out. It was no doubt, as the surgeon told her, too late to drive away in search of plasma, and where would she go anyway? The seemliest thing was to wait with Ludwik, so close to being gone he seemed to be lying in state, awaiting military honors; but she was impatient to go, to head back to Kazimierz and do something about the children. She could fit them both in the sidecar, and they could all sit there until starvation took them, warbling together in the shade of an old tree far from town; or she could try for the ravines, although no doubt the Germans, having cleaned them out, would keep a patrol in the area lest resistance fighters, or regular Polish soldiers, turned it into a redoubt. I might even make a dash for the border, she thought, and her belly quailed: even Hungary, not to mention Rumania, was at least three hundred kilometers away. And that journey, she schooled herself as if rehearsing her ABC, doesn't even start here.

20

"Am I free to go?" The major seemed surprised that, having found her husband on a hundred to one chance, she would be eager to leave him behind. "Why?" he said, but as if saying *You can't mean it, you have duties here.*

"I'm not much use here. Our son is—with friends not far from here, just past the Lublin bridge." He said nothing, but motioned at Ludwik. "And he?"

"I have to save somebody if I can." She thought she was going to break down and cry, not to persuade him, but to empty herself of too many contradictory feelings: the vinegar and milk inside her, the sense that some ghastly underside of her personality was masquerading as herself, and out of control.

"The novocaine helped, even the food. I have a good chance of being shot, for not shooting Polish wounded, for taking—I mean accepting, inheriting, enrolling, harboring, succoring, indulging, undertaking—" he stuck on the verbs as if to bury the noun in the acts, "the so-called enemy." He laughed with miserable poise, making his throat cluck, once, twice, three times. "I should have used all our supplies on our own personnel, as the manual calls them. But I'm a fatalist, I suppose; I had no desire to be in Poland, I never dreamed we would cross the border. And here I am, doing my best. Messing around here is the equivalent of the condemned man's writing a last letter. You can have the motorcycle, for all I care, if it works, which it no doubt will, we make these things to last."

"And go. Without being shot from behind?" She stared at him as if peering into a block of ice, able to see only herself in how her question changed his face.

"Who would shoot? These are medical personnel. They could not even defend themselves, except maybe with a few hypodermic needles. By the way, there was blood on the needle, which I haven't used. The syrettes didn't fit, they have a needle of their own. Did you have ampules too? We could use them. Some of these men are going to feel a lot of pain again quite soon."

Shaking her head at the only part of his questioning she chose to heed, she decided to push him even further. "Then, if it still goes, the machine, I would like to take my husband with me."

"Take them all," he said. "There is no hope here, and when I am hanged I shall think of you. The Pied Piper of Poland—a German legend, of course, but you speak German so well."

"Of course," she told him in a wince of fury, "part of the point in knowing it at all is to be able to get on with your territorial neighbors, like waving at one another over the garden wall, or having people like my husband spend half of his life in another country so as to talk to death such messes as this. It's called diplomacy, or is that the word heard only on Calvary hill these days? Your country," she hammer-blowed him with each word, "has, a, madman, in, charge." I should have kept the ham and cake, she thought, amazed at her mind's recoil from what she had just said.

"Well," he said, spreading his arms wide as if to encompass all the surgical-political sorrow of all the ages, "this belongs to *him* too. This—is—*his*. You can imagine the pride he'd take in it. I am wasting resources, Madame, and when my head rolls, it will land at my mother's feet, not yours. Take your husband, you can have his gun. I suggest also, resent it if you must, that you take a couple of the helmets lying around here and put one on him. Tunics too. Then you'll have a tenth of a chance. Most of the bullyboys you'll run into will shoot first. And then there will be no need to question anybody at all. It's a growing national tradition. Fast-growing into one of the cornerstones of our culture." Clearing his throat with stale vehemence, he spat a little free-form saliva onto the asphalt, watched it dry, gave instructions to the orderlies and then, gripping her shoulder as if getting ready to propel her to the main highway, watched them test the motorcycle. The number plate on the front fender was bent, the light was smashed and the reflector caught the sun briefly and became a stud of scalding light which, for ten minutes, she saw superimposed on everything: Ludwik's body being raised into sitting position, his face lolled forward in a ghostly bow until the helmet hid it, while they merely draped the tunic coat about his shoulders, and then lifted him into the crude little sidecar, all this with not the slightest seepage of blood. He looked light, airworthy, like a stretched-out boy, but also he reminded her of something, someone else, whose image she could not quite catch until she remembered how they lifted him: "The unknown soldier," she said impetuously, "he's just like that. All we need is a cathedral," but she did not see that any more, that image of holy cloistered quiet with indecipherable lettering on a stone flag over which people walked, whether tourists or rapt believers taking communion, but instead, as earlier, the nose and cabin of an elementary glider, with a tow-rope attached beneath, all ready for launch. And Izz was with her then, watching his own father being readied for the azure ether, never to return, never to land, but to go on and on spiraling for ever where nothing could let him down, the impassive pilot allowing the dead-silent airplane to wing him from Poland to Ecuador, from there to Samarkand, and thence to assorted countries of the heart's desire.

"Not quite," the major was saying. "Military etiquette, if you believe in such ludicrous fanciness, prescribes that the body of the unknown soldier be truly unknown. The choice is usually made from six, from among which a blindfolded officer taps his hand on one, and then the cask is sealed. Ideally, I suppose, if you subscribe to such madness, the officer is then put to death by rifle fire, the blindfold already being in place, and the other five bodies are burned at sea. I shock you. Well, it is all senseless, but the procession through the streets provides a focal amount for thousands of separate individual griefs, to occasion which a sheep or a heifer would do just as well, so long as the container remained shut, unopenable, untested by X-rays. I have no flag for your husband, who, the surgeon says, is quite dead. I am sorry. In another world he might have been saved. You have him still, which is something, at least it is not nothing. Take him, and your love for him, and go." Wooden with fatigue, he handed her the pistol with a debilitated, lazy smile. "Otherwise I might be tempted to save the SS a job. Or even several. Their view of the dignity of human life is at least erratic. You may not know."

Oh *I know*, she thought. I know too much, trying to muster the grief that had already gone, the energy she had poured into her long attempt to bring him back with kiss and call; all she did was, in helmet and army tunic just like him, to go and stand in front of him, looking down at his invisible face, murmuring "My plunger through the darkness, wait, don't go, don't be gone now, there's life left in all of us." Viewing her dead, clad in another dead one's clothes, she too wore the clothes of the dead, and it was too much of one irreparable thing, sapping and stunning her all over again, as if she hadn't even tried, his first sweetheart and his last.

"You realize," she said, trying to be dry-mannered, even in front of this so-called enemy, a malcontent make of peace if ever she'd seen one, "he went to try and find his mother. In Warsaw, who refused to leave, and that left him with very little. Picture yourself, in the dawn, going off to war, dressed as he was. You have a mother. What's your name?"

"Ranke," he said, fascinated, nervous, and appalled. "Otto."

"Going out into the dawn, with not very much chance of coming back. Poor bastard. My poor bastard. He really wanted a medal, not for finding his mother, though I don't think that's a bad idea, we should strike more medals for men who find their mothers, but for being brave, which diplomatic officers and assistant military attachés rarely have a chance to be. And it is not just that." She was astonished at how formal she had become, addressing Ranke with one hand on Ludwik's shoulder, as if drawing physically up from him an insight he hadn't dreamed of. "One of your SS deviants, Major Ranke, is going about his business with a body-belt loaded with trophies. Money?

Jewelry? Don't you believe it. His name is Haarkünstler, his nickname, really, and what he has round his waist is a collection of swab samples from the private parts of women he has interfered with, and clippings of pubic hair as well. When you write to your mother next, dip your pen in vomit and tell her that. Some things go bad before they ripen. I hope one day, just for the fun of it, you'll arrange to have your husband killed, your friends of a lifetime dragged out of their homes and done away with, and yes," resorting to a word so foreign she nearly mispronounced it, "one of your balls taken as a sample. *Eine Hode ja.* You don't happen to have a medal handy, do you? For Ludwik?"

"Do I," he said, chewing his lips to keep them from twitching, "look as if I would? I am not the type, whereas your Haarkünstler.... His chest no doubt groans with them when he's in full dress. The only medal I'll get is the one between the eyes." He slammed his upper left pocket with the flat of his hand, almost as if to beat ribbon and metal from the weave of the cloth. "Go as far as your fuel will take you. I take it you know how to shoot the pistol?"

"I have been using firearms all my life," she told him sarcastically. "As a matter of fact, I do, *this* one anyway. My husband taught me how, though he never let me hold it for more than a couple of minutes." What need of a pistol, she scolded herself, when you're deadly with a needle? A needle is a womanly thing, sure enough.

Major Ranke was saluting Ludwik with dapper slowness, perusing the gesture while he made it; perhaps his last chance to do something harmless and meaningful, and thinking deepdown *His life is no more annulled than mine, he is my counterpart, he has reached the limits of his viability, and yet by the merest tweak of fate he might have been alive now, going home and putting up with things because there was nothing else to do.* The woman, that ferocious bosomy new widow who knew more about Berlin that he did, was already preparing to go, walking round the sidecar with a limp after adjusting her husband's body to a sitting-back position.

"You'd better button up that tunic," he said. "Yours." Inside the helmet, most of her head was hidden, but she looked very much a woman with the tunic open like that, and he could not forget the dislocated, ice-cold ravening in her eyes. Nor, as an observer of himself, could he rid his mind of how ludicrous he really was, officially in charge of a playground hospital where the wounded died, the healthy had nothing to eat, and the conquering army—at least its local delegates—behaved as if nothing mattered in that margin of time save rudimentary first aid; to the children it was a game, and they were right. We are just a bouquet of leftovers, he thought, as the motorcycle crackled into life and Wanda, without even asking how to change gear, cruised unevenly away, not looking back, neither waving nor calling out, but intent on ferrying her beloved to his next destination. A Charon of the wheel, she raised the dust and was gone, speaking to Ludwik quietly in an impetuous whisper, without the goggles now, and knowing only that she must keep the sun on her right, it was early afternoon. Again the road was empty, as if it might have been cleared specially for a funeral party, although she knew better and drove one-handedly while she clasped the pistol in the tunic pocket, recognizing that a woman with a child awaiting her underground could not afford to use a pistol on herself even though the temptation began to grow on her the more she talked into the wind.

"It wouldn't be like turning my back on you, you know that, only getting alongside you in a different, a more complete way. I'm not that brave a woman, and surely not brave enough to kill off a couple children first. There are thousands of hooligans in Poland at this very minute willing to do that for you without even being asked. They do it with a cigarette dangling as if they were brushing a fly away. I didn't expect to find you at death's door, and then to watch you going through, but I didn't expect to find you anyway, anywhere, in any condition, and looking so purple, so old, so spoiled and emptied out and not just for having left on an empty stomach. Some wives would have insisted, oh we can scramble something together, fry a piece of bread and ham scrapings from the last can, or from the chicken we made the sandwiches from. I'm an hors d'oeuvres woman, I suppose, except that everything is fast changing, and I might well end up in that hole in the ground, jammed in with Izz and Myrrh, with you and your marvelous body parked alongside us, one of the dead to three of the living. That would be slum living, all right, and maybe even your old mother would show up, knocking at the pigsty for entrance, with a hot kettle in her hand and cucumber sandwiches to cool us down. I feel as if I am driving through one season of the year after another, with spring and summer and autumn all come and gone within half a kilometer. Perhaps it is otherwise, though, and we are both quite still, with the engine firing just for sound effect, and the landscape of all the seasons is flowing past us backward to teach us both something about time, maybe that no one can go vertically to God, you have to get there on the flat, not even thinking where you are going, because you are not, it is coming toward you, although not at you, the oxen-ploughed field, the big heap of sugar beets, those tall wicker baskets. Call it a floating to nowhere, I seem to have been up and down this road all day, and I cannot stop to refresh you with a tumbler of root beer begged at a farm, or milk warm from the cow, not because they have burned the farms and shot the cows, which they have, but because we are bound thither, you and I, in poisoned inertia born of loss, in a going that differs from standing-still only as dying from being alive. Far away, with between us and it only the dumbfounded faces of peasants watching for Satan in outhouses and from behind broken windows, there is a little spot of countryside drawing us to it like a lodestone, past the music-less taverns and the iron verandahs where the flowers go unwatered, and we would not recognize it in any other stretch of land, from the feel of its soil between finger and thumb, from the exact moldy loam-sick smell, from the violets and the clover and the radishes that grew in it, which makes us much more like munching cows than we were, just expecting the land to provide as village gives way to village, and village to town, then town to village, with nothing to come save that slight variation in human settlements, making us feel we are the true nomads turning the clock of progress back as we rumble along with our camels and tents and the unbreakable desert crockery in which to boil the tea. Saving the men with guns, who, looking vaguely at us, their eyes prickly and watery from the last of the pollen in the air (it is not grief at what they've done), see two of their own, slovenly and wandering all over the road from fatigue, but they know how it is after a long day's plundering: you want to get your boots off and make the crashing engine hush. They do not shoot. Nor do they halt us, never mind how quizzical they feel about that female-seeming driver and that passenger with the slump of a dead one, they let us pass, they let the foreign landscape go touring past us on both sides like some giant's tray of salad, round all the way to the horizon, but here on the right catching fire, not from the accumulated insult of it all, but because they have not yet invaded the sun, whose amber salmon gold twinkled the thin skin of your face back to life and teased out the reddish tint in your mustache." Without even checking the road for enemy or friend, she steered the motorcycle right onto the grass, all the time looking hard at his face, but seeing him only in profile which was nearly silhouette as well, she stopped, obliviously obsessed, with the machine still pointing south, but dismounting and walking limping round to where she could see the sun playing mellowly against the pallor of his cheeks and jaw, once again giving him that outdoorsman ruddiness, and, with his helmet off, almost persuading her that life could start again, so real he was, so ripe, so close to becoming an affable Lazarus with a twirl of grass in the corner of his mouth and holding a ripe raspberry up against one eye, at exactly the right distance to blot out the sun entirely so he could watch a small, buzzing, puzzling biplane slide into a bunker of cloud and vanish altogether, with not even its engine sound to track it by. But his eyes did not respond, open and still and silver-plated, so she slid the helmet down low, got back onto the seat and started up again, hearing almost in prelude to the chatter of the engine the sounds of gunfire as, behind her, a crew of zealous Polish survivors came over the roof of the schoolhouse, fired from the eaves into the playground, and captured (if captured was the word for a feat so tame) the first-aid station: something German they could have, including the body of Major Otto Ranke, cut down by the opening burst.

The German surgeon, stethoscope round his neck like a silver-plated noose, stared in contemptuous fury at the leader of the Polish force, wrinkling up his mouth in careful shades of loathing, then gestured with his arms spread wide at the prize taken by gunfire. "As attacks on hospitals go," he said in German, "this one was almost competent, No one here fired back at you. There was virtually no one to fire in any case. You have killed the installation commander, a major, and, as best I can judge, put several wounded Poles out of their misery. You are lucky you didn't kill these children too. Don't you ever do reconnaissance of your objectives? Are you going to take us over or not? It matters little to me *who* runs things so long as I can tend my wounded. I have seen a lot of everything today, very little of it good. I don't know much about war, but," he went on, more loudly and becoming more rhetorical now he realized the Pole understood not a single word, "I do know that nurses have a right to do their work without being shot at. How this unit came into being, only holy God alone knows; it blew together on the wind, and up to now it has been working fairly well with almost no supplies, you overgrown boy scout, and now you've turned it into a symbol of your bloody pig-headed obligation to resist. All you've done is disrupt good work being done with an open mind, on behalf of the living. You, all you want is to convert the wounded into the dead, and the dead into martyrs. To hell with you and your popguns. Would you like to give some blood? We don't need sharpshooters here, we need liters and liters of good fresh blood." Out of breath, he paused, then turned away in disgust, plucking his befouled white coat after him like a loosened sail.

Having seized the first-aid station, the Poles had to decide whether to stay put or to move on, and their commander, having understood none of the surgeon's harangue, held a sheepish conversation with one of the nurses, who knew some Polish. "We will give the blood you ask for, to make amends," he said, "then move on. The only force you need to be defended against is people like ourselves." So another bizarre tableau began to form, this time on the floor of the schoolhouse, in the appalling accumulated heat of mid-afternoon, with the surgeon supervising the procedure, on his face a look of disingenuous indifference, a sort of boyish gloating which intensified when he turned and looked the Polish leader (a sergeant in uniform whereas some of his men were wearing summer slacks and short-sleeved shirts) full in the eyes, his blue hitting the other's brown, his mind involved with something not so much far away as locally severed, something aloof which did not know the names of the wounded and the dying, the dead and the healthy, but fixed instead on the systems that maintained them, linking up all the blood vessels of each into one gigantic maze of runnels which was the circulation of the communal patient, in whom the surgeon gladly felt himself submerged, and the beating of all the hearts thumped a ragged rhythm in his ears, reminding him not be so self-conscious about being, here as everywhere, impersonally and unswayably, the custodian of life against all the nets of harm that fell from above, or the calamities generated from within: the *Ur*-Surgeon ministering to the *Über*-Patient not that far a cry, or a patriotic shout, he thought, from the nearly abstract greed with which his country's psychopathic leader pounded his thumb on the map of Europe, howling baby-like *I want, I want!* Between his greed, the surgeon told himself, and my own calling there isn't that much difference: neither has to do with people as people, any more than this Polish fathead paused to consider what might really be inside the ring of stone he was attacking—no, it was something on a map to be taken, it was something worthless to be doing in a world in which to be doing something, no matter how despicable, counts for more than just sitting on your hands and watching the harvest ripen, the young grow up, the middle-aged get older, the old ones die. For instance, the dumbshow with which we asked them for the blood: it was something beyond language, beyond who I am and who he is (neither has the other's name), and beyond who the German wounded are, who the Polish are, which of these four children has had enough to eat today, and if the nurses are having their periods or know how to spell, or like food fried or poached. If it isn't godlike, it's certainly better than being only just one person. How strange that most of our life is lived for us by what we have in common; individuality's just a handsome light-effect on the landscape of the race. Like when that Polish woman on the motorcycle blew in here, by outrageous accident, and then blew out, taking her dead husband with her; part of a pattern, she blunders on into the next pattern, taking her bloodstream with her, that hydraulic mystery which hasn't the faintest idea who she is. "It's all chemistry," he said aloud to the row of Poles, to the nurses, to the walls, to the framed reproduction which showed Copernicus gazing heavenward with rapt alarm, seated at the crouch with one crudely-shod foot in front of him at an awkward angle, his hands lifted shoulder high as if trying to steer some vehicle with an invisible wide wheel.

"It's chemistry," he said. "Personalities don't come into it. Or they shouldn't." He turned his smock inside out at last.

When the blood-giving was over, the Poles assembled outside with hushed voices as if having taken communion or left a deathbed, then set off again in an untidy file, no longer seeming to have the impetus to attack anything, yet obliged to search the countryside, horseless, causeless, and, since they had expended an undue amount of ammunition during the needless attack, with only three hand grenades and about eighty cartridges among them, frequenting the scene of their dissolution like addicts, haunting themselves in their own backyard, and ultimately (as the surgeon in his blank diagrammatic way perceived) just looking for some place in which to surrender without losing face, having already lost heart, and utterly unrefreshed, unrestored, by the routine cup of weak tea forced upon them by the nurses. Nobody knows his blood type in this childish land, the surgeon thought, vaguely aware of something vampiric in having taken blood for taking's sake, just to have it in reserve. I cannot type it here. But it will serve some poor German bastard sooner or later. After all, this is a first-aid station, not the Charité hospital in Berlin, not by any manner of means. I wonder who will attack us next; I could work wonders with a telephone or some decent equipment. All I am here is a sexton with hindsight. He bustled back to work, astonished to find the same bodies, awkwardly bent to fit into the wooden drawers, or plastered flat on the asphalt, being patrolled by the four children, who gaped and giggled and, at a word of command from the older boy, withdrawing suddenly to a corner of the playground to chant something unfathomable, like collusive mockingbirds with nowhere else to go, no other playground in which to wipe out time.

Cruising down the valley of the Vistula on the east side of the river, Wanda tried to summarize the route that lay ahead, familiar enough, of course, but when she and Ludwik had come south from Warsaw in previous years it had been Ludwik who did the driving, casual and given to sudden lunges of speed as if impatient with the land bound quality of land itself, wanting to fly or at least achieve an unthinkable two hundred kilometers an hour. "If only willing got us there!" he'd said. "All willing does is keep you where you are."

21

South to Deblin, she instructed herself, half-mouthing the formula to Ludwik where he sat, "and don't go back northeast where the road bends, go through the town, if you dare, and cross the river, still heading southeast, to Pulawy, and then it's only ten kilometers to where the children are. Keep east of the river all the way, and pray you don't run out of gas."

Yet these words were not so much words as palm leaves brushing across her mouth with a fragile dry clash; words belonged somewhere else, in a world of weights and measures and explicit labels, where so-and-so was a colonel, say, and this lump of cheese weighed exactly the same as a calf's heart. What Wanda felt, an awful crisscross commotion of the heart like the buried foam a torpedo leaves behind it, did not belong in words, unless she had an unused lifetime ahead of her and rights to invent words of her own, but stayed vaguely sayable through gestures such as burying the face in the hands while butting the forehead against the knees, or pulling both eyelids downward by their lashes, or pushing her face hard against a wall or a tree and howling with lips that touched the brick or the bark. There were other ways too, which included holding her breath as long as possible, as if somehow to deny grief expansion, to tamp it down, down into the zone under the heart, whence it would never return save as an eruption of bile, a mental gash made physical and thus disguised. For some reason, the air rushing past her didn't cool her (or she rushing through the air), but the nonstop vibration of the handlebars did not make her hands unsteady either, and the road wasn't in too bad a state of repair; when a crater appeared in the stretch ahead, catching the light wrong or not catching it at all, she gave it a wide berth, in the process moving down shrubs and knee-high bits of defunct fence.

For a dead man, Ludwik moved about a lot, toward her and away, back and forth, and sometimes, when she hit a rock or an empty can (this slung away by the invading army that went up this road, to Warsaw), he appeared to take a waggish bow, rising to meet the inaudible applause. She would have preferred him still, as yet unable to bear the idea of his being again in motion; but it was either seeing him bounced about like that or not having him with her at all, which latter was so unthinkable that she addressed him throughout, in a stream of side-mouthed tender, fussbudget scolding, as if he were a little boy, smaller than Izz, who kept leaning out to look, or twisting round, and then up, to watch something that was receding fast: *Hush your limbs now, son, and don't leave your mouth open or you'll catch flies.* Or she told him to squint his eyes against the flying grit. *Hold on tight during the turns, or you'll end up across a cow's back.* It was more navigational mutter than a heartsick attempt to deceive herself, and it served to keep her more or less alert, giving her the mouthable noises of a mental continuum within the uproar of the engine, and it kept her company besides, just when the kind of company she needed wasn't human but sort of metaphysical—say a strong rumor about an absent god, or an affable ghost who listened better than he talked. That this conversation always came from and returned to herself, unmodified by another's words, disturbed her not at all; it was a good preparation for widowhood, she thought, in which nothing is real but the empty space above the chair's seat, the single plate on the tablecloth: a widow learned about all that was not her, the big fanning V between her legs, often thought of as part of her, but in fact, when no one entered it, as cold and vacant as the Russian tundra. Most folk, she decided as she whizzed along the deserted road into Deblin, already able to discern over on her left the curl-back of the same road northeastward, most folk regard the air under the arms, in the pits of their arms, the air under their chins, inside their mouths, behind their knees when they bend them, as part of themselves, personalized through being close, like the raw apples which peasant women keep under their arms for a month to soak up their sweat for their loved one to inhale. But that air is nothing of ours; just floating through, recently under somebody else's arm, soon to be under some other's—a little puff of the vast, nameless, unloving, inhuman, invincible—she stopped, said "Lordy me, Wanda, you're going to pieces," and reached over to pat Ludwik on the shoulder, in somewhat cautionary reassurance, as if he had spoken and not she.

A long way behind her, his face fixed on the tight, skewed smile of one psychopath who relishes the abominations of another, Haarkünstler was speeding along at the head of a fighting patrol sent south to quash Polish resistance in the area of the first-aid camp. That was his official mission, but he also had unfinished business with Frau Czimanska, whose driver had been found blinded in a sugarbeet field, minus his motorcycle, and raving in a high-pitched cough about being jumped by the Polish sow and some partisans who had been hiding in the hedge, at which explanation Haarkünstler had nodded accusingly, then slapped the driver's face, demoting him from *Sturmmann* (lance-corporal) to *SS-Mann* on the spot, which was as low as an SS soldier could be.

On the outskirts of Deblin, which seemed less a preliminary to something than leftovers from a village which had failed, Wanda realized that her problem was to get through the town without going through the center, where she was bound to run into pockets of occupation troops; but she had to cross the Vistula and pick up the road that came in from the west and then branched at a right angle southward. So what she did, having a vague idea of the bridge's whereabouts, was to thunder in and out of the dirt tracks which were the back streets, constantly aiming for the river. All the houses were blank, with curtained windows (some boarded up against blast) and closed doors, while the one-story shops were shuttered tight. A couple of dogs barked at her without having the heart to pursue, and at one place she bumped over a horse's leg without knowing what it was, the rest of the horse having been removed. Sooner or later, she thought, I'm bound to reach the central square, and to bypass that is going to be more than I can manage. When she reached it, however, it was by accident, and she came into it at speed, thinking that what lay in front of her was yet another side street, but there was a group of Germans, not SS she noted, standing drinking bottles of beer around a small field gun, with not a Pole in sight, although there was standing room only behind the shutters and curtains. Unable to stop or to slow down, she aimed for the opening opposite her, but not without attracting boisterous attention which in turns became sardonic, wheedling, and lewd; but no one fired after her, although a tall young soldier with his helmet off, his tunic open, reached out from the watering trough in which he sat and flung something into Ludwik's lap: a bomb, she thought at first, but it was a bottle of beer. *They let me through,* she told herself unbelievingly, *and they must have seen I was a woman. So maybe they have woman motorcyclists.* There was the bridge, unguarded because the solder appointed to that post was carousing in the town square, and so she crossed the tawny-looking Wieprz, still warm enough in which to swim; passed the sentry box at the other end of the bridge, again untenanted, and she had a flash of Ludwik at the first-aid station, when he was alive, flat on his back in a sentry box that had fallen over. Yes, she thought, it is his day for being cooped up in small places, but that's usual with the dead; not many of us get a pyramid. I'm coming, children, I'm only thirty kilometers away now. She saw the entire distance between the motorcycle's headlight and the hole at Gnonka's farm as a line along which the waves of her approach bustled closer and closer together, like thousands of shallow cones preceding her and pulling her after them at what seemed increasing speed, although the engine was flat out already, and she moved through the windless air like a cleaving lopsided obsolete bird, or an airborne kangaroo with her husband in her pouch, past rubble, severed power lines, and motion picture set houses with no fronts and all their insides prolapsed down to the ground floor in a mess of cupboards, baths, and beams.

If I survive this, she said, I'll let myself get fat and greasy, I'll whiten the doorstep like a peasant woman, I'll make the forks and the doorknobs shine like nobody's business, I'll eat tripe with paprika sauce. Behind her, Deblin lost its identity long before she turned around, it became invisible, town once upon a time of trains, with a fort and a beguiling Loreto chapel, but there only because the River Wieprz ran into the Vistula, and the mind of man, ever afflicted by the lack of precision evident in sheer space, doted on intersections, where the endlessly unrolling points of separate lives collided, and so the Deblins were remembered, even if as nothings, and she remembered nothing of it, not even the square and the bridge, nor the carousing soldiery, the bottle of beer that landed as a bomb, open and flushing foam into Ludwik's lap. As she got nearer Pulawy, for which their street in Kazimierz was named, she murmured only the name, requiring an almost babyish mumble with thick lips for its perfect pronunciation: *Puwavy, Puwavy*, evoking nowhere in particular, except a street, and the few words that began the same way: *poo-wap, poo-wapka, poowk, poow-kovneek*, the words for ceiling, trap, regiment and colonel, all four of them like barbs in recent wounds; and, such was her degree of bare obsession, she rode from Deblin to Pulawy with her mind's eye choking on the image of two children beating feebly at the ceiling of a trap and a colonel (SS or Polish, German army or Polish Military Attaché, she wasn't sure) coming after her with a regiment, all of them howling for vengeance on the well-spoken murderess on the stolen motorcycle. On her left, a broad stretch of woodland tapered away, caving suddenly in like a book left open in the sun at the valley of Wieprz, but she took in none of it, nor of the jetties, the boat houses, the swimming pools along the Vistula to her right, all strangely intact along one of the war's main arteries, and thing-like willing to accept anyone who chose to use them. With each kilometer, she reassessed her chances of being intercepted, from behind, in front, or from either side, or of her fuel giving out, in which event she would have to wheel the machine, if she could, all the way home, with Ludwik in his makeshift coffin that had the spare wheel mounted flat on the back with the anchor rod pointing skyward; and, all of a sudden, everything seemed much more difficult. There would be no getting past Pulawy, or even into it, and Kazimierz itself would almost certainly have roadblocks manned by serious servants of the Reich: no songs, no beer, no lewd entreaties.

So, she would drive straight into the Vistula, with her last drowning bubble her only apology to Izz and Myrrh, who were not expecting her anyway. Or she would stop, park in the middle of the road, and wait to be captured, beaten, shot. Or she would charge whatever barricade she found and go down fighting. Or somehow set both herself and Ludwik on fire and, with her last sinew of conscious will, propel the motorcycle into a cluster of the enemy, two vermillion figurines mounted on a blazing dray, giving the soldiers a scare at least, singeing a face here, a hand there, but not enough, not nearly enough; she might get better results by just screaming, or driving up to them and falling on her knees before them, saying as if in indistinct cryptic mutinous-toned apology "Ceiling. Trap. Regiment. Colonel," at which point one of them would kick her gently in the chops, correcting her punctuation even as it fell out of her mouth, not abusing her but boot-chiding an impetuous child who would not hush.

Pulawy she knew: the palace, once Baroque, but repeatedly converted like some continually obsolescent giant's kit, and never right, never fixed in style or form, but hovering in the seven veils of its successive misconceptions, with, in the English park, a temple to Sybil. Her snapped nerve took her off the road long before she could account to herself, and she was jerking and cavorting along a cart track heavy with untrodden dust, her theory, when she at last registered it, being to go around Pulawy, through the grounds of the palace, and then somehow sneak south and west to Kazimierz. In her grief pummeled mind, the open road spelled danger, whereas the ampler habituations some distance away not only seemed safer, a haven, but also offered a place to half-hide while still keeping on the move, and the inappropriateness of roaring among the lawns, the follies, the derelict stone gnomes and the sundials too tall to be inspected, never occurred to her, or got buried in her craving to be somewhere again that was the faintest touch genteel, shaded, unpoxed by the invader or even zealous partisans, to whom a temple was an air raid shelter, a palace a barracks. In this, however, she had underestimated the perverse craving of the military mind for exactly the same things, especially among Germans of a certain generation among the officer class; her dreamy logic and their brisk addiction to the sumptuous (no matter how tasteless) had overlapped. Without knowing it, at first, and never quite realizing why, she had re-entered the milieu of diplomatic Berlin in which for a long time she had thrived, although no one traditionally approached that citadel of high fastidious ease on anything so crude as a motorcycle, unless a dispatch rider, and he of course never reached the lush holy of holies upstairs, where deep rugs deadened the sound and dark, uncleaned varnish made the hawk-faced, bulging-eyed portraits recede from the viewer into some somber no-man's-land behind the canvas, where ancient reputations vied with moths and woodworm for tenure of the next half-century.

Turning from the dust-laden country track into a gateway with no gate but flanked by two humanoid obelisks with globe heads whose faces seemed to have been erased, she found no wooden pole across her path, and would have crashed into it anyway. As it was, she overshot, past the two sentries, who sat unconcernedly on a wooden bench at the foot of a gigantic unpruned hedge which, instead of being blunt-cut, tapered skyward. Not hearing their indolent shouts, she drove on, not even braking, and vanished behind a chunk of off-white masonry set in a small, low copse of trees. Only half-discerning something familiar, the sentries resumed their idle patter, one of them actually waving his hand in belated recognition after the noise of the machine, although he could see it no longer. They had not slept properly for several days, or been out of their clothes (which reeked), and they were going to bathe in the Vistula later on, after the officers had gone to dinner in the chandeliered dining room.

"Covered in dust," the twenty-year-old said. "Another poor bastard who'll want to swim." He spat out the grass blade on which he had been chewing and selected another, just wide enough, creased it sharply along the middle, and began to pinch it again with his front teeth, as if notching memories into its grain.

"This is a better job," the nineteen-year-old answered. "Have you noticed? They keep on coming in, hot from the front line, wherever that is, but they never go away. The palace must be chockfull of drivers by now. Maybe they'll all leave at once, in convoy, and take us with them. Who needs this shitheap of a palace anyway? Germany is full of palaces." He raised one arm as if to indicate the extent of Germany and the number of palaces therein. To this youth, Wanda in her helmet and field-gray tunic had seemed another youth only, oddly stern of mien, of course, but dispatch riders always were, ever self-important, yet probably mailmen in another life officiously insisting on the exact amount in change for postage due. "I think I'll sit out the war here," he said ruminatively.

"War? It's only a policing action."

"And grass grows on officer's faces. You'll believe anything, Hilscher." He would soon be twenty and was thinking of the army as a career, and not a peacetime army either, but one that bristled, went places, made the civilians hop. Having heard about camp followers, he kept wondering where they were. "No gash," he said resentfully. "Where's the gash?"

"In the officer's bedrooms," the twenty-year-old told him. "Where else? They'll give us the used condoms to wash: that'll be as near as we get. You know what? I'm a country boy, you're a city kid. You know why, back home, why the old men who go out with stools into the fields at dusk, for youknowwhat, fuck nothing but sheep? You don't know? Well, it takes them too long to go round and kiss the cows on the mouth."

"As I said, you'll believe anything, Hilscher. Why do they take a stool with them if they go for sheep?" He smirked.

"It's the tradition, man." Hilscher liked that word a lot.

"You country people," the other said, inoffensively dismissing all peasants and rural folk, "are full of shit. You go after cows because you're scared of people."

All Hilscher did by way of response was to spit out his blade of grass and replace it, wondering where all the dispatch riders went. "It's simple," he said. "There's another way out."

"Into the river, huh?"

"If you like. Into the river." Hilscher's eyelids fell.

"Big fucking Polish river," the nineteen-year-old said to himself. "What the hell are the Poles doing with a river that big?"

"God," said Hilscher vaguely, neither exclaiming nor sighing.

"Nah. Politics. Not God. What the hell kind of name is 'Vistula'? You ever heard of anything like that?"

Hilscher had not, he didn't care, he wanted to bathe in any water, holy, or hot, or dish, it didn't matter. And then sleep. "A bit of solid shuteye. And wipe my ass on paper."

"Hilscher, you're a lousy chorus-girl. *Paper!* This is the army, dimwit. If you're finicky, save it up. It's allowed." Yet, he thought, perhaps after all the life of the dispatch rider is better, especially with the sidecar empty. You can park in some crafty place, get off the saddle and into the sidecar, stretch out and sleep, and sit a big naked peasant girl's ass in your lap, all while the war goes by, and then you're off again, in black riding leathers with goggles that dangle, when you're off the road, over the big death's-head plate that dangles from a chain over your chest. One look at that and they all shiver. You never have to walk. You're some kind of speed car racer. You break records. You get attended to right away wherever you go. Beef and onions, I bet, when the rest get soup. His future had clarified itself without warning, and he would be in the saddle, in every sense, long after the peasant bunglers like Hilscher had blown away, buried under a root crop, turning into fine-quality manure. Yet something nagged at him; the motorcyclist who had come in here ten minutes ago, or was it five, had not looked right, without goggles and chest-plate, and no rifle on his back, whereas the other guy had been asleep, no doubt an officer, hence the speed, they couldn't have stopped if they'd tried, if they'd had to, which means that the bastards have no respect for a sentry, not those two anyway, blasting past us as if we didn't exist, we don't let anybody in just like that. Off he went, rifle at the ready, after the ghost of the sound of Wanda's machine, not because he thought he could accomplish anything, but to appease the military reflex around which he was eagerly rebuilding what he thought of as his mentality, and just in case some officer came to ask. There he would be, the aggrieved sentry, in the alert volatile crouch of the gate-guardian who, having challenged the intruder, had fired a first warning shot into the upper trees (teaching the goddamned thrushes and blackbirds a lesson too) and was looking after the noise, grit-and-cinder stench of the vanished rider, waiting to challenge again and, this time, shoot for the heart. There on the gravel he stood, a misplaced unknown soldier, stranded frozen among unkempt lawns and overgrown ornamental pools, wondering, worrying, quietly and inarticulately raging about a possible major mistake that might already have cost him his career, unable to find the words that said, as if to another, the rider's face had about it something soft and bleached, a touch not of puberty (although that came to mind: the someone was too young to be in uniform, the skin too young anyway on an old enough assembly of convex planes), but of undominated panic merging into steadfast headlong resolve, and the passenger had seemed to tilt, fall, forward at the turn, not like a sleeper but someone anesthetized, enough anyway to reveal a fleck of blood on the face: no, the whole face had been both red and purple, the fleck of blood had been a patch of pink, and the face itself grotesque in a kind of forlorn, snubbed rigidity, the thing the two faces had had in common—yes, now he was beginning to get it—being lack of splendor, as if life had left them behind, cold and unseeing as cement figurines from a graveyard. Even had he fired, the shots would have pinged away off their insensate backs as the two of them ground onward, inhuman as stovepipes, to cannon into something soft as himself, barring the way with flesh and blood and nineteen years, right at the beginning of a trim career.

But it was too late for all that. He could not hear the motorcycle's engine, or anything else except, brought to him in little wafts by the dying breeze, what seemed snatches of talk, both distant and near, none of it in a language that he understood. It sounded fancy or coy, from what he could make of its tone, and he concluded that officers were once again touring the extensive lawns, cognac and cigar in hand, collar-clips open, caps and belts left behind in the big greenhouse-like lobby of the palace's main building. What he did not know was that Wanda Czimanska had driven all along the gravel walk that ran the full length of the palace (whose rear faced the Vistula and so was more imposing than the actual front), had been unable to continue because of a crater in the road caused by a stray bomb, and had not found the makeshift way out through which all the other motorcyclists had gone. So, with the engine churning full blast, she had made a detour, right along the river, with the big lawns between her and the palace façade, maneuvering as best she could, taking whatever way was open, grinding down bushes, catching her face against low branches, and (though her heart fluttered as she did so) leaving a track across several beds of defunct-looking flowers. *They're ours*, she told herself, *Ludwik's and mine. I can mow down what I want.* For a short while she actually mashed up flowerbeds on purpose, frustrated at being in what felt like a maze, although the palace had no maze proper, with a brassy, acrid taste in her mouth evoking a childhood lick at the clip of a treasured fountain pen, given to her as an Excalibur with which to confront a whole series of examinations, which she had passed with flying colors; at least that was what people had said.

Tearing around in a crude ellipse, she could not find the way back, first encountering a long crumbled wall, then a series of low greenhouses which should have told her she was far from any thoroughfare. Where there were tracks at all, they were getting smaller, so round she went again, aiming vaguely at the silhouette of the palace and faintly amazed to see no gardeners, no groundsmen, no soldiers, no police, no grooms, no horses, no dogs, no cats; it was as if the world had come to an end, and quietly so, and hers was the only noise in the vicinity, enclosing her in an only too familiar jagged uproar that functioned as her own special silence. No sooner had she formed the thought, *I don't know how to stop, I haven't stopped it of my own accord,* then she heard the engine beneath her cough, falter, and cease, although its echo revolved about her head, came back off the façade and almost persuaded her it had started up all over again. But it had not, and here she was, marooned in green, hearing for the first time in hours the bees about their less than urgent enterprises, the crows arguing in the tree tops, the smaller more diffident birds warbling as if to say hello: now we can hear one another again. If she had driven on, she would have hit the apple tree right in front of her; she had been driving without really looking, and now she was blocked, with nowhere to go and no means of locomotion. So she reached over into Ludwik's lap, found the bottle, and drank what was left of the beer, puckering her mouth at the dry, mildly nutty flavor, and then sat there holding the bottle as if it contained a clue, or even a ship to take her the rest of the way to Kazimierz. Beer and motorcycles belonged to another world than hers, and so did dental tools, steel helmets, the pistol, being a widow, and the entire ridiculous course of the day thus far. In this semi-idyllic setting, even with the bomb crater not far away, she suddenly saw how everything was terminal, telling herself *When a day comes along as much out of character as this, you cannot go beyond it, you have to come to the end of the line, and the day has come to tell you just that. Sit here, Wanda, and let the rest of it happen. The children are peaceful where they are; be peaceful yourself.* But she tried to thump the starter into life, almost spraining her ankle, and quite failing to see, first one, then two, followed by an untidy file of slow-moving rather portly figures taking up station behind the distant trunks, almost camouflaged in greenish gray, and not calling or signaling, not approaching or going sideways, but alertly staring, wondering what on earth she was. They might have been deer come to sample the apples in the uneven gloom beneath the full-blown trees. With an unself-conscious sigh, she lifted the helmet off her head and let it fall to the ground with a slack, cushioned flop. The bottle she flipped thoughtlessly back into Ludwik's lap, as if he were no one any more, and she imagined she saw deer, gray-dun, but twin-legged, poised there with outsize white envelopes in hand, just watching her and making gestures so minimal as not to matter. After rubbing her eyes fiercely, which only blurred them worse (the dust, the wind, the grief, the constantly thrusting sun had all combined to make them sore and red), she looked again even as the figures, too tall for deer and too wavery to be statues, moved and stopped. Still no sound. She fumbled for the pistol, reminding herself how to release the safety catch, wishing she did not have to try to kill again, or frighten, maim, whatever the irreducible purpose of a pistol was. Those waiting for her to move saw her in the non-act of waiting for them to do the same; both they and she had time. When she looked again, seeing a bit more clearly, she could not believe it. These silent, immobile creatures, visibly men, had here and there a hand in a pocket, a tunic unbuttoned all the way down, and a couple were smoking pipes. Ludwik? No, these men looked older and plumper, perhaps, and now one of them was gesturing not at her, but at the man nearest to her, one of those with big envelopes, an amateur mailman en route to a big child's birthday. Without thinking she made a low gesture of the hand, something between a wave and the wrist-flick that fends away a fly. And now she saw the glistening knee-boots, the sunburned top of the face crowned by hair that flashed almost ebony, the enormous length of him sauntering toward her among the trees, casually, almost happily (it was a beautiful day still), and waving her to start toward him with a buff-yellow manila file that wasn't an envelope at all. If these were soldiers, they were unduly civil. Then it all seemed like a reception, something she understood, and, while the tall officer walked less casually up to her, stared into her face without a word, then grinned, only to lean over and lift up Ludwik's head, she tried to think of what to say: how formal, how silky, how impersonal. She saw flashes of red on the collar, stripes of red along the leg. Yet, torn between two responses, she took the pistol, cocked it, aimed, only to find the incredulous face in front of her smiling again, saying her nay with a left-right shake, as if to make it plain that the protocol excluded shootings, and then the manila file reaching toward her, finding the pistol and gently depressing the barrel until it pointed at her foot. "You don't need that," he said in a language she at once understood, in which she could answer, and did.

"I never did," she said with the invincible candor of a child caught red-handed. "It's his," pointing at Ludwik. "Major Ludwik Czimanski of the Polish Army, until recently Associate Military Attaché in Berlin. Perhaps we have even met on a previous occasion." The officer, visibly a staff major, nodded at what she said about the pistol, slid it from her grasp, stuffed it behind him somewhere, then shook his head to show they were in fact unintroduced strangers.

"Such lovely German," he purred.

"You all say that," Wanda sighed. "I ran out of fuel, you see. I am on my way to Kazimierz, to bury my husband and find my—children, a boy and a girl."

"By motorcycle," he mused. "In uniform." At once she peeled off the tunic, tousled her hands through her hair with a motion akin to anger, and then dry-washed her face in her hands.

"I even drank beer, which I loathe." The other officers had now drawn close in a group, a monitoring arc of intent, amused, unoffended faces, glad of an event. "It goes to my head at once, whereas, oddly enough, stronger drink has less effect. It all depends on the circumstances. Quite early, I think it was this morning, my husband put on his uniform and left for Warsaw, since then I have had a great deal to put up with, for none of which I was prepared. I was brought up to believe in another way of life. I come before you filthy, degraded, widowed, and just about at my last gasp. It would be a lovely thing on your part if you could only get me to Kazimierz, which is not far away."

22

Those who stood admiring her, which is to say wondering at her rather than being impressed, saw what looked like one of the taller lawn statues come to melodramatic life right next to a gray stone version of a wine or harvest maiden executed with an almost aloof generality which had hung a flagon at her right hip, horizontal but corked (at least no stone flow of wine was gushing forth unless it had gushed before the so-called sculptor began) and swathed her loins in bunches of grapes so close together that nothing of what was underneath showed through, or was made to do so. Had she, some of them wondered (glad of this relief from maps and documents) actually chosen to station herself there, with the statue for company, for moral support, for echo, even for some harsh Biblical reminder of what she had almost become? Wanda's bosom, they noted with languid eagerness, exceeded that of the stone maiden, although less visible, and thus far she remained unspattered with bird droppings, although caked with dust from the road. Off to one side, like a carefully planted discord arranged by a sculptor from an altogether more recent futuristic school, the motorcycle with the inert passenger sat and cooled, the very personification of nowhere gone and nothing gained. With a sly downward pat of his hand, the officer at the far end of the admiring arc sent away Private Hilscher who, exercising right of seniority, had come to investigate, himself having sent his inquisitive partner back to superintend the gateless gate. Off he went, convinced now more than ever that officers had all the fun and already fantasizing upstairs scenes of ingenious depravity with polished belts, rubber gloves, long heavy leaden tubes of cold cream flown in fresh from the Kurfürstendamm for just such an event as this. Next day, her ruined body would be found floating in the Vistula, fungus white where it was not red-and-yellow bruised.

"An SS officer named Haarkünstler," Wanda was saying. "No, that was his *nick*name. He..." and then she told no more of him even as her audience shuffled and smiled, whereas the tall young captain close to her kept his face grave, tuned in to the exact required degree of neutral stare, which was commanded by a very civil major, "they gave me the motorcycle so that I could travel south. And here I am, but I ran out of fuel." What *was* a lie?

The tall officer, tugged by some invisible string, bowed a little, either to her or at the evoked image of the now dead major, and then stood even straighter. "That was most understanding of them. Of him. We are not all rabble, as you can see, dear woman. Most of us have homes, children, wives. We all have parents. We have not come from some parallel

Red in Tooth and Claw

race of louts, spawned in the estaminets of Antwerp or Ethiopia. The pistol was your husband's, you say. It has not been fired."

"At whom would I fire it?" Those watching looked incongruously like a firing squad, she noticed, yet had no rifles and were still smoking pipes, although a couple had cigarettes in their hands, which they seemed to tilt and air for inspection even as they watched. Then she realized that *Ludwik* had not fired it.

"And you are not a spy." It sounded like a joke, yet his face was not smiling but peering beyond her, past the Vistula as if the answer lay in that dark hinterland where the Polish divisions had made their stand. She did not answer, not at first, but then, snatching at her wits, told him "A spy would hardly bring along her husband's body for camouflage, would she?"

Did he amend her phrase to *she*, or had she done it mentally? *Would* she? Wanda suddenly felt faint, reeled, caught at the motorcycle, gasped at what sounded to them like a long serrated diphthong, and found a glass of cognac under her nose, proffered by the captain. "They call me Zollerndorff," he said with an amused wrinkle of distaste, "and sometimes other things as well. I used to play the cello, Madame; I knew the poet Stefan George rather well; I am an expert horseman and have even defeated Olympic equestrians at their own game. I dote on Latin, which I'm afraid I nonetheless tend to keep on losing. There is nothing to be afraid of. Drink this. Then we will escort you inside. So, your husband was the Assistant Military Attaché?" He turned aside, motioned to one member of the group, who approached him to converse, and then the two of them looked at Ludwik's face, his uniform, the identity papers still in his front pouch pocket. "This gentleman confirms it. So do these papers. We are genuinely sorry. How did it happen?" Awaiting her answer, he stared at the truncated arm as if mesmerized, half-wanting to touch but only while looking away, as if the vacant clear blue sky matched the space left by the missing hand, a familiar vacancy complementing the harsher one within his reach. There was even something heraldic in the dead man's posture, with the one hand touching the opposite thigh as if awaiting the other hand to cross it at the wrist, while the head bowed forward again, after having been lifted back for identification, in mute diffident homage to the victor. "*Bras sans main,*" he whispered, "now whose coat of arms was that? The arm without a hand?" It seemed preposterously familiar to him, yet from nowhere he could name, a curt simple indecipherable icon of enormous dignity and undeniable poignancy, the core of a musical dream dreamed by an executant doomed henceforth to undertaking the few piano concertos for one hand only. Was there one by Ravel? He could not remember, himself not having slept fully either, but he knew that, for the dead just as for the living, there would always be appropriate emblems, and works of art which anticipated how you were going to have to feel. Here, in Poland, this: out of the dust and out of the blue, like something he had tried to close his mind to since being a child.

"No trouble to you, but I would appreciate some food," Wanda was saying; this high-spoken, vestigially ebullient, full-breasted woman with the filth-caked face of a street urchin was telling him. "No cognac, if you please."

A voice from somewhere in his head informed her "You cannot have the motorcycle, it is Army property. Well, it is SS, in fact, of course, I can tell that from the number, but I still must deny you further use of it. Where did you learn to drive such a contraption?" I don't really care, though, he was thinking.

"I didn't," she said. "Only how to start it. It stopped first when I ran into a wall, and then just now it stopped of its own accord. Are there still, good Captain, decent burials, with the proper flag?" Her voice had floated high and brittle.

"Over the next few years, Madame," he told her as if goaded to speak something awful but also responsive, "there will be nothing else. We shall all run out of flags. The mouths of the priests will be speechless from overuse at gravesides. Coffins will be in short supply. Allow me to escort you into the main building. This was once a palace. Pulawy Palace," he said, pronouncing it, as a German would, even one who professed some Latin: "Pulavy." Once a German, she thought, *always*.

"Pu*w*avy," she corrected him, astounding herself by taking his arm, leaving Ludwik behind, the dead pilot in the nose of his crashed glider, as if she no longer bore his name, telling herself she was arriving at yet another reception although with the dental tools still secreted inside her blouse, going clink-clink as she walked.

The other officers, having waited with inflated punctilio, now fell almost into step behind them, and Wanda, still reaching up to fit her elbow into the downstretched cup of his hand, began to wonder why the two generals, the colonels, the majors, in the group allowed this stately captain to take charge of her, almost as if deferring to him, as dew to a cloud. Stateliness alone did not explain it, nor did his honed manners, his deep slurred baritone, his impossibly dark blue eyes under the plastered-down dark hair that still caught the sun as it had when he first approached her tall and slow, like a man walking forward to lay a wreath. He likes children, she told herself dreamily. No, that has nothing to do with anything; you thought of that because he said about the Latin, which reminded you of darling little Izz, and *his* Latin. His love of airplanes, Pulawsky, and I think his love of his own precocity, at table. Where was I? They defer to this young captain because he is so handsome. Is that what's called natural selection? He belongs in moving pictures or on the stage, not here, as the bureaucrat to an atrocity. On she walked, as best she could (her legs still cramped from hugging the belly of the motorcycle), absentmindedly noting that he had cut his stride short so as not to pull her forward after him, and this made him sway sideways just a touch, at which sensation he appeared to smile, unless what he smiled at was the total incongruity of this approach, the svelte Rudolf Valentino captain with the grimy refugee widow in tow, to the down-at-heel façade of yet another Polish palace grabbed for use as a classy, home-from-home HQ.

Amazed that her mind still worked at all, although to no worthwhile purpose beyond staying alive, Wanda kept reminding herself of what had happened during the day. I am a widow. The word does not fit. I do not feel like a widow. I am on my way to another reception and Ludwik will be already inside, doing the honors or whatever it's called. My husband is dead back there on the lawn with one of his hands missing; I couldn't bring him in here in that condition. I couldn't bring him in at all. Where would they seat him? No, you upper-class cow, Wanda, this is no reception, you are going to be interrogated by the enemy, of whom this suave, debonair, personable captain is one. They defer to him (not deferring really) because he's the one who does their dirty work, he being the most junior, I saw no other captains, I know the badges of rank, I know them in my sleep, whatever that is.

"Still hot," he told her, having pondered the notion for at least a minute. "But your Polish summers end suddenly, I hear."

Biting back the sarcastic answer which fatigue provided, she nodded, glad to be rid of the steel helmet and the tunic, though wondering if he could hear the metal music of the hypodermic and the probe within her blouse's front. "Oh, I don't know," she said, rising to climatic agnosticism, "some of them go on for ever; but I have spent more summers, recently, in Berlin than in Poland. If you belong here, then surely I should be there." He seemed surprised.

"Is that a political statement, Madame?" His walk quickened not faster but somehow livelier.

"Merely making conversation," she told him. "I am far gone."

"You will see. There are big marble baths with big brass faucets like tire levers. Not one of the ancient clocks keeps time. There are entire storerooms full of ceremonial robes. The kitchen is gigantic, but there was no food in it when we came. There was nobody here at all;

the staff had fled. But it's not bad as a bivouac for a few officers a long way from home."

Why, she wondered in yet another splintery daze, does he talk to me as if he's writing a letter home? Does my merely knowing German put him at ease? You would never know from him and his manner that there's a war going on around us, begun by him and his friends. She almost fell on the deep steps, but he caught her in time, murmured something encouraging, and ushered her through three pairs of double doors, with each of which a certain aroma became stronger, in part the semi-funereal leather-mold must of little-visited libraries, in part the last flight of the defeated mothball, emitting one last bouquet of camphor into a room where all the earlier camphor had gone stale. Yes, she decided, it smells like the Polish Embassy in Berlin; I am back among civilized people and their out-of-date trappings. Then she was in a chamber with no view at all, but only three high windows of stained glass, which gave her an underwater kind of light, three steady spectrums which met in the air above the center of the chamber and made her feel the subject of some chemistry experiment. An orderly in a white jacket brought her a tray of bread and cheese, a silver mug of steaming black coffee and several apples, none of which she tried before testing the door, not locked but guarded by a soldier with no gun. The tall captain,

Zollerndorff, had vanished, a courier whose obligations had met, and Wanda, unsearched and uninterrogated as she was, began to devour the bread, which she dipped in the coffee, half-smiling at the mild vulgarity of doing so.

Through the door, or even the walls which were bare save for two indeterminate honorific portraits done in sludge and varnish, came a faint relay of voices like a concertina being squeezed: no doubt, she mused, the general staff debating which piece of Poland to grab next, unless they already had it all. This is when, she reassured herself, this is when prisoners take stock of their surroundings and try to decide what to do next, how to escape. But not even the coffee enlivened her, nor even the thought of Izz and Myrrh, safe but profoundly wronged by being where they were; as she ate and drank, her spirits, rolling in high maniacal gear all day from crisis to crisis and event to event, began to fail, and, in a fit of acquiescent melancholy, she envisioned herself waiting on tables at dinnertime, scouring pans in the palace scullery, or, even less dignified, swathed in a purple toga unearthed from some eighteenth-century cupboard and positioned centrally on some flea-bitten ancient rug to be admired by cognac-swilling officers of dazzling high rank: a pet! These were not rapists, she knew, but men who had prospered and had sons elsewhere in the army that invaded, daughters at home learning how to do dressage, and high-born wives who wrapped their husbands' pajamas in a national flag until the jubilant return on leave while the rank and file went on storming through Poland, plundering and deriding. That, and nothing else, was the true opiate of the masses: the chance to ridicule the culture of others, whether Slavic or Jewish, whether intellectual or aristocratic. At least, she told herself as the coffee began to work, I am among the possessors here, not the dispossessed. At home these men have more than enough already, and Poland is an exquisite butterfly for the asking, a collector's item they want to fondle and eye, optional and quaint, to be appraised and then left behind in good order with hardly even the dust disturbed. Am I a prize or a diversion, one of the spoils of war or just an encumbrance? Their manual says nothing about the likes of me, the cosmopolitan diplomatic widow, doubling as a dentist, with her dead husband in a sidecar and appalling stories to recount of pubic hair lopped and intimate swabs taken, not to mention SS drivers probed through the throat and.... She doubted if she had remembered it all, not all that had happened to her this day, but also what she had done, aiming always at the children underground, while loose ends kept on dragging at her mind, such as Ludwik's unwitting mother now stranded in Warsaw in the comfy old apartment like a lighthouse keeper with the light gone out and the sea receded and unable to walk away over the ribbed sand below sea level. Suzanna and Wilson had gone for ever, and the world held only the Gnonkas, the Haarkünstlers, the Zollerndorffs, and ghosts, like that of her idealistic Ludwik, like that of the omnipresent but invisible Admiral, the ghosts of the dead and the living, adjacent in gruesome concert.

    Then she saw it, like a trumpet of vertical light set on a high, precarious table so as to catch what light there was in the gloomy antechamber that seemed to have tightened round her like one of Edgar Allen Poe's shrinking rooms. She stood on a chair to look into the lily's face, then managed to lift it down, set it on the rug in front of the empty, soot-thick fireplace, and marveled. Whether one of the amenities or not, it was a splendid thing, dank-perfumed and in full flower with three more buds bulging under the impetus of even that fragile, oblique light through the multicolored portholes high up in the frieze. One through five, she counted the stamens, noted the tiny purple half-nut of the pistil's end, the tiny protruding freckles like the rasps of a file on the face of the petals themselves. Hybrid lily, oriental mix, she whispered, I know these things by heart. What is it doing here? It says this room is not severed from the universe, where business goes on as usual. She tapped the nub of the pistil, dismissed the frivolous thought that the lily seemed to have retracted a multi-petaled foreskin until the ends tapered backward with histrionic urgency, and touched her little finger's tip to the deep ocher of the stamens, which at once gave up their dust, transferred in an unthinking trice to her cheeks like best-quality *Kur'damm* rouge. A minute later she had the complexion of an American Indian: *Apache squaw*, her mind muttered, I can apply it to my eyelids too, it will cover the lines beneath the eyes, it will wipe out the day and transport me to another continent: wigwam, hatchet, beads. When they come for me, I will be so different they'll turn away in revulsion. One lily later and I am a changed woman and any bees that still remain will nose me till I drop. Then she stood admiring the undusted flower, stroking its petals with and against the grain, palping the pistil with exactly measured tenderness, willing to do so until the crack of doom, or until the door opened and they took the lily away, property of the German army.

"Madame," Zollerndorff said when he re-entered, "your face."

23

"I made up in your absence; every woman needs makeup of some kind or other. I used what was at hand." How, she wondered, did she look, and tried to use his bemused incredulity as a looking glass. Did she look savage, or silly, or merely as if she had applied overlight makeup on top of a sunbather's tan? All that Zollerndorff saw was a face that might have sprung up out of the clay underneath the broken concrete of the palace floor, less human than ponderously mythic, as if widow's weeds had turned to powder, setting her face ablaze with landlocked sunset light, turmeric and gold dust, and—this part his educated essentially unmilitary mind resisted like an undertow—as if, in some long-forgotten primitive society, the sacrificial victim had daubed herself with victim-dust, pre-empting the high priests and their acolytes. Where, he wondered, had he read that some primitives painted the face of the victim red? Then he decided to make a conversation of it, for his own part as willing to let Wanda go as imprison her here among map-shufflers, flag-pinners, and strategists who savored the shifting lines of the advance like those of a poem.

"The amazing thing," he began, "is that lilies have appeared in several rooms. We ourselves are not responsible, oh no. Someone put them there overnight, perhaps an infatuated displaced gardener. When we arrived, there was nothing, and they keep on appearing, usually in such places as draw immediate attention to them. Not that we mind, we have not entirely taken leave of our senses. And, of course, we don't have so many men that we can appoint one of them to keep an eye open for whoever it is smuggles lilies into the dining room, the anteroom, the map-room itself. We don't. But, when you find a lily at least a meter and a half high, in a pot that stands on the map exactly over Warsaw, then you begin to wonder. It is easy, sometimes, to believe that one has not had enough sleep, and is dreaming the whole invasion, the lilies, the damned palace itself. And then you: you come from, and go into, the same dream. Would you," he became abruptly facetious, perhaps to cover embarrassment, perhaps because the whole proposal was outlandish (he himself was not quite sure), "consider an appointment, by order of the local general staff, as keeper of the lilies?"

"I thought you just told me you already had one." Wanda knew what he meant about the dreaminess of things, but her own dream was harsh and caustic, in which the lilies died and the husbands turned to powder and the children, if not retrieved in time, just moldered away.

He told her he was joking, but she took him seriously, with what to her seemed a natural counter-suggestion. "When they die, when they wither and go mahogany brown, I'll tend them then. I'll make a potpourri and stir the dry stuff with my own two hands."

"Mysteries," he said, concealing his amazement by pretending not to have heard. "We took down the flags that flew between the two cupolas on the main roof, but someone put new flags up there during the night, so we had those taken down too, and that was the end of it. Whoever it was ran out of flags, I suppose. Several people could hide in this place: it's full of bolt-holes, tunnels, underground chambers, and secret doors, and I don't doubt for a minute that someone is actually living alongside us, roaming about at night. We hear things, but see nothing. Dogs have picked up the scent, but they never find anybody; the scent is everywhere by now, so it is almost like looking for snow in the Alps." He talks, she thought, because he is lonely. He likes to talk to me. His eyes water. Is that strain or lack of sleep? Or is it feeling, rain in the crimp of a lettuce leaf? He's a decent man. What a pity if he has to do something dreadful to me in the end. That's one thing he won't mention on a postcard to his wife. It will be his duty. They take down our flags. They shoot us by walls. They steal our food, our homes, our beer. They kill our husbands and drive our children into the earth. Then they go on living as usual. They can produce coffee and soup and bread and cheese. They sing. They bandage. They bleed. They die. I am upset because there is some distinction between us, one that I cannot find, other than the two languages, and even then: I speak it almost as well as he does. I too know the crows that haunt Berlin, soaring in a black cloud across the sunset; *fog-crows*, or the *Nebelkraehe*; birds of passage who breed in Poland but spend the winter in Berlin, making a proper use of the border in between. And the nightingales that come back to haunt the Tiergarten in the spring, singing liquidly in the small bushes on the islands dotted about among the boating lakes.

"The year after April," she said remotely. "I was thinking of what the year is like once April has come." Zollerndorff stared at her appreciatively, his mind full of speculations that ran into one another and petered out: She talks this way because she is overwound, being no fathead, and she no doubt thinks I am short of intelligent conversation here, which is far from true; I am an outgoing person, I talk to everyone in the same way, I keep almost nothing to myself, which in the long run means that all my thoughts are groomed, they can all show their faces without shame. If you put everything you think into the open, it develops a polite face, and people begin to confide in you; my affability is bait.

"Whereas," he said, at last picking up the thread of the conversation, "the year until April is—what? Too much of the same thing, whereas the year after is full of fine gradations."

"You could let me go," she told him abruptly. "About my business. Be on my way to what little I'm going to."

"But you are a refugee." It sounded sensible, it seemed more or less true; and she looked the part too, although she was the first refugee he'd seen whose face was orange-brown with lily dust. "You belong in a refugee camp."

"I belong at home, Captain. I know where it is. Our summer home isn't far from here. Let me take my husband home, there, and bury him." In her agitation she had rubbed her face, not rubbing the powder smooth and even, but baring her skin again in a few places. Now she seemed patched with scar tissue.

"You cannot have the motorcycle. It is what's called military property. Someone somewhere has it on inventory."

"That is not the point. I am a hindrance to you here. You surely don't want a woman in your way. You already have someone who tends the lilies. You already have a ghost. I am more use to myself and my children."

"But you are on the run, Madame; you are not at home."

"I would be at home now if you hadn't, you Germans, invaded Poland. Or do you too subscribe to the mealy-mouthed philosophy that no invasion has taken place? *If* that's a philosophy."

In his face the soldier fought the mean of common sense and lost. "Certainly there has been an invasion. It is almost over and done with. But, inasmuch as it has happened, the situation is changed. All situations are different. Even at home you would be a refugee of sorts. There are two kinds: those on the run and those at home. The whole of Poland has refugee status. Sorry, I mean it. You are a refugee like all the others."

"Captain," she almost shouted, "I wouldn't be on the road going back if I hadn't been kidnapped at gunpoint by the SS!"

"Then, at least by their bizarre reckoning, you are a suspect. I am a soldier, a professional one, and no part of the SS, but I have to concede they may have had a point. In a word, you have escaped. You are a fugitive rather than a refugee."

Now, she thought, he *is* going to grill me about the motorcycle. Lord, she rehearsed, strike me dead if I tell a lie: I was taken away by the SS officer, Haarkünstler—all Germans love a *Künstler*, it is one of their vital words— because he felt sorry for me, with my husband gone off to Warsaw to look for his mother. No, that's too glib. In fact he took me away with him for some filthy purpose of his own, and when they stopped en route I ran away, hid, and they couldn't be bothered to come looking for me. Then I blundered into the first-aid station. How, then, did I come to have the motorcycle? They gave it to me at the first-aid station, to take my husband home in.

"Captain," she began, instead, "I am a bad woman. I killed my SS driver with my bare hands and stole the motorcycle just like that." He had not even asked. He had been waiting for her to lie, but not to joke, not to invent melodrama such as this.

"Of course," he said calmly. "Why not?" They just dumped her, he decided. Even SS officers with peculiar tastes have enough sense of self-preservation to do that. He thought better of it and let her go, this Haarkünstler whose name is not a name. "If it were up to me, Madame," he added, "you could go now and take the motorcycle too. Unfortunately almost nothing is up to me alone. You are right: charming as you may be, you are a nuisance here, although a diversion from mapwork. This is by way of being an interrogation, without duress, of course. We would like to be rid of you, but only to our own satisfaction. Two very famous generals have instructed me to determine your status, as the jargon has it. *I* think you are a refugee. That makes you innocent. A fugitive is something else."

"I," Wanda told him in German, hammering each syllable home, "am a fresh-made widow.

Wdowa in Polish. I have no other status under heaven."

"But you have taken refuge, then: here, there, and almost everywhere. Which makes you a refugee." He almost prodded her.

"Captain," she said, warming to the semi-academic nature of the debate, "why must you insist on adding a category to a category that's already comprehensive enough? A widow is a widow. My husband is the refugee. He needs the refuge of a grave."

"Then we can bury him here, decently, and hold a military service at the graveside. Everything will be decorous."

"I want to bury him at home."

"But what's down the road, as you say, is only your temporary summer home?" He shaped a summer chalet with his hands.

"Home was in Berlin, believe it or not. Or in Warsaw."

"Then you were taking him to Warsaw, in the wrong direction?"

"I could hardly take him to Berlin." Harder than a slap.

"Where did you live in Berlin?" Said with a trace of a nod.

"Tristranstrasse, 23. We also had quarters at the Embassy."

He was gaping, with a slow radiant mellow smile that came right out of the sun. "In Wannsee?" He savored the very word.

"In Wannsee." He looked floored, at the least convinced, but also dreamily jubilant. "Not only that," she went on, "we had an arrangement with the Admiral. You know of *him*." She said the Admiral's name in full, without going into detail, but implying the entire arrangement—the money, the promise, the words daubed on the walls of the house in Pulawy Street, the morning rides Ludwik and the Admiral had taken together in the Grünewald during which the scheme had been arranged, the sly bond between Izz and the Admiral, who talked about toy trains together—by sheer emphasis. "Oh, there was an arrangement all right."

"You mean the Pied Piper of Europe? This—Admiral has so many fingers in other people's pockets he sometimes touches one of his own fingers without knowing it. One day he will sell Afghanistan to Sweden, mark my word. So you made an arrangement. I wouldn't count on it, Madame. Look, you are still here. I speak as an aristocratic socialist; the Admiral is neither an aristocrat nor a friend of the people. Now, if you had a horse in trouble, he would raise heaven and earth to move it to Switzerland, whereas his record with people is much spottier. He helps some, not others. I share his love of horses, but I do not, as he seems to, confuse horse lovers with decent people. Your Admiral, *our* Admiral, is Proteus with teeth. Now you see him, now you don't; now you know him, and mostly you wonder if he's a myth, manufactured by the same company as created Olympia, the dancing doll. Don't let me discourage you: he may well deliver the goods, sooner or later, but don't count on it. A man so busy, and so proud of being busy, is just a born interferer. Not that I know him, but I know of him, as indeed everyone knows of him. He's the Santa Claus," he almost giggled, "of the Tirpitzufer, where his office is. We call it the 'Fox's Earth'. You know your way around Berlin, of course."

"Then the so-called arrangement," Wanda persisted, ignoring his jokes and allusions, "is already too late for my husband. I mean, if it matters to him at all, in the circumstances, he should want to go through with it twice as much."

Zollerndorff sighed, battling his skepticism into a polite shrug. "Or with only half of his original zeal—if zeal there even was. There must be scores of people, maybe hundreds, in exactly your position. The Admiral has stashed the loot in Spain or Switzerland, or so I'm told. He calls it his Retirement Fund. In one or two per cent, at most of these cases, he's gone through with the arrangement, but mostly not. In that way, I suppose, he covers his tracks. Just when nobody expects him to do anything, when they've given up hope, along he trots on his white horse and hey presto, there you are in Brazil, going to the theater as usual, reading the latest books, concocting menus, getting a suntan, and making new friends who find the so-called invasion of Europe as far away as Pluto." Wanda felt the core of her brain sink down her throat into her heart, and then her overloaded heart sag into her stomach, kneaded and churning; it was as if thousands of years had knotted together and begun to rot, just there below her ribcage, with a death followed by blow upon blow of frustration, whose taste in her mouth, right then even as she peered into his candid, good-host's face in which the boyishness had lingered on. "Then I should go. The children."

"No," he said, imperious but gently so, "you wait. We must have been neighbors in Tristranstrasse. One does what one can for one's neighbors. Now, tell me about your children. Your husband won't mind waiting, will he now? There are ways of reaching the Admiral— I mean of contacting his office, which isn't quite the same as actually getting something into his own private special head. What can we use?"

"Use?" Wanda already wondered if he meant by boat, car, train or plane.

"Something unique which would save us from having to use your name. I mean Czimanski. You do know the Admiral?"

"Of course," she said furiously. "Otherwise why—"

"Understood," he said concisely. "Did you arrange a password?"

"Only with the children, who are...cached."

"*Cached.*" He shook his head and she explained, which made him shudder. "Like young foxes."

"If there had been a password," she said in a defeated whisper, feeling at once preposterous and sadistic, not only a poor mother but an improvident one as well, "I'd have known."

"Nicknames, then. Your son is obsessed with this Pulawski, the designer of the Polish fighter plane; would the Admiral connect the name with your son?" Now he sounded softly irritated; curt.

"Who knows what they talked about? It was toy trains as well as aircraft. It was horses too."

"He promised to find you in Kazimierz. How unwise of all of you. Never mind. Were we to send, in cipher of course, something such as *Kazimierz—Pulawski—Izz,* might that tip him off enough?"

"The Admiral, so far as I remember, never used nicknames; he was outrageously formal in all things. *Izydor,*" she said. "*Ee-zi-dor.* That would be better. He said nicknames diminished people, made them into masks."

"Well," Zollerndorff, arguing with himself, went on, "the wonderful plane your son is obsessed with, this Pulawski fighter, it has a nickname, doesn't it? They call it *Jedenastka.*

Or *eleven*. We could try that. No, I think the nickname is new. It does not antedate the invasion."

"We aren't getting very far, Captain. Why don't you just go the whole way, be hanged for being a sheep rather than for being a lamb, and drive me down to where the farm is, just to let me check. I can't exactly see a German officer wandering around saying the codeword to two children under a pigsty."

"I haven't even offered to go. Provided your children have not taken a direct hit from a shell or a bomb, and have sufficient food, toilet paper, and the collected works of Marcel Proust, they should be all right for a day or two. Forgive me, Madame, I was not being sarcastic, it just came out. I have never heard of anything so ridiculous. German parents would have—"

"Browbeaten the Admiral into doing his job, his part of the bargain? I imagine Germans could have. We are Poles. In case you hadn't noticed. We wait for favors, of which the biggest one you could have done us is to have left our quiet, muddling country alone in the first place. None of this would have come about—" but she collapsed her sentence and ended it right there. "Would it? Would it, now? Would it ever?"

On the point of flaring up, he seemed to tauten from within and frowned what she knew was a covert apology. "No codeword, you say. It makes no sense. It gives him all the initiative, which is no doubt how he wants things. If I had my way, which I will, I'd make it explicit, just saying *Military Attaché*, I beg your pardon, *Assistant Military Attaché, has foals*. How about that? As for your question, I come from a military family and I relish the chance of getting about and seeing things, even if—forgive me—it tears up a bit of Poland here and there. That is my schizophrenia."

What staggered Wanda was not so much his casual assumption of the right to use her country as a plaything, a sandbox, a set of Gothic ninepins to be bowled over, so much as his other assumption, no it was a commonplace fact, that he could pick up the telephone or send a cable and at once reach the old seafaring duke of dark corners in Berlin, or the Admiral's staff, his office where the dung-encrusted rug smelled worse as the weeks went by. And he, Zollerndorff, would do so out of some so-called neighborly whim, because they had both lived on Tristranstrasse in the garden suburb of Wannsee, as if he would not have stirred at all had she lived in Lichterfelde, say, or even nearby Zehlendorf. Oh he was bored all right, and perhaps he was showing off his power, his clout, his influence over those two very famous generals; but he was doing something else, he was experimenting with her present and her future, both offering and bluffing, both generous and niggardly, as much enemy as friend, and his warmed-over chivalry had something fancy about it, which she nonetheless resolved to ignore while she used him in the insane atmosphere of a palace where night-revenants haunted new-come generals, tall lilies like celluloid spinning wheels endured thanks to the ministrations of a two-hundred-year-old ancient servant touring in the wainscot like a knight in fluffy cotton, and the ungainly radio masts, erected on the roof where the flags had flown, been felled, and had flown once again, sang out into the wounded air above the map of Europe into which, on a daily basis, the officers stuck pins round which they twisted little colored threads, like children at long last tinkering with a yearned-for toy, part sewing machine, part crochet, part bloodbath as well.

He was asking her something, but the voice seemed to come, velvety and expansive, from the mouth of the high lily, and she stared into his stare, reconstructing from his face what he might have said while he measured her guessing and got ready to say it again, in exactly the right tone. Confronted with an interesting lunatic who, undeniably, had been your neighbor, in whom you felt an interest amounting to mental transvestism, you had to get things across, even when doing a favor, with an air of complicity, an eye that was weak enough to blink, a hand that halted in mid-gesture as if convicting itself of histrionic excess, a mouth which made the words stay put like skywriting, level and legible in a windless zone between them. "Then I will send it plain. And you will wait."

"Have I a choice, Captain?" If she napped while waiting, she might never wake, drugged, gassed, and shot, or merely dumped into the Vistula tied in a sheet strapped to a piece of broken masonry.

"Plain," she said. "It's just as well. Busy men don't like conundrums, do they? I could use a nap," she said, reckless in spite of herself. "I really could. Fatigue has caught the coffee up."

Airily he swung one hand at the couch by the wall on which hung the portrait obscured by varnish. "Of course. You will not be disturbed. There is a lavatory across the hall, and the guard will take you there if necessary."

Oh, she thought, I drank beer. That is what is wrong with me, and she made her request there and then, feeling cork-light as she trudged behind the guard to install herself on a gigantic mahogany seat flanked by polished wooden leaves; the whole thing was wide enough to be a table, and the twin, unfused odors of the place—creosote and furniture polish—took her back to the Berlin Embassy again, renewing the same sense of fustily baronial splendor amid which she had wearied of the clicking heels in the corridors, the well-bred dry barks of the officers, whether German or Polish she had never been able to tell when merely listening. I am a mother who has come a long way, she explained to herself; but never being able to go back isn't half so bad if there's a guaranteed going-forward: going home, going back to duty, taking a train, getting into position in the receiving line, going to hospital to have a baby, escorting your son to his first school with his fists clenched and his eyes closed off. When she emerged, Captain Zollerndorff was nowhere to be seen, and she settled down to sleep, or nap, grateful for the subdued tints of the light in the anteroom, but wishing the air smelled breathable, and haunted at the very last by Ludwik, as she envisioned him, still in the sidecar out on the lawn, and developing minute by minute the dismal, peppery, cogent aroma of death, whereas he was lying in comparative state on a stretcher in one of the stables, carried there by the two soldiers from the gate, of whom one, Hilscher, mumbled to the other that, while such labor was right for the lowest rank of all, he was a *Gefreiter*, which other armies dignified with the appellation Private First Class or Lance-Corporal, and such menial trade was not for him. Just because he was a country boy, they put on him, and he was going to let the sergeant know. None of this impressed his comrade in arms, his fellow stretcher-bearer, who told him, "Hilscher, you'll soon object to having to carry your own shit around inside of you. Even the generals have to do that, and the only one who doesn't any longer is this poor Polish bastard. You can whiff it in his clothes." They left Ludwik in his German tunic, his German helmet, alone to bubble and seep on the stretcher, next to a broken harrow, himself like a length of discarded equipment, settling into terminal rigidity with no one there to hear him out.

24

Only half an hour's drive away by road, south to Bochotnica where Casimir the Great had built a castle for Esterka his paramour, then west, along the south bank of the Vistula to Kazimierz itself, Izz and Myrrh had squabbled about going up into the daylight, to where the pigs had first of all crunched around at feeding time, and then with lumbering mumbles settled into torpor.

"The coast is clear," she said. "I can go."

"Clear enough for you to be seen. I know it's horrible, like being sick in bed and having to do it into something underneath. But it's better than being captured or shot."

"Germans don't shoot children. Izz, we're *kids*, just kids."

"Well," he said, feeling himself grow older, more in charge, with each word, "that damned farmer, he came by and he didn't even shout down to us. Not even a hello. Is he just sullen or was he scared even to do that?"

Myrrh finally gave in, praying to be released by evening, and finally, after they had made up, urging him to blot out time, and light, and smell, and an ache in her lower back amounting to pain, by playing games they had played from years before, in one of which she was a fledgling wren who raised her mouth high and cheeped incessant little cries of *meek-meek-*

meek! for food, always to have him still her cries by clamping his mouth on hers, in the role of mother wren; but the instant he raised his mouth to breathe or relax, still within the game, she chirped hungrily again at him, and he silenced her fast, as if his very life, or hers, depended on shutting her up with food. As he played, his mind not on their game at all and thinking he was past all this fol de rol, he realized how his stilling of her cries matched their near-emergency: the cheeping wren might give the game away, heard by the wrong person on the outside, and get them dragged blinking into the terrible daylight, up among the polished ebony boots and the fry pan in which a mayor had sat.

"They're bound to come and save us," he lied. We are going to be here for days, with food enough for nearly a week; and when our folks come for us, all will be well upstairs, everything will have settled down again, except the Germans will be delivering the post, printing the newspapers, being traffic policemen, marching us to school, watching our teachers teach us, the history lessons especially, and there won't be a single Polish plane in the sky. Where are the bombs and the shells? Is it over so soon? Already, he reminded himself, the sandwiches smelled stale and tasted incongruously sweet. He yearned for someone, anyone, to apply his or her mouth to the other end of the speaking-breathing tube and call "Pulawsky," and then he thought he heard a sound, but it was only Myrrh, histrionically plaintive, asking him to kiss her nose, upon whose bridge his mouth found tears like tiny salt pebbles, winning substance from the gloom. He tickled her navel, which always made her cross, and today more than ever. He tap-kissed her eyelids, which made her murmur furtively, and for longer than he had ever heard her do so. He even resurrected an older game than the wren-feeding one, in which two panthers figured, a genial one known as the *kawus pantera* (the kissing panther) and another, Zygmunt, a bad-tempered one as apt to claw and rend as to kiss. To begin with, as always from the dawn of their parallel childhoods, he slept, snoring and gutturally purring, as a panther must, then waking up in a rotten humor that made him paw the air around him, snatching and slashing while Myrrh cowered away from him although held firm by his arm about her neck. At this point, the game went either way, but most often it was the kissing panther who awoke, celebrating its first glimpse of light with a roar while still flailing and slashing, but with the tiniest access of accuracy, or so the panther was supposed to feel. At last, out of the corner of its feral but essentially kindly eye, the panther caught sight of Myrrh, freezing her with a savage squint, then doing nothing further in order to prolong the agony, until, snarling only a hand's breath away, it fell upon her and plastered the bridge of her nose with ritual kisses while she squeaked the delight of voluptuous reprieve: it had not been Zygmunt at all, who would have torn her into unloved shreds. On the rare occasion, and never without warning, when Izz played Zygmunt, he pretended to be insatiably ferocious, not by battering her nose with his jaw or clawing at her with his fingers curled, but just by roaring louder until his throat hurt. Over the years his roar had changed, actually becoming more effective, but the only difference between the two panthers was in the volume of their nastiness, and, as Myrrh got older, she began to wonder if the panther game were not the very best way of unfanging a world that snarled always more harshly. A hypnotized, dozing lamb against his arm, she went through the terrors of an ancient human, ecstatically shocked out of her wits, and then kissed to death as a survivor.

"Jekyll and Hyde," Izz had said a year or so ago, when they had played the panther game in a derelict windmill and experimented sexually while the February wind whined, "but Hyde's a nice guy too. What a lovely game, when you just can't lose." And he had kissed her nose again, as if trying to butt into the sinuses behind it.

In that same deserted windmill, at night busy with rats (as he knew), he had seen a spider's web arranged across the lower angle of a ladder's bottom rung, and had marveled at the detritus on the ground beneath, the cold carnage of husks from beetles, flies, harvestmen, sucked dry by the tiny toiling maw of the smallest spider he had ever seen, almost invisible in its net of gossamer and froth. Is there something just as small, he thought, which can do that kind of thing to us? Working out the ratios, he thought it must be an animal, a spider even, about the size of his chest, or maybe his head, and then realized that it wasn't so much the smallness of the spider vis-à-vis the size of its used-up prey which had daunted him as the smallness of the spider, hung like a dot, above the accumulated leavings, a month's worth at least. A much viler comparison came to him then, of one human suspended in its web above a month's worth of cattle skins, cattle bones, cast-off leaves of cabbage and cauliflower, potato peelings and opened cans, eggshells, greens from beets, and, mingled in, a month's excrement. He gagged. All of a sudden the spider looked clean, like a blob of cake decoration afloat in a weather-haze, and he held back the foot he would have tapped it with to bring it down to squash, and turned to Myrrh again, stifling her complaints with a mother-wren kiss and closing his mind to analogies he could not bear, or couldn't bear to work out to the very end. And now, as he thought of the spider, brought to mind by the filth they would soon be living in, he saw coming toward him, unwinged and like a red-hot pea, the bullet that had landed on them earlier today, which could kill them no less certainly, but took nothing from them for itself. Does the baby, he asked himself, suck its mother dry? He gave up that entire line of thought, intent now on something that seemed simpler: We have been in here only one night and part of a day, and already we are growing down instead of growing up. We aren't as grownup as we were, we are going backwards when, actually, we need to be stronger than ever. Or is it the other way round? The more helpless, the more passive, the more infantile we become, the less we'll resist what's happening to us. We will bend, we will give, instead of snapping. So long as we are not brittle, now, we will be able to grow up again, along the same lines as before, with not a single quirk of all our previous development missed out. Now and then, as he'd roamed through the fields and woods of his childhood, the Polish part anyway, he'd seen the occasional grass snake right in front of him, utterly still, like a coil of dog-doo, and therefore something to step round so as not to mess his shoes, when the snake uncoiled and went away with its head no longer resting across its interminable arm, he was amazed, wondering if it had really tried to look like something else. Well, he and Myrrh would try to be like the snake; that was the only thing to do, passing for something inanimate until it was time to slink away again. And then (although he did not formulate it thus, not exactly thus), those noisy, innuendo-ridden meals at his parents' table, or at Myrrh's house, would go on exactly as before, full of crackling repartee and full-mouthed laughter, with genial parodies of how Berliners talked, lithe barely tolerated excursions into Latin or aeronautics, and giddy trips to Samarkand or the Caribbean Sea, each of the six longing for a favorite food, but making do with what was served. It would all come back, of that he was certain; and it would be better than ever, while the parents made the most of their precocious offspring before losing them, for much of the year, to college, even as, he recognized, they had lost them already—little Izz, bigger Myrrh—to each other when they were only toddlers. It was all there in his head, in Myrrh's, and it was all ready to be renewed at the drop of peace's feather; no, earlier than that, *in a few days' time*, he'd bet on that. And being underground, alive among the worms and beetles, would be something to chatter about over stuffed cabbage, meat turnovers, roast duck with apples, and tons of fungus-light pastries, for years to come. All he and Myrrh needed to do was wait and stay in love, as it was called, nourished by each other's awkwardness until the overhead planks went flying back, a small brass band played the Chopin Military Polonaise (if they could), and a crowd of Poles and Germans welcomed them back with open arms as if they had just been to the Moon with Jules Verne.

Crooking his middle finger rather less than the other ones (which actually touched his palm), he made for Myrrh a trembling angular animal that nibbled below her middle finger, and she cupped her hand around it, caging a butterfly or a cricket, letting it nudge and flicker for her delight, but hoping that this time it would not escape to cross her wrist and hobble its way up her arm to the pit, where it usually threatened to tickle, which always made her giggle before the knuckle touched. Away in Pulawy Palace, Wanda prepared to dream that the two of them were dreaming about her and for the first time felt she was part of the main building, with its twin Doric pillars on the second floor, sandwiched between two blind-looking belfries with onion-shaped cupolas. It was the college to which the children would go, Izz to study the science of flight, Myrrh to study dance, which made it an unusual university indeed. Five doors away, down a corridor thick with pipe- and cigar-smoke, Captain von Zollerndorff put through a priority call to 'Caesar,' as the Admiral was known, not so much to speak to him direct (he, Zollerndorff despised him) as to set on his desk, where the two infamous wire-haired dachshunds Seppel and Sabine could not rend it, a cryptic message from advanced staff HQ in Pulawy Palace, jogging the Admiral's labyrinthine memory, and informing him that the Czimanski mare had foaled.

25

For all his outward primness, the Admiral had never been squeamish about Sundays; so far as he was concerned Sunday was just another day of the week and anything had the right to desecrate it, whether family uproars with trays and goblets thrown, little children drowned in shallow streams on their way home from communication with the deity, or old friends all of a sudden insisting that he never again address them by nickname. This Sunday, however, a mere seventeenth of September, his telephone rang at dawn to inform him that the Russians had crossed the Polish frontier between Polotsk and Kamenets-Podolski at four in the morning; he was hardly surprised, having for some time expected them to make a move, egged on as they had been by Ribbentrop, and other lugubrious brains, to come and get their share of Polish spoils; but he had been unable to go back to sleep, and he just lay there palping his heavy face with his small hands. To him it felt brittle and light, ready to be blown away or pecked to bits by the next bird.

Born on the first day of the year fifty-eight years ago, he had started as he meant to go on (and, he knew, as he was meant to go on): he expected his days to begin every bit as well, and he loved to say *From the very first*, as if he and he alone had such things as primacy, or precedence, at heart; he knew, almost as if by divine right, the initial causes of what happened, both at home and abroad. He prided himself on being crisp, acute, and wise until mid-afternoon at least, which explained his regimen of pills: pills to get him to sleep on time, and pills to get him alert before his counter-intelligence staff was quite awake, and then he dazed them with stances so absolute and cogently concise that he seemed a consummate specimen of the human ability to make up one's mind. That was when the Admiral truly loved himself, pronouncing with unbrookable finality "The British Empire has to go" or "One is a serviceman and must obey." As the day wore on, though, he began to qualify what he said, and the icebrick exactness of his early-morning dicta became eroded; by lunchtime he was a muddling dog lover again, vaguely aware that his mind had, for a few short hours, been visited by the ghost of immaculate reasoning sent by Plato from his cave. So, while this visitation lasted, he trounced others mentally, but grew to loathe the inferior Admiral who surfaced with the soup at lunch, wondering into the vapor why (he was not that old) his mind could not always be crystalline and deft. The power was always there, of course: he could do what he wanted, but he could not be sure it was what he would have wanted to do while he was superlatively lucid, with that cleansed, amiably cool sensation reaching from his buttocks to somewhere beneath his liver.

On this particular Sunday, during coffee and biscuits at eleven-fifteen or so, the telephone rang again. It always did. He never minded, and he had never thought of Sunday as a day of rest; but this was a call bringing personal bad news for the family. Somewhere near Radom, deep in that accursed Poland, his nephew, Rudolf Buck, had been killed in action. "At least, my dear," he told his sister Anna, "it is a piece of bad news that will not have to come again. He is a hero, God be thanked. He is at peace, a peace we cannot even guess at. You will never have to be afraid for him again. At least, his suffering is over. Ours has just begun." Rubbing crumbs of powdered shortbread from his mouth, but somewhat upward, against his septum, he shook his head miserably at Erika, his wife, who never knew what to say to him anyway: far from the rhythms of his mind, to which she had made only an average effort to attune herself, she filled the distance between them with sarcasm, except when, as now, she said nothing at all, knowing that in his piggish, cumbersome way he would make the best of things, as he always did, defusing bad news with a quotation from Frederick the Second, tempering the good news with a sly reference to the disasters the morrow would bring, and adjusting to the in-between times when the phone rang and rang, delivering information of only medium interest, with the additive shrug of a hobbyist, glad of a few new stamps for his collection, even gladder that any old thing was happening rather than nothing, and in the innermost cells of his heart relieved (like so many Germans) that a *Führer* had come along to break the monotony. "Heil Hitler," said the Admiral with a cagey wince as he brushed past her on his way to the open French windows, meaning it was all Hitler's fault, yet it brought as much honor to Germany as it did grief to his sister, and it was a part of the ongoing ruckus that the Fatherland needed to persuade itself that it still existed after the humiliating Peace of Versailles, which had made it the wholly-defeated, utterly responsible nation. "And," he said out on the lawn, "*Heil* Rudolf too," making a mental note to have Rust, his blind masseur, loosen up the cords in the back of his neck tomorrow, after which Rust would gambol on the floor with Seppel and Sabine, growling and yelping as well as they, and freed briefly of the obligation to pass for human in a world, a society anyway, that would have put him down long ago had the Admiral not given him a job.

He is having another of his days, his wife told herself as she watched the Admiral's back recede. Wilhelm the Cantankerer. How did I, a cultivated woman, ever manage to tie myself up with a man who shudders at the mention of illness, who backs away from anyone taller than he as if they had the plague, who rattles with pills, is more superstitious than a peasant, will only shed one imaginary complaint in order to contract one even worse, and, God help me, needs twelve hours of sleep, thirteen if the preceding day has inflicted too many small-eared visitors upon him. He looks well enough until you see how much less than average height he is: almost a dwarf, not quite 1.6 meters tall, although what he calls his mariner's tan and his white hair deflect the eye from his body to his face, that sundial on the rotten pedestal of his intentions. Death to him is a breach of decorum, something his masseur must shovel up or brush under the rug along with the rest of the filth. So long as his eyebrows remain bushy, as if they could really hide what terrible things happen in his eyes, he can stand anything, and he just happens to be in charge of German intelligence worldwide, which is like giving an ostrich the entire Sahara to play with. If only he wouldn't lisp and, even in those nice gray suits with the metallic sheen, pat the place where he wears the Iron Cross when in uniform.

"What are you *doing*?" she called after him in a voice thinned shrill by exasperation.

"Getting out of your way," as if he had been waiting his cue to answer with something unsubtly wounding. "I am going *out-thide*." That un-Admiral-like lisp. He isn't far away at all, just lurking behind the corner of the door, which means he walked away large as life and then sneaked back, to see if I am talking to myself. "And on Tuesday," she heard him call, whether spies were listening or no, "I will be off to Poland again. I am going to Lvov with Yary, Piekenrock, and Lahousen, to see what we can do for those godforsaken Ukrainian refugees." He lisped, she was certain of it, only when he wanted to, in order to catch her off guard, distracting her from what he said by making her mix motherly sympathy with baleful amusement, only to exploit the moment by accusing her of not listening at all, a role into which he delighted to compel her, converting her into an ogress while he played at being a child.

In the end, as always, there was only Motte he could tell, only Motte who could assimilate without levity or disgust the full gamut of what the Head of the *Abwehr* felt from day to day, having to put the world to rights from the cramped, gloomy office behind the metal grille, at the end of the longest corridor in the Fox's Earth. The balcony with a view of the Landwehr Canal did not help much (canals were stagnant), nor did his few personal belongings: all those books (mere recombinations of the dictionary, he had begun to feel), the model of the light cruiser *Dresden* (it only made him long for the old days, like the time the real *Dresden,* only survivor of the Falkland Islands naval battle in 1915, had dodged the Royal

Navy for months and had finally found haven off the Pacific Island of Más a Tierra, exactly where Robinson Crusoe had been marooned). Nor did the trio of three bronze monkeys from Japan, supposed to embody the code of the top-flight intelligence officer—"see all, hear all, say nothing." No, canals, books, model ships and bronze monkeys only reminded him of the career he almost never had, when the official report on the lieutenant who became an admiral said he was too irritable, too high-strung, too much of a man of opposites, unpredictable and in manner hypersensitive; the nose was big and long, and the jaw was dour, but his brow receded above the soldierly sharp angles of his oval face, and they said he could not be counted on, being both down-to-earth like his mercantile and entrepreneurish forbears, but, like his mother an ascetic dreamer as quick into a volatile dither as out of it, leaving the world about her in a daze. Yet, he told himself out there in the sunlight, tapping his shoe on the dry grass of the lawn, I prevailed, I am here. I once escaped from internment on the island of Quiriquina; I had not joined the Navy to rot on a Chilean island, or to ride the horses provided for the officers to ride while our men laid roads or tinkered to improve the water pipes; up into the rough ground I went, and then down a path to the beach, where for twenty pesos a fisherman rowed me away. I would not mind that beach again, or that escape, arriving quietly in Concepción en route for Argentina, with only the snow-thick Andes in between. For the Admiral it was a cheerful enough daydream, so long as he suppressed the presence of Más a Tierra, way back then, of a factory that canned crayfish.

The best memory of all, though, was his parents' villa, whose grounds he toured in a little goat cart with his brother and sister, past the tennis court and the stables to the choked magnificence of the kitchen garden: a witty child who astounded his father with boned-up allusions to something so far-fetched as the history of geography and who, when his mother peered at him severely, just before scolding him for going too far with his madcap dry humor, would say "Mother, Mother, there are X-rays coming out of your eyes!" Even now, in his Admiral's uniform or the plain gray suits that blatantly understated his importance, he was still the smart-mouthed young enigma whom a carriage delivered at the Duisburg Gymnasium every morning and took away each noon, an aloof and haughty boy who eventually did so well in the university entrance examination he was excused the oral. For his teachers and schoolmates he came alive only when the annual outing took them all on more or less military expeditions into the gently slanting woodlands along the edge of the Ruhr, and there he became a leader and an organizer, leading boldly across the distance his taciturnity had set up, and joking as if all along they had been caught up in the same surge of quick-change conversation. And then, in Greece, he discovered the sea, and a monument to a Greek admiral of the nineteenth century, Constantine Kanaris, whom he thereafter idolized and made into his seafaring holy ghost.

Now, he was still aloof although given to fits of organizing genius, but he had come to see himself in an access of gracious candor as a bit of an eccentric; his wife had told him so, and not without reason after seeing him, usually at weekends, trudge out to the apple tree with the screwed-up bundle of his pajamas, handwashed at the basin by his own hands with expensive toilet soap. Then he faced the tree as if taking position in some parade, re-wrung the pajamas, unfurled the jacket and let the wind billow into it once or twice, shook loose the legs until he could see the ground beneath through each, and deployed the laundry on the lower branches, attaching it with bulldog clips, taking enormous care not to scar the bark. Sometimes he did the same with a shirt or his underwear, almost as if washing away a contamination which others must not touch, but really, as he saw it, to do something small and humdrum after hours upon hours of rearranging Europe or even the world. If he had time, and on weekends he often did, he would stand and watch the laundry dry, appraising its float and twirl, glad to see the dark patches of wet or wet's ephemeral transparency disappear (depending on the fabric's color). Deep down he guessed that he missed messing about in boats and fiddling with sails, and this way he could sail on the lawn, but he wondered if the whole thing wasn't also the result of one terrible sleepless night when he had perspired in the dead of winter, and had washed the pajamas through to keep Erika from asking questions. If ever in doubt about his motives, he attributed everything to the secretiveness for which he knew he was renowned. In winter, though, or when there was rain, he let things go, just to thwart the pattern, somehow pitting the variability of weather against his reasons for doing what he did; sooner or later, what he thought his reasons, and what others *knew* were his reasons, just didn't apply. His life and his mind were more complex than that, and whole chunks of his being just did not pick up where other chunks left off. A dislocated man, even in his own eyes, he had no wish to be made whole, to be irrevocably connected up in all his joints, and, when he did other things just as unusual, he enjoyed telling himself that anyone spying on him would think them rather symbolic, whereas they were nothing of the kind. Tapping beetles off his roses into a jam jar with a screwtop lid, and then shaking them violently to stun them (motions of the cocktail shaker with his short slight arms) might have seemed omnipotence gone mad, or a substitute for control of the world at large, but he simply liked to hear the beetles rattle against the lid, some of them still coupled in rut. The jar stood for days on a rustic table by the apple tree, but from time to time he let in the air and tossed in a bit of leaf, at least until the jar became too smeared with droppings, and too clouded with vapor, so he then sent it out in the garbage for someone else to play with.

On this particular Sunday, however, neither his pajamas nor the beetle jar suited his mind; he could not dismiss the thought that, somewhere too far away, his nephew's face had ceased to move, to murmur, and would remain still as a tortoise shell until the end of time. A million years of fixity, of deadness, he could not conceive of that, or of its mathematical equivalent, which was that in a billion billion trillion chances (what *was* the American word for an unstateable number?) there wasn't a fraction of a shadow that any human being would ever come back to life. Each would lie cold and unstirred, at least by reprieve, through successive ages of ice, even until and actually into the incineration of the planet by its sun: just so much fodder, tinder, trash, which was why he insisted to the point of boring even himself on the role of the German nation as a survivor, as a framework in which interminable death did not matter so much. Telling himself he was being obvious, giving in to a morbid impulse, he twisted the lid off the jar to let the twenty or thirty beetles do as they pleased, settle if they wished where his pajamas might have been had he been less distraught. Damn, he said quietly, as a couple of beetles flew sideways away, because I know a lot I'm supposed to know everything; because I manufacture secrets I'm supposed to crack the riddles of the universe; whereas, of course, as this miserable day teaches me, I cannot even manage my own grief, my own indignation, just another man with a reservoir of tears, a few dress uniforms in the closet to make me feel invulnerable, a whole network of spies from Hong Kong to Mecca to persuade me that I am in charge of things. Wars exist to distract us from our own deaths: we inflict on strangers the very thing we fear for ourselves, so that, as millions fall, we can keep on saying *Not I, not we*, it will never be us; but it never works out that way. Here I am, for better or for worse, a man with special task forces at his command, which are nothing but Gestapo butchers on temporary loan to combat what's blithely called activity harmful to the nation, in particular espionage, treason, sabotage, propaganda and subversion, all *in the theater of operations*. What they do is ferret people out, behind the lines, and hand them over to the SS for execution. I go along. My nephew has his brains blown out. I go along. I wash my pajamas, I free my beetles. I behave quite automatically, somehow mustering an adequate front so long as I am clean-shaven, short-haired. I go along, I sweat into my pajamas, I tip new beetles into the jar. Then someone else gets his brains blown out, and I don't feel like telling my field police to stop arresting people. I am a specialist in displaced retaliation but what I do not know, will never know, is why I began, before I had any grievances at all. For what was I getting my own back at the start? For having to eat, to breathe, to work? For having been born at all, like a New Year's gift? As if, before leaving the womb, or being conceived, I should have had a preview tour with the archangel Gabriel showing me around like a salesman: 'What do you think, fetus? Can you take seventy years of this? Or would you like to go back and read for ever?' And, when you have to leave it, when your time's up, you go out squealing with pain, writhing like a frogspawn pancake. Father died of a stroke while taking the waters at Bad Nauheim, cut down at fifty-two, just because he was glued together wrong to begin with, and I have outlived him by six years, I am already six years older than my father ever will be, and I am living the rest of his life for him, like the tenant farmer of his undischarged ambition, yet far too small, too inward, too nervous, too mixed-up, to be living a life of any kind even my own, still less that of the man who was dead-set against my joining the Navy in the first place. His going freed me, that is clear, but my doing well (if well it's been) is broken glass and ordure on his grave.

Checking the sit of his necktie, and shooting upward at the summer sky a look of mutinous bittersweet deviousness that implied he wasn't responsible for anything today, he strode a dozen paces past the apple tree, paused to flick a few beetles off a cluster of irises, and began again, resting his hand on a low whitewashed door and talking into the space above it as if he had found a focus the apple tree, the beetles, could not provide. "It has begun to happen again, I knew it would, the matrix is never still, the dead have started to die again, it is all Hitler's fault, it all began when the message came in 'Grandma's dead' on the afternoon of August 31st, only two weeks ago. It feels like years of stone. Naujocks attacked Gleiwitz radio station and Hellwig's troops pretended to attack the German border, and Trummler's fired back at the so-called invaders. That was it: a charade, the put-up job of put-up jobs, and there we sat in my office, listening to his awful voice telling us there had already been fourteen border incidents and that was fourteen too many, a sleeping giant cannot stay asleep that long. Then Piekenbrock said 'So now we know why we had to get hold of those Polish uniforms!' and I did not even answer him, I who had known all along. What was done was done. And that was only the first day. At nine-fifteen on the morning after, I called the staff into my office and tried to cheer them up, invoking my own thirty-four years in the service of Germany, the relative poorness of private life, and our obligation to be loyal. Since there was no going back, we had to go forward with the mob; no one else was going to hire us, and we knew too much to be allowed to go our own way with a few favorite books and a sleeping bag under our arm. Not only that: when you are familiarly called 'Chef' (and try to ignore the French overtones of the term), you are literally the head man, in charge of everything, and that calls for a certain amount at home, and responsible abroad for entire *Abwehr* units, often far ahead of our invading armies. I had to have hourly accounts of what was happening, which may surprise you—you who never think farther ahead than the next meal, if you think of that—but when you have men out on a limb, supposed to seize this rail junction or that coal mine, you have to be on top of things, especially when your telephone rings all day with demands for such things as a special strike force to wreck the three main railroads from Romania to Poland. All this is hacking at the map, a hard-nosed resolve to change the map in the act of staring at it, melting and reshaping while the silly shiny thing sits there on its table as if it had a right to life, and you tell yourself *There are people there, right under the steel points of the compasses*, but their faces do not shine out, the smell of their breath or their clothes does not leak through the pores in the canvas backing. No: the message of maps is that humanity is unmanageable without some degree of formal symbolism. Only the mountains and rivers go unscathed. You would have to have heard and seen Groscurth, our liaison officer with the Army General Staff, clenching and unclenching his fist while he denounced the *Führer*, calling him 'Emil,' at the same time sweeping his other hand over the map in delighted incredulity: 'Just look at that—the Poles encircled at four points. Let's hope they don't get out.' It was like watching an angel and a panther fused in the same body. Always, when I could, I let the others voice sentiments which, coming from me, might have seemed compulsory just because I'd uttered them; and, if my staff seemed muddled at times, six of one and half a dozen of the other, then it was better for them to seem so to me, than I to seem so to them. Wanting it both ways, we also left open the possibility of a third way; when your mind has chosen one thing over another, you are less disposed to think again, but when two complementary opposites have you impaled, your mind is busier, and a better thing than either might turn up. Britain and France declared war on us, of course, but an invader will always have enemies, even if only on paper. It

Red in Tooth and Claw

was only in Poland itself, however, that anyone got a true, physical sense of how well Rundstedt's armies were doing. You should have been there, Motte, at Army Group South's headquarters, near Zloty Stok, on September 3rd. You would have been well cared for, and, back home again on the fifth, you'd have relished the memory of that whiff of smoke, the map ever changing like molten wax, the thunder of bombers overhead—the constant, overall sense of single-minded mobilization. After that first visit to the rear of the front, it became clear that we would have to foster the malcontent among the Ukrainians, the Caucasians, the Irish, the Welsh, the Scots. Persia, India, and British-run Iraq were ripe for shaking, and it was high time to get good old King Amanullah of Afghanistan back on the throne simply by staging an anti-British revolt among the mountain tribes on the Indian-Afghan border. For the first time in decades, the sun's rays were hitting the field of the cloth of gold, and that field was in my head, where ideas sprouted and flew at all hours of the day and night. Imagine: we could turn the Tibetans against the British and provoke some kind of uproar in Thailand! There was nothing we could not do. At our bidding, all foxes would run backwards, all clouds would come down to sea level and moor themselves there like barrage balloons, all armies would surrender as soon as their politicians declared war, and a deputation of the world's admirals would arrive to pay homage to the smallest admiral known. Of course you, my dear Motte, with your poor grasp of Latin (although your speech is lucid enough when you want it to be), you will not be as attuned as I to the *admirable* component in the word *admiral*, but it is there; an admiral is to be wondered at, marveled at, quite simply to be admired, and to that he's entitled without doing anything further! Is the word perhaps even a relative of the title *Emir*? Can one be an Emir of a Navy? I sometimes think that, no matter how shoddy what a man has to do in the exact performance of his duty, a decent-sounding title helps him through, whereas Mister or even Doctor fortify him precious little. I envision the day, when the dawn has come up like oil poured into a flaming brazier, on which a man such as I can go quite beyond himself, and his being short and having a lisp don't count at all, not in the glorious final sum of his deeds while his golden name surrounds him like a vapor. Fame is the spur, but greatness is the horse."

That seemed to clinch it, verbally at least, and the Admiral fell silent, having received no answer; Motte knew how to listen as well as how to obey, and was accustomed to these long crescendo voluntaries coming, it almost seemed, from above and behind, and usually during an early-morning saunter in the Grünewald. What the Admiral needed was an audience, not an interlocutor, and today more than ever, conscious as he was of death and maiming all around him, he felt like a lightning conductor for trouble. It was not only his nephew: young men called to the colors had about one chance in three of surviving, and losses in Poland had been light overall. Grief had begun, and grief would go on, but grief in this instance came on top of something else, about which the Admiral and his wife rarely spoke even in private. She went her way in cultivated society, fixing on Heydrich's talent as a violinist and playing duets with him while her husband, who had no ear for music, disappeared into the kitchen, where he donned his chef's hat and prepared the meal, most often saddle of wild boar cooked in a crust made from red wine and crumbled black bread, served with a special *Abwehr* salad in which the secret ingredient was a fleck or two of *Abwehr* paper. Caviar and cognac accompanied it. Sometimes, while preparing the meal, arranging his tools and the makings with symmetrical precision on the big scrubbed central table, he heard his wife laughing in the other room, rejoicing in the music made, especially if Heydrich's younger brother Heinz was there to play the cello and the Heydrichs' friend, Ernst Hoffman the chemist, his viola. Lina Heydrich, who spent most of her days pregnant, listened with voluptuous intentness as if what she was hearing weren't music at all but (as the Admiral concluded after watching through the crack in the door while taking a breather) the lovemaking of unicorns and manticores, to which she from time to time added a little whispered "Bravo!" in time with the music. Yet the man out there, that whispering earth-mother's husband, the man playing first violin, was none other than the Blond Beast, a nickname which the SS themselves gave him, an expert fencer in all senses of the word, whom the Admiral regarded as a son. They had been in the Navy together, they despised Raeder its Chief, and they both had the same aloof, lone wolf streak. Each thought the other was spying on him, and took due precautions.

The presence that no one mentioned was that of the Admiral's first daughter, Eva, sixteen years old, a chronic mental defective whom he had been obliged to remove from ordinary schooling and install instead in a Protestant mental home at Bethel, where she gradually went to seed, into an intermittently violent blank that enclosed no one knew what and shut out all well-meaning attempts at endearment, as if tuned in to harsh music from a distant star that made her yelp or coo but never quite gave pleasure other than that of a new pain interrupting an old one. As for Brigitte, the other daughter, just in her teens, she was already a gifted and utterly persistent musician, smart and brash and, as some of her contemporaries thought, a bit batty, but she got on well with her mother, as if what was aggressive in Eva found an echo in her mother's hard-boiled unmotherly ways. So, with one offspring shut away like the best-kept secret of the *Abwehr*, and one violining her way into her mother's leatherbound heart, the Admiral felt somehow wounded, not with a wound that stank, but one that several times each day brought him up short as if he had forgotten something: a spiky ache with accretions of moss around it, a missed heartbeat which made the whole orchestra of life seem wrong, and then he remembered the face that knew him not, the slowly weakening and failing sphincter within the pretty frocks, the stupendous loss of knowledge from week to week—not so much grammar, or anything so complex, but the role of a noun, say, or the increased meaningfulness of words when grouped. There at the core of his being, where he knew no rain fell and no seed swelled, her image remained, like a voodoo doll wrapped in sackcloth and getting bigger all the time while her mind ran down, fuller and fuller of hormones while the electricity in her brain fell below that needed to make a flashlight glow dull red; an erotic, self-pleasuring jelly who could not count, or learn, or smile, or heed, or salute, or wipe, or weep, or even know what death-in-life could mean to those who lived their lives morbidly, as the Admiral did, much to his sprightly wife's displeasure.

"You need some anthroposophy," she'd tell him, furious that he never responded to what she saw as the mutations of spirit during pagan pressure, whether at cocktail parties (where she bloomed like a monthly amaryllis) or during rehearsals of their string quarter. "Like Brigitte."

"Astrology," he'd answer. "When I need a supernatural aid, I'll check my chart. The fault, dear Brutus—no, never mind. I have my lucky stars, I want no mumbo-jumbo from southeast Asia. I get enough of that on my desk each day as it is. Now, if you mean anthropo*phagy*, which is flesh-eating, or cannibalism, we can talk turkey. I see it every day. What do you think of this? All parents of mental defectives should be obliged to kill, cook, and eat their defective offspring? A sort of family clean-up? Like doing the mental dishes?" He could never leave the notion alone once he'd started, and he could stop only when, with all the considerable asperity at her command, she outdid him in a word or two.

"A lisp in the sperm, Wilhelm. What's rotten's *there*." The Admiral had not asked for leave in twenty-six years, and, when returning from a trip he'd had to take without his dogs, he asked his staff, "How're things at home?" he meant the dogs only, whose bites were duller than her bark, whose barks to him were better tunes than Brigitte's on the violin. What a relief it was to get back to bloodletting and atrocity, invasion and sabotage, from the indefatigable spitefulness, which over the years had ridiculed his entire body until he felt like a museum-piece in her presence: something found in the wastes of the Arctic, warmed up and got going again in an electric chair as a species of subnormal Levantine (Heydrich's word for him).

When she became truly vicious, he just said "Mush, mush," as if addressing a dog team. To which she always responded, "Don't think you can put me off like that. Do you cock your leg at every lamppost? If you were a sea urchin, your lack of spine—"

"The dogs, and the bitches, may bark, but the caravan passes on. In your case, Madame, it is the caravan that's barking; but the dogs and I, and even the bitches, will go our way."

"Heydrich says you've been snooping at his desk. You even got Brigitte to look through the papers in his study."

"I did, did I?" he said, "I would no sooner set her to snoop on the Goat than I'd get a banshee to shovel up dogshit." *Goat* was Heydrich's most common nickname, in recognition of his high-pitched, unsteady voice. In these encounters, the Admiral almost always retired hurt, but his capacity for blunt filth usually shut her up and drove her away, into more esthetic company, where she ascended into the conjectural spirals which relayed what Heydrich thought of what the Admiral had supposedly said about him after hearing something that Heydrich himself might have said. Flummery, all of it, but it told her how dangerous both these men could be, but she had always thought Heydrich the deadlier, the more dedicated, the languidly murderous first violin who gave her blood a fillip while making it run cold. She no longer wondered what the Admiral was thinking when he fastened his gaze on the corner of a given room and appeared to recite something with his mouth closed and his clenched fists on his collarbones, in fact rehearsing what he'd tell Motte later on when the house was quiet: "When she looks at a window it becomes a screen like wood. When she goes to the lavatory, what she came to leave behind her moves back into her body and stays put. When she tries to eat she chews her tongue instead as if it swells up at the presence of food. When she drinks, it runs away out of the sides of her mouth. When she sleeps, she sweats until she wakes and then she flails around and sweats even worse. When she tries to speak, a big white fungus climbs her throat and chokes her off. When she blinks, the lashes refuse to part. When she crosses her legs, the muscles freeze. When she stands up she gets vertigo. When she lies down, the bile flows from her stomach into her mouth and sets her coughing. When she wakes, the daylight terrifies her. When someone comes in, to see her, she thinks they are birds or frogs or walnuts.

When I try to think about her, I doubt the power of thought to mend itself. And when she dies, as she will, she will die as numbly as she lives, like the peel on an orange. She lives under a dying star which has never come down to warm her up with its indifferent, red-hot breath. Now, let's play hell with Afghanistan."

He was often that way. Sometimes it came out clipped, succinct, as then, dominated by being cut up into sausages (the image was his own); sometimes it came out like ectoplasm, a long white silky-slithery tongue drooping from the tip of his own, messing his lap and his shoes, and when it came out like that it was tinged with wishful thinking: the wretched images had a rosy side, the child's physical degeneration was a boon. When he was this way he saw her as the only lighthouse keeper to a shipless ocean, praying for a ghost ship to guide toward her, a skeleton crew to keep her company. Erect there, behind the windows of her phantom pharos, she seemed already a saint in colored glass, two-dimensional and frozen, heedless of his frantic beckoning that cried *Break out, there still is time* and, eventually, making him brainsick with incurable yearning, far sicker than he was when craving for the *Dresden* again, upon whose deck his commendable English, his acceptable French, his bit of Russian, served him well, always at the captain's beck and call. In almost every crisis he translated, gradually wearing away the first impression he made. "He is small of stature and very modest and retiring," wrote one of his superior officers, "so one takes a little time to get to know him. But extremely efficient and conscientious—he promises to be a good officer once he acquires a little more confidence and self-assurance." Then he added Spanish to his repertoire and felt as if he had the League of Nations in his mouth, on one occasion dealing so articulately with the Venezuelans that President Juan Vicente Gomez invested him with the Order of Bolivar, Fifth Class, in 1909, his first decoration, which in a sense made him a Venezuelan for life and fanned on what some began to regard as his pan-exoticism. The more foreign a thing was, the better he like it, and in that passion lay the seeds of his uncontrollable appetite for foreign intrigue; yet, later on, there was no way in which he could tap the dark continent of his Eva's inertia: there was no language, no semaphore, no Morse; not even the tawdry old expedient of a warning shot across her brows (a tweak of her ear lobe, a bellow from close up) got her attention, and he began to see her as his albatross, took to reading Samuel Taylor Coleridge's *Rime of the Ancient Mariner* until he had it by heart, actually in that September of '39 daring to repopulate the poem with contemporaries—himself as "Caesar," Hitler as "Emil," Heydrich as the "Blond Beast" (not as the "Goat"), and travestying the wedding scene by fusing the cacophony of the violins with the rending screams of dive bombers. The albatross survived, removed from blame by one of his tenderest and most maudlin turns, in which she became that year's angel who from heaven fell (they fell on the average of one each year), a transit best described in the Admiral's own words, fudged into the poem as one line: "Truth by dreams made true." No wonder, he told himself only half in bluff, I fell for Hitler, who made things come true again, who showed every intention of tidying things up, who showed us a grid and told us that upon it everything would be perfect, in perfect position. When your daughter becomes a basket case, your other daughter turns into a bumptious Tzigane, and your wife is wrapped in cultural barbed wire, upon whose barbs she chews for fun, you settle for your country right or wrong.

On September 9th he headed for Dresden (whose very name was promising) with Lahousen and Piekenbrock, there consulting with Colonel Homlok of the Hungarian General Staff. For a long time the Hungarians had been awaiting their chance to invade Romania, to win back land given up in 1919, and now the Polish invasion seemed just the moment. There in the Hotel Bellevue he made his point, at first seeming pliable and amenable, but then toughening up until he came right out with it, while Homlok was sipping his coffee: "Just hold off, will you? If you don't, the *Führer* will hit the roof, and then we might have yet another invasion to worry about."

"Well," said Homlok, "a nod's as good as a wink, isn't it? Just so long as he keeps us in mind."

"There's a good chap," the Admiral told him. "Our *Führer* isn't the forgetting type." Only a day earlier Heydrich had spelled out Hitler's Polish policy as if discussing a musical improvisation: "We'll spare the common folk, Wilhelm, but the priests, aristos and Jews will have to go. Once we've dealt with Warsaw, I'll arrange with the Army how to squeeze them all out." Even if I am going when I'm coming, the Admiral thought, and coming when I'm going, I'm still in a hell of a mess: I'm in between, and they've already made their move. "Did you know," he asked the Army Chief of Staff on the same day, "that SS officers are going about boasting quite openly about having shot two hundred Poles a day, there having been no trials beforehand? What about divine justice? Doesn't anybody care? You've turned a war into a turkey shoot. Now, where is the dignity in that?"

Pottering about in Krakow, he asked the local Abwehr chief "How many Jews have been shot in this area?" but the man had no idea. "You ought to know," the Admiral told him. "It's part of your job to know," which sounded somehow wrong, as if the Admiral did not so much object to the shootings as to careless keeping of the books. Behind the scenes, however, he began to maneuver against the SS, talking the corps commanders into curbing its worst excesses. He sent out a stern memorandum, deploring unsoldierly activities, and the Army severed itself from Heydrich's most notorious unit, commanded by a von Woyrsch. The Fourteenth Army's Abwehr officer submitted a report claiming that young soldiers were demoralized by having to "test their mettle on defenseless people instead of fighting at the front." It was a small start, a minor interference with the machinery, and typical of the Admiral's way of doing things: he usually lay low and left it to others to speak out. On September 12th, however, he tried his best, actually visiting Hitler's private train, which was parked at Illnau in Upper Silesia—twelve cars and two locomotives—on a branch of the Opole-Kluczbork line. His ostensible purpose was to discuss the plight of Ukrainian dissidents who were moving westwards.

"It's no good," Lahousen told him. "They're only running into an area—Galacia—which the bastard's going to hand over to the Russians anyway. They might as well stay put. Imagine, leaving one place only to find it's the place you started from. It changed overnight. I've entered the whole thing in your diary. Except for my own blasphemies. He wants the Ukrainians to rise up in revolt and accept some degree of

German leadership. But it won't happen. You may think that the Ukrainian staff and its units will become part of the Fourteenth Army, but that's only window-dressing. *I* think he's going to strike a bargain with the Russkies and hand the West Ukraine over to them tied in a pretty ribbon."

"Surely not," the Admiral whispered, fondling his Iron Cross as if it might melt right there on his chest, "Mel'nyk's been told to keep himself available to talk with me."

26

"If I were you, sir," Lahousen told him, always willing to steer and disabuse his cautious chief, "I'd think up something else to talk about. Ribbentrop and Keitel keep on saying opposite things, a sure sign the *he's* already made up his mind another way. It's just a bloody smokescreen. Admiral?"

Flicking his head sideways, as he often did when willing himself to come out of a trance, the Admiral nodded and, with a look of superhuman forlornness, said "Then I will speak to him about the atrocities. All those shootings."

But he did not see Hitler at all and was able to register his protest only with the obsequious Keitel. "I hear the nobility and the clergy are to be exterminated. They will blame the Army for this. I mean the world will judge us. It will happen right under the Army's nose. You're Army and you ought to care."

"It's all settled," Keitel told him with a bored shrug.

"The *Führer* has already informed the Army commander in chief that, if they want no part of it, then they can hardly object if SS and Gestapo put in an appearance alongside them to do their dirty work for them. What could be more reasonable than that? The Army's lucky it can back away."

"But," the Admiral persisted, although becoming less precise, "there's a moral issue involved in this, which has nothing to do with who does what for whom, or alongside whom. What about the morality of the thing? Am I alone in caring?" His face was flushed, but he felt balsa-frail as he stood before the tall, burly Keitel, who not only looked high above the Admiral's head but averted his gaze to look even higher, into the ceiling of the railroad car itself. "Then you must ask the *Führer*," Keitel said. "About that I have no authority." Denied access to Hitler, the Admiral left, telling Lahousen "Get it down, get it all down in the diary. That was an important conversation. One day it will count a lot."

"What was the fellow driving at?" Keitel looked incredulously at von Vormann, the *Wehrmacht* liaison officer. "Could you make head or tail of it?"

"I've no idea. I think he came to say something, but he's too clever to come right out with it. He's one of those, *Herr Feldmarschall*, who get what they want deviously, which means they often get something they never bargained for, but pretend it was what they wanted all along." All the way home, the Admiral argued with himself, telling Lahousen to add this or that remembered phrase to the account in the diary, the more he recalled what had been said, feeling increasingly helpless. What he had with Keitel was not a conversation at all; the man simply spouted the official line and only pretended to listen. The reasons for doing things never came up and when they did Keitel, or someone like him, set them aside as so much academic taradiddle.

"Was I forceful enough?" The Admiral had often asked this.

"Of course, Admiral. But some things just cannot be forced. Either there's tacit understanding about certain things, or there isn't. You can't bludgeon an ox into sensitivity. To anyone of conscience, a quiet recital of the facts is enough. If something is scandalous, it can been seen to be so; it doesn't have to be blown through a tuba."

"Then I was too diffident. Is that what you're saying?"

"What I'm saying, if you'll forgive me, is that the conversation just could not begin. It was in the nature of things that it couldn't. There is no need for self-rebuke."

"I'll never have the opportunity again, Lahousen."

"Even if you did, sir, it would have destroyed itself before you even arrived."

"Emil did not even deign to see me."

"Same difference. You'd just be angrier. He lets the toadies talk for him. What we do is useful, but he doesn't want to meet us face to face. You don't interview a cobra."

"Is that what we are? Cobras?"

Lahousen grinned, glad his chief had picked up the image; now he could deflect the Admiral with colorful tangents, and the whole business could be over. The Admiral would end up grateful he hadn't seen Hitler, relieved he'd not pounded away at Keitel in the presence of the wily, brittle von Vormann. Yet, while Lahousen, ever the expert poulticer of psychic boils and the defuser of explosive moral anguish, plied him with comfort, the Admiral brooded on, telling himself that Hitler in his train in that godforsaken siding was like a reptilian infestation come from another planet, curled up invisibly awaiting his chance to strike, to strangle, to engorge. The Admiral yearned to be home, riding in the Grünewald, preferably with a touch of fog in the morning air, or on the lawn, brushing an ant off his suit and wondering if it, in its turn, found gray serge as alien as he himself found the likes of Keitel. At some point in every human transaction, reason failed: that was it, and the rest was emergency improvisation, *sauve qui peut*, and no embarrassing questions asked. It was one thing to sit with Lahousen over a mug of Turkish coffee, squinting at the map after coming the morning reports from *Abwehr* outstations, and then deliberately disrupting the status quo with half a dozen strategically placed phone calls, but it was quite another to have spent hours with the bully boys on their private train, like some gentle-mannered fanatic reciting the New Testament to the proprietors of the Old. The image of the snake came back, then went, and the Admiral thought of Hitler and his crew only in terms of the train, which slunk through the countryside unseen or at least unidentified, pausing at a series of little-known halts in the back of beyond, lurking and snooping and fanning out radio signals to all points of the compass, and all the time sheathed in steel while the madman smashed his fist through the broken jigsaw puzzle of Europe, behaving like God with the universe—with it, at least according to rumor, but *of* it not in the least.

27

Something in the Admiral snapped: one of the minor rubber bands that held compassion close to instinct, or self-preservation close to logic, and there ran through his mind, as so often, a piece of something he'd heard recited, or read in one of the journals in his desk back at the Fox's Earth; he hadn't imagined it (he told himself he wasn't that good with prose, for all his knack with languages), and he certainly hadn't read it in a book. It was something irretrievably serene, something lavish in which his early picturesque naval career came together with something to which he looked and leaned forward: a vision of the South Atlantic, or the Azores, or Punta Arenas, or even the islands of Más a Tierra, tinged with the Aegean. He wore his cadet's uniform, dark blue with gold buttons, and inhaled a scene that was both epitome and something unique, making his heart go fast and his mind scud about like a dinghy in a high sea. "Steel-blue and light," he remembered, "ruffled or rippled or rumpled by a gentle, hardly discernible or perceptible crosswind, the waves of the Aegean or the Adriatic—or was it the Tyrrhenian?—poured or streamed up against the imperial squadron as it stood at anchor or veered/steered/aimed toward the harbor." But which harbor was it? How could he be so moved without knowing the exact location? Or the exact text? Like someone longing vaguely for the flower sellers in the Berlin streets, or for an evening listening to Brahms violin sonatas with the sound of the cicadas drifting in from the garden as a dark busyness in Nature, he felt an emotion he had heard about from others, but his and theirs never quite matched; his was poignant, theirs was fun. He began again to remember the seascape, changing it now to "Ice-blue and frail, troubled by a mild crosswind, the waves..." but then gave up; some day, when he was not trying to think of it, the exact wording would come to him, not here, on the lawn, on this awful Sunday of the Russian invasion, with his dead nephew's face afflicting him with the regularity, the callousness, of a metronome. Here I am, he said, back from yet another trip to Poland, as much at home here as if I had never gone away, and what I felt is locked away in the diary, in the safe; perhaps, if I didn't give so much to Lahousen to put down, I'd feel things more. No: I feel them all right, but in the wrong idiom—not that of pain, but of dawdling anesthesia. Something in me keeps me from feeling things too keenly, and maybe being fifty-six is the key to that. You pay internal homage to your pain, but you don't exactly go through it as you used to. It's no use asking Heydrich, who doesn't feel such things at all; Lahousen's too young, or he behaves it, and Piekenbrock, the bantering ironic Rhinelander, he's ten years younger than I. What would he say? What is the predictable decline, I'd ask, in the intensity of emotions felt after fifty? All Pieki will do is laugh and say something in algebra. Once I asked him why he transferred from the 11th Hussars to General Staff work, and he said "A bit liverish, sir."

"Do you drink?"

"Only at undefiled springs."

"And where are *they*?" I said, doing my best to sound blasé.

"Ultraphotography," he said, meaning the technique by means of which we could photograph enemy installations through fog or camouflage nets. "And Bruckner's Fifth."

"Ah," I told him, "you are in retreat from the philistines of the lance and saber, the beerswillers, the hearty songsters."

"Not quite, Admiral: I need a job at which I can try to be clever, I want to be ingenious. When your heart dotes on complexity, you don't just want to charge about; you want to wind things up, then watch them go."

Yes, the Admiral decided as the telephone rang once again, Pieki has a sense of toys, he has a feeling for clockwork. Out came the Algerian butler, Mohammed, who heard fluently in German but never spoke it in company; the Admiral had recruited him in Bordeaux for a reputed twenty marks (according to Heydrich), but Mohammed had cost much more than that.

"A Captain von Zollerndorff," he said with his Berliner accent, "calling from Army Group South, to which he is temporarily attached. He says it's urgent. The Czimanska mare has foaled."

The Admiral blinked. He knew no Zollerndorff, a name which sounded wrong to begin with. But the other name.... He remembered something about it; his conscience pushed it into the front of his seesawing, punch drunk mind, and he saw Major Czimanski clearly, a paladin of sorts, witty and volatile and in love with his work, and on his arm that ebullient slightly dotty wife. Then he caught mental sight of a small boy, bombarding the three bronze monkeys at the Fox's Earth with a toy artillery gun, and asking for a dive bomber to finish them off with.

"If," the Admiral had told him recklessly, with more than a hint of boyhoods he had known, "you don't leave those monkeys alone, they'll come after you in the night."

"*Et tu*, Uncle Wilhelm." Had the boy been *that* frisky? Of course: the little foxcub had quoted Horace at him, in the same breath venturing to translate, as if in the presence of a philistine, such as Pieki who had fled from the Hussars. "*Aere perennius*—more lasting than bronze, Uncle Wilhelm!"

Then the Admiral, entering into the spirit of the game, had pretended to call the Luftwaffe for a Stuka dive bomber, which never arrived, so they had both, with the door closed and the two dachshunds leaping about in consternation, mimed the bombing attack with their hands, their thumbs out-tilted for wings, and nosing their palms at the monkeys while making buzz noises through whistle-pursed lips. And when Grimmeiss, Pieki's insipid predecessor had come in because the Admiral had left the phone off the hook when he raised his finger after the fake call to the Luftwaffe, the Admiral with hare-brained abandon had shot him between the eyes with the tin artillery gun: a thin metal pellet the size of half a matchstick.

"Who the hell is Zollerndorff?" the Admiral asked Mohammed. "Is he still on the line? A Zollerndorff I must sample, I really must. Zollerndorffs do not grow on trees, Mohammed. A captain, you say? He's not one of *ours*. It's not long since I myself was at Army Group South, and then it was at Zloty Stok or somewhere like that. I wonder where it is now. And now this business of the Czimanska mare." On he fussed, conjecturally relishing what awaited him on the line connecting him to Poland, almost as if he preferred the prospect of the call to the fact of it. There had been days when he flung his overcoat over the telephone, both at home and in his office, moaning "Why don't they just use the teleprinter and encode it in the usual way. I detest being importuned by a mere machine; I like to think an answer through—though there is one man, the *Führer*, who never once has telephoned me, either to ask or to tell. You can say that much for him, at least." Finally, after letting Zollerndorff dangle for a couple of minutes at least, he went inside, trailed by the enigmatic butler. Once again the Admiral had flirted with the chance of the connection's being broken while he dawdled, thus inviting a whole series of voluptuous guesses as to what the call had been about: meat for a full day's wondering, which tuned up his imagination and, quite often, brought him ideas he otherwise might never have had. Anticipation was honey to the Admiral; and, if this Sunday's facts were anything to go by, he preferred it and never wanted to be told anything again.

"Yes, this is Caesar," he whispered into the mouthpiece. "Whatever you wished to say could have waited for me on my desk until tomorrow morning, couldn't it?" The telephone, he gathered, made his lisp more blatant, so he was never at ease and actually went out of his way to avoid using words that he knew gave him trouble. And this made for longueurs in his talk; he had already said "Caesar," ironic codename for a man who lisped, but he had not chosen it himself and he found the high sound of it outweighed the trouble he had in saying it.

"Where is the Army Group now?" he asked faintly, and Zollerndorff told him. "Most impressive," the Admiral said, thinking *Yes, the move has cost one of us a nephew.*

"A mare and *two* foals," he mused into the phone, echoing what Zollerndorff told him. "You are using an official line for what is essentially private business. You must be mighty sure of yourself, Captain." Zollerndorff allowed that such a thing had been said of him on more than one occasion, then added, "I have the generals' confidence, of course. As far as *I* am concerned, this is an Army matter only."

"You certainly don't waste much time on protocol, Captain. You have heard of the *Abwehr*, of course? I happen to be its titular chief. So the matter, as you call it, has something to do with the *Abwehr* as well."

"Or with yourself, Admiral. Hence my call."

Damn the man, the Admiral thought: he is pushing me, he is presuming to remind me of something. His awareness of something is more important to him than my discretion. For all I know, he could be another of those benighted crypto-communists who mask their leanings behind a *von*. "Zollerndorff," he said, puzzling audibly. "It has a Swedish tinge to me. Or even Yiddish. Who exactly are you?"

What he heard sounded like a military parody, full of words like *liaison, seconded, acting, attached, adjutant* and *posting*. Was this Zollerndorff all of these? "Captain *Count* von Zollerndorff," the drawling, bumptious voice in Pulawy said. "Detached from Wielun to serve as temporary adjutant for posting and protocol: staff work, of course."

"Is there," the Admiral asked for lack of something to say, "an umlaut on the first syllable of your name—Count?" *Those damned bluebloods are looking after their own again,* he thought: *Find a big fireplace, some satin sheets and a four-poster bed with a servant's room down the hall, and your aristos will begin to gather like warlocks. They run the war for their own comfort. And our nephews are dying while these finely-spoken gentlemen play chess over cognac and big cigars.* "Yes," he grunted in his muted way, "if there is an umlaut you would pronounce it Zö—, would you not? We are sticklers for detail here, Captain."

"A cover name, actually," the telephone said. "No umlaut. But who cares? By drawing attention to itself, it removes attention from me, the bearer, so to speak. That's the theory, at least. Who the hell dreamed it up, I have no idea."

"Then, umlaut or no," the Admiral said, getting tasty as Seppel and Sabine perked up and began to yap, sensing their master's agitation, "who *are* you?" Zollerndorff told him, but the name meant nothing to the Admiral, who decided to call him by his cover name anyway, and began to evolve the kind of complex summary utterance he was famous for. "Captain," he said in the tone of someone perorating as obliquely as possible, "the case of the mare is not unfamiliar to experts here, the word *here* denoting both the formal establishment and its informal satellites. Not that there was, as I recall, any exchange of vows—nothing so ceremonious. But a series of interacting words, umlautless if you will, the upshot being one of those casual agreements easily paraphrased in such everyday parlance as *I'll see you when I see you.* Or *sooner or later.* Mañana would not be irrelevant either, provided you seize all its implications. A Latin language, as I'm sure you know."

"Romance," said the voice. "As in *sub rosa.*" The Admiral winced: one of his own cover names was Reed Rosas.

"What," he went on, "of the sire? There is always a sire, is there not?"

"I too love horses," Zollerndorff said with a glitter in his tone. "Dressage, not racing. The sire is off in the happy hunting grounds, I regret to say. With its ancestors. The mare is quite desolate as a result."

"The foal, then?" The Admiral did not like the sound of this, although perhaps it obliterated the bargain altogether.

"The foal is not in evidence. The foals are elsewhere, away in a manger." I could use this man, the Admiral thought: he picks up on obliquity and converts it into creative idiom. He's wasted in the Army, aristo or no.

"Next week, he told Zollerndorff, "I'll be going to Lvov by way of Krakow," mentally rehearsing the map and the chronology of the invasion: Pulawy taken on the fifteenth, after local bombing on the tenth, and this is the seventeenth, so things must be getting back to normal, if any picture with the Russkies in it can be said to be normal. I am so much in demand by those who wish to be elsewhere than their native land, their native continent.

"Tuesday or Wednesday," he said. "How did you know about the sire? Put down, you say?"

"The remains are here, Admiral. *Sir?*" The line seemed dead, but there was the Admiral talking again, in a slow calculated murmur—"*Pu*—the name is hard to say," but thinking I have been to Hitler's train, I have seen Poland on fire and have gone back to that landscape of horror as if enslaved by a drug, I have lost my nephew and the Russians are on the move, I have talked to Heydrich and seen the butcher-shop mentality he hides behind that squeaky voice and that disarming cankered smile, and I still have not asked Pieki about a man's emotions after fifty. I have no more lust in me, Pieki, is that normal? Dogs and horses are my one desire, yet I have power over the back doors of an entire continent, I can infiltrate Hong Kong, and Tokyo, and the wilds of Kalamazoo. If I were already an also-ran, I'd be out to stud, but here I am in the saddle with a thousand things to do. Lives, like music, move into different registers without warning. There are harmonic improvisations within the soul. "Are you musical?" he said.

"Cello, a bit," Zollerndorff replied, wondering why the man sounded so laconic while rounding off the conversation. "I would gladly surrender a month's pay to hear the Archduke Trio once again." There was a silence full of static and clonking sounds while the Admiral inhaled.

28

"I am not musical at all," he said. "Some regard that as an unforgiveable failing, but I do not. Small ears, which I happen to admire, hear less music than big ones do. Is that right, Count? I realize that several honored proverbs cover the situation, depending on one's need to feel vindicated."

"*Chacun à—*" Zollerndorff suddenly felt light-headed.

"*—son gout.* You quote on cue, Captain. Some of my associates allow me into their private train and then deny me access. As if God Almighty had snubbed one of His leading mystics. Some of my associates," he went on, as if the preceding formulation had taken a wrong turn, over the edge of some headland and down, down, "do not quote at all, which means they have utterly no ability to be allusive. They are so direct they do not suggest. No mystery at all. I have always thought," he continued even as the war went begging for lack of at least one radio-telephonic line, "that, if the universe is mysterious, as it is, then we are entitled to our little models of it in everyday procedure. What do you think of that? Before we end this little exchange."

"God has never snubbed a mystic yet, Admiral."

"There are gods and gods," the Admiral snapped. "Some are of tin, and some have the holiest creamiest refulgence to them, and are not to be trifled with." That half-submerged dessert image made him wince, so he abruptly said, again, "Tuesday or Wednesday. I promise nothing but a—tour of inspection. Understood?"

"Inspection guaranteed," said Zollerndorff. "The stables will be cleaned in your honor."

"Augean, no doubt." His voice felt sapped and frail.

"Herculean," Zollerndorff answered, then took the initiative and said goodbye, which the Admiral echoed in a whisper, wanting to say over the phone that bit of prose which haunted him and which he never could get right. If only he said it down the wire, it might come true. "Steel-blue and feather-light," he crooned, almost to himself while Zollerndorff awaited dismissal, "frayed by a gentle, hardly felt offshore wind, the waves of the—sorry, Zollerndorff, I can never remember the named of the damned sea! Tuesday, then, or the day after, as far from the piano as possible. Until then. I shall demand a full report." There was Mohammed at his side with a small tray on which stood a cup and saucer of black coffee, his pills, and a small box of throat pastilles. He sipped, he swallowed, he sucked, then he drank the coffee in a gulp, but his mind was on the days when he had played soldiers on the floor of his office with the small shy, but really quite rude and unutterably clever Polish boy who, surely not as a sop to another Caesar, planned dive bombing sorties in Latin and exclaimed in Latin too at the results while the dogs barked and Grimmeiss tried to barge in through the locked door because the phone, the phone, was out of order, and the *Führer* simply had to speak to the Admiral at once. It never happened, but it would. I am tired of being Mahomet, the Admiral decided; but soon the mountain, that puy of shit, will come to me, and then, and then, and then, and *then.*

As for Zollerndorff, walking through the lofty cavern of the main hall to check on Wanda Czimanska, he thought *Go bid the soldiers shoot,* as in *Hamlet.* The old bugger's got *me* quoting things now. If quoting he was. It did sound like something by—somebody else. I have never heard anyone so close to having a nervous breakdown, not on the telephone. Living so close to the *Führer* must be a strain. Thank God I'm out here among the soldiers—well, if not the shooting soldiers, the ones who do the deciding. Maybe he'll come, maybe not. It will be like meeting Marco Polo. This chap likes to flaunt his languages a bit. He likes to chat. It's company for him. He'd be happy in a zoo, reminiscing with all the answerless animals, or in a wood, opening his mind to the trees in weird little contorted sentences. I can see him now, on the other end of the line, wondering whether to get involved or not, shuffling imaginary situations like a madman at a casino, and working out all the contingencies that will follow if he does D or E instead of A, B, C. He spends his life in a dither of backhanded interference. Will he refuse once he gets here? Will he even remember? Will he, maybe as a cover, go looking at the stables on the estate? Will he take them away, the live woman and the dead major, in a horsebox? Do invading armies run to horseboxes, as if the whole thing were a day at the races? And then her children. You can't evacuate *her* without *them.* They say he'll go anywhere there isn't music, and I believe it. But who am I, a lowly captain, to debate with the Admiral? With *any* Admiral? Dammit, I am not even Zollerndorff, and he smelled it, he smelled the ersatz quality in the name; but he must be used to *noms de guerre* by now, answering to half a dozen different names himself, like an international gangster, who's probably had killed, bumped neatly off, more than he's actually saved, smuggled out, given jobs in his own organization. Would I accept if he took me on himself? My English alone would qualify me. No, the *Abwehr* outstation in London or Dublin isn't for me; I'd rather be home in Bamberg, with all my dear ones round me, children and wife and mother and uncle, my twin brothers. The trouble with too widely known an alias, like Zollerndorff, is that when you really need an alias you have to get a new one. When did that nickname become an alias? Or when did that alias become my nickname? The amazing thing is that he seemed to recognize the Czimanski name, masculine form, whose feminine takes an *a*. He almost collided with a general who burst out of the library, slamming its ironbound oaken door behind him.

"Ah, good! Just the man I was looking for! Bad news."

Zollerndorff just looked at him, counting one, two, three, and a half lines in the crow's foot that fanned backward from the corner of his eye, the ample nose more curves than lines, the oh so accurately trimmed moustache above the beet-dark sensual mouth. This ruddy extrovert had a dashing face.

"The SS insist on moving in with us. Something Heydrich's dreamed up in the cesspool head of his. Lions do not lie down with cobras, do they now?"

"The general knows my views. I thought it had been agreed that they would get on with— whatever they'd persuaded themselves they should get on with." He loathed the SS's pompous names for different ranks, the bogeyman black of their tunics, the callow mystique that pretended to elitism when all they were was a clique of toughs, misfits and psychopaths; overeducated in inconsequential subjects at inferior schools (those of them who'd been educated at all), and pumped full of clichés, porridge, and racist vinegar until they burst. "At this rate, they'll soon be running us, and not just sitting alongside us, tapping their heels like divas."

"All files to be locked up tight, and signed for. No lists to be handed over to them." The General seemed out of breath.

"The only lists we have are theirs." He pointed at them as if they were outside, beyond the palace walls. "That's their kind of thing. Sneakwork, nightwork, baiting traps, asking the children what their parents say. Does the General envision trouble?"

"The General envisions some uncomfortable meals, with them at one end of the table, and us at the other. Surely we can find them separate quarters in a place as big as this."

"The grooms' quarters? The stables, perhaps. Or they might be quietly installed in the Vistula, overnight, with black gags and death's-head handcuffs, just to maintain the status quo. By the way, if the General is wondering, I spoke to Berlin about our lady visitor and her late-lamented husband. She wasn't lying. The Admiral seemed to recognize the name. He will be here Tuesday or Wednesday. She'll be off our hands in no time."

"And so will he, thank God. You spoke with him today? With *the Admiral?*" The General had never understood the Admiral at all.

"One of my vices," Zollerndorff said in a confessing tone that also bragged a bit, "is that

I like the personal touch. Face to face, ear to ear. Memos wear me down. I yawn, I die." He yawned and pretended to die: another of his winning ways, especially when he died upright on slowly trotting feet, his face averted in a fit of clamped distemper, his eyes frozen at the bulge, his mouth the deathbed of the yawn.

"They'll tap the phones," the General said, laughing in spite of himself. "They no doubt have been listening in for days."

"Let them listen," Zollerndorff chortled, bumptiously intimate. "We'll talk Latin. Greek. Some of us, like the General and I, will even talk Swabian dialect if we must, with a Swabian brogue to thicken the brew! All they know is jargon and gutterjabber. I have always thought that one of the advantages of being educated is that the rest of the world hasn't the faintest bloody idea what we're talking about. And one of our problems is always trying to *mean* what we've just caught ourselves saying just for the hell of it."

The General breathed harshly out, as if to strain the exhalation through his cropped mustache, behind which his whole face seemed to aim itself when he spoke; the nosetip felt ahead, but it was the sprig of bristle that led the charge. "Speak for yourself, Zoll. Some of us went into the military as boys. Some of us are not *von*s either. You exaggerate: we're not that creamy, you know, not that top-drawer, whatever we think we are when we're in full dress uniform. We're horsemen and gardeners at heart, hunters of elk and boat. Which of us last read a book I wouldn't like to say. That's why we have the likes of you around—to give us a little tone, a little class." He laughed within his chest.

"The General makes of me a royal fool? A coxcomb?

"*Fool?* No, I meant it. You also happen to be a gifted organizer. Please close the files to the SS. It would help if you ran off the orders now. Dictate something suitably woolly, in German if you please, and circulate it to all personnel of field rank and above. Me too, of course."

Yes, Zollerndorff was thinking as the General turned his big amiable walnut of a face away and plunged back into the smoke-laden air of the library, they must listen in to the Admiral all the time, but maybe not when you phone him at home. No wonder he wraps everything up, no wonder he nearly breathes in code. I bet he shits in cipher. Hitler hates horses, he hates the horse-owning, horse-riding classes; but I doubt if he's primed the SS to list all matters involving horses for intensified interrogation. Not yet, anyway, though it's bound to come. All they're likely to do with the Admiral is get him pensioned off, safely put away in a field full of dogs and horses. And, as for such altruists as me, scuttling between family estate and stolen Polish palace,

I think they'd leave me to tie myself in knots with the red rope of protocol. All they want is to take over, shunt the Army aside; but they might not, if they knew about it, take too kindly to the export of a Polish lady, *en famille*, and with her dead beside her. It would look too—too much like collaboration, too much like collusion between neighboring social classes.

Then, in his feckless wholly retentive way, he remembered Wanda Czimanska's story about the SS officer whose *nick*name was—Haarkünstler, the SS driver she airily said she'd killed, the SS motorcycle she'd arrived on, thickening her personal myth like a cloak to wrap around her, like some exotic variant of Saint Elizabeth, Landgravine of Thuringia, offering a basket full of roses to the poor, eventually renouncing her titles to go and live in the forest in a hut of wood and mud, to which lepers came and were welcomed. No, he corrected himself, get your medieval dreams right: she gave up her wealth, but not her rank; her husband had died of the plague, and it was her children that she renounced. After she died singing exquisitely through tight-closed lips, oil began to flow from her body, and the Teutonic knights collected it for distribution to churches and monasteries. Frau Czimanska was quite different; something aggressive, or combative at least, gave her an edge, so maybe she had told the truth about killing an SS driver and being degraded by this Haarkünstler. Whatever the truth about her was, he could not shake off the feeling that, in dealing with her, he had involved himself in a bewitching, fragile pattern, no not myth exactly, nor anything so bald as conspiracy, but a weave of life-in-death, perhaps merely an illustration he'd seen and forgotten of a wife and her husband's corpse on the verge of entering into heraldry, becoming stylized figures under the dome of an armorial tent cluttered with lances and ermine linings, helmets with visors raised and almost illegible mottoes in gold on blue. Or Frau Czimanska had just stepped out of such a design, her face still theatrically daubed with lily dust, her features and her voice still full of what she had been through in the course of a day not yet over. The woman they had to save from the SS, or at least enable to find her children, spoke and behaved as if she had suddenly happened upon an abstract sense of herself—not that she suddenly felt symbolic or allegorical (it wasn't that neat, he knew). It was simply that, on a single day, forces had come to bear upon her which she had never dreamed about: she had been stretched, she had been tested, she had been tickled by fatality and coincidence until she could stand no more, and perhaps Pulawy Palace itself had made her feel so strange, as it had him, when he arrived, finding himself abruptly transferred from the smoking rubble of Poland to a dimension of antique rigmarole, where lilies thrived amid the damp, tended by night-stalkers from another century. My God, he thought, in this place a pear falling off a plate would seem resonant, far more than itself: a cannonball of wool, plopping onto an ermine field.

And then he saw it. He saw what lay behind the things he saw. He remembered a phrase from his optional studies at the military school, where things had reached him best, and stayed with him longest, when he was half asleep, attuning his mind to the drone of a bee outside the leaded window while one of those superannuated officers for whom "a job had been found" droned away about heraldry, in particular about *a complete achievement*, which meant when all the elements of a design had come together in the right places: the imperial banner on top of all, the king's crown beneath it, then the armorial banner, and the dome of the tent with, underneath it, the king's own helmet flanked by (usually) two wild men, their heads crowned and their loins girded with oak leaves, and their beards blown sideways by contrary winds, one to the left, the other to the right. What was he remembering? Something sexual which overlapped the red-hot blotch which was the helmet's front while the visor was up? All he knew, for now, was that the phrase *a complete achievement* plucked at him, much more than a mere two-dimensional design, as if it summed up, at least in Pulawy Palace pronounced *Puwavy*, the whole of life, with fact and rumor and yearning and thought all distributed correctly throughout the main design. *Madame*, not *Frau*, Czimanska and her dead husband replaced the two wild men holding up the dome of the armorial tent like two girded Father Times nestling in the flaps like labia majora tugged wide apart in some Hindu setpiece for incitement. She and her man were real, but they easily became two-dimensional when he thought about them, and he was nervously grateful that life, from time to time, instead of mixing things into a bloody mess, gave off hints of order which made him want to move with inordinate slowness like a doped ant crawling over a military badge whose motto said "Rather die than be soiled." *Potius mori quam foedari.* It was easier to say than to do, if you could say Latin at all without feeling you had a mouthful of chessmen.

As he paused at the door beyond which she lay sleeping still, no doubt, he told himself to calm down, to be more military, to remember his job. Give nothing away. But what did he know? Ask the right questions again and again. But she had told her story already, including the lies she intended to stick to, and did these even matter? Practically speaking, he was supposed to keep her out of the way for the time being. And, in other matters, to dictate that memorandum about locking up all files, all signals, all lists. They know it all already, he told himself; the horse has gone.

"The Admiral?" she said husky from sleep. "Not like the other officers at all. Gentle-voiced and not always straining to stand erect. He even wobbled a bit. He seemed to shiver a bit even when it was insufferably hot indoors. Did you actually speak to him?"

Zollerndorff made a careful selection from what he and the Admiral had said. "The day after tomorrow. He will probably come by train, if the tracks are still intact. Do you realize, Madame, that the Russians are now invading from the east? And the Ukrainians are running westward in front of them, from them? No, how silly of me. How could you know anything of the sort!"

"Blazing blue eyes," she said, still intent on the Admiral, "in a thickish face. He seemed to talk in what people used to call double Dutch. No one could understand him. He'd say something utterly banal or obvious, and, while they gaped at him in amazement, then said something they couldn't even begin to fathom. He'd say what they wanted to hear, or what they knew already, and then add something so private it didn't get through. And he didn't mean it too, either."

"I know," Zollerndorff said. "You have to keep your wits about you. He goes to Moscow to reach Wannsee!"

"There were always Luftwaffe generals too," she said, back in pre-war Berlin, "at the military attaché's house."

"They say," Zollerndorff mused, "he actually had dealings with Mata Hari. They say he used to fly to Spain and back in stripped-down Junkers 52s, perched among the stores and the reserve aviation fuel. Always by night. He came and went all the time, high over France, and he always cheered up when he'd crossed the Pyrenees." *I make him magical*, he thought, *just by talking him up*.

"You know more than I do," she told him. "They used to call him something behind his back. *Peeker*. That was it. Because, I suppose, he peeked a lot. I don't think he peeked at all. He often looked away as if thinking about something quite private."

"Tuesday, Madame. We'll see. They do say, they also say, that on September 1st, after German convicts dressed as Poles pretended to invade Germany—a miserable bit of history if I may say so—he was in the Tiergarten with his horse, and he saw the *Spanish* military attaché driving past, and waved at him to stop. The ensuing conversation went something like this. Spanish Attaché: 'Of course, Germany has calculated this whole enterprise down to the last detail, all the way to the final victory?' The Admiral: 'Calculated nothing at all.' That's what he said. I do believe, Madame, you have a discerning friend."

"Who loves children. That's important."

"Loves Germany too," Zollerndorff said, "hard as that may be for you to accept. Once upon a time, you had a soft spot for us yourself, I wouldn't doubt."

"Don't doubt," she told him in Polish, then in German, "it's a luxury you can't afford." Then, in a different, girlish tone: "Just imagine! Coffee makes me sleep!"

"Don't doubt, but just imagine!" He spoke it like an old friend, chaffing her after long years apart, and she felt his tone was just a bit too forward, too smart, and she slammed him with one of her mouth-puckering frowns, from which he mentally backed away only to stumble over what had been nagging at him for some time. Yes, he reassured himself, she is right out of the medieval tournaments, when they sat the helmets of the participants on the floor and the assembled ladies paraded past them, four times each, and if the wearer had ever said anything offensive about them, or any of them, the offended woman tapped his helmet with a stick, and then the trouble began. Well, she has just tapped my helmet with her stick. She might just as well have thrown a beer bottle at it. But is it me or Haarkünstler of the SS? *My* offense is minor, but his sounded pretty bad. And, after all, she has only just been widowed today. What is it that prompts me to joke? Because she doesn't weep, being wept-out? Or in total shock, and conducting herself, automatically, by the standards of embassy protocol? He once again tried to interrogate her, fending off in vain the thought that the Admiral would have her story in three minutes just by pretending to talk about the Pyrenees, Mata Hari, or the abominations of music.

29

Naked from the waist up, however, on a small mattress that overlapped a table, the Admiral was having his back and neck kneaded by Rust, his blind masseur, who spoke rather than sang folksongs while about his work, even while the Admiral, with moans suggestive of long-delayed climax, reviewed the events of his day, burying them in his haphazard mental flow and, in a lunge of heartsick resentment, wondering why he of all God's men should have to play the part of "Logothetes: one who places words," which had been the title of Piero della Vigna, the greatest Latin stylist of the Middle Ages and the mouthpiece of Frederick the Great. In the end, however, not even his intentionally obscure Latin saved him; blinded, and almost hacked to pieces, Logothetes entered prison at San Miniato, asking the guards who led him to his dungeon, 'Is there anything between me and the wall?' Told there was not, he flung himself with such violence against the prison wall that he split his skull, only to end his days permanently in Dante's Wood of Suicides. Is it true with me, the Admiral wondered, as with him, that a blunder merited extinction rather than mere banishment or rebuke? If anything, Frederick the Great had been less whimsical than the megalomaniac lance corporal who ran Germany and, for all his excesses, dispensed a greater charity.

"Deeper," the Admiral told Rust. "Feel for where the muscle joins the bone, then tempt the blood to flow again. Yes, there, either side of the spine. Where the neck meets the shoulder." Rust leaned on his thumbs and the Admiral felt a sudden hot flow as if something had indeed been released, whether blood or electricity he didn't know, but he fancied it sped his mind up, made him see things more clearly, able to sift the trivial from the weighty. Perhaps that was why the Japanese admiral, Yamamoto, had always, long before he attained exalted rank, developed the habit of standing on his head on the deck of whatever ship he commanded, usually near an open hatch: to get the blood flowing where it ought to flow. But the Admiral knew he himself was no physical paragon; if he stood on his head, other than mentally, he'd look like an upside-down mushroom, with his jowls touching the ground, or the deck, and the near-punitive shortness of his legs made blatant. He'd look even more like what he was: a rather old boy, and that was an idea he found hard to face even the right way up.

Tomorrow, then, he would do a blitz on his paperwork. At the prospect of that diet—dried and bitter leaves—he shuddered so much that Rust, deciding he had truly found the spot, dug his thumbs in even harder, making the

Admiral jump and curse. No, a pox on the paperwork; he would hand it over to his secretary, Fräulein Schwarte, and to hell with low-grade security—she never understood half of the material she typed, anyway. The main thing was to keep his private diary up to date and lock it away in the safe. Then, with his past dumped behind him, as it were, he was free to go off yet again to Poland, on Tuesday, en route for Lvov, by way of Krakow, yes, then Kielce, Radom, and *Pulawy*, of course. Then off to Lvov after seeing the Czimanska mare. He tried to picture the map in exact detail, but only the colors came through, while the towns, the roads, the railways danced about in sketchy disarray as if to tell him he couldn't make the journey after all: Poland had been garbled.

On previous trips, the devastation and the smoke had made him sick to his stomach. Surely much of all that had been gratuitous, the work of ill-trained Waffen SS, who did everything by extremes. Yet, whether Poland were a hell-hole or no, it would be a relief to get away again, to be on the road, disencumbered of papers and files and the telephone, with only his stomach, his mind, and good old Pieki, and the lanky Lahousen, for company. He might even (he thrilled at the prospect) attempt an act of good will, a feat of rescue, not merely because the woman herself had been charming, or because he had indeed taken her husband's money (another lump sum for Eva's future, if she had one at all), but because, by doing some such thing, he proved he could do it. An act of mercy was within his gift, whether the subject of a bargain or not. He mused on the operation V7, by means of which friends of his own, among the seven or twelve, had been enrolled in the *Abwehr* itself, ostensibly for infiltration as agents into the United States; but they had all stayed in Switzerland, with a hundred thousand dollars sent after them, and a bulky bag of jewelry as well. *All Jews*, he smiled. Not only that: *Abwehr* outstations in Poland had had word from him to conduct prominent Poles to places of safety. One rabbi had already arrived in New York. The Ukrainian Archbishop of Krakow had vanished from Poland too, and so had the Bishop of unpronounceable Przemysl, Dr. Josafat. Not so bad, he thought: but sooner or later they'll crack down—Himmler and Heydrich will—and then the holiday will be over. I'll lose my head if I don't watch my step; I'll lose it anyway if anyone finds out what I've been up to. A helping hand may well drag the entire body after it, as Piero della Vigna found out. Would *I* split my skull by leaping hard against a prison wall? Maybe not, my skull is too thick for that, and I am too old for such athletics. Will I ever figure in some twentieth-century Dante's *Hell*, whispering dryly about my fate, in the Wood of Suicides, perched on a broken branch of the *Abwehr*?

Once he had imagined how his final years would be. Obliged by poverty to wear all the discarded clothes he'd saved over more prosperous times, he wrinkled his nose at the idea of the mothball aroma that spilled from drawers left unopened for entire decades, where all those old pajamas—mostly tops because the pants wore out first—awaited him in his dotage like leaves pressed in books he knew he would never open again. Once they wore out, he'd be unable to buy any more, so he'd die naked in a cold bed, on sheets brown like charred paper, unless.... Was there even an unless? He suspected not. Any pension that depended on Adolf Hitler's survival would never be paid, and, after Hitler was gone, all previous arrangements would be off, and the survivors, instead of catching up on their reading, mowing their lawns and sipping coffee at the outdoor cafes or even (his heart leapt at the very image) living quietly over a small bistro in Piraeus harbor, would be on trial. Now there was Poland, there was Hitler, there was his dead nephew, there were the Russians moving in for the kill, the loot, and he wondered if he had enough emotions left to respond to it all. It was no use looking backward, in a cozy dither, to his ancestors, who'd spun exquisite silk in a village by Lake Como, or forward, to war games on the rug with that little Czimanski boy, Izydor, while the dogs kept trespassers at bay. It was like living within the covers of a cheap thriller, with all emotions foreshortened and made crude: a time for the Heydrichs, not Reinhard-and-Lina, but for the Reinhards, who wept crocodile tears while they played the violin after a hard day plotting the extermination of the Jews.

"That's enough, I think," he told Rust, who today heard something tight and granular in his master's voice. "Himmler's masseur, Kersten, is going to publish his memoirs one day, or so I hear. Imagine that!" If Rust had similar plans, he'd have to talk to the Admiral more and coax him out. "I don't give you much to go on, do I?" Rust said nothing, helping the Admiral with his shirt while Mohammed advanced into the small study bearing yet another pill and a glass of water; Rust had been blinded by a back-firing furnace in the bowels of a destroyer on which the Admiral had served; Mohammed had been a wine-taster and in his spare time a language tutor. "Is it true," the Admiral asked the room at large, "that behind my back they call me 'Father of the Persecuted?' I wouldn't like a thing like that to get around. You never know where it will end up."

"*Mon Chef*," said Mohammed, taking the emptied glass, "it would only end up where it was, quite deliberately, begun. A rumor from on high returns to its source encrusted with the lies of amateur slanderers, like a branch that has been dropped into a coal mine and, years later, comes out phosphorescent. I am citing the great Stendhal, of course, to whom I am distantly related through a military connection of some unorthodoxy. A bastard always takes pride in a distant father, never mind how many removes he's at."

Working late, sometimes, in the Fox's Earth, the Admiral sometimes strolled the hallways, lost in thought, not snooping as some supposed, but adjusting the automatic motion of his limbs to an inner restlessness, like someone tapping or drumming his fingers in order to concentrate. It was then that he noticed, even in seasons remote from autumn, the tiny dried leaves always on the floor, making a sere whisper as his shoes stirred them. An afflicted hawthorn tree somewhere in the outside world had shed its leaves out of season, and the footwear of secret agents had brought them in, tiny emblems that belonged on outsize playing cards. When he was very tired, at night, he caught himself looking at them unusually hard, watching them change shape or nature, becoming arrowheads or unknown insects. In time he began to know where they were and steer round them without so much as a look down. Or, instead of putting his foot directly on one of them, he crooked his knee and checked the motion, which gave him the idea that, on his most demanding days, he walked the corridor like Christ walking on water, no longer subject to ordinary laws in a place which no one ever swept. Yet, even when he went round them, or above them, the leaves responded crisply to his passing, drab confetti of being wedded to his work, but also his solace, a reminder that he was more or less real when not even the gold rings on his sleeve, one wide and three thin, convinced him the blood which ran in other people's bodies ran in his as well, and that he was not outside the race, a chameleonic freak, an also-ran with no jockey, a chunk of flotsam which had floated out to sea and should never have floated inshore again. He would have gone home, except it was not home in a profounder sense; he could hardly go and wake a horse from its sleep, just to pour soliloquy over it about the impending doom of Germany, or the mighty network of spies he controlled and sometimes, just to see what might happen, allowed to get somewhat out of hand through a spontaneous betrayal here, an unplanned kidnapping there, on occasion a document leaked by drunkenness, an agent not saved at the last moment, a rendezvous forgotten, a bribe squandered on silk and sin. One of the privileges of holding the reins tight was to let them slacken.

  The Admiral wished with all his heart he were once again in Madrid, as Reed Rosas, shunning the German embassy in Calle Castellana for reasons good and true, having wangled his way through France and northern Italy by posing as a consumptive Chilean on his way to the sun after having treatment at a Swiss sanatorium. He was even willing to be caught again, and jailed; he would simply, as before, lock the Italian prison chaplain in his cell, take his cassock and escape in that, noting tersely in his diary, as he sat by a raging fire in the terrible fastness of yet another Berlin winter, "Detained in Italy during return journey, very harsh conditions, rigorous questioning, badly treated; escaped again, God be thanked for being on my side." He had escaped so often he couldn't always remember the exact geography, or which alias or passport he had been using at the time, but he sometimes enjoyed returning by U-boat, usually off the port of Cartagena, yes, meeting it in a sailboat that carried a red flag and, by way of signal, kept dipping its mainsail. For more years than he could count, he had roamed the world with casual finesse, obliviously riding the bicycle of his charm, as often as not shabby enough to go unnoticed, but gently arranging the downfall of every country he wandered through, and undoing every town—Montevideo, Santos, Rio, Bahia, Pernambuco, Lisbon, Falmouth, finally winding up on the doorstep of his Aunt Dorothea's home in Hamburg, quivering from the accumulated strain, gasping "I have just been through hell again. Don't ask. *Another* secret mission." Then the malaria would lay him low for a few days, after which, nursed back to rosiness, he would find his way to Naval Staff and report as much as he thought fit. The name of each place he'd been through elicited a different smile, depending on what he had managed to undo while there, and to him a map was a tableau of whimsical manipulations akin to a schoolboy's little book of train numbers discerned amid smoke and cinders, but manfully written down while the engine blasted by.

It was all a follow-through from Frederick the Great's enlightened decision to found the first organized espionage service, back in the middle of the eighteenth century; the many-souled Admiral, as some called him, was the most recent heir of Bernard Wilhelm von der Goltz, the first *Chef.* That the Admiral, as some also said, resembled the impresario of a worldwide music hall agency, was all to his advantage; it helped him to slink and wander unremarked, yet full to the gills with nationalistic pride, and with secretive joy at consummating the line from von der Goltz. Just so long as he did not have to deal with people who had colds, he was happy; just so long as there was always a Kasper to replace a Seppel when a Seppel died (as even wire-haired dachshunds did); just so long as he could catch a snooze on his leather couch during the afternoons; just so long as he had time to sneer at the bad English when a colleague wired him "All catched," as von Reichenau had after the SS murder squads wiped out their SA rivals in 1934. As long as he could recruit porters, chambermaids and waiters to spy for him in the best hotels in the civilized world, he felt secure and, as he liked to say in Spanish, plugged-in: *enchufe*; just so long as he could persuade film directors like Karl Ritter to make the occasional propaganda spy movie, such as *Traitors* (1936), he felt he was not being overlooked; and just so long as he did not have to make speeches to audiences, or cope with people in the mass in other ways, he felt within himself, at ease, and warm, and every inch the boss. "*Kürzer! Kürzer!*" he liked to say, telling people to get a move on. "Make it snappy now"; yet asked for a raise while he ambled vacantly down the hallway at the Fox's Earth, playing games with the leaves beneath his feet, he often came through on the spot and, to his detractors, seemed to run the place on whim. Anyone who buttonholed him when his mind was off-duty won his favor, but tackling him in his office, when the conspiratorial filament in the big bulb of his head glowed white-hot, was a different matter, and he usually said no or nothing at all. With blue pencil he loved to scrawl "This is utter nonsense!" on anything that came his way at the wrong moment, or even just out of juvenile spite, knowing that anything important would fall into his in-tray again within the week.

Once, on holiday *en famille* in Corfu, he had complained about the drain of love on his nervous energies and had gone to kick the sea in a fit of temper, not quite like a latterday Xerxes (who, the Admiral knew, had thrashed the sea with rods after losing an important naval battle), but enough like him to make the Admiral feel important in a long tradition predating even Frederick the Great.

This Sunday, September 17th, after Rust had helped him on with his shirt again, the Admiral had sat by the telephone and begun to doze, as if daring the bell to sound, but lured into swoon or sleep by Rust's talk about the branch in the coal mine which returned to the light encrusted with—with what? Dew? Diamonds? Had the branch been there that long? Since the Age of Coal, when the first roaches tried out their newborn feet? He asked, but Mohammed disclaimed the whole thing. Already he was deciding what to pack for his trip to Poland, was it his fourth or his fifth? What I need, he thought, is more men who tell the truth, because in my branch of the service no one believes it. Neither Rust nor Mohammed could be counted on for outright truth or outright lies: they mingled the one with the other prudently, always listening to him hard for signs of storm, like the times he wheezed viscously like a flexible pot of glue giving up the ghost. This time he would travel light. "Isn't that the thing to do, Mohammed? Rust?" They both agreed, glad they would be staying in Berlin. He sometimes thought Rust could see, never falling over anything, always finding at the first grope what he'd dropped, and evincing the most remarkable ability to divine the Admiral's mood by vibration or smell—he heard the facial muscles move, he sniffed the acid of his pique, the alkali of his cheerier moments. No, the Admiral told himself: that's dreaming. Now: how to settle this business of the Czimanska mare, and company. I'll improvise when I see what the situation offers on the spot. What amazing memories people have. They always remember that they do not want to die, they never forget a cash deposit. Perhaps, just perhaps, she might be induced to take an interest in invisible ink, the discreet use of a radio transmitter, or of microdots. Never waste an obligation or a gift. Wherever she went, she might prove of use, and one can never have too much intelligence, in any sense. Teach her the uses of obliquity, and she might work wonders, especially if we install her near some frontier and equip her with a photophone; just imagine, sending phone messages by means of invisible rays of light! Is there a woman alive who could resist it?

Already caught up in pragmatic speculation, he grew more cheerful, and dined early on sandwiches while Mohammed took his evening off in a dark suit, a bottle from the Admiral's private store under his arm wrapped in Christmas paper. The Admiral telephoned Anna, his sister, and they mourned for Rolf together in disjointed, conventional sentences; he was glad to be able, for once, to say things uninhibitedly, and to hell with who was listening in, but instead of the rush of patriotic grief, as he expected, he heard himself speaking almost cagily, as if Anna herself might trap him in some self-indulgent thought about the regime. The conversation with Zollerndorff came back to him, and he wondered how much Jewish blood might account for so non-Aryan a name; after all, it had been he himself, in 1935, who said that German Jews should wear a Star of David to identify themselves as "special-category" citizens comparable to resident aliens, and this would save them—so he'd argued—from the worst excesses of fanatics. What he really had in mind, however, was the eventual resettlement of German Jews in the old German colonies, so all Jews were Jews-in-waiting, and he wanted the Star to designate that status. Jews were not to be persecuted while still waiting to go. That such a line of thought exactly matched the racist doctrines of the SS occurred to him only on his worst days, but he always reassured himself that, instead of trying to single people out, he had tried to provide them with a token of safe conduct: not a scar but a visa. His life had been full of such casuistries, and he was accustomed to the rip tide emotions they provoked in others, the churlish perturbations they caused him when he woke at three in the morning, wondering if he were a feeble Nazi or an extremist liberal, and if putting on a bold show for his *Führer*—really for Germany—made him less of a liberal, less of a patriot. Fortunately, nothing got him back to sleep faster than having to set his conscience in order: he found just as many sheep to count on Hitler's side as on his own, and how could a man who took a pride in his work, loved his country, and knew he was no desperado, betray the keenest patriot of all? The how came to him at once; he'd salve his soul quietly behind the scenes, getting this or that person out of harm's way, making a special case for that woman in Pulawy, and her entertaining little son. Next thing, this Zollerndorff would be asking favors for himself, with one eye on his commanding general and the other on a chalet in Switzerland! "If only the *Führer* knew!" This, the fervent exclamation of a people who thought their leader his party's dupe and sentimentally supposed him more helpless than he was, came to the Admiral as naturally as breath. Everyone had little secrets that did no harm: Hitler, the Admiral, Pieki, Mohammed (a woman in a sleazy Berlin suburb), even Rust. Secrets were the salt in the national soup, and, after all, they were his stock-in-trade.

Who more than he had the right to a couple of shady whorls of truth here and there, so long as the national security went unscathed? If the master of national secrets couldn't rise to a fib or two, or do a little private business on the side, then he'd find another polity to serve. Savvy colleagues in the outstations often kept a dog in reserve for his visits; if things weren't going well, out it came to be fondled. Now that was a minor secret, but he didn't mind, except when the dog was less than friendly. British agents monitoring radio traffic had been baffled by constant references to an agent called Axel, who in fact was a dog assigned to agent Caesar (not the Admiral, of course). The next two transmissions were "Watch out for Axel. He bites." and "Caesar is in hospital. Axel bit him." All this diverted the Admiral, reminding him of life's crosshatched complexity, into which, without even an apology to himself, he gladly introduced—for his favorites—Spanish strawberries flown in from Aranjuez by courier planes codenamed "Strawberry Swansuit"; diamond-studded tobacco jars all supposed to have belonged once upon many times to Napoleon; rugs and paintings and miniature perfumed dogs. The Bulgarian outstation was the most corrupt, he knew, but the one in Munich was close behind. Racketeers were part of reality too, he reassured himself; so long as the main job got done, none of this black market stuff mattered a fig. He even knew that the British knew so much about the *Abwehr*, its corruptness and inefficiency, that they went to enormous lengths to make it stay that way. Two sets of eyes dreamed the day when the

Führer finally awoke to what was going on in his famous intelligence service and brought the entire house of cars tumbling down: the Admiral's, and those of the British Intelligence Service. Both sets watched and, repledging themselves to the need for a touch of badness in all things, looked the other way. So there was all the more reason, the Admiral persuaded himself, to get out into the field and lay his traps, retrieve his rabbits, bury his gold, riding the confidential rainbow to its end, before heads began to fall. The very thought of going off to another country, there to meet an old friend (if such she was) and her son, excited the Admiral more than he could credit. I still thrill to it, he mused: the foray, the confrontation, the bargain struck, the wires pulled to make the marionettes work an ocean's width away. I am not nothing. I make the truth curve. I run contraband to hell and back. In the end they all come to me, begging or boasting, and I suffer them all. I'll go in uniform, of course; it adds to the pageantry. If only the smoke and the rubble could have been removed by trucks to Russia; I have been close to tears, yearning for old-style naval engagements, with cruisers slogging it out over the mild meniscus of the open main. Burning horses and sundered houses are not my idea of war at all. One bright spot, though: when you reduce a country to rubble, you can count at least on not having to eat its dreadful food.

One day, when things have been cleaned up, Mohammed will have to come along with us, with dishes, linen, and silver. Poland will fill with aromas and the saintly Rust will rub my back. I will come into my own again. This Admiral will sail.

30

"Four nights," Myrrh whispered in a voice of sodden straw. "It's four nights, Izz. I'd give anything to see the sky. There's no sky in here. Nobody can live under a plank."

"Planks plural," he told her gently. "And we're just coming up to the fourth night. It's only three: Thursday, Friday, Saturday. We've still got Sunday night to come," as if it were something to look forward to. His voice too was weak from lack of use.

Already they lay in the ground as if they belonged to it; something in them had given, not in blind scrabbling at the soil for a horizontal way out after the fashion of demented miners, nor in suffocated recoil from contact with earthworm and sow bug, but in the quietest, meekest way imaginable. One moment they had been trespassers, misfits, and then they became denizens against their will, gradually changing all they thought to include the soil component. They were closer to planted wheat, to barley and oats; the blood that moved in the thinnest capillaries of their skins had more in common now with the blood in the mainstreams of the spider and the earwig. In a few days' quasi-captivity at ground level, they had come to the uncouth oneness with things that mystics tried for, but it wasn't something they bothered to voice. Each knew that the other knew it. The panic had drained away. The need for preposterous chatter, just to assert their differentness from the creatures around them, had seeped down into the water table somewhere, and they sat not so much tight as loose, Izz having discovered that the most soothing and the most comfortable thing he could do for hours on end was to make for her "a chair," so that while they lay on their sides she curved into the line of his lap, which cupped and reinforced her. On their backs they were too much apart, while on their fronts they felt they were breast-stroking deep into the earth.

"I can't take this," Myrrh had said. "I don't want my nose this far down, this close. It doesn't feel like me. I might inhale some dirt."

"But if you lie on your back," Izz told her with a show of antic bravery, "just think what might fall into your mouth through the cracks in the planks."

"Well, it's not dignified," she said. "It's something I can't bear. I don't care what the reasons are. Why hasn't somebody come to take us home? I'm willing to give myself up. I don't care what happens now."

"You're not a felon, Myrrh. You could surrender, yes, but not give yourself up. And don't give up anyway. It's not been as long as it feels. It's bad, it's worse than anyone could have imagined, just thinking about being underground as an idea; but remember this, and keep thinking about it, like something you'd whistle while milking a cow: We're still alive, we haven't been found."

"What do you know about milking cows?" It was a flash from a Myrrh he no longer knew, at any rate no longer heard from. "If you'd said milking a plane, I'd have believed you."

"I haven't seen a plane in months. I haven't seen one in years. I haven't heard anything but that farmer."

"You called." She had begun to have the shakes again, as if the full burden of the night's cold had gathered into a ball that rolled through her marrow. Not a ball, a ball-bearing the size of an eye, she thought: it moves slowly, as if in oil, bigger than the bubble in that leveling device called a spirit level, but just as fast. When you tilt one of those, the bubble goes the other way; but a bubble is a cheerful thing, it's a bit of the sky trapped. "Izz, give me the sky," she blurted. "Any way you can."

He cupped his hands, then shut them tight. "There's sky in that, Myrrh. Can you see it?"

"It's almost night. What did you do?" He told her, and she shaped her hands round his, resting them where he rested his, on the top of her right hip. "We could go to the farmhouse and give ourselves up. Nothing would be as bad as this."

"We promised," he reminded her.

"We've just about eaten it all up."

"We were greedy," Izz said without a hint of blame. "Do we burn food faster just lying still down here?" He pushed his legs out long to still the cramp, and felt his foot touch the empty can of ham, split in half along the peeled-back seam like a machine-age oyster. The sandwiches had gone, as had the individually wrapped toffees, the broth in the hot-water bottles; but they still had water and aspirin, and, after each meal, they had brushed their teeth, spitting white foam into the corners, the exact art of which he schooled her in, saying "Old men in summer do this when their pipes back up. They build up a column of air in their throats and then get it behind the spit, see. It travels enormous distances. But you have to do it as if you believed in it. Tighten your face muscles, and then it go whang."

Gradually she had learned; but they could not brush their teeth all day, or talk, or sleep, or hug or get into heavy petting. Something, neither of them knew exactly what it was, had vanished from their lives—the casual element that sponsored wasted time, the combined array of things too trivial to mention one by one, but which enabled everyone to fend off the sense of being alive and being too keenly aware of it. At the far end of their endeavor was the volunteer suspended in his immersion tank, bereft of sound and sight and feel and smell, with only the frantic circling of his mind for company, like a dog preparing to sit without ever getting down. Forced up close against the process that sustained them, Izz and Myrrh found it difficult to fix on it: their minds kept on going past it, to something more apprehensible, like sky and food, but on it went, the pulse and the lymph and the continuous mop-up in their lungs and liver, something to lie very still and tune in to, but easily lost in the thumping doldrum of a headache, the gurgle of a stomach not so much empty as unaccustomed to lying down for so long at once. Izz had tried to listen to his blood, his breath, even his sinuses and his knuckles, but mostly he heard the friction of his fingers against one another, against Myrrh's, a velvety scrape, and that was that. How secret it all is, he decided: You never hear a tenth of it, where it all glistens and seeps, where it skims and dilutes, and breaks everything down with acid. Where does the mucus come from? How does the saliva form, and know what to do? In Biology class, he, and she, had studied these things in a trance of near-indifference, content to let the body look after itself ad infinitum, simply because it now occupied the space where it never used to be, not that many years ago.

"Give me some sky!" she pleaded, again, as eager to see what he improvised as to breathe fresh air, which was out of the question.

"Atoms for sale!" he quipped, trying to come up with something he hadn't tried already. "Well, the pilots of the Japanese and Italian air forces have open cockpits, which means they have a greater sense of exposure to the elements. The same is true for the Polish pilots of the good old Pulawski Eleven. You sit with your head visible inside something like a bit a giant has taken out of the top of the body, see, and behind you there's one of those long stream-lined tapering things, like they have on some racing cars. It's the continuation of the headrest, actually, and I guess if it weren't so cold up there, even if you have a helmet and leathers, it might feel as if your head is a comet with the long streamer behind it. Hey, that's not bad, because where comets go it's even colder. Anyway, you have the wing right in front of your chin, which means you can see just about everything in front of you. A bit like holding a dinner plate up to your mouth. Your eyes have a clear field of vision immediately above it."

"Get to the sky," she moaned. "I've heard all this before, Izz. You do go on. And see how much use it all is."

"Wait," he said cheerily. "I'll soon have you flying. Aloft. Imagine yourself in one of those Elevens, then, all olive-green on top, and pale *sky*-blue underneath, which is how they are, so that when someone on the ground looks up at you, you really do merge with the sky, provided the sky is blue, which doesn't mean they only fly them in good weather, when the pilot won't get rained on or get cold. No. The rim of the front cowling is a maroonish red, and so is the propeller, not that you notice the color when it's spinning round, although the whir in front of you has a reddish tinge. Behind you—now wait, Myrrh, these are the preparations for take-off—behind you there's a white patch, a triangle, with a black owl painted on it in profile. See, you are a member of the Owl squadron, Number 113. I ought to know, I've been flying with them for years. Now, let's pretend the Eleven has been converted to a two-seater, and you're the passenger in the front seat, with the better view." Using her hands as cockpit instruments, he tapped her knuckles, eased her thumb back gently, squeezed her fingernails into the palm of his hand as if in simultaneous measurement of something too technical to explain, and began to buzz the engine noise through the strict pucker of his lips, making the pitch higher as the revs increased, the tail-wheel lifted clear, and the little high wing monoplane began to trundle forward underground with its wing at right angles to the water table, as if the Jack on a playing card had drifted free, still two-dimensional, but no longer mute, his grin just as fixed as the flickering fan of the propeller, but grinning in a new place.

"I didn't taxi, I forgot," Izz explained. "We took straight off. The wing is reinforced with parallel struts that join with the undercarriage struts. And struts hold up the tailplane too.

It's all struts, and that costs us a good many kilometers an hour. We can climb to ten thousand meters, though, pulling ourselves up while the Earth tries to tug us down."

"Take me to ten thousand meters, Izz. The seat is hard and I'm right in the wind. My eyes are watering." She sniffled.

"We call that the slipstream. It slips past you from the propeller. Can you get these goggles on?" He bent his head over her eyes, maneuvering the left one between her head and the blanket, then bringing it round.

"I can't see at all." So he opened a V between his index and middle fingers. "That's better. There's less wind, and I can see."

"What can you see? It's a clear day."

"The horizon is pink, it must be sunset. The horses look like brown loaves. The windmills are like bottles."

"You asked for sky. Are you getting enough sky? Can you smell the blue? How does blue smell? It smells like ammonia, a bit, and purple ink, a lot, and starched new shirts kept in a drawer that hasn't been opened in ages. Is that how blue smells to you?"

Busily inhaling to test the smell of blue, she didn't answer, so while she was quiet he pretended to steer, banking by pressing her right shoulder down, but keeping the Eleven's nose up by easing her forehead back. "It's like having a cold," she said finally. "When you feel there's more space in your nose and where your nose goes into your face—more space than there ought to be. And it feels sort of drafty in there, a bit like old smoke, I think, like a damp with edges. That's what the blue's like for me."

31

"Now we're going to fly upside down," he told her. "I'm glad you finally found some sky." With both palms against her forehead now, he pulled her head back and back, reminding her of the swingboats at the fairground. "Up you go, and back, and you're looking straight up, and you think you are going to fall right from the top of the arc because there seems to be nothing under you and you're sitting with your legs high up, ready to slide out. But the belt will keep you in." Quickly he clasped her waist with his right arm. "See how tight it is." They actually made a slight joint movement on the blanket, perhaps thirty degrees, which corresponded in their minds (Izz's stage-managing, Myrrh's going along for the ride) to the complete three hundred and sixty. They looped the loop horizontally, and Myrrh actually felt her stomach upturn its load behind her lungs. "I'm dizzy!" she cried, opening her mouth wide as if to swallow air which then might give her back the sense of balance.

"You asked for sky!" he yelled against the wind. "Hold on tight." Upside down, they were looking up at the ground, which suddenly for both of them pushed the ground to where the ground belonged, away from under them, where it had lain for four long days. It became a canopy, a tent, a thing as optional as a parasol, newly made lighter than air and drifting away southward or northward, it didn't matter. Then it went vertical as Izz hugged Myrrh's knees and firmly drew them up against her breast with her eyes closed to get the maximum from the sky, the blue, the thunderous air, she felt like a wet fly against a window pane, flailing with drunken splayed legs against the smooth nothing that reared up and stayed put between her mind and all she'd wanted life to be. But nothing lasted. The ground canted back, the Eleven's engine ceased to cough and nearly stop, the blood in her head went its proper way again, and she began to cry, not just because the dream loop was complete, the flight over, but because Izz had tried so hard to bring the sky down into the hole, folding it and making the creases sharp. Joined thus, like two spoons mated, they lay still, breathing hard and waiting for the ground to stop spinning as if they had spun around horizontally.

"North is still up," she said at length.

"North is only up when you're looking north," he said. "You can look upward and be looking south. There is the top of the celestial sphere, as seen from Earth, and the bottom. If you look at Sagittarius, the teapot shape of stars, at night, then you are looking south, to the Carpathian Mountains. If you look back at the Great Bear, which is north, you're looking towards Warsaw. Or, if you want to be accurate, my darling, Mragowo, to the east of which is the Lake District—the Mazurian Lakes. Up's not always north."

"And down's not always south. Australia's south, isn't it?" She had stopped crying. After aerobatics, geography too had begun to work, and she was glad it had, dimly ashamed of being so emotional, and of having to make him find things to spruce her up. I do not like sleeping underground, she thought. I like my frills, my clothes, a window to open and fall through.

"Yes, but someone in Australia could look into the northern sky, trying to find the Great Bear, without ever seeing it. They'd still be looking in the right direction, though."

"Izz, how did you become so wise?" Now, she sounded older, more robust, readier for a diet of aspirins and water, toothpaste and candle wax. "Will they ever come for us?"

"Any day now," he said with forced good spirits. "Any hour, you might even say."

"Izz, I have a confession."

He murmured invitingly, still high up in the Eleven, although far beyond his range, his power to return the way he'd come. "What?"

"I don't believe in that Admiral chap. They invented him to shut us up. He's no more real than Saint Nicholas."

Izz bridled, obliged to look away from the quivering needles on the faces of the dials in front of him, encased in glass but seemingly blown by the same wind as froze his cheeks. "He's a nice old fellow. I've met him. A bit weird, but who isn't? He's real all right, they didn't just invent him. Maybe, though, he invented them."

"I don't believe in parents anyway."

"You mean you don't hold with *having* parents."

She agreed, but he persisted with the boyish pedantry that irritatingly pleased his parents themselves. "You didn't mean that there aren't any parents anywhere. It's 1939, September. I've forgotten the date. But it's all real. Oh, there are parents, all over Poland, all over the world." He laughed dryly.

"You know what I meant. You don't have to be so huffy."

"It's cold in here. When I'm cold I fidget, and when I fidget I get sarcastic. Sorry. Wasn't that a nice flight?"

"What are we going to do for the next five hundred days? If I have to sneak out at night and fall over a sleeping pig, just to do you know what, I think I'll lose my sanity. Izz, it just isn't right. Something's wrong. Nobody's come. There are no more Germans, no more bombs. No guns banging."

Knowledgeably, Izz just said "Curfew," and left it at that.

"They can't leave the house?"

"Just like us. They'll be reading books and playing chess. Playing dictionary games. Seeing how many words you can make from one. Killing time until things ease up again. We have to do the same. I've even heard that some tribes eat soil."

"Didn't we have some cheese? What time is it?" Izz had neglected to wind the alarm clock, but he could tell from the light between the planks that sunset was near. Over in Pulawy Palace, Captain Zollerndorff had just told Izz's mother that the Admiral would be on his way next week, by no means exclusively to see her, the Czimanska mare, but from Berlin to Poznan and Lodz. And by way of Radom and presumably Pulawy, en route for Lvov, a route which Izz would have rejoiced to trace on a large-scale map so as to overfly it in his battered Eleven, whose pale blue underside was gray from smoke, whose olive green was almost black. The white squares in the red and white quartered emblem on the wings and fin looked merely empty now. The red was maroon, the black owl on the white triangle had lost its head, scratched off by an itinerant woodpecker which had tried to peck through the metal skin while the Eleven had been hidden behind a ruined haystack. That was on the left-hand side of the fuselage, where the white 11 was still intact, whereas by custom there was no owl at all on the right-hand side (starboard, he corrected himself with a grimace: *prawa burta*), and the aerial, from fintop to the top of the wings had been shot or blown away, he could not remember exactly when.

"Cheese?" he said, picking up the echo of what she'd said. "We ate that yesterday." He rummaged in the sack, humming self-consciously. "There's something in here that feels like—" he was going to say *ants,* since he could feel them crawling busy-light on his fingers—"a pineapple!" There was nothing edible at all. "No, sorry. A toilet roll. And no chocolate cake, no German pastries, no beer, no mead. Wait." He had found a single toffee, which he unwrapped and bit in half although it had hardened in the ground.

32

"Izz," she said, instructing herself to suck it and not chew, "is this Sunday? Have I counted right?"

Izz was listening to a pair of feet advancing above, ponderous and uneven. The walker cleared his throat with what sounded like an antagonized word, then spat. The pigs thumped on the planks, and one seemed to fall while getting up from where it lay. In one motion, Izz arranged his body over hers, coming out of his sideways hunch and straightening out to face upward. Now someone stood on the planks, heavier than any pig, and blocking the light in a different way because taller too. Yearning for a hint of language, Izz prayed not to hear German; but not a word came down to them, only, as the middle plank tore back and let in a slice of rosy evening light, a lump wrapped in sacking. The plank had already slammed down again, the feet that weighed its neighbor down had gone. The bundle almost hit Izz in the face, making him recoil as if from a hand grenade tossed incuriously in, but it was meat, old and dried, but far from rancid: a bone with the best cuts already gone, yet a better bone than a dog would get.

"It's beef," he said. "The farmer threw it in."

"He read our minds, then. He can't be such a bad old stick after all."

"Conscience," Izz told her. "He's feeding his conscience. Here, ladies first, but don't eat it all. Three mouthfuls, and then it's my turn. There's water too. Quite a banquet."

"Sure it isn't horsemeat?" Myrrh made him sniff at it again. "Well? You have a good nose, Izz."

"I," he said after taking a deep breath over the bone, "never quite believe the evidence of my senses. Once, I saw a seed on a shelf at home, see, and I thought it might just be a worm or an insect egg, so I crushed it, and it opened its wings exactly down the middle. But it was a seed after all. I'd just broken it clean in half. I looked at it through my magnifying glass, the one for maps; but it was a seed all right. Funny, I expected it to fly, even after I knew what it was."

"You still haven't said." Myrrh pushed him off her, no longer needing protection. "You don't even know, you're going to lie, aren't you?" He had heard this formula before, in fun.

"Beef to me," he said, "but I'm no expert. It could be deer, or dog. It isn't pork. I say, if we were really desperate, we could go up there and slaughter a pig."

"How far do you think you'd get before that wolfhound was at your throat? It isn't bad, but it's days old. I know: the dog refused it, so he threw it in." She was nearly shouting.

"The bastard. He owes us more than that."

Her mouth full, she asked him something she had to repeat. "Is it dark enough to go up anyway? I have to *go*."

"Did you think it was the Admiral? Our parents?"

"Answer my question, Izz. Is it dark enough?"

"How about some meat? It'll be another hour. I'm not your keeper, though. Go if you want, but don't blame me."

"But you *are* my keeper. You'd never let me out. You're only pretending you would." She made as if to reach up and shove the planks apart, but only to see if Izz would stir, which he did not, being intent upon his bone, swallowing fat and gristle as well as meat, wondering why their food had given out so soon, when all along he'd been sure they had more than a week's supply. After all, who expected them to be in here for more than a week? The farmer, Gnonka, had come and gone with not a word: not even a guffaw or a sneer, not even a loutish thump of the foot to say We are all three in the same world, you pampered upstart brats from Warsaw or wherever you wipe your mouths on fancy-pattern linens. Izz knew more about diplomats and couriers, economists and metallurgists, than about farmers, the Latin word for whom brought Agricola to his mind, the rough-hewn Roman who had settled the hash of Britain in the first century A.D. Sensible or not, Izz's way was to get to know things, and people, better by making something of them, something homemade in his own head, not by getting intimate; he imagined novelties about people until the people became somehow more intimate to him, although never with him. Things were easier, having nothing to say by way of contradiction. Oddly enough, Izz's near-explosive charm was his means of keeping people at bay, and on things he didn't waste it; as for Myrrh, his soul-sibling and adversary, he dealt with her (at least up in the daylight world of old) almost prophetically, assuming something else, and so everything he said or did had a throwaway quality both impatient and forlorn. Until they were both grown up, or at least had no hope of getting away with being childish any longer, he didn't see the point in saying or doing anything serious, even if the subject were only ancient coins, the butterflies of Africa, the secret vocabulary of plumbers. All of his life so far had been five-finger exercises, a limbering-up, a Grand Tour with his eyes closed, almost as if, like certain soldiers in certain wars, he were going to carry the same egg along with him for months in hopes of boiling it one day in his helmet, or finally getting a chance to light and make coffee on the tiny stove he'd lugged around with him for years, campaign to campaign. Izz was a series of old soldiers posing as a single greenhorn, whereas Myrrh, lacking his experience of the embassy, the set in which the Admiral moved, had just assumed that life was going to be good to her because she was harmless, bright, and like Izz an only child. When beef thundered in through the gap left by a lifted plank, she was not surprised; it was all part of the fabric in which gratification and good luck wove themselves together. Hearing Izz regale her with bits of Latin, the unquenchable legend of the late Pulawsky, two stars called Sualocin and Rotanev (really somebody named Nicolaus Venator in reverse), and four others quite inappropriately known as the Bull of Poniatowski, she told him "You don't need to have so much information in order to get by! Being clever and loved is enough," which he poo-hooed, believing that knowledge was like heads of bison mounted on wooden shields in the hall. It was good to know, but it was better to let others know you knew you knew, and this trait in him the Admiral had enjoyed, warming to the boy as if to a miniature of his quirky, retentive, unfathomable self.

So when Izz chose to recapitulate, as now, he was a demon, airily informing her, while trying to pick his teeth with the rubber spike built into the end of his toothbrush, "Yes, Myrrh, it's Sunday, a week since Kazimierz was bombed. I'm sick of the damp in here. We'd be drier underwater. That was the tenth, this is the seventeenth, unless the Nazis have changed the calendar, like certain Popes. Last Friday, the day after we moved in here, they took over the town—you could tell that from the noise. So it took the soldiers five days to catch up to the range of their bombers. It's a wonder they didn't give us a second plastering just before they moved in, but maybe they thought we just weren't worth it. Are we going to die down here? Not with beef being slung to us as if we were dogs in a kennel. Are we going to get out, then, and not just for bathroom purposes? Numero One, Numero Two. Answer: very soon. Things will soon be back to abnormal." He was revving up, she could hear it in his tone; the accumulated boredom had begun to sharpen his edge, and he would soon begin to talk experimentally, just to see what effect he could have, and this time round she wasn't going to stand for it. "Izz, will you please shut up?"

"I was only trying to distract you from your bladder."

"It isn't bladder anyway, knowitall."

"Aha, name one ancient Greek whose liver made him cough," She sighed, prodded him hard in the belly, and turned her back; but this time he did not make a chair to fit her in.

"Prometheus Linctus. It's not bad for underground, low oxygen, no nitrogen, week-old beef, and sick with worry about my folks. Sorry, Myrrh: all of a sudden, I'm scared to death."

"I know. When you start making that kind of joke, I know you're getting on edge. Farmer or no farmer, Izz, dog or no dog, Germans or anybody else, I have to go. Look, it's nearly dark, I'll risk it." For the past five minutes, she had been peering at the finger-wide crack between the planks, amazed at how little she could see through it, yet knowing how much more she could see if she had her nose right up by it; distance and perspective, she decided, had altogether too much to do with what you did and didn't do. All of life was a leap in the dark according to peculiar laws having to do with the roundness of the eyeball, the speed of light, the inescapable way in which everything, just everything, tapered away from you as if loathing your presence, determined to reduce all visible things to a point, and that was tantamount to nothing. If you thought life stayed put like grapes in an arbor, then you'd have to learn about the fox in the night that took them all. The only way was not to look ahead, and then the preposterous narrowing of everything did not happen, as it did in those drawings of Albrecht Dürer. The peerers, the anticipators, the long-viewed students of the horizon, got no relief until they shut their eyes. How unlike me, she thought, I always feel low when some sort of physical need begins to take me over, and then I bounce back again. If only we could travel at the speed of light to the other end of perspective, to that point, and then look back to where things are still as wide as ever, knowing that what we'd supposed a mere point isn't that at all, and still able to enjoy the place we were standing in, still as large as life as when we left it. But we can't have it both ways. One end always dwindles. Life is a wedge, and not a lovely series of parallels like those railings on bridges where you can close your eyes and walk over the water, or the railroad track, trailing your hands quite loosely along the iron or the wood. If all bridges really came to a point, we'd never get across. The thought defeated her, then emboldened her: it was no use thinking about it instead of doing it—doing anything.

As if called, she sat up with a slight shiver, using Izz to push against, and shoved hard against the plank, which gave way easily. Her hand and wrist were in the open air again and warmer for being so. Izz growled something at her, but she kept her impetus and, with a slow-motion heave, flipped the plank on its back while he marveled at her strength. Up she went, roll of paper in hand, and Izz was not even saying "Wait, wait for me to check things out." One pair of eyes, for what it's worth, is as good as another, she thought: at our age, certainly. Her head and shoulders were in the open, and the light was amazing, like something creamily violet that had been squirted about: liquid, uneven, like the light at the top of looping the loop had been. Then her dark-adapted eyes calmed down. Objects—the rough parchment-colored mortar of the sty, the low bushes like something rolled pale green between someone's hands and then let fall where they grew, the distant strawstack like an outsize loaf between herself and the low September sun—sank back into their places as if their colors had darkened. There was nobody there: no shout, no soldier, not even Gnonka's dog.

"The coast is clear," she whispered down past her chest.

"The seacoast of Bohemia," Izz responded with frightened levity. "What now? Myrrh?"

"Our parents are out here—they've been living up at this level all the time. You know what? It's like being born again." Only a short bicycle ride away, she told herself.

"How do you know? Are you going to hang on the parapet all night, just talking and taking the evening air?" He made as if to drag her back down again, but she was already moving, thrusting herself fully into the open where swarming midges cruised like motes and, as her ears seemed to come back into use from long numbness, a distant crackling radio voice came on the breeze, a mix of old Caruso records and a crow up high scolding and complaining. It was curfew time in Kazimierz and what she heard, distorted by trees and distance and the megaphone itself, was the customary sundown threat: Stay in your houses. Curfew breakers will be shot, all in a Polish she could not precisely hear, although the *dzhee* of *godzina* and the *pol* of *policyjna* reached her skewed and faint.

"Somebody talking in the town," she said quite loudly as if determined to create something audible in her vicinity.

"*Nazis*," Izz grunted. "You see what trouble you're getting into? This isn't the day of the school picnic, Myrrh. This is the twentieth century." How old he sounds, she told herself as she actually stood, wondering why the pigs were all inside. Would one or two of them come out to see who the intruder was? Expecting to be fed? She could hear them in the sty, heaving their bristled bulk in sleep, exhaling with a tightened mellow drone, obeying the curfew. No sooner was she over the wall and walking up the slight slope to the bushes, beyond which a low fence with a canted white boundary marker vanished into the trees, than Izz was after her with a scrambling, noisy leap, just to stand guard, he said, but also to punish himself for hanging back.

33

"Wait," he called in an expanded, long whisper she remembered from early childhood, when she had been the faster runner of the two. *Wait for me, Myrrh, wait for Izzy.*

Without answering or slowing up, she flitted into the bushes, wishing she were home in bed again, reading by the last of the light, with a glass of milk or lemonade on the small chest of drawers beside her bed, low enough to reach from sitting position. First she flailed to rid the area of midges and mosquitos, then with a quick twirl of her clothes moved into squatting position, thinking *Even this is better than down there. I can breathe. My nose isn't blocked any more, I can see boughs and nests and the charcoal scribble of the town over there. No lights, that's funny. No, there's probably no electricity, but if so why the radio?* Not radio, she told herself, ceasing to think or evaluate, hoping spiders or earwigs wouldn't get into her sandals while she was stranded there. For a girl who lives underground, she rebuked herself, I'm a scaredy-cat on top.

Not far from the wall, and doubled up so as not to make a target in the landscape, Izz began to worry about a dozen things. The hole was open to the stars, if stars there were, but it was too light for that, although he could see Venus over where the sun was almost down. If the dog were out, it would come after them, and he had left the knife behind. Then the farmer would be out with his shotgun or, on the quiet, fetch the Nazis to take them away in a dark green van. What if (this became more and more real as he thought about it) they both fancied life upstairs so much they decided not to go back, and then picked their way carefully home. What would happen then, this being curfew time? Who would be there? Where were the ravines exactly? It would be right, wouldn't it, to send a message? Sneak up to the door, in the night, and slip a piece of toilet paper under the door, saying *All well. Need sandwiches and soup.* Could he shout? Tap on the windowpane and so use the Morse code? Or just burst in, laughing *Look who's here!* No, the only way through was to go disguised as a dog, on all fours, or do a Tarzan-of-the-Apes swing on some gigantic creeper, all the way from Gnonka's farm to Pulawy Street, with none of Tarzan's agonized yodel of course. Would the curfew police shoot them on sight? Children? *Polish* children. A cuff would do. A rude, German shove in the back. Or would they be interrogated, sat in a red-hot skillet to make them talk about their parents, who were tucked away safely in one of the ravines, deep in a cave with a candle and some old newspaper, cans of ham, hot-water bottles bulging with broth, a whole chicken to pick at. What would Poles do if they had really, as they were supposed to have done already, invaded Germany? How would they behave with German children? Sit them on red-hot pianos? Make them say unpronounceable Polish words for hours on end, on a stage, with a jolly beer-swilling audience to make fun of them? I know what's hard for Germans to say: I've been there: *zdziecinniec* is to grow childish. *Zdzhe – cheen – nech.* That would stop them. If only Poland had stuck its most awkward words all over the landscape, written enormously big, the German tanks would never have gotten through at all. He fancied the image of a Panzer tank stranded on the verb which meant to grow childish, and honor regained flowed through him.

"Don't be scared," he called, full of new-minted bravado. "I'm here."

Myrrh shrugged in huff. "I'm just fine myself."

Izz felt beneath one arm for his moles and tweaked them. They seemed to have no nerves in them at all: quite numb, as if nature were already rejecting them. Then he made water against the wall, as before, wondering if in time he would create his own private stain. He cleared his throat and spat, partly imitating Gnonka, but lacking Gnonka's tobacco sludge. He kicked the wall and managed to dislodge a chunk of mortar, on which he stood in the gloom, waiting for it to crumble. Nibbling a blade of grass, but unable to define its taste—

like spinach beginning to rot, but not quite that, it was too somehow silvery, if silvery was the taste of anything. Of course their parents were all right, comfy in their armchairs, observing the curfew and quite amiably thanking God or the stars they'd hidden the children. If so, he persisted with himself, if all was well, then why had no one come?

A curfew was one thing. Risky to attempt it then. So what about the daytime? Was it just as risky then? Was there no time of day suitable for rescue? This could go on forever, until their skeletons were found by archeologists of the twenty-first century, who would say this was how some dwarf specimens lived, even in the age of jet propulsion, in underground hovels, denied literature, friends, light, and air, although allowed to come out at night to forage and leave their droppings in a designated spot. Pig-minders of the last century, these outcasts had no offspring, no culture, no language. They just died out, sucking on hot-water bottles of broth dropped off each morning by the Neanderthal delivery truck. Or, he speculated, if the Nazis found them, experts of that future time would say that a merciful society had humane-killed them out of their misery; or, if the Nazis sat them in the red-hot skillet, had tried to use them as an edible resource, justifying the cannibalism involved as maximum use of resources after hydroponic gardening failed. What would Professor Stanislaw Pawlowski, of the International Geographic Union, say about that in time to come? *A small and helpless people who retreated from the machine age and became cave-dwellers again: troglodytes.* Izz's mind blazed with the names of those who, if they knew about Myrrh and him, would come and get them without delay. Where was his father? What was his mother saying to him? Did they qualify as orphan parents now? As he stirred to ease a foot gone almost numb with inert waiting, he felt something tindery and still beneath his shoe. This was Poland. Poland in near-autumn. Soon it would be snowing. He had stepped on one of those big fanlike leaves that lost heart before autumn properly began. It crackled, but it resisted too, and its shuffle sound was robuster than it should have been. In the brimming dusk, which made all things wobble and gently melt, he could not see the outline, there on the turf by his foot, but now he knew it was stuck to the sole of his shoe, no doubt with mud from the sty. Bending to retrieve it, he almost toppled over, but surely he wasn't that weak, that light-headed, after gnawing on a bone of beef. Uneven ground has made him reel, made him let out an incomplete, almost jocular cry. He tried again, almost kneeling, and there it was, a piece of torn paper, tougher than newsprint, but lacking that armored quality of passport pages. Screwing it up one-handedly to pitch it into the darkness, he checked himself, no more than idly curious, and stuffed it into his pocket, wishing it were his ticket home magically transported to him from his destination, where the first fire of the season hummed and glowed in the hearth.

"Well," Myrrh was asking, "shall we go back? We could sit out all night and get moonstruck!"

"Poor moon tonight," he said absently. "I'm ready."

"I'm not. Is there a law against an evening stroll, like the ones we used to have, looking for birds' eggs, ferns, bits of fool's gold, minnows in the streams? All that isn't over, is it? I mean, life's going to go back to normal soon. They won't abolish walks, and strolling past the stores just to see—window-shopping, things like that. I don't see how they could."

"We may not even be allowed to kick a ball about. They have funny ways, invaders do. I've heard."

She scoffed, unable nonetheless to dismiss the mind's-eye view of herself hunched on a bit of Poland, with a toilet roll in one hand, waiting for something to happen to her; and, when it did not, the reprieve of living on as before wasn't quite enough because she still hadn't learned (she chastised herself) to prize the beat of her pulse as an end in itself, or the sleek enclosure that her skin was, or the way her eyes continued to work according to the laws of perspective which got on her nerves. "Izz," she began, "it's all going to be all right, isn't it? We won't be here forever. I think I'd rather walk off into the night, wolves and all, than go underground again. Our ancestors came down from the trees, and out of caves, and going back sticks in my throat. You know German. Let's go and try."

"You really are tired of life," he said with sly disdain. "They'd bump us off on sight. I just wish I could play some of my records, the Duke Ellington and the Louis Armstrong I bought in Berlin. Y'know, liven up the dungeon a bit. It's having to be quiet that gets me down."

"And there's nothing on the radio any more. Why," she said, stretching and yawning, "have they shut everything down? What do they want that we have?"

"Just Poland," Izz heard himself saying in the voice of an aging politician, "that's all my sweet. When a country's involved, you just can't say *It's my ball, I'm going home, you can't play any more.* A country is a sitting duck. They can come and get it whenever they want to. If you've read your history, you know they've been coming and bloody well getting it for centuries, ever since Mieszko the First stopped Margrave Hodon's Germans dead, at the River Odra, in 972. Sorry to sound like a book. Poland's like a cake, and there's never been anybody in history who didn't want a piece." He took her hand as if to walk her back to the pigsty, but she tugged free and began to walk about, blatantly strolling in a circle.

"Izz, just so long as we keep away from the farmhouse, couldn't we just walk about? It's a lovely night, just a bit crisp." What dumbfounded her was that, not far away, entire families were sitting down to the evening meal, never mind how meager, and even the Germans were clustered round their portable canteens, grabbing black bread in hunks and swigging hot thick soup in unbreakable arm mugs. "I'm homesick for lying in bed and *then* wishing I were whole continents away, in South America or the Fiji Islands. What I miss is the chance of wanting to be where I'm not, as distinct from being obliged to feel that way all the time—just because where I am is awful. In my bedroom, there's a little block of something like glass, but it isn't glass, and there are two globes of the world in it, one very up-to-date, the other old-fashioned. The new one's sort of abstract, just ocean and white or yellow land, but the old thing has palm trees and little square houses, and a big prickly fish half as wide as the South Atlantic is swimming right into the coast of South America, and there's a Chinaman down by Africa, I've no idea why, unless it's a cobra rearing up and the hood is what I thought was a Chinamen's hat! There are old-fashioned galleons on the sea and the land as well, and even a small rosy crouching animal with whiskers like a cat, only it's not a cat at all. The trouble is when I try to look at North and South America, the other little globe gets in the way. It actually bulges out when I tilt the block, and then, all of a sudden, half the old world's gone, just because of something funny in the way the light goes through the stuff they're sealed in. Anyway, what I started to tell you is that it says Nubia on Africa, and on where Poland is—guess."

"Transylvania. Right?" Izz cannot believe she was sometimes a pleading wren, a girl whom he cheered up by patting her rear end with the slack slapping sound of a loaded paintbrush.

"*Polonia.*"

"Which gave us polonium," he said snippily, wanting Myrrh to go back where she belonged, or at any rate where she was supposed to be. "Madame Curie was a patriot. If she'd been from Patagonia, it would have been patagonium, wouldn't it? A metal."

"I *know* it's a metal, silly. Sorry, Izz. I adored looping the loop with you."

"Then let's loop again. I found something on the ground. A piece of paper. That's my evening, all of it. It's been nothing but thrills all the way."

Myrrh sensed that another curfew was coming into force, but, just as if she were half a dozen years younger, she wanted to stay out to play even though it was almost dark; the long summer nights had always entranced her, as if a new day had dawned at seven in the evening and a midnight sun, of supreme irresponsibility, had come into being just for her, to make her play for ever.

"Listen," Izz said. "Something coming." He had heard a faint buzzing sound from the road two hundred meters away. "They're on the prowl, checking the outlying districts. Time to go home."

The home in Myrrh's mind was not the home she returned to. Even in the gloom, she felt for the glass of milk, and even when Izz flicked on his flashlight after making sure the final plank was in position, she still thought she was dreaming in her bed, a dream of blurred deprivation that made her roll in dirt like a dog trying to cool itself down.

Once again they settled down to the bleak hiatus between seven and eleven o'clock, in which they tried in their different ways to face going to sleep again in the ground, Izz with a vestigial sense of adventure although already he felt chilled enough to faint, Myrrh with a gathering hysteria barely contained; she had been in the open, where she belonged, and nothing else would do. A dispassionate observer, reporting their time underground merely in terms of hours, might say they had only been there since Thursday, and this was only their fourth night; but, in terms of time inflated through indignity and sheer worry raised to childish maximum, they had been there at least as long as Robinson Crusoe on his island before he found the footprint. Even during the years of peace, camping out on the lawn in June in a makeshift tent improvised from a sheet and an old clotheshorse, a single night had been enough for Izz, and Myrrh had refused altogether: "You just tell me about it, Izz; I'll make do with that." He hadn't been able to sleep at all and had got up repeatedly to look at the stars, a bold and sleek display that night, but they had merely excited him and he'd ended up thinking he might miss something if he closed his eyes. "Oh, it was fun," he'd lied the next day. "You'd have enjoyed it a lot. I watched the stars, and they were watching me."

So now, for him adventure had sunk into boredom and morose indignation, for her claustrophobia had begun to affect her very breath. Each now saw that, to every underground preliminary, there was something preceding even that. Having no exercise, they found their limbs itching to go, and the prospect of never beginning to sleep drove them into successive preludes that only led to other preludes. They became immature insomniacs, unwilling to talk, too tense even to cuddle, rammed up against the old human dilemma of not knowing what to do with the in-between times, for which the outside world had evolved complex cultural remedies from tale-spinning to chamber music, from the monastic illumination of manuscripts to chess.

All Izz had was the bit of paper, which he now examined by flashlight. "A torn page from a book," he said, "and burned. It's hard to read the words." A curl of brittle black, not having broken off before, disintegrated in his hand, but he took a firmer hold and read aloud what he could see: "...to it, that by your great and frequent urgency you prevailed on me to publish a very loose and uncorrect account of my travels." That was all. "Some kind of travel book," he said; not even things that found their way into his hands were interesting. "There's a date. April 2, 1727."

"Not exactly a good night's reading," Myrrh said, toneless and distant.

"Could you be bothered to read anyway?" His mind filled suddenly with the intimidating idea that what people did, in fixes such as this, was to go over and over again the same things, fingering the fabric of what they knew would never change—a death, a loss of limb, a house burned down, a tree snapped in half by wind—yet continually hoping that it would. A kind of death arrived when nothing new happened and you had stared and stared at something until, having become abruptly strange with too much attention, it changed back into itself unenhanced. Thus his pulse, his breath, his itching skin bumpy with hives. What people found to remedy all this, he decided, was something trivial—a menu, a newspaper, a knitting pattern—which enable them to kill time, of course, but to go even further and somehow empty the space they occupied. His own version of this idea was lacksadaisical, whereas Myrrh, having come to it in terms less abstract than his, lay there in a hot whirl of agitation, too jumpy to fix on the blank as Izz had done, and beginning to feel more abandoned, in the sense of left, with each minute. Obsessed with going to sleep early, they found sleep vanishing behind their eyes, drawn up through the gaps between the center plank and its neighbors into the September sky. They wanted it to snow, to rain, lightning to strike their burrow, the Nazis or the farmer to come and haul them out, helpless as oysters. Izz fumed, and drummed his heels against the blanket. Myrrh sighed, then sighed about having to sigh, quite selfishly now wanting her parents to be captured and to blab about where the children were; and Izz's parents too, at last telling the invaders to go and get their darlings, it was all only a game they'd played together, it was nothing bad, no kind of subterfuge at all, they had nothing to hide except one partly Jewish child, and who cared about something so fractional as that?

"Listening to my muscles," Izz told her grandly, "You have to listen hard."

"I can hear my mother and father talking," she told him. "They bore each other. They even talk about how much they bore each other. Is that what life is like? Life to come, I mean."

"And my ears, a sort of pearly whoosh," Izz resumed.

"I wish they'd just shut up," she said dreamily, "and switch on the radio instead."

As if cued, Izz tried their own radio, but could find only static, the most anonymous electrons of all, serving nothing human, but maybe God's own breathing. Was that of interest, enough to get him through the night? No, the pearly whoosh in his ears was *his*, more intimate, whereas this crackling aural flash behind the tiny grille that masked the speaker was nobody's at all: a sound almost designed to make you nervous, to make you miserably aware of all the stuff that surrounded you and didn't care. April 2, 1727 haunted him, though: wasn't that around the time a Swedish king of Poland abdicated? The time of fancy garden layouts and palaces embellished like Christmas cakes. Two hundred-odd years ago, but to him as far away as Adam and Eve. Such a page had come from the school, no doubt, so had the school gone up in smoke? He felt a pang that truly stung, not that he treasured history lessons, or lessons at all, but he adored the ceremony of going to school, he adored devoting so much of each day to what seemed like doing nothing: sitting down and reading, or drawing maps and cross-sections of crocus corms. That was one form of inertia: the best, whereas cooling off underground, with nothing to fiddle about with, no light, no food, and an increasingly tight-lipped Myrrh for company, that was quite another. Myrrh, in her turn, felt Izz was unsympathetic, in his high-spirited secretive way surviving very well because he'd found private things to while away the time, things he wasn't sharing.

"Tomorrow," she said, to interrupt whatever reverie he was enjoying, "we'll have to look for food. Go and ask the farmer. Hunt for potatoes and beets, apples and cabbages. Or we'll get light-headed, and then do something stupid."

"If we go looking for food," he said, "we'll have to go out at night. It's no good wandering around in the daylight."

"How much longer, then?" she said as if talking through stiff paste.

"As long as we can stand it, and then a year. Sorry, I was feeling glum. Know what, Myrrh? The word Poland means those who till the field, people of the fields. We're Poles who've gone back to the fields, the first of a new breed. We'll be legends in no time at all. We'll even be famous in Africa."

Unimpressed, she asked "Do you ever get the sense that, against your will, you're being made to live inside a fairy story of the *nasty* sort, with a wolf to swallow you up and an ogre to grind your bones to dust and an old witch who sews up your mouth with spiderwebs and bees who use you as their queen and feed you fat until you almost burst?"

"No, none of that at all. *If* it's like anything, it's like what happens at the top of looping the loop. It's like the moment when gravity hasn't even begun to drag the plane down again and its upward momentum has only just worn out. It's almost stationary there, at the top of the climb, upside-down, see, and all the forces that affect it cancel one another out. But that sensation's great—I *know* it would be, whereas being down here, well it's creepy and moldy and slimy and lousy. I suppose there are fairy stories that tell about such things. I just don't know of one, and I don't get that put-upon feeling, not like yours, with wolves and such. That must be a girl's response."

Had she been attending to him at all? He held out the palm of his hand for her breath to touch, but she seemed to have stopped breathing altogether, and her nose, her chin, were as cool as meadowgrass at night. "Myrrh?"

"Izz," she said, still without any breathing he could feel, "when somebody tells somebody to go to hell, what kind of hell do you think they have in mind? Fire? Or just very unhappy?"

"Cold in a manger," he said, feeling smart for once. "The serious answer is: I've no idea. They want that person not to exist, it's as simple as that." Then he saw what she was driving at. He agreed. "I suppose we could very slowly turn into nothing, until we're only a pattern of whitewash in the soil. Like where a snail has died."

"A snail?" Myrrh sounded amazed.

"A big-type snail, then."

"One that even talked now and then."

"A snail that read books and liked spaghetti."

"An Italian snail. A snail from ancient Rome."

"Wherever," Izz said, letting his mind come free.

"When they die, they all look the same. They wither."

"Izz, we're not snails, we're sort of people."

"To the snails we might be snails. I guess we're so big they don't have a special word for us, see. And anything that's too big to have a special snaily word, they call it a snail to save time. They're real slow."

Baring his teeth, he mock-bit her on the nape of her neck, pulling a large chunk of skin and flesh at least a few millimeters out of line.

"What was that for?"

"That," he told her with his nose still firm against the mossy fur where her hair began to grow, "was the panther's good night kiss. If we think about being awake, we'll end up going to sleep. Try it."

"Izz," she wailed in that echoless place, "I will never go to sleep again until I'm safe between clean sheets in a bed made of polished wood. I'm too prim for this."

"Think of when the Admiral comes," he said soothingly "He has a parrot in his house. He's everybody's uncle, with a toffee in his pocket, and a surprise in every drawer. You'll see."

"I don't believe in your Admiral," she said in a sullen half-voice, "he's somebody you invented so you wouldn't be lonely in Berlin. Didn't you know that children invent imaginary playmates, Izz? They talk to that sort of playmate all the time, and their parents get upset because they think the kid is crazy, and all she is is lonely. Or he."

"You could ask my mother. She *knows* him, and my father knows him too. He was sort of a family friend, although some of the people he knew were very creepy. Not his friends, but people he dealt with a lot. You saw them coming and going. I've even seen the Admiral in his pajamas, getting the bottoms all wet, walking on the lawn in the dew to take his dogs to see his horse. Now, would I have invented *that*?"

"Izz, you invent all kinds of things. *My* mother and father don't know him, though—we've moved in different circles, as they say, I mean as *people* say."

"I bet you'll see him soon. He has two daughters, one you never see, another who just stares at you, and then buries her face in a big doll's house. She's a violinist, and she knows absolutely nothing about planes. I think she's really a dwarf he uses to pose as a girl, whereas in truth she's one of his spies. And you know what a spy is."

Myrrh snorted at him sarcastically. "It's a kind of flower that you plant, but it never flowers. Izz you aren't the only one with an imagination. I suppose he talks to flowers, then."

"If they're spies, he has to. He even sends them to Lithuania."

"And he's coming to get us out."

"Any day. Do you think, if he knew where we are, he'd leave us here any longer than necessary?"

"How long is necessary?" Her voice seemed to be coming from far away, and something tinny, something that reminded him of toothache, was in it. She was going to cry again, he just knew it.

34

"I'm *not* crying," she said, shoving his hand away from her face.

"I didn't say you were," trying to push his hand as far behind him into the earth wall as he could, but managing only to cause a little crumbly landslide. Soil fell into the back of his hair. "If we stayed here long enough, Myrrh, we'd start to grow roots, like potatoes, and when they came to get us we'd have to be chopped loose with a spade. There must be hundreds of kids who'd enjoy this—you know, a sort of adventure they could talk about when school started up again in September! Just imagine. *What I Did Last Summer, An Essay*, by Isydor Pulwasky."

"Changed your name, Izz? Are you a spy too?"

"One day the Admiral might take me on, as a cadet spy, you see, an apprentice, and he'd set me up in an attic somewhere with invisible inks, a radio disguised as a Bunsen burner, and all kinds of little yellow oilcloth tobacco pouches to hide secret messages in, in chimneys. That's what it's like. And a pill to swallow if I got into trouble. What they call a lethal pill."

"With sugar on it so you wouldn't pull an awful face? Izz, *lethal* means it would make you dream."

"It means you'd forget, it doesn't mean dream. Don't you remember that poem, it wasn't Polish, but it was in the Czechowicz anthology we used at school. *Go not to Lethe—* meant *Don't forget* or *Don't die.* I can't remember any more than that, but it was there, black on white. It made me shiver, and I actually thought that Lethe was some awful place north of Warsaw, where all the houses were full of water, and you drowned if you opened the front door. And there were snakes with sleep in their eyes, a sort of crust that snakes get. You could only get to Lethe in an old squeaky carriage with a horse, and driven by a wrinkled old woman who smelled of rotten apples. If you waited for her at any crossroads, whenever there was nine in the date, she'd pick you up and take you north of Warsaw. I used to imagine all that, and then my mother or my father used to pull me back by the arm and say *Come back now, Izydor,* and they meant from wherever I'd been—I used to get that faraway look and they knew what was going on."

"Will we have school again soon? What would we do without it? What would we do with all the time?"

"Make love." He said it fast but distinct, like a password.

'We don't know how."

"Oh, don't we? You just try me. I've *studied* it."

"I'm trying to go to sleep. Shouldn't we be going to sleep? All you're doing here is scaring me to death. And you don't *study* it, you just do it, it has to be all of a sudden, when you can't help yourself any more. It comes over you and you have to do it. Nothing else feels right. Did you study *that*?"

When they argued, never mind how mildly, their sharp duet built into a crescendo of heavily emphasized words which, supposed to be more than words, were lumps of feeling slammed down, like the letters somewhere in the Bible, made big. In the end, what they countered each other with was rival intensities, not really arguing at all but stressing clincher words such as "study" and "know" and even "heart," sometimes resorting to important words like "impetuous" or "instinctive," but always coming back to how deeply they felt what they knew.

"I can't prove it, Izz, but I *know*."

"Can you prove you know?"

"I can prove that I feel it, even if I can't explain."

"Myrrh, you can only prove you feel it, you can't prove that what you feel—well, makes you know. They're different."

"Then shut up."

"That *then*, my precious, is what the Romans called a *non sequitor*. It doesn't follow, it's just an emotional turn of phrase."

"If you can't shut up, then just shut up."

"Nonsense, Myrrh. You're asking for it twice."

Now, however, in so-called strained circumstances, they were using words as relics, as trophies garnered from above, in a world less verbal than they had ever known, less verbal even than those afternoons passed on top of haystacks, chewing on stalks of straw or tasting flower petals at their bottom tip, which always reminded Myrrh of that little bleb at the inner corner of the human eye: what it seemed to be fastened with, like the flower, although surely the eye would fall out if held only in that place. But she never asked him what the name of the bleb was, because she knew he would know, and sometimes she didn't want to know things, not as Izz knew them anyway. So, in the half-light of her defiant dream about eyes, she almost expected them to come toppling out, and was too lazy—she told herself it *was* laziness—to look it up in the biology textbook she only too rarely opened.

"Izz," she said, having squeezed the tears away by scrunching up her face, "let's go to sleep. Let's try."

"And not to Lethe."

"Turds to Lethe."

"Sounds like a proverb or something."

"Izz, you're more nervous than I am, you're all wound up."

"I'm waiting for the Admiral, and our parents. There's bound to be a picnic, with champagne. I've tried it, and it's grim. It sort of spits at you as you drink it."

"Be a camel, then."

He made a camel's face in the dark until she found the flashlight and illuminated his bottom lip shoved right inside the upper one. That was his camel.

"You're not a very good camel any more. Use the rest of your face as well."

"I've forgotten how. I'm the only camel you've got anyway."

"Then don't be a camel at all. Be grownup."

"I don't know how." She switched off the light. "Camels are easier to do. Now I'm doing it. Look."

She refused though, knowing he should not only wriggle his contorted lips about as if in camel mastication, but also furrow his brow and so slightly depress his eyes into his cheeks.

"I'll take your word. Be a camel in the dark."

"I could be cheating."

"Talk me to sleep."

"That's what I'm doing. Calm down, now, and I promise not to say Lethe again."

"Do you love me?"

"Why not? Will that do?" He liked her to wring it out of him; it always sounded premature, and so the later he admitted it the better. "Say it."

He giggled. "Yes."

"That's not saying it." Her voice dark-brown gentle.

"Then what must I say?" A bit giddy.

"That you love me. Just like that." Coercively inviting it.

"Well, I do."

"This isn't a marriage service, Izz."

"Then let's not rush things."

"You won't say it?" Tense and splintery.

"Love, love, love."

"Not like that, idiot." That breaks the ice, she thought.

"Izz loves Myrrh."

"Still not right. Start with *I*—I'm sentimental."

"And I'm affectionate. I really am."

She gave up. "I know you love me, I don't care."

35

But sleep would not come for either of them, nor any of sleep's substitutes: trance, daydream, stupor, so they lay there in conversationless closeness, each hoping the other would detect in the earth a rhythm which lulled and soothed, and which the other could then pick up just from being close. First they lay flat on their backs, holding hands, then they turned on their sides. Izz once again making a chair for her and, from time to time, at her request, the sounds of panther; mother wren; looping the loop. Then they began to fidget, especially with their feet, at first sticking them out full length until they hit the earth at the far end, after which, in unison, they cocked their legs up and each raised a plank, only to let it fall with a gentle clonk. On and off went the flashlight. Static from the radio only made them feel more isolated than before, as if the radio were broadcasting its own blank mind. Soon they began to get hungry again, but they could not go out to forage, and they had only water to sustain them. Briefly, and with mounting aversion, they discussed catching earthworms, burning them with matches, or over a candle flame, or even in the fat-caked lid of the ham they'd eaten, but they weren't that desperate, they decided: not yet. Izz lit a candle anyway and told her how cozy it was in there, hadn't she realized it? She was cold, she said, so he found the gloves and the long socks for her, asked if he should set the mousetrap or brush her teeth for her, only to hear her saying, No: there didn't seem much point in interfering with fellow creatures or doing goodie-goodie types of things. The world was going to end soon: children would be parentless, parents would have no children, the Germans would be gone, the Poles wouldn't know what to do while waiting for the end, and the air all over the Earth would be as foul as it was down here. Leave her be, he told himself, she has to get it out somehow, and, anyway, I'm not convinced she's all that wrong. There's an unbearable sense of everything's having gone wrong; it's in the air, it's in my heart, it's going through Myrrh's mind like wildfire. It's nothing you can hear, like sirens or explosions, it's more like hearing words spoken and feeling that all kinds of other words are lurking behind the words used, or hovering above them, spurned or inaudible. What did Mother always talk about? That fancy-sounding thing about the end of a cultural epoch had always bored him, but it had sunk in. She had come home one evening in Berlin, full of the idea, which some acquaintance had picked up on the radio from Vienna. Now, to Izz, it made more sense, and there in his cave, like primitive man reconstructed, he began to juggle the pros and cons, the vague notion that the type of human rights for their time in history hadn't yet been born against the even vaguer notion that, somehow, the unforeseen repercussions of human behavior had outstripped the human scale. A madman was on the loose in Germany; you didn't have to study history or even go to school to know that; and the Poles hadn't stopped him yet, although the French and British might try.

He forgave himself for having no highfalutin' ideas about the invasion. It was immoral not to care, just to have in mind getting out of your hole in the ground and up into the sun, the not yet extinguished flowers, and to sit at the family table again even if it were only for bread and preserves; but, he decided with grave adaptability, he was immoral, some boys were, and some even stayed so. They became gangsters, Nazis, ne'er do-wells, but they always seemed to get out of the way before trouble really warmed up. Just knowing an admiral wasn't enough, nor even paying him a certain amount to make sure the bargain stuck. What kind of a man took money anyway just for helping people? The Polish Army could hardly do it, they were too busy fighting; but wasn't there anyone, other than a German, who could whisk them to Sweden, say, or Switzerland? All of a sudden, against his will, he became part of his family, but indifferent to the fate of Poland, and, weirdest of all, wanted to be back in Berlin again, where he had been happy enough: exotic, fussed, and indelibly special.

"Are you asleep, Izz?" Myrrh sounded parched.

"Drink some of this, not too much, mind."

"I hate warm water. I just can't sleep. Not that my mind's going round and round. It's not. I'm just twitchy from not having had enough exercise, that must be it."

"If you need to sleep," he told her, trying to be sage and useful, "then you will. If you don't, you needn't worry. I'm a bit lively myself tonight. Our fourth, you know. Even Jesus Christ only stayed put over the weekend, Friday through Sunday. Do you think they'll find religion after us? No jokes? All right, I'll watch my mouth."

This was the worst night of the four. Looking at the illuminated face of the alarm clock, Izz wished it had a complementary opposite called a calm-down clock, whose hands ran counter-clockwise, taking the sleeper back into the previous day. Perhaps, he reasoned, instead of trying to sleep, the trick was to do everything to stay alert; if trying always failed, as it did with going to sleep, then sheer busyness would make them nod.

"You're fidgeting," Myrrh told him peevishly.

"You don't have the monopoly."

"But I'm better at it, I do it more often. Whereas you, you itch, you're better at that, better than I am, I mean."

"What," Izz wondered aloud, "are our parents doing? Where are they? I feel as if my imagination's failed or something—I can't picture them doing anything. It's as if I don't know them all that well."

"Waiting it out," she said, "with bad grace. Fuming and fretting, rubbing one another raw and practicing their German."

"I bet they never went to the ravine."

"Don't be silly, Izz, they wouldn't leave town with us down here. It wouldn't make sense to go that far. And they're emotionally tied anyway."

"I'm surprised my father didn't sneak out to see how we're doing. It's almost as if we were an investment or something."

"That isn't how *I* see it. Funny, it's not even as if we've been planted. You go outside to see if anything's coming up. In our case, you'd go outside to make sure we were staying down. It doesn't make sense at all."

"I've been told we're almost adults, Myrrh, so we're not even seeds, as children might be thought to be."

"Then it's all over."

"What is?"

"Being kids."

"No way: if you postpone any bit of your childhood, it bursts out later on. You always have it, one way or the other."

"Doctor Czimanski has spoken."

"I'm just keeping busy."

"Then you're not too busy to tell me you love me. We're almost grownups anyway."

"It's true, I do. In my childlike way."

"In a few days' time we might be dead, frozen or starved. Would you like your lips to be sealed for ever without having said that little thing?"

"You're exaggerating. We're just uncomfortable." But, even as he said it, he knew it was just possible that things might go very badly indeed for them, more for Myrrh than for him. The very thing which made her seem riper than other girls, which gave her hips a slightly more voluptuous roll and her manner a touch of histrionic animation—in a word, her part-Jewishness—made her a target. His problem was that he thought of her as Myrrh, sister and childhood sweetheart in one, and never in any category; indeed, he didn't even think of her as Polish, having privately arrived at a view of people (intimates in particular) based wholly on how they were with him. So what they did away from him, hobby or work or other relationships, counted little, and in this way he came to dote on such things as skin texture, hue of eye, vocal mannerisms, and gait and grin and grip, as so many *poems* given him to enjoy. And when he really grew up, he wouldn't care (he told himself) about someone's politics or their status in the world. Moving in diplomatic society, mostly in its at-home manifestations, had made him feel this way:

nurtured among tribes whose main concern was with the pecking order, with nationality and heritage, he had rebelled more or less unwittingly against the day-long ladder of colonels versus majors, butlers versus maids, Germans against Poles, and Teutons against Jews, not to mention the well-bred versus the boors (one of his mother's favored topics) and the articulate versus the rest. Not that he had no standards; he did, but they were his own, designed to apply within a limited radius, and best summarized as how he came to know and treasure another organism. Or not. So the physicality of someone's presence, and how the mind made that body behave, mattered a lot, and he often found himself ignorant of things that others cared about: someone's name, address, group, family, or, at school, which of the rival gangs. At life's banquet he was an oblivious dipper, by some standards a short-sighted sensualist or sybarite, and of course this truncation of appraisal helped him in emergencies: he couldn't see as much of the wood as of its trees, so he could be calm—calmer than Myrrh, for this as well as other more obvious reasons—because the overall design of things didn't much interest him. As long as he was alive, he discovered immediate joys that blotted out things that would obsess most other people.

Some of this he knew. He had been told about it. Not that he tried to mend his ways;

he just tried to relish criticism for its energy, its sheer direction, the ripple it provoked in him, the glee it generated in those who told him off. What bothered him now, however, was that if all this were true, and he suspected it was, then he ought to be having more fun with the beetles, the spiders, the worms, the potato bugs; he ought to be looking forward to the time when the first vole scurried over his face as it tried to go somewhere, and he ought to be lapping up the frayed-wire nerviness of being unable to get to sleep. Quite a lot of the old Izz survived, but he was already responding in a more conventional way: pushed nearer his limits than he realized, he was becoming, at speed, more of an ordinary boy or youth than he had ever been at school, in Berlin, even in private with Myrrh, and this irked him. There is a point, he decided, at which you get so close to life-and-death, or losing mental control—so close to the naked programmed organism, as if you were a dandelion or a centipede—you undergo a personality change akin to having a limb amputated. Is that it? Not exactly. It's more like how a tooth suddenly hurts. All is chemistry, and pain makes you do things that aren't part of your natural personality. And when the tooth is out, what wasn't natural with you falls away. The difference between me and Myrrh, I ought to know, is like that between an optimist and somebody who just hopes. Not that I'm an optimist and she just hopes, but it's that *type* of difference. Optimism being an overall attitude not necessarily based on the available facts, or on facts at all, whereas hope refers to certain cases one at a time. The optimist belongs among those who make up their minds beforehand and don't change, the hoper allows circumstances to decide much more—sometimes there's hope and sometimes there's not, so I belong among the visionary ignoramuses, and Myrrh belongs among the people who go by experience, as no doubt a partly Jewish girl must in a world that calls her a Jew first and discovers who she is later on, or never. The trouble is that the ignoramuses, among whom I belong, also include in their number the racist maniacs the Admiral talked about and introduced me to, thinking I was just an ordinary boy, a bit precocious here and there, whereas I'm precocious all the way through, and it's even precocious to think so. Or does precocious mean that you much too early assume the ways of a stupid adult? I'd always linked it with brains, but no doubt I'm wrong again. I pay for it in spite. So does she—not that her parents have shoved her heritage, her Jewishness down her throat, they're hopelessly vague about it themselves; but there have always been plenty to remind her, negative and positive, and I know how they both go: because you're a Jew, you can't...because you're a Jew you can always...it's as if they'd told her she was a giraffe, and she tried to steer clear of doorways, to keep on looking for higher and higher trees. They should break the mold you're made in and not try to fit you into it for the rest of your days. He broke off, wondering what piece of the natural world had interrupted him, but the tiny rapid squeaking was from Myrrh who, with her back to him, was being a non-ethnic baby wren, avid for food and comfort and his peculiarly maternal hug.

"Good night, wren, I love you," he said softly, finally.

She was not asleep, but sheathed in a cozy farness, a fledgling nestled fluffily in his love, with her mind all but inaudibly remembering *He said it, He said it,* I needn't worry now. Germans might have invaded Poland, but they could not invade her not even when it began to rain lightly, and a slight seepage began to come through the gaps between the planks, drawing an intermittent invisible line down Izz's chest, which felt like gentle anesthesia, he thought: the water-torture before the stone knife in the hand of the Inca priest. When, finally, he dozed off, it was through nightmare such as that. Deliberately envisioning all the horrors in the world, including some he didn't know had virtually come true (his father dead, his mother dead, the Sakals locked in a cell with snakes and rats, Pulawsky crashing not in a light amphibian but in an *Eleventh* that spouted flame), he found they did the opposite of what they ought to do, and he faded out, damp, exhausted, his own best exorcist, with one hand numbly clasped on Myrrh's head, the other stretched toward the earthen wall, which was the top of their bed, to keep off those creatures who lurked in there and bided their time to come out and bite.

36

Seated calmly in her little detention room in Pulawy Palace, Wanda Czimanska found it hard to believe she smelled the aroma of toast and cheese, but she did, and it surged into the room on a tray carried by the same white-coated orderly as before, who brought her a plate of sliced canned ham, a bottle of nondescript white wine that smelled of cloves, and a couple of polished apples. The ham had a sheen in which various fish-like hues came together until she scraped them away with the dental mirror, almost queasily watching the scrapings in the glass as they were born. Snack time at the Palace wasn't her idea of gracious living, but it did very well as a way of keeping body and soul together. The smoke of toast was preferable to the cloying smoke of all those cigars, suggesting as it did, to her at least, not a tribe of officers having a bivouac picnic amid the mahogany and ivory of the dining room, but the close of a summer evening in Kazimierz, after a long day swimming in the Vistula, and that curious sensation of the sun's having given them nothing at all, but having taken, so that they all three felt sucked dry by it, not just of moisture, but of substance too. She crunched her toast, some of it burned black, and meditatively gnawed the cheese, salty and congealed in a bevel-edged flood (they had toasted the cheese on top of the toast, she realized, which was why the corners of the toast were overdone). Amazed at how slowly she established this, she decided to try not to think at all; then she would not notice how slow she had become. But things kept occurring to her, ideas and memories in somnambulist procession: the swish of wet bathing shorts as someone walked into the house straight from bathing (Surely not outside the door? Surely not one of the generals after a dip in the Vistula, walking in wet as if he owned the place?); then the plop-flap sound as she patted Izz's little wet behind with a partly cupped hand and urged him to get into something dry. Once he had found a fallen bird and tried to rear it in a can full of cotton wool, feeding it slugs and caterpillars, which for a day or so it accepted and converted into soft thick rods of pure-white toothpaste blurted from an anus wide enough, at full distension, to fit a cigarette; but at length it had choked, gone still, although with a faint tremor in the beak, and then sagged sideways, at which point Izz had cried, saying "You said I'd become it's mother! And now it's dead, and its real mother has left it, and its other mother has let it die." The bird's mouth had been the color of fried egg; the tiny jaws had clacked astonishingly loud; full of grubs and other unmasticated food, the bird had quivered in a stoked-up trance, gradually cementing the white wool fluffs together with its hourly squirts until it had seemed in pale gray cement both soft and stiff. And she had said, "Izz, darling, only a mother bird can rear its young. There's knack. Once you've touched the baby bird, the mother won't return." She hated herself for remembering something so obvious, which seemed to rebuke her almost allegorically for having stuffed her own baby into the ground, where presumably he was feeding himself, if he was lucky.

"Everything all right?" It was Zollerndorff who stuck his immaculate, groomed head round the door. He explained she would have to sleep where she was, but the orderly would bring her sheets and blankets. "I warn you," he laughed, "we've unearthed them from upstairs closets, and we're not responsible for mold or moths!" If this was war, it was a chummy, offhand thing, and the force that had slaughtered her own husband that very morning was also the one apologizing for the bed linens, as if she had wandered into some long-closed Alpine *pension* and insisted on spending the night there, even though moths the size of hummingbirds cowered beneath the uncased pillows, and colonies of red mites scurried about in the mold cached in the seams of the sheets.

"Thank you, Captain. Bed and board. My husband would have appreciated your sense of scruple. I am sorry that you never met. You are both amateurs, I sense." *Were*, she thought. What tense do you use when one of the subjects of a sentence is dead, but is still very much present in the flesh, and the other is alive in front of you? The two domains necessitated different verbs, of course; Ludwik was no longer an amateur soldier; death had somehow completed him, had made him an accomplished professional for ever and ever, and when this Zollerndorff was dead he too would be no longer an amateur. Death was the last promotion.

"What are a few moths to us?" she said in fixated severity, almost in tears, and desperately pointing to the plates of toast and cheese and ham. "We are the defeated."

"Then this is honorable amends," he said gently. "But we have only come here to defeat ourselves. We have gone to the house next door to do something disreputable. You have fought us tooth and nail, with swords and guns. But we were ready and you were not. There will be no more interrogations; but—" he seemed to ponder about speaking further, then made up his mind, "—if the SS come interfering here, as well they might, we may not be able to protect you. The Admiral, yes; but he won't be here until Tuesday or Wednesday, and I hear rumors that the SS have plans for Poland as a whole. They're bound to show up. The Army, as I think you know, has no more use for them than for the devil's claws, but they prevail, they prevail...."

"Then what?"

"We'll put you in the wainscot."

"With a cask of Amontillado," she said with an hysterical flick, trying to master her mind, to make it settle into a dignified mood no longer available to her, she could not fathom why.

He nodded, "So long as you didn't get lost."

Then she blurted out. "Or get me away to Kazimierz at once. To my children?"

"Too much trouble to get you back. The Admiral will arrive by rail, from Kielce and Deblin. His itinerary's just come through. Poznan to Lodz, and then down here. The tracks have been repaired."

"It's not 'Lodz,' it's *Woodzh*. Don't you think, Captain Zollerndorff, you should learn to pronounce things properly before you take them on?"

"Begging your pardon," he said with debonair chagrin, "but the question won't arise. We are going to change the name of everything so we *can* pronounce it. I mean, the Army is, the men who make the maps. I'm sorry, but that's the way of it. Why worry? You'll soon be in a different landscape. How's your French? How's your Italian? No, I don't *know*. I didn't mean to imply that was where. You're just as likely to need Romansch, or Rumanian. The Admiral runs Babel, you know, like a private boarding house."

"But I'd like to go to my children now. It isn't far." She saw herself getting into the hole in the ground, squashing Myrrh to lie alongside Izz, or to kneel contorted at his side, or becoming the children's mattress, hip-deep in mud and slime. It was raining, and for the first time she understood what rain could do to a hiding place. "Listen to the rain," she said. *Tell him.* No, wait for the Admiral. This Zollerndorff was affable and firm and decidedly unmilitary, but he ranked so low he might be overruled at the last moment, and where would she and the children be then? Temporize, she told herself: he is your conduit, he's the go-between. Wait it out.

After Zollerndorff had gone, with a carefully shaded bow somewhere between acquiescence and punctuation point, she tried to fix her gaze while holding an apple, and what she found to hold her was the face of a crowned king on the wall, first of all seeing only her reflection, which is to say herself looking at nothing to begin with and then watching herself looking at herself, after which, through the veil of the old varnish, she saw the outstaring king in the act of looking at her daring to stare at him, who was dead, almost as if she were the original painter of old and saw the king in the flesh as he glowered at the eyes which were going to fix him for ever, exactly as those eyes perceived him. Then she again noticed her own face peering at all of this, unable to believe that so much could pass between herself and the two-dimensional king just because there was light in the room, and not very good light at that.

She almost readied herself for a miracle: if looking hard could set all that overlapping successiveness in motion, then a hard look at Ludwik in the stables might bring him back, oh not to life, she knew that remained in the hands of necromancers, but to—she had no idea, having all the emotions that would fit, yet lacking the word for the state she so longed for him to be in. Neither a death mask nor a painting would do, not even if Ludwik, like this curmudgeon of a narrow-shouldered king, had a big yellow shield that trapped a black eagle emaciated as a violin stand with feathers. Come back now, Ludwik, she mouthed. I am convinced. The demonstration has worked. Life can end. Please do not dress up and sneak away into the dawn of Friday the 15th of September ever again. Let us go and pick up the children now and get them out of their wet bathing suits. The waters of the Vistula reach through the pores. These newcomers cannot even pronounce Kielce properly: they say it with a soft *c* instead of as Kieltze, which, if they only thought about it, they could easily manage like the *ts* sound in *Seif* or—again her mind had wandered off into the maze of grief, where it heard itself unproductively sobbing behind a hedge as high as a castle: "Oh, my love is slain, under false pretenses, in the flower of his manhood, and my children I have buried first." It was wrong, of course; it wasn't true, not that part of it, but so much had happened so fast that Ludwik was not irrevocably dead (the fact was so new it might yet be changed), whereas the longer the children stayed where they were the less she could envision their coming out.

If only they could all go back to, of all places, Berlin, to the fragrant small house in the Dollestrasse, nestled in the sleepy suburb called Sudende, where it was all gardens tended with almost British fanaticism and architecture in the chalet style. The houses were houses, of course, but their style had given her a breath of the Alps, and she longed for the sleepy afternoons when she could nearly hear the beams creaking in the summer heat, or, in winter, pick out the tinkle of sleigh bells or wind chimes within the fat muff of snow. A military suburb or dormitory, it revealed its severity in only the mildest way; it was where junior diplomats and medium-rank officers kept their unofficial dreams; no one wore a uniform there. In good weather, whole families strolled up and down, showing off a new baby, or retreated to the back gardens to play croquet. Once, the Admiral himself had lived there, almost next door to Reinhard Heydrich, but had then moved to a villa in Schlachtensee, as befitting his rank, and the Polish Embassy had soon after that moved Major Czimanski to Wannsee in order to house his assistant in Sudende. The new house had never quite won her over, though, and she always homed to it as the place where Izydor was truly little, had banged his personal little croquet mallet on the manicured lawn, had actually set up his train set by the goldfish pond (transporting, as he said, ants' eggs for the fish to eat), and on occasion had romped with the Admiral and his dogs, crying "Mush! mush!" as the Admiral had taught him. How, then, could a man who had known them so intimately, for so long, not yet have—what was the word?—*exerted* himself to get them out? Now Ludwik was no more and Izz and Myrrh were at risk, and the Admiral was somewhere in Germany, blathering at his dogs while serious people tried to get answers out of him with voices raised. Or, when he finally paid attention, he put to them such naïve questions, the responses to which he then twisted and elaborated until his interlocutors couldn't remember what they had said in the first place. No doubt the parrot rattled on, the violin and the flute drove him from home on Sundays to spend the entire day at his office, and the Polish masseur—formerly Rusztowanie abbreviated into Rust as being more German—eased the Admiral's muscles and Mohammed the butler lined their stomachs. Had he really dealt with Mata Hari in the old days? Did he still, as rumor claimed, maintain an undercover force of deaf mutes in all the capitals of the world? To pick up every secret conversation that took place over a dinner table. Or were they just people who could read lips? Or even (all the energy drained from her at this) read *minds*? What had he said to the Polish Ambassador, Józef Lipski, on the day of a large reception held in a high wind? "It's better outside, in a wind like this: what's said carries further, and what's lost gets blown even farther away." He always wanted to hear, but he never wanted to say. His mane of white hair blown awry forward in the breeze was his only message. His periwinkle eyes filtered all, missing nothing except what he wanted to miss. Right there, with the face of the old king outstaring her on one wall, and the outsize lily which strained toward the light away from her, she willed the Admiral to do his part, not merely to make the journey, but to put an end to a mother's misery. Uncle Wilhelm, she almost prayed, using Izz's phrase for him, Come and get us soon. Our help in ages past. Strong to save. And in the years to come. I am a widow now, thanks to your despicable invasion. Surely the tremor that ran through her was not the vibration of the Admiral's answer; no, it was only the final collapse of her nerves, pushed beyond their limits by this final overload of care, this punitive long-distance act of will. She realized that what she wanted almost as much as to have the Admiral give the three of them safe passage (she had forgotten about the Sakals since arriving in Pulawy Palace) was to yell at him, slap his face, tear his floating hair out by the roots, and teach him what not to do when in power. Their meeting would be a diplomatic collision, not a reception: Don't you realize, man? You have killed a friend. If you Germans had left well alone, my Ludwik would be doing a crossword puzzle by lamplight after a day on the river, but he's beginning to rot in the barn out there. You could have spirited us out long before things came to this. We needn't have put our children underground at all. Then she thought of the Sakals, wondering, wondering, and raised the seating in the escape airplane to five, plus the pilot. *Five?* Five: Ludwik made five, and if their Daddy's body upset the children, then they would have to stay upset—it would be the last thing for him that they could do.

Wanda Czimanska, she said aloud, you are really losing your wits. He was Izz's father only, he is; not Myrrh's. Why is it that I think he's the father of other children too? I have been trying, and trying, to keep things straight, but my mind is epileptic, and all this—lily, portraits, coffee, ham and cheese and toast, the non-stop Zollerndorff from Wannsee, the talk of the SS, the dental mirror and the spike, my Ludwik dying right in front of my eyes, my son buried underneath a pigsty—comes together like a fireball into which I'm made to stare. And then there's nothing. There's less than that. Only the scald from too much crying, and a hollow which is not that of the stomach, or the lung that cannot breathe, or the heart through which no blood can go. I shall be empty as long as I live, another ghost in this house of ghosts.

37

"It's me again," said Zollerndorff easily. "The rain has stopped. You had enough to eat?"

Why should he report the rain unless he knew about Izz and Myrrh under the planks? "I'm glad," she said without moving her lips. "Not that I have anything against rain."

"If they come tomorrow," he said in a different tone, "we will *secrete* you somewhere. You are the Army's prisoner."

"*Prisoner?*" She was aghast, having thought of herself as a refugee perhaps, maybe even an injured party, but as someone taken prisoner, never. "I gave myself up, Captain. I surrendered."

"Very well, then. Prisoner of peace. How is that?" He smiled the smile of the overtaxed bureaucrat: forbearing, tense, and bland.

"What about diplomatic privilege?"

"In your own country, Madame?" He almost stood to attention.

"It's yours now, isn't it? You can't have it both ways. You can't come and take it and still pretend it's ours. It would be, if you'd stayed out; but you came in, you took us over. So I *can* claim diplomatic immunity, and that includes immunity from being called the wrong thing. What I am, Captain Zollerndorff, is a stateless person. Have you heard of anything more diplomatically immune than that? Have you now? Do you know what I mean?" All this, in German, took him by surprise, and he began to think he had never thought anything through at all; every phenomenon made him feel stupid, unpracticed, lost in trivial zeal. The woman had a nasty habit, in her truculently dreamy way of being always nine-tenths right.

"We still have to get you through Monday," he said. "I mean tomorrow. Tuesday the Admiral will be here, and then we'll have a new set of problems. Never mind. The Admiral carries more clout with the SS than most generals do. He's close to them without being exactly of them."

"He was always good to me," she told him, surprised to hear her voice saying what it said. First get him here, she was thinking, then we'll sort things out. "So: I'm to go into the wainscot. Is that it?"

"Through any one of some dozen secret doors."

"Then, Captain, you should hunt up a ball of thread, or I might never find the way out. What would you do then, with the Admiral cooling his heels and me lost in the walls of the palace? Would you send him in after me?" Another voice was talking for her, brittler and more imperious than her own; a voice that breathed her grievance in deep, and spat electric flame.

"He has others to do that kind of thing," he said unguardedly. "I mean, he wouldn't enter the wall himself."

"My God, man, what if he did, and we neither of us came out, ever? A mouse would marry us inside the plaster, and we'd live happily ever after, on dust and copper wire."

"I'm sorry, truly, if I have frightened you."

"After this day's doings," she told him haughtily, "what with one death and some others, I don't think I'll frighten easily again. It's my children I'm worried about. And all this delay. You know, if you'd sent me down to Kazimierz when I mentioned it, we'd be back now, and the children would be asleep in a bed at least as damp as mine, as damp as these sheets and things."

"No," he said with an acid pucker. "I asked. The General said no."

"General who? May I speak to him?"

"He would not speak to you."

"Do you mean he wouldn't answer me if I spoke to him? Or did he refuse to speak to me at all?" She pointed at her blouse.

"The latter. Which takes care of the former."

"General *Guderian*, then? Is that who it is?"

He shook his head. "Such information is restricted."

"Ah," she said, trying to recall embassy parties, German rather than Polish. "Most of the high-ranking officers we met were from the Luftwaffe. Do you know why? But I recall General Freiherr Geyr von Schweppenburg, and Bader and Wiktorin. How strange it is, Captain, to find your hosts at a rather charming party have become, almost overnight, the plunderers of your native land. As if the drink had gone to their heads, and they started to smash windows and demolish houses just for a student prank. Was it perhaps General von Küchler? When I arrived here, I didn't—"

"It's official," he said wearily. "The Army is taking a stand, you see, but only in an informal way. Any outright confrontation with the SS, we would lose. And lose face as well. But, behind the scenes, we can work a miracle or two. It is not necessary for you to know the intricate workings of the entire maneuver. Even if you have done nothing, and not what you claim to have done, the SS would grab you just like that. You even stole one of their motorcycles: a capital offense, in time of war."

"In time of war," she said as if tasting the words.

"Just an expression," he said. "You know what's going on."

"Just an invasion, Captain? I don't see many Germans running hell-for-leather for the border, just to get back home again, to their steins of beer, their corpulent butter-cream torte-sucking wives, their revolting politicians and their—"

"You know Germany better, Madame. It is not Germany which has done this to you, it is the Party."

"And the Party is a completely self-supporting thing, for whom no one is responsible. It pleases itself, and you all go along?" She was amazed at herself. When someone died, when your husband died, you expected to feel dead yourself, and not be able to make sense, to argue; yet here she was, taking on Zollerndorff in a spirit akin to that of repartee, as if some still-adroit part of her being had lifted clear of circumstances and had begun to function out of sheer defiance: not to scream or to weep, though she had done both since reaching Pulawy Palace, but to do the sort of thing Ludwig himself might have done if confronted with a Zollerndorff. The more she said, the more Ludwik's vigorous living image came into her mind, to fuel her and boost her for debate. Now he was standing on tiptoe to stretch himself out vertically, with his fingertips prodding skyward, in order, as he said, "to get the kinks out of my system." Now, in an altogether different mood, he was working every evening of the late summer in the garden of the house on Dollestrasse, building a cage of laths and chicken wire to protect their one small vine from birds, squirrels, foxes—whatever it was that, the year before, had taken all two dozen bunches of the crop in one night, leaving only the skins. First he built the cage, using a few screws and a lot of nails, then he enclosed it in bendable wire, smoothing out the corners with his bare hands, getting more than a few nicks in the process, but thrusting on, hammering the nails halfway in and knocking them sideways over the wire, down firm until the head of the nail went beneath the level of the wood. After he had painted the cage white, for appearance's sake but also to waterproof the wire and the coarse unfilled grain of the wood, he lashed it with creosote-treated cord to the lattice up which the hardy little vine grew, then screened the back of the trellis with another layer of wire. That done, somewhere about the fifth evening, with sore fingers and sweating into his eyes, he began to hang what he called "baffles" on those parts of the cage where grapes were growing perilously near the wire, making the bunches harder to reach because each of the baffles was a good twenty centimeters deep. With his pliers, he squeezed most of the holes tighter and smaller, at least those directly in front of the bunches, so making some of the other holes even larger; but these were away from the danger zone, as he called it. By this stage in the process, the wire-cutting edges of his pliers had blunted, and in order to cut he had to twist and pull, which left several jagged edges, to be bent outwards as far as possible. In effect, this made a sort of barbed wire against the night marauder, and he warned her not to get too close when collecting the grapes. Seeing the blood on his hands, she believed him, wondering at the same time why he had not painted the wood before hammering the wire home; some of the wood was still bare because the brush had missed. "I forgot," he said with a boisterous laugh. "I got carried away!"

"How," she had asked him then, "are we going to get the grapes out? No one can reach them now." But that was the final part of the work: cursing the blunt pliers, he cut three sides of a rectangle into the front of the cage after first positioning himself close to the wire and making, to all areas of the cage where grapes were growing, the motions of reaching and gathering. That was the door, which he tied with cord, a figure reattached to its ground. Next came the padlock, fastened in place while he allowed himself a jubilant grin, and the last line of defense: a motley collection of opened, washed cans, whose lids were still connected by a flange of metal. "No labels," he told her. "I tore the labels off. The sun on the shiny tin will reflect even more sunlight on to the grapes, and it blinds the birds as well, if birds it was." Izz began to laugh at such completeness.

"At night?" she said, reluctant to speak at all, wondering how well he had planned the whole operation, hastening to have the whole thing done so that he could stand and contemplate it with one of the most complex smiles in the world; proud, gratified, boyish, daring the wildlife to come and do its worst, to dangle for ever from a paw trapped in a loop of the wire, or impaled through the wing by one of his thin jagged spikes. The sunset glowed against his features as he turned to face it, looking through the front of the cage at the grapes and past them, beyond the reinforced trellis, to the vermillion spill along the western horizon, like red leather in a cocoon of thin saffron glass. Then he changed position, slipping one hand into the top of his trousers, and she at once knew she had seen him before, in another life, at enormous altitude, where it was windless and no one breathed, as a male angel leaning against a granite pillar, with one hand just as nonchalantly thrust into his loincloth, capping the glans that grew heavily upward from the dimpled clove of the scrotum just beneath. Until then she had believed in the sexlessness of all angels, and this hadn't mattered because she didn't believe in angels anyway, so their having organs or not had been merely a funny annotation to a myth. Behind him, though, as she had studied him during that sunset as he surveyed the grape-cage, with Izz beside her looking appalled and anxious, she saw how the foliage behind him seemed to absorb him into its pattern, making him oddly two-dimensional, while above him, on the cross-bar supported by the twin columns, she saw something else which only her own mind had supplied. Ludwik was there, half-melted into the image of some preposterous angel she had remembered from a book of parodies; but this other thing was not, and it came from no book. Two leaning figures in hoods and cloaks of purple were dragging sideways, in long loops of skin-like fabric, the eyelids of a woman's face whose mouth remained open, downcast in a roaring ellipse of grief or pain. The whole tableau had frozen. It was not her own face, or that of any woman she had met; but it felt so close, so familiar, that she let fall from her hand the little stones with which she was going to cover the inside bottom of the cans, to make them rattle when bird, fox, or phantom touched them.

"You look as if you've seen a ghost," he'd said, at last blinking the sunset out of his eyes.

"No, I think a ghost has just seen me," she said, unable to explain or make excuses, "I sometimes see things strangely. There was a head above your head, with coarse blond strands of hair almost like piping." Now it had gone, a skein of vapor in the blue.

"You've been looking at books of heraldry again," he said with a shallow laugh. "You're superimposing. Take it from me, Wanda, those shields exist to simplify—there's no human situation that corresponds to them. They're to show off with, to brandish. Why, even a human name is more complicated than a coat of arms. Usually, anyway. Now, what about those stones? Let's make a rattle for whoever comes while we're asleep."

She picked them up from the lawn, pensive in slow-motion, wishing she might never see again what wasn't there, and wasn't prophetic either, and wasn't even—she didn't know what she was trying to think—*was I trying to say "true"?* She wondered, dimly, what truth there could be that wasn't factually past, present, or to come. Nothing is ordained, she scolded herself: *nothing at all.* Then, as if nothing had happened, she and Ludwik and Izz were dropping stones into cans, almost as if playing the children's game which cast a pebble into a well or a defunct mineshaft and waited for the distant splash after the long fall. When that was done, and the cans had been tied to the cage with lengths of wire passed through holes punched through the top rims, Ludwik with a mysterious callow cry ran indoors for something, which he found after a quarter of an hour, while she and Izz tested the cans and pretended to be birds or foxes trying to reach the grapes.

"Look what I've found," he called as he approached. In a small cardboard box, nestling on tissue paper, six Christmas tree bells caught and reshaped the evening light and tinkled faintly as he stirred his elbows.

"Not outside, surely," Wanda had told him. "There's no need." Did he want to frighten whatever took the grapes? Or was he eager to greet them instead? "They're only glass," she'd said, "they'll only break."

But fasten them on he did, humming something indecipherable, and the glossy blue and red and green bells at once picked up the evening breeze, creating an effect of wry delicacy, in contrast with the hamfistedly hammered-together cage, the patchy white paint, the improvised look of his entire contraption.

"You don't even like grapes," she had said, forgiving him.

"I'll try one, if any survive." He'd almost blushed just then, popping a finger against his lower lip to show where the single grape would go (and perhaps no farther, since mere contact with fruit had always made him shudder, it was the acid in his already acid mouth, he claimed, which is why so much calculus built up on his teeth although he never had a cavity).

'They're already starting to purple," she had said then. "Your timing's perfect." And, indeed, not a bunch was lost; she, mainly she, and Izz, and the Sakals had polished off the grapes in a couple of weeks with Ludwik looking on, his face wreathed in I-told-you-so euphoria, and the little glass bells went back unbroken into their cardboard box on top of the wardrobe (one of the few places safe enough for them). The cage stayed put, against another season, through the snow and the spring rains, looking like something frail—something that should have been horizontal instead, over rows of plants—which had been blown against the trellis and had stuck there, left to its fate by people too lazy or too incurious to venture out through the upheaved drifts of the Berlin winter and the rains of spring.

"The Party," Zollerndorff was saying, why and to whom she could not establish for at least a minute, "is like an iceberg in the North Atlantic. You always have to go round it, unless you are some sort of Titanic. It drags all of use in its wake."

"You mean the Titanic going down?" She wanted to sleep, to sink away now, from the one mood of impossibly painful nostalgia into another, in which peaceful death was congruous, with not another word spoken on her behalf, by anyone, as long as time endured.

"No, the iceberg floating." He was staring at her still ocher-colored face.

"I don't care about the Party," she told him wanly. "My husband was killed this morning. Nothing is serious any more. Only a child." She corrected herself with lazy huskiness. "Only two children. Child is generic, you see."

He saw he would have to go. Had he told her what he came to tell? He thought so, but she had so bemused him, first appearing to attend, then floating away from him almost, it seemed, into the back-furled superstructure of the lily, like an inebriated bee. The pungent sadness of almost everything came over him as he eased the door shut behind him and motioned to the guard to resume his place. Tomorrow she would have to hide inside the wall.

When she at last began to drop off, the process reminded her of something she could say in French: *reculer pour mieux sauter*—stepping back in order to jump better. With each sudden sag into sleep, she twitched awake again as if jabbed, the victim of a double state, at least until she began to curb the sag in anticipation of the sudden start that followed, and this wearied her even more, making her crave the long fall from which she never came back. Haarkünstler, or his minions, would be coming for her, she just knew it; no one got away for long with the kind of thing she'd done with what still clinked against the mirror inside her blouse. The Admiral would come too late. It would be no use hiding behind the wall. Zollerndorff had no hope of protecting her, and indeed was not obliged to do so. A whim had got her into trouble with Haarkünstler; *his* whim. A lunge had taken her still deeper in. Another whim, no doubt, though fortified by her mention of the Admiral's name, had earned her a stay of execution at the hands of the generals who hid behind Zollerndorff, But, in the end, all luck ran out with the sands of time, she thought: you always find the Old Testament on your track if you wait long enough, and anything done to her would apply to Izz and Myrrh as well, and their children's children who would never come into being. Oddly, the horror of that prospect acted as a sedative, and, with a sense of floating sideways, she began to go, felt the going gather momentum even as, quite irrelevantly, she longed for the finishing rinse she used after washing her hair. She ached to be clean, before she dirtied her hands, her face, her mind, again.

Certain members of the military staff worked through the night, setting the palace a-twinkle with yellow lights banned by the rudimentary blackout regulations; but the Poles had hardly any bombers anyway, and most of the *Eleventhi* that Izz doted on had been lost already, one hundred and eight having been lost in the course of shooting down rather more than that number of *Luftwaffe* airplanes. Six more *Eleventhi* would be lost before the end of air fighting, and the final number would be 114 Polish fighters lost against 120 aircraft of all kinds from the enemy armada: no disgrace in that. It was rather as if the cavalry that had fought the tanks on the ground had fought them in the air as well, with stoical benighted chivalry, unable to stop the aerial tide but determined to even the score. Captain Zollerndorff slept badly in a bedroom too vast and too stuffy; all the unoccupied space tugged at his mind, as if he should get up and occupy it as part of the invasion, and the mothball smell tickled his nose almost as hay fever did, making him sneeze himself awake with a startled whoop. If the SS came to interfere, he thought, chalk and cheese would meet, and he was cheese, young and ripe for the knife. So, then, why was he, well beyond the scope of his orders, doing favors for this Czimanska woman—the mare—instead of protecting his rear? Boredom, charity, the urge to interfere and to draw attention to himself, all came into it, and he already knew exactly how she would get into the walkway behind the wall, where the nocturnal ghost patrolled the palace. *Ghost?* He knew nothing of ghosts, but the word would do for someone as yet unfound. Surely not an SS spy already installed, waiting to link up with the main force? No, they were too shrewd for that, and not imaginative enough. Perhaps, though, one of the Admiral's deaf mutes was already at work, although how anyone read lips through a wall he had no idea. It would be just like the Admiral to have a whole team of them posing as mutes, as deaf, after a rigorous course in dissimulation conducted in the Alps somewhere. Carefully rehearsed, they would never flinch when a tray crashed down or pay the slighted heed to thuds and thumps, or even uttered words. With such a shadow force, he concluded, the Admiral would have raised his three brass monkeys—who did not speak but heard all and saw all—to exponential maximum, and the world would be his, at least on the level of information. Yet the strong always inherited the meek who inherited the earth. Information was not everything, and one day, he felt it in his bones like an expanding suet, the SS and the Gestapo would run everything, with carte blanche to know as well as to kill and maim. And this military career of his, begun in a spirit of fidgety adventure and in accordance with family tradition, was merely a badge of ice in a slowly warming oven. There was no honor, no *honor*, in half the things the Army did, and it was beyond his own personal power to save his conscience repeatedly, like the Admiral. There were limits: once lucky but caught out the next time, and there would be only the scaffold, being seized and shoved headfirst into the machine, and then the unspeakable second before the thundering blade bit into his neck. Was chivalry worth that? Was anything worth that? Back in 1935, two German women, Frau von Falkenhayn and Frau von Natzmer, both of whom he had run into casually on the beach of Wannsee Lake, had become involved in spying; the former, of Swiss birth, talked the other, a secretary in the War Ministry, into filching secret papers to be photographed, including the outline plan for the German attack on Poland. Frau von Falkenhayn had plied the other woman with gifts from expensive stores, and had then tried to talk her into enlisting the aid of all the other girls in the Ministry as well. Caught, they were condemned to death. "I die gladly for my new Fatherland," Falkenhayn had cried as she was led away from court.

Not I, he thought. Spare yourself the ax. The Poles didn't even credit the plans they eventually received. It was all a waste of time and lives. I'll make this one my last and then shuffle papers for a year or two while I think things through. With his hand over his eyes, he thrust his head deep into the early twentieth-century pillow that reeked of mold and smoke, all of a sudden wishing he too, like the then Colonel Guderian, could break off all social relationships with the Poles, as Guderian had in 1935 after the Falkenhayn-Natzmer case, only to come back at the head of an invading army four years later, as a lieutenant general who this very day was in Brest-Litovsk, raging at an order to retreat because Brest was going to handed over to the advancing Russians, who in turn would halt at the River Bug.

All that's far away from here, he told himself. It's in the east, and this is really the last day of the war, bar a few wordy surrenders here and there, bar the removal of German troops west of the Bug. The thing is over. It hardly even began. Seventeen days. We overran them like ants. We have brought them the culture of the ax, the bomb, and the curfew. All they had was Chopin, Madame Curie, and Henryk Sienkiewicz, author of historical novels. Unfair: they have much more, but we shall in all probability forbid it, banning all forms of Polishness, just as the Prussians did in the 1870s. The wolf and the bear will quarrel over the guts of the Polish eagle's corpse. *Heil Hitler.* We came all this way, although in one sense only over the backyard fence, only to let the Russians loose. Can I go on thinking without using words? Is it possible to think of things as abstractly as that? At least things that don't bear thinking about? If you were more of a warrior, you'd be glad; if you were another Fortinbras, you'd be glad of a lump of Poland. *How purposed?* says Prince Hamlet. *Against some part of Poland,* a captain tells him. Were they just marching through Poland, then, to get their hands on something else? Nah, says the prince, the Poles won't even defend it. Yes, the captain says *it is already garrisoned.* Fortinbras was a Norwegian, Hamlet a Dane. They were going through Denmark to get to Poland. How could I forget? How get that wrong? "A little patch of ground," the captain said. "That hath in it no profit but the name." Not worth defending. That was what Prince Hamlet meant. *Goodbye you, sir.* It has been squabbled over since the dawn of history. It's only where other nations overlap. A crossroads, a culvert, the place where the wakes of ships that pass one another in the night mingle and vanish. It's a playing field, that's all, for games that have no rules.

Then he knew that, once the Admiral had been and gone, he, Zollerndorff, would wash his hands of the whole thing. Never again would he meddle, never mind which general deputed him to make a show of military civility just to throw a sop to the Army's badly bruised conscience. He too, like Guderian, would stage an orderly withdrawal, but on his own initiative. He could hear footsteps going up and down the hallways, those of guards or night clerks or, the lowest-ranking troops of all, manual laborers in uniform appointed to sweep and wash, to dust and polish, just to keep the palace palatial, as if nothing untoward were going on, neither here nor on the maps. The only dead man on the premises was an imported Polish major, killed in a war so far from here it might have been in Denmark, or in the Norway evoked on the fringe of the play. When he went home, he not Fortinbras, the children would mob him, asking for presents, and his wife would hug him close as if he were a myth that had finally come to earth. I, he schooled himself, I administer, I do nothing else. I'll say she slipped away again. No, the Admiral will do that, unless he escorts her out with bugles and banners. He's done it before, he's got them out, so he might not mind the ax; he's earned it, whereas I, losing one head for one fit of altruism, I'd be a patchwork fool. He butted his face into the pillow as if the stuffing held oblivion, and its dank aroma were the status quo of August 31.

38

Awakened from their shallow sleep by some night sound, Izz and Myrrh lay with the battery radio between them, and a bulky thing it was, making them slide their legs sideways to give it room. All they heard, though, was the procession of static, as if the radio had finally found its own voice, or voices, one of which was like the flick-flack of a loose strip of rubber attached to a wheel somewhere and hitting something as it went round and round: a casual, languid rhythm with nothing of the war in it, almost sedative; or it would have been, on its own, but the other sounds, amid a background snarling of summery atmospherics mixed beyond recall, had much more agitation in them, especially what sounded like the quivering, electric shudder of a big machine shoved to its maximum and being drained nonstop of all its power, so that it emitted a massive whine that changed pitch only slightly. Wherever it was, it must have been ready to explode or to trundle away from its mooring, made mobile by sheer vibration, but it stayed, hogging the airwaves with its unappeased agony, pushing slacker noises into the background and making Izz more nervous that he'd been all day. It was like something waiting to get them, ready to creep out from the low shed that housed it and advance toward them.

"Just listen to that," he said, dry-mouthed. "What do you think that could be?"

"A generator," Myrrh said in her practical way. "You only hear it at night. We've heard it before—but there were always other sounds like music or talk on top of it."

Izz yawned laboriously. "It's like the noise of whatever it is that runs the world. I wish it would quit. I don't mind the other sounds at all, but this one hurts my head." She mentioned aspirin, but Izz couldn't be bothered, trying instead to fix his ears on the other noises in the gigantic bowl of night above them while the invisible sun played on the atmosphere of the earth's other half that faced it. One noise went *chuddudah-chuck*, relaxed and almost invitational against another one that was the sound of frying with no crescendo, no variation, and yet another, the frailest noise of all, just a little tick-tock of a tiny energy source lost, but persistent, in the recesses of the universe, like a reminder that it, and it alone, would survive; the other sounds were mere extensions of itself, the signature-tunes of clowns, whereas it was the key to everything, the little tune of hydrogen, oblivious of absolutely everybody, even two children cached alive in a grave not far from the Vistula, where other forces, with only power of life and death, waited to work on them. The night was full of chance.

"A great writer."
—Hector Bianciotti, front page, *Le Monde*

"One of the most consistently brilliant lyrical writers in America... [West is] possibly our finest living stylist in English."
—*The Chicago Tribune*

"West has been for several decades one of the most consistently brilliant writers in America. His aim seems to be the rendition of an American odyssey analogous to Joyce's union of mythic elements in which earth-mother, shaper-father and offspring, as well as the living and the dead, all achieve communion. The language is Paul West at his best.... shows perfect pitch."
—Frederick Busch, *Chicago Tribune*

"West, prolific novelist and critic, is a literary high-wire artist, performing awe-inspiring aerial feats with language while the rest of us gape up at him in dumb amazement."
—*The Boston Globe*

"Out on those risky ledges where language is continually fought for and renewed—that's where Paul West breathes the thin, necessary air."
—Sven Birkerts, *American Energies*

"A rich, often astonishing meditation upon how a particular human culture can represent a source of 'otherness'—imagination itself—that persists even in a world that other modes of thought and desire have made almost uninhabitable."
—Thomas R. Edwards, *The New York Times Book Review*

"Paul West's epic touches upon the most powerful human themes—the meaning of home, the desecration of war, the quest for a curative past out of spiritual exile."
—Bradford Morrow, *Trinity Fields*

"West's enormous pastiche of yarn-spinning, meditation and sheer wordplay is precisely the sort of work that can help us understand the ways in which we approach and avoid the realities of being human.... Paul West is a worthy custodian of a time-honored tradition."
—Alida Becker, *The Philadelphia Inquirer*

"West's astonishing new novel, which maps the lives of Indians in the American Southwest, reveals a Joycean genius in its exuberant play of language, and its epic and mythic resonances.... West's prose, dazzling in its fecundity, affirms the erotic nature of the literary act."
—*Publisher's Weekly*

"Intoxicated by the novel's unparalleled capacity to connect life and ideas in an unholy mix, he likes fireworks in his fiction, the blowtorch of art that brings reality to the boiling point.... Thorough, passionate, opinionated—West never lets his judgments interfere with his considerable ability to evoke the texture and character of the work under review."
—*Washington Post Book World*

"A writer of distinction and originality."
—The Los Angeles Times

"West is an original and daring writer...he has never written anything so risky and triumphant."
—Richard Eder, *Los Angeles Time Book Review*

"No contemporary American prose writer can touch him for sustained rhapsodic invention—he creates a hyperbolic hymn to joy, a swashbuckling swirl of sentences. West stands as an authentic voice in the wilderness, a visionary who plugs the ghosts of history and morality into his textural dream machines."
—*Boston Phoenix*

"In his many works of fiction, memoir, and criticism, West proves himself to be a writer blessed with a cheerfully mordant wit, an acrobatic way with words, ebullient learnedness, and a deep if wry perception of

the human condition. Each previous *Sheer Fiction* volume has offered pleasure, revelation, and provocation, and now, in West's fourth collection of biting literary essays, he again covers a remarkable breadth and complexity of terrain."
—*A.L.A. Booklist*

"West argues passionately for a literature that reveals brilliant minds at work shaping it, that incorporates the world we know today—quantum physics, computer technology.... [His] argument is likely to provoke much disagreement, especially from the academic community... Yet his argument needs to be heard. ...*Sheer Fiction* demands the attention of any reader seriously interested in the purposes of fiction."
—*Wilson Library Bulletin*

"This kind of infectious enthusiasm is rare to the point of non-existence among modern critics. ...Sheer pleasure."
—*Kirkus Reviews*

"The inimitable, brilliant Paul West never ceases to amaze. *Love's Mansion,* orchestrated with Proustian care, offers unforgettable episodes of familial dark and light, bittersweet recollections activated by empathy and sexual

awareness. A revelatory book of extraordinary power."
—Walter Abish

"*The Tent of Orange Mist* is a bold, shocking book, filled with cynical brilliance and sensual power."
—*The Boston Review*

"Paul West is one of American literature's most serious and penetrating historical novelists. *The Tent of Orange Mist* is a gorgeous assertion of human life."
—*The San Francisco Chronicle*

"If there are no 'men of letters' any more, there are innumerable figures writing now…who move easily among the fictional, the confessional, the polemical, and the critical. If Paul West is not the most conspicuous of such a group, he is the most stylish and intelligent."
—*Journal of Modern Literature*

"A towering astonishing creation."
—Irving Malin, *Pynchon and Mason & Dixon*

"Paul West's book is transformative. West's immense narrative gift has transformed a traumatic historical event into art. He has re-imagined experience and made literature from it. His book will live."
—Hugh Nissenson, *The Song of the Earth*

"It takes a writer like Paul West to explore the deep psychic lacerations occasioned by [9.11]... Anyone who thinks he or she knows anything about that harrowing moment should read this novel; it will change their perceptions forever."
—David W. Madden, *Understanding Paul West*

""West's phenomenal command of language and the flux of consciousness, and his epic sense of the significance of 9.11 are staggering in their verve, astuteness, and resonance."
—Donna Seaman, *Booklist magazine*

"Not since Proust's *Albertine disparue* has a novel explored the subject of anguish and loss with such unflinching persistency and such annihilating force. This book will have you on tenterhooks and will break your heart."
—Mark Seinfelt, *Final Drafts*

"Paul West, among our more formidable literary intelligences, is not afraid to take risks. His ability to give original expression to complicated ideas about culture and personality is gargantuan. *The Place In Flowers Where Pollen Rests* presents a stunning, hyperbolic vision of men between cultures, between darkness and light, groping for authenticity."
—Dan Cryer, *Newsday*

"Extraordinary in its scope, inventiveness, and prose.... spectacular writing."
—Gail Pool, *Cleveland Plain Dealer*

"An exciting and evocative tale of love and treason."
—Andrew Ervin, *The Philadelphia Inquirer*

"While this biting, scatological tour de force will appeal mostly to West fans and more experimental poetry readers (many of whom are already West fans), it deserves a prominent place in poetry collections."
—Rochelle Ratner, *Library Journal*

"An exhilarating collection.... West's genuine excitement for this fiction is contagious and his own language is as splendid."
—*Review of Contemporary Fiction*

"[This novel] thrusts us into a rich domestic situation that reflects the complexities of our century like a prism. *Love's Mansion* is the late 20th century's contribution to the great, classical love novels of history."
—Elena Castedo

"[*The Tent of Orange Mist*] is both a terror and a joy to read."
—Kathryn Harrison

"The rest of us will despair of ever being able to write prose so immaculate as that of Paul West."
—Jonathan Yardley

"Most intriguing is the overarching narration told by Osiris, god of the Nile, who comments on this swarm of events with hilarious and humane authority. Profound and entertaining, *Cheops: A Cupboard for the Sun* is perhaps Paul West's greatest novel yet."
—J. M. Adams

"West, a writer of finesse, amplitude, and wit…describes his father in startlingly tactile detail as he recounts the wrenching war stories his father told him…. West's sensitivity to the vagaries of temperament is exquisite, his tenderness deeply moving. Writing of wars past in a time of war, West creates a portrait of his father that has all the richness of Rembrandt as it evokes the endless suffering wars precipitate."
—Donna Seaman, *Booklist*

"For beautiful sentences fed on brainpower, there is perhaps no other contemporary writer who can match him."
—Albert Mobilio, *Salon.com, Reader's Guide to Contemporary Authors*